HOCHSCHILD'S PASSPORTS

Hochschilds's Passports
First Edition in English
© Verónica Ormachea Gutiérrez, 2019
© Translated by Katie Fry
© Lazy Publisher

ISBN-13: 9781623751357

Visit us on the Web:
www.lapereza.net

HOCHSCHILD'S PASSPORTS

VERÓNICA ORMACHEA

To my father, Victor Ormachea Zalles

No thoughtful man can doubt the fact that the Jews are beyond all question the most formidable and the most remarkable race which has ever appeared in the world.

Winston Churchill

My deepest thanks to my dear writer friends—Darío Villanueva, Javier Moro, and Carlos Mesa—and to Eduardo Hochschild, for promoting arts and culture.

Chapter 1
Warsaw, 1939

I know what I want . . . but I have an even better idea of what I don't want, and what would happen if I continued living here in Warsaw, thought Boris. How can I make Dad see this? You don't have to be a genius to see what lies ahead for us. I have to convince him to open his eyes . . . but every time I try to talk to him, he changes the subject or tells me he's busy. He's avoiding me because he knows well enough what I want to say to him. The awful thing is that with each passing day the political scene becomes more complicated, and the safety of my mother and siblings more precarious. And because of his obstinacy and carelessness, he refuses to even listen.

He's always thought of himself as the owner of truth. His word is and has always been law in our family, and the worst of it is that my mother acquiesces in everything he says and has no influence over him whatsoever. And my brother and sister, younger than I am, don't have much of a say (not that they would let them anyway). If Dad refuses to listen to me, will we be able to escape this calamity? Maybe it's already too late, but nothing's worse than doing nothing. Later, we won't be able to say our fate was sealed; we're the ones responsible. There's nothing more dangerous than tempting fate or leaving it up to chance. One must take charge of one's destiny, at least that's what my heart tells me. Many people simply say "it was written in the stars" without doing a thing. That's nothing but a saying. I can't just sit here and wait until we're forced to face the inevitable, unable to escape desperate times and circumstances, and no longer able to flee the war.

I'm afraid. I'm terrified of what might come, and of how Dad, who's so terse and awkward, will react. But now, I'll force him to speak to me. When he arrives, I'll take him into the study and we'll speak face-to-face.

Dr. Kominsky opened the door with his key and entered the comfortable, spacious apartment on the top floor of a three-story building with two apartments on each floor in the center of Warsaw. He closed the door and his son stepped in front of him; his demeanor intimidated his father, who wasn't smiling (which wasn't surprising because he never smiled). They greeted each other and he asked if they could go into the study to talk. The doctor had no other choice, and Boris closed the door.

No one noticed that the head of the household had arrived. The doctor put his medical bag on the desk and they both sat down in the somber but impeccable room.

"I'm leaving, I don't care where to, but I'm leaving Poland," Boris said to his father, his hands and forehead wet with perspiration that he tried to conceal. "Sir . . . won't you accept that we Jews are considered deicides, the killers of Jesus? And what's worse is that this has been embedded in the collective consciousness and unconscious of humanity for millennia . . . Hitler hates us to the point of obsession . . . and why do you think the Nazis wouldn't get rid of us, the Polish Jews, just as they're getting rid of the German Jews?"

Boris was glad to be confronting his gruff, laconic, and impenetrable father whom, out of fear, he even addressed as "sir." The doctor was left speechless by the determination of his eldest son. Marek Kominsky began to crack his knuckles; this exasperated the young man, but he remained silent. He knew that his nervousness showed. Dr. Kominsky was tall and thin, with a scruffy beard and wispy gray hair that gave him a certain air of distinction. His intelligent eyes were visible behind thick, square-shaped glasses with black frames that he only took off to sleep. He was unusually sharp, quick, methodical, obsessive, and proud. When he spoke, only his mouth moved; the rest of his body remained motionless. Blue veins bulged from his hands, and his fingers were so long, thin, and bony that they resembled those of a skeleton. He always wore dark suits—which he had in all shades of gray—a spotless white shirt, and a dark tie; it was like a uniform.

"Come on, Father!" Boris continued with unease. "We need to escape before it's too late! It's an open secret that Germany will invade Poland any day now. Father, I beg you, let's sell the apartment, if there's still anyone who wants to buy it, and let's leave Warsaw as soon as possible. The Joint, Hilfsverein and HICEM have helped more than three hundred thousand Jews emigrate, and they can still help us get out of Poland. I've also heard of a Jewish magnate who owns mines in South America, a man named Moritz Hochschild, who lives in Bolivia."

"Bolivia? And . . . where on earth is that godforsaken country?" he scoffed arrogantly.

"Father, please let me continue. Hochschild has helped hundreds of our people emigrate to South America. I've even heard that when he takes business trips to London and Germany, he helps people he doesn't even know escape. He even hires our people in his companies and obtains visas for them and their families. He's some kind of godsend. We could go to him; obviously, we'd have to travel to one of those countries because I doubt he'd come to Poland. The stories are true—the Hirsches and other families have gotten out of Warsaw thanks to his help. And he doesn't even charge a cent, and even if he did . . . he's a true patron. Father . . . I beg you not to sacrifice Mama, Sonitzya, Sergei, and me. This is life or death! I'm just asking you to look reality in the face . . . don't you know what it means to be a Jew, and even worse, a Polish Jew? It hurts to accept it, but we're considered the scum of Europe and the world."

"Son," the doctor said, his face purple with indignation, "Since when do fathers obey their children?" He was stuttering, left almost speechless by his son's determination; deep down, though, although he didn't say it, he was pleased to see that his son was now an adult. "What's more, I refuse to allow you to question my ability to procure the safety of your mother and siblings. And I warn you: I'll never leave Poland. Listen well, Boris. I've lived here for most of my adult life, and I'll die here. My family, my life, and all my interests, everything I've earned with the sweat of my brow, are here, in Warsaw. You, your mother and I are Catholic; we're not practicing Jews, so they'll never hurt us. Besides, you know that the Vatican signed a concordat with the Third Reich protecting the rights of Catholics in Germany."

"But not in Poland, Father! Besides, everyone here in Warsaw knows that we converted to Catholicism and that you fled the Soviet Union. Father, you chose a bad destination and an even worse religion to convert to because Poland has historically been an anti-Semitic country. It's not only the Church that promotes anti-Semitism, but also the government and most political parties. How many pogroms have taken place in Poland? And at the Catholic school, they even insulted Sonitzya because she has Jewish blood; they yelled *Jüdin* at her just a few days ago."

"How dare you say that? They will never discriminate against my daughter!" his father declared, shaken and raising his voice. "Besides, she doesn't even look Jewish. The Catholic Church actually wants and has always encouraged Jews to convert to Catholicism. During

13

the Inquisition you could save yourself from being burned alive if you converted."

"Father, there's nothing worse than denying reality. Face the facts. I'm begging you, Father! We're not Polish or Russian . . . we're Jewish, and we'll always be Jewish, even though Mom is Polish and doesn't have a drop of Jewish blood. And you insist on denying our origin."

"Listen carefully, boy. We had no choice but to flee the Soviet Union. If we hadn't fled, we wouldn't be alive."

"Father, if you want us to stay alive, we need to leave Warsaw," Boris said, wiping him hands and forehead with a handkerchief. "Forgive me, Father, but the urgency of the situation compels me to insist. Even though Poland has more Catholics than any other central European country, it also has three and a half million Jews—three fourths of Europe's Jewish population. Sooner or later, Hitler will invade us."

"What a stupid thing to say. Our entire family could pass as Aryan," his father responded forcefully. "All of us, me included, are white, tall, blond and blue-eyed."

"The Nazis don't care just about what we look like; they detest our blood, race, religion, customs, and surnames. They even accuse us of being communists. Look, Father," he said as he held out a piece of paper. "I've worked it all out. We can also flee to Palestine and start a new life there. David Ben Gurion, the president of the Jewish Agency, has made it possible for us to emigrate there. We could turn to him."

"You're wrong. Palestine is an English protectorate, and the English are Arab allies. Don't be naïve. Palestine is a no-man's land where a mere three hundred and fifty thousand Jews live surrounded by forty-five million Arabs. Don't you realize that we're historically stateless?" he replied without even looking at the document.

"But we'll make it ours! We'll start out living in a Kibbutz, and then we'll see. Father, doctors like you are always needed. You won't even be allowed to practice here."

"I'm licensed to work at the hospital. And if they kick me out, I'll take care of my people and the Poles in this room or at their homes."

"Father, if you don't like the idea of going to Palestine, there are countries that are still giving visas to our people. It's too late to go to the United States because they closed the quota, and most other countries are only granting tourist or temporary visas, which wouldn't be of much help to us. The only ones giving unconditional refugee visas are Bolivia, China, and the Dominican Republic. The latter has a limited quota and you have to pay a fortune. I've been told that in Bolivia, in the heart of South America, a ruling was passed last March requiring their consuls all over the world to consider applications for admission from Jews."

"Absolutely not!" bellowed the doctor. "The Catholic Church will protect us. Their power and authority are so great that, if necessary, we could take refuge in their temples, which are sacred places where armed people are prohibited from entering. The Catholic Church doesn't even turn beggars away. Listen, son. I'm no longer of the age, nor am I willing, to emigrate wherever, to live however I can and start from scratch. Besides, our life is here, and I'm at the peak of my career. And what's more: your mother suffers from asthma, and to leave Warsaw for some unknown place, without even knowing if they have acceptable hospitals, would be extremely risky."

"That's all the more reason, considering what you've gone through. Father . . . what about me . . . us . . . your children? We have our lives ahead of us," he said, frightened.

"What are you insinuating?" he said, staring him straight in the eye through his thick glasses. "You're trying to break up our family. I'm disappointed in you, son."

"Father, it's not like that," he said, trying to reassure him. "I'm just trying to get you to see the political situation that's developing."

An eerie silence fell. The doctor stood up and lit a cigarette to break the tension; Boris followed him with an ashtray. He was still cracking his knuckles. Both men began to pace around the small room whose walls were covered with books, mostly about medicine. There was also a fireplace, unlit because the weather was mild; spring had begun. In truth, the room looked like a doctor's office, since it always had a stretcher laid out with clean sheets where he treated patients outside the hospital. He never charged his people or Russians; it was different for Poles. There was a desk with a table lamp, a prescription handbook, a telephone, a clipboard, and a crucifix, which was purely for show because the doctor had never become a true Catholic. He had converted for convenience—unlike his children, who had been baptized and were followers of Christianity because of their mother's influence. There were also two easy chairs and an armchair in which, when he could, he would take a nap on the weekends or on the rare occasions when he didn't have to deal with an emergency at the

15

hospital. The study also served as a refuge at night. It was a kind of sanctuary that no one entered without first knocking on the door, not even his wife Olga when she brought him a tray with tea and pastries. At the end of his workday, after promptly having dinner with his family (and even saying grace), he would retreat to the study to read, updating himself on the latest advances in medicine. And like a good Jewish scholar, he had an important collection of books and documents that he guarded jealously and never lent to anyone. If someone wanted to obtain information about something, they would have to read it in his study.

"Have you spoken to your mother and siblings about this, son?" he asked, exhaling a puff of smoke after they both sat down again.

"Yes, Father. But Sergei and my twin sister are confused and scared, and they'll do whatever you tell them to. I don't have any power over them, and they're not able to grasp the situation. Mama told me that she'll also abide by your decision."

Dr. Kominsky reflected on and remembered his life in silence. He was too proud to tell his son. He preferred not to relate what had happened in the past, and he had forbidden his wife to tell their children. Before emigrating to Poland, his last name was Horovitz; he was the son and grandson of Jews on both sides. He was an atheist and a communist, and deep down he still was, though he denied it. But to keep up appearances and to please Olga, he attended Mass on Sundays with his whole family. He never listened to the sermons, but he received Communion so everyone would see. He had fought in the Soviet Communist Party mainly to defeat the tsarist regime. The tsar's secret police had written a pamphlet denigrating the Jews: "The Protocols of the Elders of Zion." The goal was to get rid of the Jews. He was also outraged by the wealth and ostentation displayed by the tsars while the people of Russia were starving to death. Kominsky took part in the October Revolution and was shot in the leg. He studied medicine not only out of vocation, but also to help the poor, since he had seen people die due to a lack of resources and support. Lenin, the only member of the Soviet Party leadership with Russian blood, revoked the rights of the Jews. And the political operator behind the revolution, Trotsky, born Lev Davidovich Bronstein, the most anti-Jewish Jew in history, betrayed his people. Both men were anti-Semites, which enraged the doctor, since many Jews had risked their lives for the revolution. The worst of it all was that many followers of Judaism were among the most radical members of the

16

Cheka. They used and abused their power. Along with Lenin, those Judeo-Bolsheviks were the very ones who increased the pogroms, persecution and massacre of their own people, whose property they confiscated. They were forced to dissolve their religious communities and close their synagogues. They were sent to Siberia to perform forced labor, where they died of exhaustion, hunger, and hypothermia. All this terrified Kominsky, and he had decided overnight to travel across the nearest border with Olga: to Poland, the ideal place, since she would be reunited with her family and her country. She supported him without reservation; she was happy to return to her homeland with him and the twins. The doctor urged his immediate family to flee with them, but they didn't want to because they felt they were too old and didn't want their son and daughter-in-law to take care of them. His siblings didn't accept his offer either. After a heartfelt goodbye, his father gave him a small gold menorah, the only thing of value he possessed. They sold the few things they had left for next to nothing, dressed themselves as peasants, and the young family crossed the border on a horse-drawn cart loaded with vegetables, passing themselves off as greengrocers. Months later a neighbor wrote to them relating how, after their departure, the People's Commissars had exiled their entire family to the Gulag archipelago. Even though Olga continued repeating that had they not emigrated, they would have been persecuted by Stalin's government and suffered the same fate, the news turned the doctor into a dry, bitter man. Despite being from Georgia, Stalin, born Iosif Vissarionovich Dzhugashvili, was also of Jewish descent. The couple arrived in Poland and Marek bribed the authorities so that they could obtain documents with a new surname. He converted to Catholicism and, thanks to Olga, obtained a baptism certificate from St. Martin's Church. When he had it in his hands he said, "Paris is worth a Mass"; this upset her. They began their new life pinching every penny. They lived in an attic on the outskirts of Warsaw, and their savings dwindled away little by little because the doctor couldn't find work. Olga gave piano lessons and made baby clothes to help with their limited finances. They ate lunch every day at her parents' house, whose economic situation was stable. Her father was a typical lifelong bureaucrat. After months of unemployment and thanks to some friends from the Jewish community, the doctor was hired as an internist at Szpital Zachodni in Warsaw, where, for years, he worked night shifts in the emergency department. His professional and economic situation improved rapidly, and Sergei was born. All the children went to the German-Polish school. Dr. Kominsky, however, chose not to teach them Hebrew. They didn't practice Judaism either.

The doctor rested his elbow on the arm of the chair, placed a hand over his face and closed his eyes. He was overwhelmed by doubts, but he tried not to let it show. "Could my son be right, all the more so considering that I already had to flee once because of the persecution of my people? Will history repeat itself? But nothing will happen to us . . . nothing can happen to us . . . we've been using different names and practicing another religion for more than twenty years now. Impossible!"

"Son, this conversation is over. I repeat: I highly doubt that anything will happen to us."

"But, Father . . ."

"Don't keep on about it. I'll never leave Warsaw."

"What do you want me to do, then?"

"Well, you'll do as I say and stay with us, with your family."

"But, Father . . . I'm already of legal age, I'm already a professional . . . I work and I have my own income."

"Don't keep on about it! I forbid you from mentioning this again, either to me or to your mother and siblings."

"Do you know what, Father? Forgive me, but I must say it. You'll be the one responsible for the uncertain destiny of . . ."

Dr. Kominsky lost his composure. He stood up from his seat and slapped his son for the first time.

"What's more, if you go, I'll disinherit you for good!"

Boris was stunned. Silence fell, and he thought: "If he's incapable of seeing the situation clearly and he hits me on top of that, then a man, or one who claims to be a man, should do what he has to do." He lowered his head, spun around, left the room and walked out of the apartment, slamming the door behind him.

The doctor took refuge in his books, but he found it impossible to concentrate. Filled with anger and sadness, he began to read Tolstoy and listen to music by Russian composers, reliving his childhood and youth in Moscow, the only place he had ever been happy. He had never been happy in Poland. He was convinced that the Poles would never have the level of culture that the Russians had. He considered them the "poor neighbors," incomparable with the great artists of the Soviet Union. His mind strayed from the page in front of him and he began to recall his few moments of happiness. One of them was when he met Olga, the light of his life. He had loved her from the first day he saw her in the college cafeteria. She had won a scholarship to train as a pianist; she dreamed of being a soloist. Life let her down, though, because she ended up teaching piano and catechism lessons to Catholic children at St. Martin's. The doctor recalled her joy, her beauty, which had conveyed so much freshness and charm. Her face was fine and delicate, her skin soft and white, her eyes almond-shaped, blue, and full of life. She was, incidentally, one of the few slim women who could be seen in Moscow. All of his friends fell for her, but Olga set her sights on him and they fell in love instantly. It was the kind of love that expresses itself spontaneously, with absolute affinity, in spite of the difference in nationality and language. She was quite outgoing. "Opposites attract," she would say, and for him, a man of few words, she was the ideal companion, because she spoke for both of them. He praised everything she said, even though she spoke little Russian. She was passionate about music and reading, as was he, and this made them happy. At the same time, however, Olga was balanced, serene, understanding and could easily adapt to any situation. She was so restrained and submissive that she was practically stoic. Her sorrows trailed in front of her mind's eye "like a procession," she would say. The only thing that worried him was that Olga had asthma; she was terrified of choking to death and would pray to God to protect her. Shortly after they met, they decided to marry civilly as well as according to the laws of both religions in order to please their families. Marek's parents were Orthodox Jews, and deep down they never quite accepted the fact that he married a Catholic, even though she had White Russian ancestry. It was the same with Olga's parents. Although they didn't say anything, they thought it was a sin for a Catholic to marry a Jew. Another moment of great joy—recalled the doctor—was when his children were born. It wasn't until Olga was in labor that they found out they were going to have twins, Boris and Sonitzya. They were almost identical. At first they worried about money, but everyone came together to help them. Their friends gave them everything from diapers to cradles. He convinced Olga to give them Russian names so that something from their beloved Soviet Union would remain with them. As they grew older, he spoke to them in Russian, a language they came to understand. Looking back, he came to the conclusion that the only thing that had made him happy throughout his life was his family. He was deeply hurt by his son's stance, and upon recalling the scene that had just occurred, he was plagued by doubt once again.

After slamming the door with a resounding bang, Boris, deeply distraught, went out for a few hours to walk off his anger. He gazed with sadness at the Royal Palace, the Lazienki Palace, walked through Ujazdów Park, looked out at the Vistula River, and thought: "How will all this end?" He continued on to the end of the Old Town until he reached the Old Town Market Place. There he entered a bar he liked to frequent with his friends and ordered a dark beer. Then another, and another; he sat there, drinking alone, not wanting to speak to anyone. He was very disappointed with his father. He couldn't understand his stubbornness, and he was driven to despair not only over the fate of his family, but also over Varinia, his long-term girlfriend. She was his first love, the first for whom he felt passion, and she felt the same way about him. He decided that, for the first time (they had always been very open with one another), he would refrain from telling her about his concerns.

Varinia's family had no Jewish ancestry; she had ancestors who belonged to the Polish nobility. They spent the summers in Ciechocinek and Karlovy Vary, important cultural centers with theaters, concerts, exhibitions, restaurants, cinemas, cafés and, in the latter, the famous hot springs, where the royalty and nobility would go to rest. Apart from being lovers, they were best friends. There was nothing they didn't share or discuss with one another. The only thing they hadn't done—at Varinia's request—was make love. She, a practicing Catholic, wanted to remain a virgin until marriage. What's more, she feared becoming pregnant because of what people would say. She would say to her boyfriend: "I must remain more virginal than Mary until my wedding day"; they found this funny, although not entirely, since they desired each other intensely. There wasn't a day that went by in which he didn't dream of taking her to bed, holding her naked in his arms, and giving themselves to one another fully. They talked about it, but they didn't do it. Whenever they found themselves alone, smothering each other with kisses and caresses, he would begin to stroke her breasts and try to touch her pubic area, and Varinia wanted to caress his member, which felt swollen and erect, but she abstained; she would stand up with her little wet panties and withdraw, knowing she had to resist. When they parted, they would console themselves by touching themselves, each one thinking of the other. "It is a sin to touch yourself," they would hear in church, which always made Boris think: "But these priests are the ones who jerk off and then flagellate themselves to appease their conscience! You can even see their members rising beneath the fly of their pants when they see a woman showing cleavage or wearing a skirt a little shorter than normal. Poor men . . . to live without sex!"

The couple had met at the Communities of Christian Life at St. Martin's Church, which Boris led by giving talks and organizing meetings. They also carried out social work for the poor. She was dazzled by his leadership, and he by her charm, beauty and lucid mind. Varinia was enigmatic and playful; she radiated energy and was sought after by most of the young men who knew her. Her list of admirers was endless. There was not one member of the church group who hadn't noticed her. She was also a leader; she was inspiring, and everything she did she did with enthusiasm and passion. She had strong willpower, and whatever she set out to do she did with conviction because her self-esteem was extremely high. She saw herself as a warrior. She was convinced that one had to make the most out of life. She was tall, perhaps too tall, although well proportioned. She had white, almost transparent skin that contrasted beautifully with her vivacious, lapis lazuli eyes and her long, curly, ash-blond hair, which fell to her waist and which she usually wore in a braid. Her face was so perfect that it looked as though it were painted; it was "as if God had painted her by hand," Boris would say. Her intensity made him love her passionately: she danced to the point of exhaustion; cried until her eyes were swollen; read until she fell asleep; laughed until her stomach ached; sang the same songs until she ended up detesting them; and prayed so often that she spoke by rote and in the end understood nothing of what she was saying. She had an aura of spontaneity that she didn't hide, and she had so much confidence that she would make fun of herself. She didn't miss out on anything; she would be first in line even for a bombing. There were no half measures with Varinia. Her personality and charisma were so pronounced that nothing stopped her; on the contrary, her candid way of speaking her mind got her into trouble sometimes. According to Boris, she was the embodiment of "spoken thought." Later she would realize her tactlessness and be forced to apologize to the offended person, as well as to God and his heavenly court. At the same time, she had a wonderful sense of humor and

21

would tease both friends and strangers. This got her into trouble because people tended to have a solemn air about them and didn't take jokes well. When someone hurt her, however, she remained offended forever. She was spiteful. She never forgave, even though she promised the prelate in the confessional that she would. And when she was having one of her "fits of lunacy" (as her mother called them), she would lock herself in her room and no one would dare to speak to her or look at her long face until her bad mood had passed. She loved to use foul language; she said that even though swearing was a custom of the common people, it was a privilege that only aristocrats could grant themselves. Her character was rebellious and—within a society as conservative as that of Warsaw—conflictive. And when she lost her temper, she would howl rather than scream, hurling decorative objects into the air that would end up in pieces, which she later regretted. But everyone loved her, and wherever she went she was always the center of attention. She was a ballet dancer and went to the dance academy every day even though, because of her height, she would never have been able to join the corps de ballet of the national theatre of Poland. This wasn't a problem, though, because she danced all the same in private performances or in lesser-known theaters. Often, when she heard *The Firebird* or Tchaikovsky's *Swan Lake* on the radio, she would move the main table, roll up the carpet, and begin to dance. She danced mazurkas with a grace that only her charm could bestow. And whenever she could, she convinced her boyfriend to go dancing in some dance hall, where she would spin like a top and he would end up exhausted. All this charm and energy ignited Boris's passion for her. Sometimes, however, he found her secretive and elusive.

When dawn began to break, Boris returned home by tram because he had drunk a few too many. He arrived at the apartment, opened the door, and found all the lights off. He went straight to the bedroom he shared with Sergei.

"What did Dad say?" Sergei asked quietly.

"He doesn't want to hear a word about it," Boris answered despondently.

"And what are we going to do?"

"We're in God's hands."

He spent the rest of the night lying awake, trying to understand the incomprehensible. But Boris was as stubborn as his father, and his dad's refusal had made him even more obstinate than usual. He decided to act. The only thing that worried him was the thought of going alone; he had never traveled outside of Poland before. And since they weren't married, he couldn't ask Varinia to come with him either.

The next day he got up as usual and went to work at the pharmaceutical lab. At lunchtime, he proposed to his best friend Isaac Levi—whom he not only had gone to university with but who also worked at the lab—that they emigrate together. It didn't take Isaac long to say yes because his adventurous spirit prevailed over any sense of danger. Boris was greatly relieved by his decision.

"And Varinia? Have you told her about our plans?"

"No. Even the thought of leaving her breaks my heart."

Once he had Isaac's approval, that same day he went to find out from other Jews in the neighborhood what the easiest and cheapest way to emigrate was. They all agreed that he needed to go to a faraway country, and they gave him several addresses. The following day, Boris got up at dawn, skipped work on the excuse that he was ill, and put on a dark suit, a white shirt, and a tie. He didn't forget to bring the most important thing: the slip of paper with the addresses of the consulates. He took the number two tram to the city center and walked towards the closest place: the Chinese consulate. He had heard about the International Settlement at Shanghai. When he arrived, he saw that the huge consulate, which was part of the embassy, was guarded by Chinese and Polish police. He went into the office to check whether it was true that Poles could emigrate to China without a visa. The secretary told him that China could indeed grant him an unconditional visa, and she gave him a number. He took a seat. As he waited in a room full of motley, tasteless decorations and lamps, he analyzed the situation. "Even if they don't require a visa, what the hell am I going to do in such a far-off country, with people of another race who speak a different language, with an alphabet so different from ours, one that looks just like drawings to me? There must be a Jewish community there, though. In fact, the only thing that would make it worthwhile for me to go there would be to pass through on the way to another country. But where? If it's in the middle of nowhere and it would cost me a fortune to move again, then . . . what the hell am I doing here? I'm going to another consulate."

He left the consulate, took the slip of paper with the addresses and went to take the number twenty-five tram to the Bolivian consulate, which was located in a more humble neighborhood in the suburbs of Warsaw. He had never heard of the country and he had very little information about it. Just the night before, when he couldn't sleep and no one was awake to see him, he had consulted an encyclopedia and a world atlas. "To go to South America, to Bolivia," he thought. "An underdeveloped, landlocked country, in the heart of America, in the Andes, where they speak Spanish . . . where most of the people are indigenous . . . but there are Jews everywhere . . . the diaspora is eternal . . ." This was his only consolation, although the fact that he spoke neither Yiddish nor Hebrew would complicate things for him. He got off the tram in the right place, but it took him some time to find the consulate, which was on the second floor of a somewhat neglected building. He found it thanks to a discolored, oval-shaped shield painted on brass hanging on the side of the building, which said Republic of Bolivia. Upon entering, he saw a lengthy line of people stretching to the main entrance door.

"How long have you been here?" he asked.

"For two days, actually. We've been taking turns with our relatives to hold our spot," answered a relatively young man. He was unshaven and tired-looking.

"And . . . are they giving out visas?"

"Yes, although they cost a fortune."

He went up to the second floor and saw people sitting in the staircase, fighting against the heat and the lack of ventilation. At the door he was met by a couple of Polish officers who asked to see his papers, inquired about the reason for his visit, and instructed him to join the line. The line was barely moving, and he waited all day. He only left to eat a sandwich, after begging the people in front of and behind him to hold his place. He came back, resumed his place, waited the entire afternoon, and when his turn was about to come up, they announced that the office was closing at five and that they should come back the next day. He left in low spirits, without saying a word. He was upset at wasting a whole day with nothing to show for it. And what would the line be like the next day? That night he didn't sleep a wink either; he decided to get up at four in the morning and walk to the consulate on foot, since there were no trains or buses at that time. He arrived an hour later; five people were already there, waiting; they opened at ten. Those who had been there the day before began to arrive and demanded their places, but those who had arrived early banded together and ignored them. Around noon he finally got to speak to someone, and he was given some forms to fill out for himself and Isaac. They made him wait until almost four in the afternoon, since the consul, Mr. Urioste, had to interview him. When his turn came, he couldn't believe it; he crossed himself. The stress of it all had left him exhausted, but he put on his best face. A secretary brought him into the consul's office. It wasn't luxurious, but it was acceptable. It had a tricolor flag with an embroidered shield, a portrait of Germán Busch—whom he assumed was the president of the republic—hanging on the wall, a desk piled with a disordered array of papers and files so full it would be difficult to cram anything else into them, a couple of chairs, and a small living room space. When the consul saw him enter, he stretched out his hand in greeting and gave him a forced smile. As he looked at Boris, he thought: "This is the type of person we need, so white and well built; people like this will improve the Bolivian race." He hardly asked him anything because, to his mind, Boris had everything except the typical Jewish face. He was an imposing man, well over six feet tall; he had inherited his father's height and his mother's beauty. People would even comment on how alike they were. He had blond hair, a lock of which fell across his forehead, a slender nose, a well-defined mouth, a cleft chin, and an almost perfectly square jaw. He looked so much like his twin sister that his friends used to tease him by saying: "You're Sonitzya with pants," to which he would reply: "Except that I don't sneeze when I'm nervous, like she does," and they would burst out laughing. His clear and determined gaze shone through his small, round glasses. The confidence he had in his physical attractiveness allowed him to move with remarkable ease, which caught the consul's attention. Boris took a seat and handed over his and Isaac's documents.

"Mr. Kominsky: are you Jewish or of Hebrew ancestry?" asked Mr. Urioste in the arrogant tone he used with everyone.

"No, Consul," lied Boris.

Boris made such a good impression on the consul that he began to explain the immigration situation in Bolivia.

"We have instructions from the Bolivian chancellery to grant 'Agricultural Visas' in order to attract European immigrants to cultivate tropical and subtropical land in Bolivia. It's an initiative by our president, Captain Germán Busch, the son of a German doctor who emigrated to my country at the beginning of the century. If you, even though you're an engineer, go there to work the land, the

Bolivian state will give you a monthly subsidy for a year, and then eventually transfer the land over to you. Many Europeans have immigrated to Bolivia, especially near the end of 1936. There is a German colony on the banks of the Ichilo River, in Santa Cruz, and another one in Colonia Busch, in Chapare, in the department of Cochabamba. The goal is to eventually form farming settlements in these places and thereby help to modernize the country. Would you be willing to take up farming?"

"Of course, Consul. I'm a chemical engineer, but I'm willing to work the land."

"Did you know that Bolivia also welcomed Polish and Soviet Jews following the pogroms in what was then Russia at the beginning of the century and when the October Revolution broke out?"

"I didn't know that, Consul."

"Are you affiliated to any political party?"

"No, sir. Please allow me to ask a question: would you be able to grant a visa to my parents and siblings?"

"Ah! I forgot. Your family can only be granted a visa once you've been offered a work contract, and the paperwork must be done in the immigration office in the city of La Paz. For now, I'll grant you a refugee visa that you must pay for at the counter in the entrance hall. But first, you and Mr. Levi must purchase your tickets to Bolivia. The secretary will give you the name of a travel agency where you can buy them."

"We'll do that. Thank you very much, Consul. Good afternoon."

After the meeting he arranged to meet Isaac at a café, where he saw that his friend was having second thoughts. In order to put some pressure on him, he told him that, unless they returned to the consulate as soon as possible with tickets in hand, they ran the risk of not being granted visas. Isaac, who was somewhat faint of heart, assented. "At least we'll get to know another country," he said.

They went to a travel agency and bought two tickets to travel by boat to America. And with their *biglietti d'imbarco in terza classe* from Lloyd Triestino in hand, they returned to the consulate the next day, where an official stamped their passports. Although they were happy at having obtained their visas, they were outraged that they had to spend a small fortune on them, as well as deposit some money whose final destination they never discovered. They supposed that a lot of money was being made off of the visa business. For them, it meant two months' salary, which reduced their already limited budget for the trip.

Boris, discreet and independent, didn't a word to anyone for days. He kept thinking about Varinia, about how he would reveal his plans to her. He felt guilty not only for abandoning her but because he had organized everything without telling her. However, the moment of truth arrived, and he had to face his father again. This time, though, with something concrete: he had a visa. He asked his parents if he could speak with them in the study.

"Father, Mother, I have obtained a visa for Bolivia, although it cost me a small fortune in zlotys." He showed them his passport. "Isaac also got one, and we're going to Bolivia to try our luck and begin a new life," he told them firmly. "But if we bribe the consul, we can all go, at least that's what my fellow Jews have told me."

"But . . . you've lost your mind!" spit out the doctor. "To Bolivia . . . a tiny country . . ."

"What you call a 'tiny country' and China are the only countries, at this point, that are giving unconditional visas to our people. Remember the Evian Conference that was convened by Roosevelt? The world leaders made it clear that they would limit the entry of our people to their countries, so obtaining one is very difficult. According to the consul, Bolivian government regulations ensure that only one family member is given a visa. And once I'm there, working and with a residence permit, I can send for you to come join me. At this point, countries like Chile, Argentina, Mexico and Brazil, as well as other countries that used to grant visas, are only issuing transit visas. Now, if Bolivia is a very underdeveloped country, then I'll move to a more developed one. But the fact is that I'm leaving with Isaac and I want you to know that I won't change my mind. What's more, I've never spoken so seriously about anything."

"Are you going to throw away your career as an engineer to become a messenger, a driver, a longshoreman—in other words, a nobody? Don't you realize that the only way to be 'someone,' to not go through life unnoticed—and this is all the more true for us Jews—is to achieve excellence in a profession, earn money and acquire prestige and the respect of society?"

"I'll worry about that further down the road. I'll start by working in the countryside, and then later, since I have a relevant profession, I'll see what I can do."

"How naïve you are . . . our people have always been known for being merchants, bankers, intellectuals or artists."

"Are you really going to abandon us?" interjected his distraught mother. "What about us . . . and your brother and sister . . ." she exclaimed, beginning to wheeze, cough and choke. She felt a tightness in her chest, which worried all three of them.

"See what you've caused? Your foolishness has given your mother an asthma attack!" The doctor went up to her and patted her back softly, giving her a massage in an effort to calm her down. "I've already told you, Olga, you're not going to die from asthma. The worst that can happen is that you faint, calm down, and breathe again."

"Forgive me, Mother," said Boris. "Father, I warned you in advance of my decision, but you ignored me. I'm already an adult and I want to try to save myself. Now, if there is no retaliation against our people here in Poland, of course I'll return as soon as possible, and I'll consider the trip an adventure. In any case, once I arrive and receive my work permit, I'll send for you. We'll need to be in constant contact."

"You just don't understand, son," cried his father with growing anger. "I'll never leave Poland!"

"Father, Mother: Isaac and I will resign from the laboratory as soon as possible. We'll request letters of recommendation and we'll travel to South America in a few weeks' time. We'll be leaving from the port of Genoa. I can't deny that it hurts in the depths of my soul to be forced to leave you, as well as Varinia, and I hope that our blessed Lord and the Virgin Mary, my Black Madonna, will bring me back soon."

A chilling silence reigned, broken by Olga's inconsolable weeping in the middle of her asthma attack. Boris went up to her and hugged her, his tears flowing as well. Then Sergei and Sonitzya were called into the office; they had heard everything through the door, where they had been eavesdropping like household employees. They were told about their brother's decision, and they cried too, especially Sonitzya, who adored her twin brother. She was closer to him than to Sergei.

"You leaving is like me being split in two," said Sonitzya, choking on her tears and beginning to sneeze.

"Everything will work itself out along the way. I'll write to you constantly, I'll send for you, and I'll be back before you know it," he whispered in her ear.

Boris had another ordeal to go through: telling Varinia that he was setting off for a new and unknown world. He called her on the telephone and went to see her. She lived in a small palace that her family had inherited from their ancestors. Her father was able to maintain it because he was a rich merchant. He was the principal importer of glass into Poland; he had it brought from Czechoslovakia and Austria. She found herself alone that night because her parents and sister had traveled to their summer house in Lodz; she had stayed home because she had choreography classes over the weekend. She received him with open arms, as always. "But how beautiful you are! You look like Anna Karenina." The maid had prepared a meat stew with rice and peas, and they sat down to eat in the stylishly-furnished dining room beneath the light of a Bohemian crystal chandelier.

"I have to talk to you," Boris said nervously.

"What is it?" replied Varinia without batting an eye, completely unaware of what he was about to say.

"My love, I didn't tell you this before because nothing had been finalized. My love, I've decided to leave for a while. I believe a German invasion is imminent, and I have no doubt they'll persecute us. I've tried to convince my parents, but they don't want to come with me. I'm going to Bolivia, a country in the heart of South America, with Isaac. We're going to find work through a colonization program for Jewish immigrants."

She stuttered from sheer surprise.

"So you've decided to leave me?"

"I'll never do that! I'm just going to try my luck for a while. If they don't invade Poland, I'll return immediately."

"Are they going to invade us?"

"How many times have we discussed this, darling? It's extremely likely."

"And you're leaving . . . you're abandoning me . . ."

"You'll be surrounded and protected by your parents, sister, relatives and friends."

"You know what? You're outrageous! You worked it all out before telling me, as if you didn't love me!"

"Don't be childish. I have Jewish ancestry and I have to leave."

"My father says anything can be solved with money."

He didn't know what to say.

"When I arrive, I'll send for you, and of course we'll get married, either here or there. But first, I want to see if I can make a life for us there."

"So now you're proposing marriage at the same time as you're abandoning me? Don't be pathetic!"

Varinia threw her serviette down, got up from the table, and went off to her room on the second floor to cry with abandon. He followed her and went to console her. She was leaning against the wall with her back to him. Boris turned her towards him, brought her into his arms, and embraced her with all his strength.

"Don't cry, my dearest love."

"You know I cry easily!"

"You know I love you."

"I, on the other hand, detest you! You're a scoundrel, a shameless bastard! What if I never see you again? What if you fall in love with another woman?"

To stop her from speaking, he planted a kiss on her mouth. Their tongues met and licked each other between Varinia's tears. This silenced her, and she closed the door of her room with her foot. He began to kiss her neck and ears. He slipped his hand onto her back, underneath her silk blouse, and unbuttoned her bra. Then he began to unbutton her blouse; he took it off and began to kiss her now swollen nipples. She began to breathe heavily and moan without pause. She felt her heart racing. She unbuttoned his shirt desperately, kissing his chest, neck and earlobes. Then she undid his pants, opened his fly and gently touched his engorged member. He moaned along with her, closing his eyes and curving backwards as he stroked her hair. "I love you; I love you," she said. She felt uncontrollable pleasure in this first experience, and she let herself be guided by him. Then, sticky with perspiration, they let the little clothing they still had on fall to the floor. He carried her to the bed, delicately opened her legs and began to kiss her. She had never felt so much pleasure; it wasn't like when she touched herself alone. She began to cry out in pleasure, and her eyes appeared to roll back. He, seeing her excitement and wanting them to come together, penetrated her. Her wet vagina absorbed him eagerly. Then he turned her around, made her kneel, and penetrated her from behind while he held her waist. This excited her even more. "I love it," she said. "Give it to me . . .

with all your soul . . . never stop." He finished with an explosive orgasm, although he wasn't sure if she ended up coming at the same time. They lay down together, exhausted.

"I love you, I adore you, Varinia. I'll never love anyone like I love you. You have given me indescribable pleasure."

"And you to me . . . and . . . I love you; I love you so much more . . ."

They kissed again as if they had never kissed before. "Will you marry me?"

"Of course. I've loved you since the day we met."

Then she felt a wetness in her crotch that made her sit up and look. "Boris, I'm bleeding!" she exclaimed.

"Does it hurt?"

"No."

"I deflowered you, my love, you also gave me that honor . . ."

"And . . . what should I do?"

"Nothing, it's another testament to our love . . ."

Boris was the kind of man who succeeded in everything he did. His perseverance allowed him to achieve everything he set out to do or obtain. He was also methodical and disciplined. Failure didn't exist for him. He was a natural leader. When it came to teamwork, he was always at the head of everything he undertook. No doubt his strong physique helped, but on top of that, his Catholic education had instilled in him a deep sense of humanity and morality, which had opened many doors in his life. Although he had very close friends, like Isaac, he became friends with people from all walks of life. "I'm neither racist nor classist," he would say, which made him accessible to everyone and loved by all. Many women dreamed of being with him, but he was faithful to Varinia. When he got angry, however, he ranted and lost control, leaving those around him speechless. The only one who yelled louder than him was his girlfriend. On his father's advice he had read the classics of Russian literature, such as Dostoevsky, Tolstoy, Gogol, Chekhov, and Gorky, and concluded that they were without peer. And as a result of his mother's influence, he loved music. He liked all kinds of music except opera, which he found extremely tacky. And to Varinia's chagrin, he hated Tchaikovsky, whose ballets, he said, were as tasteless as a man who puts a ring on a finger for reasons other than signaling marriage. Of all the arts, he liked music the most because it reached the depths of his soul and had the ability to transform his emotional state. As a

31

good believing and practicing Catholic, and because of his mother's influence, before setting off on his journey he traveled by bus to the Shrine of Our Lady of Czestochowa in Silesia, the miraculous Black Madonna, to pray and place himself in her care. He was so devout that he even carried her image in his wallet. He prayed, kneeling before the altar: "Queen Mother, I know that everyone makes their own destiny . . . I hope I have made the right decision. But . . . what can I do if my father doesn't want my family to emigrate, and I can't bring Varinia because we aren't even married? Where would I be bringing her to, if I don't even know what Bolivia is like?" He thanked her from the bottom of his heart for the opportunity to travel in the company of Isaac and prayed for his family's protection. He loved his country, the land of Chopin—Poland's greatest treasure—and identified with his concertos. When the opportunity arose at parties, where both young and adult women gazed longingly at him, he didn't need to be asked twice to dance mazurkas. He loved his city; his neighborhood; the fresh bread from the bakery on the corner; having coffee with his girlfriend; going to Mass on Sundays at St. Martin's and then going out with a group of friends to have a beer and *zurek*; horseback riding in the countryside; getting around on his motorcycle, his bike or simply on foot; going to the theater and to concerts; listening to music with the volume up high on weekends, accompanied by his family; and his mother's cooking. It truly wasn't easy for him to leave his homeland, his family, and least of all Varinia.

The night before his departure, his mother gave him an unusual gift. "Take this, Boris," Olga said as she handed him a flat package wrapped in wood-colored paper.

"But what is this, Mother?" he asked, unwrapping it.

"It's an oil painting that Wassily Kandinsky gave to me when I was studying in Moscow. We became friends despite our age difference. You'll see, on the back, that it's dedicated to me."

"And how is it that we knew nothing about the existence of this painting?"

"Because I've been saving it my whole life to use in an emergency."

"But, Mother, it's worth a fortune," he said after examining the avant-garde, abstract and geometrical brushstrokes that characterized the painter's style.

"That's why I'm giving it to you. I don't want you to ever go hungry or suffer from the cold, and this painting can get you out of trouble, if it ever comes to that. All I ask is that you hide it at the bottom of your suitcase and never lose sight of it."

"I don't know how to thank you, Mother," he said, deeply moved. He gave her an affectionate kiss.

That same night Boris went to say goodbye to his girlfriend. She received him very formally, in the living room, since her parents were home. He suggested they go for a walk because he felt uncomfortable saying goodbye in front of them. They went out to walk through the garden surrounding the mansion, where her mother grew roses as well as other kinds of flowers and plants.

"You were wonderful the other night."

"It was an experience I'll never forget . . ."

"Are you still sore?"

"A little, but recalling how we made love with such passion makes the pain go away."

They smiled at each other mischievously, and their desire for one another stirred.

"Once I've found a decent job and I've gotten to know what Bolivia is like, I'll send for you and we'll get married."

"What are you talking about? We'll get married here, when you return. My family and I will prepare everything. You'll be back before you know it."

"I hope to God you're right. I swear I thought of bringing you with me, but your parents would never have allowed it since we're not married and they don't even know anything at all about Bolivia."

"It's true. They're too conservative. I'll miss you every minute that goes by."

"Me too. You know how much I love you, and that I can't imagine any woman in my life other than you."

"I can't imagine another man in my life either. I'll write to you every day."

"I'll do the same."

"I'll love you forever. I'll wait all my life for you . . . come back . . . come back . . ."

He unclasped the gold chain with a crucifix hanging around his neck (which he had never taken off) and put it on her. "This is so that I remain in your thoughts always . . . a symbol of the indissoluble link between us . . . never take it off."

"I promise, I'll never take it off."

They kissed beneath the full moon, which shone like a nocturnal sun, and they embraced with all their might amid tears and sorrow. After saying goodbye, and with his heart in tatters, he went to his apartment to pack his bags; they were departing the next day. He hid the canvas in a secret compartment and packed four changes of clothing; a few novels; two dictionaries he had purchased: a Polish-Spanish one, and a German-Spanish one; the Holy Bible; a small crucifix; a rosary; and photos of his girlfriend and family. He didn't want anyone to accompany him to the train station to say goodbye so as not to attract attention, as he knew many Jews would be emigrating. He also knew that there was a strict currency control; they weren't allowing people to take out more than two hundred and seventy dollars, which made him very nervous. Therefore, early in the morning, he said farewell to his family in the apartment. The goodbye with his father was brief and cold; they merely shook hands. Things were different with his mother, brother and sister, who refused to let him go, embracing him tightly and drowning in tears. The last thing he said, without his father hearing, was: "The first thing I'll do when I get there is send for you." He left, wiping away his tears.

Isaac was a smart, good-natured young man, always in a good mood. He was one of those people whom everyone liked, and he made himself loved by both friends and strangers. He was clumsy, with curly red hair and a face full of freckles. He wore a small hat that he never took off. He also said farewell to his widowed mother and sisters at home, and he and Boris met at Warszawa Zachodnia train station. Both were wearing a suit and tie; it was as if they had planned it in advance. Once they boarded the train and settled in, the full weight of the trip they were embarking on hit them. They exchanged a sober glance and took a deep breath. They felt scared and nervous. It was the first time that either of them had taken a trip to such a strange, faraway place. Boris told Isaac about his mother's gift, and neither of them took their eyes off the suitcase. Isaac's mother had made each of them a flat cloth bag with a zipper that they tied around their waists and wore underneath their pants. There they kept their documents and extra dollars, which they had exchanged on the black market at triple the going rate. Out of compulsion, every now and then they touched their abdomens surreptitiously to make sure the bag was still there.

It took them all night and part of the next morning to arrive at the port of Genoa. As they were traveling on a tight budget, they couldn't afford a sleeper car, so they slept poorly, sitting up, without taking their eyes off the suitcase. As they crossed through Czechoslovakia and Austria, their hair stood on end upon seeing that these countries were occupied by the Nazis. When they stopped at the train stations, they observed dozens of armed, uniformed guards and an enormous flag with a swastika hanging from the roof. The border stops were terrifying because they made them step off the train, leaving their luggage in the car, and line up to show their documents. At the first border crossing, the Nazis stamped Isaac's passport with a red "J" to mark his Jewish status. Isaac wasn't bothered by this, but it scared Boris, all the more so because of the tense and hostile atmosphere surrounding them. After checking their documents, they told them to reboard the train and they crossed the border. The first thing Boris did after getting back on the train was to check if his suitcase was still there. He kept thinking about how wrong his father had been in deciding not to emigrate however and to wherever he could. As soon as he had a free moment, he would phone his parents and beg them to leave Warsaw as soon as possible, even if it was for China.

When they arrived in Genoa they went directly to the port, where they found the ship Tiberius that would set sail that same night for Arica, Chile. They were approached by members of the Aid Committee for Immigrants (LEB) and given two lire each so they could buy something to eat. Boris ran to find a telephone and called Warsaw. It was his father, by chance, who answered the phone. After barely greeting his son, he heard him say:

"We arrived in Genoa and we'll be boarding in a few hours. When we entered Czechoslovakia they stamped Isaac's passport with a red 'J,' for Jew."

"And did they stamp yours?"

"No."

"You see? Didn't I tell you nothing would happen to us?"

"Father, emigrate! Go to China, even, but leave now! It was terrifying to see two countries occupied by the Nazis."

As they boarded the ship, they were asked to show their transit visas for Chile, a requirement no one had told them about. They went pale and were asked to step out of the line. They didn't know what to do. They waited until everyone had boarded the ship, and when it was about to set sail, they approached a naval officer of a certain rank who was standing on the ramp checking documents. Boris showed him his, and the officer turned him away, indicating that he lacked a transit visa for Chile. Seeing the situation, Isaac presented his documents, but he slipped a gold ring his mother had given him for an emergency into his passport. The Italian officer accepted the bribe and told them: "Get on quickly and don't tell anyone." They finally boarded the Tiberius for a trip that would last three weeks. Later, Boris told his friend: "It was only thanks to your cunning and courage that we were allowed to embark."

Chapter 2
Bolivia, 1939

"It doesn't matter whether they're violinists or doctors; we must continue rescuing Jews and their families from the persecution of those damned Nazis. We'll place them wherever we can. What's the count so far?" asked Moritz.

"About two thousand have arrived recently in Bolivia," replied Adolf, his faithful executive and closest friend.

"I've re-instructed the directors of my companies to employ as many Jews as possible and, if necessary, to invent positions so that they grant them visas in the Bolivian consulates in Hamburg, Paris, Warsaw and wherever else," he said worriedly. He was sitting at a desk cluttered with papers, an unusual situation for a millionaire used to making executive decisions and signing documents with a gold Parker fountain pen.

"I've asked them to inform me daily regarding how many they've employed and how the process is going."

"Bribe the president of the republic, if necessary, to obtain the passports," he said firmly. "How many did you buy?"

"Two hundred and twenty. Our contact went to the printer and we've already paid the man who forged the immigration authorities' signatures. It cost us no small sum to buy their silence."

"And the stamps?"

"I have them in the safe."

"And the contracts and work permits?"

"They're all ready, just missing your signature."

"Then I'll head to London the day after tomorrow."

"I'll instruct the secretary to reserve a seat for you in Panagra."

"Perfect."

"Extraordinary man, Moritz . . . men like him don't exist anymore . . . he has a kind of vocation to serve others," thought Adolf. "Since 1935, thousands of refugees have entered countries where he has companies, thanks to his efforts."

In their view, it didn't take a prophet to see that the Second World War was coming. Hitler's hatred for the Jews was no secret; it had been published for all to see in *Mein Kampf.* The most pressing matter was that the situation for his people had gotten worse since

Kristallnacht, the moment in which war was openly declared on the Jews.

The directors of the company Mauricio Hochschild & Cia. Ltda. in Bolivia (where its headquarters were located), Peru, Chile, Argentina, and Brazil granted work contracts to Jews so they could emigrate to South America and thus be saved. Moritz Hochschild, whose presence commanded respect because of his imposing size, direct gaze and undeniable authority, was the richest German Jew in South America. *Newsweek* had called him "fabulously rich" and dubbed him "Bolivia's Top Boss," which outraged a succession of Bolivian governments, especially since he was a foreigner. He was one of the Tin Barons, and they also called him the Bolivian Rothschild because his wealth rivaled that of the Guggenheim and Getty families, whom he had no reason to envy. He was a legend in the Bolivian Andes. They called him "the Silver Table with Golden Legs" because he was always ready to climb to the snowy peaks to extract ore. Even when he was told that the seams were exhausted, he would enter the inundated mine shafts to dry them, open enormous galleries, scan the highest points of the land and discover new seams of ore. He never surrendered to the adversity of nature, and he pulled tin, silver, wolfram, antimony and lead out of the bowels of the shafts and the land. And since he was a miner by vocation, he did everything on his own initiative.

That night, Adolf Blum—tall, thin, around fifty, with firm and elongated features and a unique lucidity—handed him the passports with the fake names that the forger had chosen from the telephone directory at random, the contracts, the work permits, and the stamps. Moritz put them in his false-bottomed suitcase. It was a leather executive briefcase he had had made by a Bolivian artisan for this purpose; it wasn't the first time he had smuggled false passports.

When he arrived in London after an exhausting trip of almost three days, two trusted Jewish associates were waiting for him at the international airport. One of them was a very wealthy and sophisticated textile factory owner. The other one worked at a bank. Both were impeccably dressed in dark suits, white shirts and red ties. Moritz preferred to hand over the documents in Britain because it was less risky than in Germany. His only worry was the officials from the Bolivian embassy in London, whose ambassador was Antenor Patiño (the son of Simón, another of the Tin Barons). On the way to Dorchester, where Moritz always stayed, he said to his associates:

"If that Patiño fellow finds out about the contraband, he won't hesitate to inform on me, and that could cost me dearly."

"We'll hand out the passports at my country house so as not to attract attention or arouse suspicion."

"Good. What's the atmosphere like? Are rumors of war circulating?"

"Don't doubt it for second. War is imminent."

The next day he got up early and went to his office in downtown London. He met with his employees, signed documents, delegated tasks, had lunch, and asked not to be interrupted during the afternoon. He returned to the hotel and a navy-blue Austin Martin was waiting for him punctually; the same men who had met him at Gatwick were inside. It was a cold, gray afternoon mantled by the typical London fog that the British find agreeable only because they are used to it. Feeling nervous, Moritz traveled with the two men to the outskirts of the city. The journey took about an hour. They passed through woodlands and an exclusive country club, arriving at a mansion hidden in the countryside of Virginia Water, county of Surrey. The associate had bought it from an English aristocrat who had fallen on hard times and found himself forced to sell because he hadn't worked a day in his life and could no longer maintain the estate or pay the property taxes. It was from the eighteenth century and was sober in design. News of Hochschild's patronage had spread throughout Europe, even to the countries in the east, and his people were already there awaiting his arrival. They had come to London for the sole purpose of obtaining the documents. They would return to their countries and emigrate at once with their families, bringing only the clothes on their backs so as not to arouse suspicion.

When they entered the mansion they found an assembly of Jews of many nationalities. Upon seeing so many, Moritz—a controlled and articulate man—became anxious, fearing he didn't have enough passports. "Two hundred and twenty, only two hundred and twenty . . . and all these people . . . how did I not buy more?" he thought. "They wouldn't have fit in the briefcase, and carrying two would have called too much attention," he told himself, trying to ease his conscience.

The lady of the house had allowed them in, asked the servants to light the fireplaces, and offered them places to sit in the living rooms and the dining room; those who didn't fit were sitting on the stairs that led to the second floor. She also offered them tea and coffee in shifts because there weren't enough cups. Most of them were heads of families, and they were given priority so as not to separate them from their wives and children. They looked anguished and anxious. A murmur flooded through the room. The owners had told the servants the excuse that they were hiring people to open a new textile factory. With the utmost secrecy, the three men locked themselves in the office along with the lady of the house, who already knew Moritz. They began to go through the cases. The list had been compiled by a coordinator who, financed by the wealthy associate, had traveled throughout Europe collecting the names and addresses of people who wanted to emigrate. He had hidden it under his belt and traveled to London, where he met with the associates who in turn got in touch with Hochschild regarding his next arrival date. Then the coordinator had informed his people so that they could travel to England to obtain the documentation. The only thing he requested from them were photographs, and to not say a word to anyone, except to fellow Jews who were truly willing to emigrate. The four of them now formed a team, and they attended to each person individually. They called them in one by one, giving them work permits with a new name that matched the one on the passports. They glued the photographs, affixed the stamp, and thus they had a new name and Bolivian citizenship.

The London team weren't fearful during the operation; they had British citizenship and they knew that the English would never ally themselves with Hitler, or so they had heard from trustworthy sources within British Intelligence. What's more, they were giving the documents to Jews from different countries, so there was little chance of them being discovered.

Those who didn't want to change their name were given work contracts so that they could process their own visas. They filled in the permits with the job titles of directors, consultants, or even mechanics to work in the Hochschild mines.

When Moritz laconically handed out the documents, he was not promising them work; rather, he was promising them the possibility of fleeing Nazi persecution. When they received the documents, they didn't know how to thank him. The eyes of both men and women filled with tears. Many offered him money or jewels, but the "Team of Four" refused them. They made it very clear that what they were offering was free of charge. The new citizens couldn't believe it. "Does anything in life come for free, especially something that saves lives?" they wondered in confusion.

The work took all night. The lady of the house offered hot soup, bread and coffee to those who spent the night. Dawn arrived, and they finished. To Moritz's relief, there were even a few documents left over, and he left them with his associates. Once everyone was gone, the four of them let out a deep sigh of relief. They were tired but happy.

"Thank you. Thank you so much," they said to Hochschild in unison.

"You are so kind," added the lady of the house.

"I'm the one who should be grateful for your collaboration. My work is done. Please take me to the hotel to get my suitcase, and then to the airport," asked Moritz, feeling exhausted but content.

They went to Dorchester and picked up his suitcase, which he had asked a chambermaid to pack. He gave her a tip and they left for Gatwick at once. Moritz said farewell to his associates and returned to Bolivia.

Moritz Hochschild was a German Jew who was born into a middle-class family in Biblis, Germany. His father was a landowner who sold cattle as well as second-hand construction materials, such as scrap metal. His charisma and personality were imposing. People fell silent whenever he entered a room, just as the entrance of a political leader causes people to begin whispering. And a political leader was what he was, in effect. Sharp-minded and visionary, he overflowed with energy and never tired. In essence, though, he was an intuitive, pragmatic, and cold businessman. He was in his fifties, balding, with a thick mustache, brown eyes under bushy eyebrows, a frank gaze and a belly typical of rich men and renowned chefs. He loved to smoked Havana cigars. He dressed elegantly; even when he was traveling to the mines, he would don a cashmere sweater, suede shoes, a tweed jacket, and a thick wool coal. He often wore a bow tie and always carried his heavy gold Patek Philippe pocket watch, which he said he had bought "with the sweat of his brow." He was a man of the world: cultured, refined and sophisticated. He spoke English, French and Spanish with equal ease. As a multimillionaire he was warm, gentle, uncomplicated, and exceptionally compassionate, especially with his own people, even though he was not a practicing Jew or a Zionist. He had studied at the mining school in Freiberg, Germany, and moved penniless to Valparaiso, Chile, at the beginning of the twentieth century, with the intention of "making it" in America. All he had was a letter of credit from a German bank where

41

his uncle worked, which he intended to invest in mining. He knew the business because he had worked in Germany, Australia, and Spain, where he learned Spanish.

During the First World War he returned to Germany and volunteered in the army. Fortunately for him, he wasn't sent to the front; they assigned him to an office job. During that time, his brother Sali took charge of the business in Chile and continued to supply minerals to their country and the Austrian army. He was lucky: copper prices went through the roof and he started earning a lot of money.

He returned to Chile with a Jewish wife, Käthe Rosenbaum, and his only son, Gerardo, was born there. His wife died of tuberculosis when the child was four years old. It was a tragedy for Moritz; it left him widowed and unsure of how to raise his son. Because of Moritz's long working hours, the child was left in the hands of Chilean Catholic governesses. He saw him very little, especially because he was obliged to travel frequently for work. Work became his obsession, perhaps as a means of forgetting her. He would tell himself: "The only way to forget my loneliness . . . her absence . . . and the sadness of seeing my small child without a mother . . . is to work to the point of exhaustion . . . to fall into bed at the end of the day with my eyes closed . . ."

He had heard of Simón I. Patiño, the Bolivian mining tycoon, during his school days. People said he was the child of a Hungarian, because of his green eyes, and a Bolivian mestiza. They also said he was making a tremendous fortune selling tin in Bolivia. When Patiño started the business, they were so broke that his wife Albina had to sell her jewelry in order to pay the miners who worked for them. He told her: "You've acted like the Queen of Spain; one day I'll build you a palace." When they found ore, she knelt before a crucifix and prayed to God: "Let it be tin, God, not silver!" The price of tin on the international market was much higher at that time. She waited anxiously for Patiño, who left for Huanuni on a mule, carrying samples to be analyzed in his saddlebags. He returned and told her that in La Salvadora—the name they had given his mine because of a premonition—they had found tin. Did Moritz want to emulate him? Patiño managed to amass the fifth largest fortune on the planet, according to *Forbes*. They called him the Tin King. He had so much money that he bought the Williams, Harvey & Co. Ltd. smelter in Great Britain and controlled a quarter of the world's business in smelters and refineries. So great was his power that he even influenced the price of metals. His great sorrow, however, was never being able to live in Bolivia again, because his heart couldn't withstand the altitude.

Hochschild, a skilled Jewish businessman, saw that Bolivia was a country with mining prospects of mythological proportions. Tin possessed extraordinary properties. It didn't rust, could be used both for building weapons of war as well as for alloying with other metals, mainly steel, and for making food cans, a novelty of the modern world. He moved to Bolivia in the 1920s with the aim of becoming the owner and administrator of his own business. At first he did everything himself, from delivering messages to managing the company. "I must become familiar with each position so that no one deceives me," he thought. He initially opened modest offices in Potosí, Oruro, and Tupiza, Bolivia, as well as in Arequipa, Peru. He also opened several laboratories in these places.

He was an avant-garde entrepreneur, full of innovative ideas. He began as a trader in minerals, and then went into wholesale. He would go personally to buy minerals from small and medium-sized mining companies, run primarily by indigenous miners. He had a great capacity for adaptation; when he traveled to mines four thousand two hundred meters above sea level, where conditions were precarious, he lived as he had to live without complaining. He didn't mind whether he made stretches of the journey by truck or mule; he did whatever the situation called for. He loved traveling, and for him, Potosí was the summit of the world, rather like Tibet. When he was there, he felt as if he could touch the sky. He probably came to know Bolivia better than many Bolivians.

He exported minerals directly to Europe because Bolivia lacked a smelting plant. He sold them to Berzelius, which was owned by Metallgesellschaft AG, whose directors he had met while doing an internship there. He therefore had a secure export niche in Germany. He transported ore via a railway line that the nineteenth-century Silver Barons—Arce, Pacheco and Aramayo—had built, both to export their ore and import virtually everything (even their sheets) from Europe. The cargo was shipped first to Arica, Chile, a natural port used by the Bolivians. Then they would put it on the first boat leaving for Europe or the United States.

Moritz was like a good hunter: he had perfect aim. He recalled that during the First World War the demand for tin was so high—it was needed for making everything from soldiers' buttons to the war weapons themselves—that the German government asked its citizens to donate pots, vases and any metal bowls they owned to be melted down so that tin could be extracted from them. Peter the Great did something similar in the war against Sweden. He had the church bells melted down, which offended the clergy and believers. Not that he cared, though; he built an empire.

Hochschild told all this to the managers of the German smelting company Berzelius, and he convinced them to buy low-grade metal at a low price, which they later sold. He was very successful, even more so than Patiño, and his fortune began to grow by leaps and bounds, especially because the price of ore was sky-high. This is how he became the first wholesaler in Bolivia, exporting forty percent of Bolivia's tin and ninety percent of other minerals.

He was in second place after Simón I. Patiño, with Carlos Víctor Aramayo following him in third. They were called the "Tin Barons," the "Clique," or the "Mining Oligarchy," a name they inherited from the "Silver Barons." At the beginning, of course, Hochschild and Aramayo were just "princes" compared to Patiño. For the land-owning oligarchs who belonged to the "Old Silver" group, they were nothing but vulgar "nouveau riche," with the exception of Carlos Víctor, whose father and grandfather had belonged to the group of Silver Barons. These men had created a dynasty, multiplying their fortune, unlike the usual case in which rich parents bring forth tired children. Aramayo, in addition, had insuperable power: he was the owner of the right-wing paper *La Razón*, the most widely circulated newspaper in the country. The new Clique practically owned Bolivia. The mining industry accounted for ninety percent of Bolivia's imports and exports, and it was in the hands of these three people. Their economic and political power, as well as their influence, were monumental. They instated and overthrew governments at their convenience, and they created the supreme decrees that were signed by whichever president of the republic and ministerial cabinet were in power. Moritz lived like a king, and when he traveled, he stayed in the fanciest hotels, ate at the best restaurants, ordered custom-made clothing from the most famous fashion houses in London and Paris, and collected Swiss watches. He surrounded himself with European nobility and was a close friend of Prince Wittgenstein and his family. Power dazzled him, and he used it with the skill of a goldsmith. It attracted him more than money did, probably because he had already too much. But he never stopped saying: "My most precious capital is human capital." And he would tell anyone who would listen that his origins were Jewish, a fact of which he was very proud.

The staff of his companies were mostly Jewish immigrants he had hired not only to help them but also because he felt comfortable working with them. He knew how to treat them, and they trusted him. Clear proof of this was the fact that many lawyers managed the mining companies.

One day, in private, seated in a soft and comfortable armchair and after a few drinks, he suddenly complained with vehemence to his business partner:

"It bothers me that some of my employees complain that they work too much and I pay them too little! Maybe I don't pay them as much as they'd like, but at the end of the day, at least they have a job. I hire all sorts of people, from engineers to artists, and I need to teach them the mining business. That takes time."

"Calm down," Adolf told him.

"It also annoys me when they say I have a preference for German and Austrian Jews, and that I ignore the Poles, as if I were racist against my own people! I don't give a damn that the ones from the east don't speak German and that people say they're lazy and uneducated," he said angrily. "Sooner or later they'll learn to speak Spanish, which is the language they'll need to know here," he added. "It also irks me when they criticize me for preferring to hire our own people instead of Bolivians."

"You're right to do that, because there's a war coming. Don't worry, Moritz. It's difficult to please everyone. In Bolivia, Chile, Brazil and Peru you've hired thousands of people, both natives and Jews, and the company has turned into one of the few multinationals that exist."

"I've loved Bolivia since the day I arrived," he would often say. He was fascinated by the Andean country, not only because he had made his fortune there, but because he felt appreciated, admired, respected and, most of all, needed. He thought that Bolivia, despite its underdeveloped state and certain difficulties he'd encountered, was a beautiful country, one that had always filled him with satisfaction. He admired the marked contrasts of nature. He could appreciate the jungle from the high Andean plateau. He was captivated by the mountains, with their different shades of brown and ocher; enthralled by the brilliance of the sun in the intense blue and cloudless sky; the winter, which didn't seem like winter because the sun made the days warm, embraced him; and he was moved by the people, most of all the indigenous people, whom he found to be humble, self-sacrificing, and courteous, and who worked extremely hard, risking and even shortening their lives. Their ancestors, children, and grandchildren had a life expectancy of thirty-five years because they died of silicosis in the tunnels. When he went to the mines, as he frequently did, he would send a cow or some lambs to be sacrificed, which he would share with them. They would have a tremendous feast during which the miners drank beer until they passed out. "What's left for them to do, given the fate that awaits them?" he thought.

Bolivia's head of state was Germán Busch, a thirty-five year old who had taken power in a military coup and was elected constitutional president by a constituent assembly. He was the son of a German man and a beautiful mestiza. He had inherited his father's white skin and blue eyes, and his mother's raven-black hair. Probably because his father was German, he wasn't racist and had a good heart. He had grown up in the department of Santa Cruz and was so provincial that, when he arrived in La Paz, it seemed like New York to him.

He had participated in three coups, instating and overthrowing presidents through his leadership and command over young officers and troops. He was a product of the Chaco War, where socialist ideology had flourished, when white and indigenous men coexisted and the indigenous ones observed their marginalization and exclusion, especially when they were sent to the front as cannon fodder. He became a furious socialist. He was unstable, fundamentalist, and schizophrenic to the point of paroxysm. On one occasion, in the Palacio Quemado itself—the official residence of the president of Bolivia—he slapped the sixty-year-old eminent writer and liberalist leader Alcides Arguedas several times in the face, until blood poured from his lip. The man had written an open letter criticizing the president. Even worse, he once sent a journalist to be shot for writing against him. He declared himself "Totalitarian Dictator." He exiled his opponents and didn't think twice about sentencing anyone who opposed him to death. Nothing stopped him. He was loved and hated, but more than anything, he was feared. In mid-1939, his government promulgated a draconian decree.

"This cannot be!" Moritz said to Adolf, fuming. "That little brat Busch wants to destroy me with this decree. It's aimed directly at my companies and those of Patiño and Aramayo. It's unbelievable!"

"What does it say?"

"That the large mining companies must deliver one hundred percent of the foreign currency earned from exporting ore and exchange it for the national currency fixed at a lower than market rate. And that the business will be run from now on by the Mining Bank, which is owned by the state."

"That would mean the end of the mining industry, particularly for the wholesalers."

"That's it. I'll ask for a meeting with Busch."

Hochschild's secretaries called the Palacio Quemado a dozen times, but they got nowhere, so Blum went personally to request a meeting with the president. He met with the president's chief of staff, as well as the head of the military, and both said: "Don't call us, we'll call you." That meant "no," just as it does in the United States when a job applicant's phone call is never returned. Busch didn't receive him. Moritz managed, however, to meet as usual with the finance minister, Pou Mont, to whom he said: "I can't believe that Germán, who's been a friend of mine for years, refuses to see me."

After several fruitless encounters, he decided to spell out the circumstances of the situation in a letter, sending a copy to the president. The letter clarified their situation and stated that the maritime freights and railway cargos needed to be paid for in foreign currency. They received no response, not even through the press.

"But . . . why is Busch provoking me? Does he want us to throw ourselves to the floor and declare a hunger strike, or go out into the streets to protest with signs? I have to defend my interests however I can! Well, if the government ignores us, we'll launch our own campaign!" exclaimed Moritz.

Hochschild, with pacifist zeal, stationed his own secretaries and messengers in several places around the city, in both the center and the periphery, to collect signatures with the aim of pressuring the government to revoke the decree. He even asked them to do the same at the mining centers. Everyone supported him. A riot broke out, stoked by the miners' fear of losing their jobs and the business going under. They managed to obtain thousands of signatures. Even the indigenous people who couldn't write put a fingerprint beside their names. Busch and his cabinet were outraged by this movement.

Days later, Moritz met again with his directors in the company's luxurious meeting room, which resembled one of those English clubs where they don't allow women. The room had a huge table carved with lion's feet, Chippendale-style chairs, and walls lined with mahogany on whose shelves stood samples of every mineral on the planet. Photographs hung in the empty spaces: some of his mines, one of La Paz with Illimani in the background, and another of Cerro Rico de Potosí. He loved showing the samples to his friends; they were the only thing he bragged about.

While they were analyzing the difficult situation, they suddenly heard doors slamming and employees running. Despite the bravery of the executive secretary—an elderly woman, who tried to stop them—a group of six armed military men stormed violently into the room.

"Dr. Hochschild, you're under arrest!" shouted a soldier.

"What . . .?"

"Yes. You and the director, a man by the name of Blum. Which of you is he?"

"Me," said Blum as he stood up, his eyes bulging.

"And what are the charges?"

"Keep your damned mouth shut!"

They refused to let them speak and they took them away forcefully. The executives in the room were left speechless, with nothing to say and no one to turn to. At that moment they received a call from the office of Philipp Brothers informing them that their director, Arthur Grünebaum, had been arrested.

The executives from both offices met to analyze the situation. They came to the conclusion that the arrest was politically motivated, and they tried to locate the detainees. Some went to look for them at San Pedro jail, and others went to the small jail on Ayacucho Street, where political prisoners were usually detained. One of the directors slipped a hefty bill to a subordinate guard, who confirmed that the three of them were there. They breathed a deep sigh of relief, because if they had been taken to San Pedro with the common criminals, they would have met their end. They tried to see them, but to no avail. Then they went to the Palacio Quemado hoping that Busch or someone would receive them, but seeing the face of the president proved as impossible as seeing the face of God. Nevertheless, they stayed in the antechamber in order to put pressure on the president. The two detainees arrived at the detention center completely disoriented. They were forced to enter a filthy cell, where they found

Arthur, and they embraced as if they were brothers. Arthur was so afraid that he could barely do or say a thing. All three were somber-faced and deeply distressed. Upon seeing blood on the walls and a mattress lying on the floor stained with God knows what, they trembled and fell silent. Suddenly a squat, hunchbacked, grimy man arrived, dressed in civilian clothing and accompanied by three armed military men. He shouted:

"How dare you challenge the government of our Captain Busch, our war hero? How dare you have been so cynical as to question the decree and collect signatures, when this measure is for the good of the Bolivian people? You have committed a crime against the government and the nation, and that is treason, a crime punishable by death! You shitty gringos! You rich sons of bitches!"

They were dumbstruck. After the dwarfish man left, they began to speak to one another in German.

"The death penalty . . .?" said Moritz.

It was as silent as if the ghost of Hamlet had appeared. The three men swallowed in unison. Protesting the decree, it seemed, entailed arrest and execution. They had never imagined Busch would take it so far.

"Busch can be reasoned with, if he's approached gently. I only hope that our managers can make him realize the mistake he's making," Moritz said firmly.

"But he won't even see them! He only meets with you," said Blum.

"Don't be negative, Adolf."

"What's your relationship with him?" Grünebaum asked nervously.

"We've become friends and I think he appreciates me. He's not a bad person, he can actually be quite reasonable, although he's certainly insane. This must be one of his fits of rage. I've had long conversations with him. I can't deny that thanks to him thousands of our people have been allowed to immigrate to Bolivia, and I've agreed to help establish a large Jewish colony. He was enthusiastic about the idea. He even told me repeatedly that he would accept twenty or thirty thousand on the condition that they colonize agricultural areas and become pioneers. He told me this in the presence of two emissaries from the American Jewish Joint Distribution Committee. It's a project we can't abandon and in which I need to be involved."

"I hope his friendship with you will make him listen to reason. Busch got upset because we're still mining and trading ore, despite the decree. The decree hasn't been sanctioned by Parliament yet, and as long as they haven't approved it, we have the right to continue working. The lawyers assured us of this."

"But how do you explain that to an ignorant, provincial military man?"

"The truth is that I'm afraid he found out that I financed the coup, at Aramayo's request. It's true that I put in half the money. How could I not, when everyone said they were going to nationalize the mines, as Toro did last year with Standard Oil? I made Carlos Víctor promise that my name would remain anonymous, but some Judas betrayed me. It must have been that, too." His head began to ache. "On top of that, the government must have discovered that I've been involved in trafficking Bolivian passports for our persecuted people. I don't regret that; on the contrary, I'm proud of it."

"Excuse me for saying this, Moritz, but you take too many risks."

"Busch most probably thinks I'm like his chancellor, that Diez de Medina fellow, who's a moron. He made a business out of selling visas and trafficking passports, charging up to five thousand dollars at Bolivian consulates in Hamburg, Warsaw, Genoa, Paris, Zurich, and who knows where else. That crook, stealing money from our people, who have given over all they have and even what they don't have. From one day to the next he went from being a beggar to being rich. Everyone knows that. They branded him a swine, saying he's a Catholic convert of Jewish ancestry. His last name confirms it. Me, on the other hand, I've lost money."

"Don't take it that way . . . Moritz, you haven't lost anything, you've saved so many people. Luckily the 'Jewish Immigrants Affair' cost him his job, the scoundrel. And you, on the other hand, have become a legend, you and 'Hochschild's passports.'"

"All that talk about 'Hochschild's passports' isn't important. What makes me angry is that the government doesn't recognize that we've created jobs for thousands of Bolivians . . ."

"The fact is that we're locked up in this disgusting cell that smells like shit and piss, as if we were thieves or murderers."

Busch was in a meeting with his cabinet members in the main office. He had summoned them to decide how to punish the "three treacherous Jews." Whenever he met with the magnate he called him Dr. Hochschild, but now that he was his enemy, he was "that fucking Jew." He was determined to give the death penalty to Moritz and two years of prison to Blum and Grünebaum. He wanted to make an example out of them.

"That damned Hochschild is a double traitor. He conspired with Aramayo to finance the coup to overthrow me and instate Toro!" cried Busch, in one of those outbursts of anger he often had. "And that Toro scoundrel managed to flee the country; if he hadn't, I would have sent him to the firing squad! For now, gentlemen, I ask for your approval to execute Hochschild tomorrow at six in the morning."

The ministers were left speechless. A few moments later, when they had recovered, they tried to convince the president to retract his sentence and release the detainees, mostly because they didn't want the execution of such a remarkable man on their conscience. Some of the ministers began to mention possible resignations within the executive, which infuriated the president even further. He repeatedly banged his hand on the table, losing control, his face purple with rage to the extent that the veins on his temples bulged.

"If you'll allow me, your Excellency, Mr. Hochschild helped to finance the Chaco War," the finance minister reminded him.

"But that was chump change to him! The Tin Barons have more money than thieves . . . they're a bunch of crooks!" he roared, as all dictators do. "That gringo bought the mines for next to nothing during the Great Depression. He became the owner of Huanchaca, Unificada, Matilde, Colquiri and Minera de Oruro when those mines should belong to the Bolivian people. What's more, he's hated by the majority of Bolivians because he got rich off the backs of indigenous people. He's an imperialist!"

"Mr. President," the finance minister added. "According to the information I have, ninety-five percent of his capital is invested in Bolivia. As long as we ensure he pays his taxes, Bolivia, to a large extent, maintains itself thanks to those taxes, and he's brought great prosperity to the cities of Potosí, La Paz, and Oruro. Roads, railway lines, hospitals and public schools have been built. Oruro owes its buoyancy today to the fact that it has become the country's mining center."

"That shameless Jew has forged passports, signatures, names, and stamps, and trafficked in them. There's all this talk about Hochschild's famous passports, even though he has smuggled Bolivian passports with the sacred emblems of our nation!"

51

Dionisio Foianini, the minister of mining, a chemical engineer and a close friend of Moritz's, stood up and spoke in favor of the condemned man with the frankness and courage for which people from Santa Cruz are known.

"What Hochschild's company has done for refugees is worthy of praise, as is what you have done, your Excellency, in helping Jews enter Bolivia without conditions, saving thousands from Nazi persecution. Eight thousand Jewish refugees entered the country from 1938 to 1939, and according to the recent census, there are currently 13,250 Jews living in Bolivia." He held up a document confirming the statistics. "The magnate helps the Jewish community disinterestedly, with unprecedented generosity and without asking for anything in return. Rarely has such solidarity and generosity been seen in a man of his social and economic status. Along with Grünebaum, he has founded and finances the Association for the Protection of Jewish Immigrants. He also created the Colonization Association of Bolivia, to which he has personally contributed one hundred thousand dollars in collaboration with the American Jewish Joint Distribution Committee. He obtained international financial aid for this project to the amount of one million dollars, which includes, among other things, the purchase of a thousand hectares in Yungas to grow fruit, cocoa and coffee. They've already built houses there for them to live in, even the new arrivals. Their organizations have a fund that provides the refugees with vouchers for food, a roof over their heads until they get settled, as well as loans for housing or for opening a business. The Colonization Association of Bolivia (SOCOBO) has become the most important Jewish company in the history of our country. Hochschild helps his people with colonization projects like no Bolivian has ever done. In addition, the detainees create jobs not only for refugees, but also for thousands of Bolivians, mostly in the mining centers of Potosí and Oruro. He has created work for twenty thousand indigenous miners, in medium sized and small companies, by buying their minerals. He himself has financed most of our people without charging interest, so that they can open their own wholesale businesses and thereby become independent. This has raised the standard of living for our people and contributed to the progress and welfare of our country. These cities have grown enormously, contributing to the development of Bolivia. He is also a great philanthropist. He has built a hospital, a nursey, an asylum, and a home for the children of his workers in

Cochabamba, especially for the Potosí miners who live at a high altitude. And he has planted trees all over the city. The site is also used as a vacation home for his employees and their families. He has made considerable donations to Catholic convents and monasteries, despite being an atheist; he maintains institutions, charities, and hospitals for elderly and destitute Bolivians; he gave money to the University of Potosí for the creation of a Faculty of Mining, and he has founded scholarships for Bolivians and Latin Americans to study at Harvard. Moreover, he has promoted our country's cultural heritage by financing an edition of *The History of the Imperial City of Potosí* by Bartolomé Arzáns de Orsúa y Vela, the most important chronicler of the colonial era, which was published by Harvard and Brown Universities. He also gives money for education in Peru, Chile, Argentina and Brazil."

"I don't give a damn what he does in other countries!" snapped Busch, trying not to swear.

"He discovered the talent of Rubinic de Vela, the indigenous draughtsman from Potosí, paying for his studies in Chile and Europe, and now he's the most famous political cartoonist in France. He has also promoted the work of the great Bolivian sculptor Marina Nuñez del Prado."

Things were looking grim to the ministers. In the midst of a heavy cloud of cigarette smoke, after hours of discussion during which everyone spoke of Hochschild´s virtues, a vote was taken. The majority of the cabinet voted against the death penalty, some in favor of exiling him, and others in favor of several years of imprisonment. The president, probably very much influenced by the words of Foianini, who was a close friend (they used the familiar form of address in private), affirmed vehemently:

"I had decided to proceed with Hochschild's execution, but because of your insistence on clemency, gentlemen, and in homage our friendship, I will grant Mr. Hochschild an absolute pardon, without fines or financial penalties, as these would be unseemly for the government to impose."

"He came to his senses, fortunately," thought Foianini. The ministers breathed a sigh of relief, went home, and slept peacefully. The president allowed himself to be persuaded, albeit reluctantly, because, like a capricious child, he liked to have things his way. He pardoned them, but he forced them to spend the night in jail.

53

For the detainees it was the worst night of their lives, because even though they were together, they had no news from outside. They didn't sleep a wink due to the uncertainty, the misinformation, the threats made by the grimy dwarf, and the fear of being tortured. The dictator was capable of anything, and they knew it. They weren't even allowed to call anyone or use the bathroom. They were exhausted from the nervous tension and had to sit on top of that filthy mattress, which filled them with nausea.

Moritz couldn't stop thinking about his profound loneliness. Not even all the money in the world gave him the happiness he yearned for. He thought: "My son Gerardo is studying in the United States and rarely writes to me . . . he simply expects his monthly allowance and doesn't even deign to send me his grades . . . and me? Divorced from Germaine . . . our marriage didn't even last six years . . . and to think that I got married without caring that she was Catholic . . . what a difficult woman! . . . but so loved . . . I fell in love with the wrong woman . . . was it because it was a forbidden love? How could I take Phillip's wife away from him! How could I do that to him, he was my cousin . . . a Hochschild . . . and we worked together . . . and now the family and the company are divided . . . I behaved like an idiot, and now I'm paying for it. I like to live well, just like the next person, but . . . perhaps I'm just as frivolous and ostentatious as Patiño and Aramayo, with their mansions in Paris, apartments in New York, yachts in the Mediterranean, and art collections? My life and my world are in Bolivia, though."

They were released the next day after a phone call from the Palacio Quemado. Word of what had happened spread quickly, just as it does when someone dies, and the day after their release the three men received a special invitation from the Israelite Circle, a center for social, cultural and religious activities. The center had a lounge, a dining room, a synagogue, a library, a cafeteria and games rooms where Skat and table tennis were played.

Moritz went to pick up his friends and they arrived together. When they entered the assembly hall they found hundreds of members of the Jewish community who, upon seeing them, began to applaud. He was so touched that his eyes filled with tears, which he tried to hide: "These are my people . . . nothing has been in vain . . ." He felt happier than he had in a long time. They placed kippot on their heads, welcomed them, and expressed their unconditional support. The businessmen said a few words of thanks for their support. Then they stayed for dinner, where they ate kosher food while the Schein Orchestra played, a quartet made up of Jewish musicians that caused a sensation in bars, hotels, night clubs and the brand-new Sucre Palace Hotel.

The freed men continued with their daily lives, but they were worried about their future as businessmen, as well as their personal safety.

Just as there was a Jewish community in Bolivia, there was also a German one, whose members were mostly Nazis. When they heard that the "powerful Jews" had been arrested, they got together to celebrate in the German club, which only they were allowed to enter. They didn't even accept German Jews, and they made this known the minute they stepped foot in Bolivia as refugees, stigmatizing them immediately. They were denied entry to the club even though they had German last names, didn't speak Hebrew, and didn't practice the Jewish religion. Many newcomers were stunned by this since they felt more German than Jewish.

The German community, although much smaller than the Jewish one, was older. It dated back to the beginning of the twentieth century, when Germans arrived to colonize the departments of Santa Cruz and Beni. After a while, many moved to La Paz to start their own businesses. The most emblematic figure, and the one closest to the Third Reich in Bolivia, was Hans Kundt. At the beginning of the century, President Villazón, an oligarch who sympathized with the military, contracted a German mission headed by Kundt. He advised and trained the Bolivian Armed Forces and oversaw them during the Chaco War. He put down such deep roots there that, during the Saavedra government, he was appointed minister of war, which did not go down well with the Bolivian people since he was a foreigner. While Kundt was living in Bolivia, Ernst Röhm joined the Bolivian army with the rank of lieutenant colonel. He was hired to instruct the military. Röhm was an ill-fated and ambitious member of the Nazi part, and he was a known homosexual. He was so effeminate that his comrades would mock him by saying that he peed sitting down. After his poor performance in Bolivia, he returned to Germany and, at the request of the Führer, took over the command of the Sturmabteilung (SA), a paramilitary group also called the "Brownshirts," over which Hitler had previously presided.

The German community was exclusive and well established. They founded the educational establishment Mariscal Braun, also known as the Colegio Alemán; it was located on Aspiazu Street, and the director as well as most of the teachers were German. They also created other schools: one in Cochabamba and another in Oruro. Both the Bolivian and the German anthems were sung every Monday morning. A picture of the Führer hung permanently in the main hall, and the Bolivian, German and Nazi flags were on display. They celebrated Hitler's birthday religiously. The teachers inculcated the National-Socialist doctrine and did not hesitate to punish undisciplined students by hitting their hands with rulers and pulling their ears. They humiliated them by making them sit on a bench in the corner, facing the wall. Such students were called "detainees," which provoked the wrath of their parents, who came in to complain. Others weren't bothered by the violence and loved the school. Upper-class Bolivians who had enrolled their children there because it was a European school learned about all this and began to withdraw them, regardless of the fact that they would miss a year of classes. They enrolled them in American establishments instead. The small and cliquish high-society circle in Bolivia may have been right-wing, but it wasn't fascist. The German school closed a short while later.

The Germans even had a Protestant church, called Martin Luther, where they went to worship on Sundays and where they also took the opportunity to chat. They were very concerned about the unprecedented growth of the Jewish community. It was growing so quickly that it had become the largest immigrant community. They wanted to stop more Jews from coming regardless of the cost. They said this to their "Commander-in-Chief," Wendler, and he replied: "I know . . . we know . . . and all because of the efforts of that dirty Jew, that *nouveau riche* Hochschild, who's in cahoots with that scoundrel Busch. It's a pity he didn't end up rotting in jail. He must have bribed God and the devil to get out," he said in a strong German accent. (He had never made the effort to learn Spanish well.) Although the Germans owned a few stores, the Jews owned more; they never bought food or products from each other, and if they needed something urgently, they would send their maids. They never encountered each other at restaurants or cafeterias because they frequented different places. Whenever they ran into each other on the street, at the market, theater or pharmacy, they would recognize each other immediately and intuitively look away. The Germans would generally cross the street when they met. The Jews wouldn't, however; they felt safe in Bolivia because they knew they had a protector and benefactor: Hochschild, whose messianic work had turned him into a legend. They knew that if their lives were threatened, they could become Bolivian citizens and emigrate to one of the neighboring countries. And some did this, moving mostly to Argentina, the most European country, or to the United States, the most desirable one. It was even known that a few emigrated to bordering countries illegally, hidden in cargo trucks, bribing the authorities at the borders. The majority, however, went through the citizenship process in order to obtain, among other things, a Bolivian passport that didn't have a huge red "J" stamp, or the name "Israel" added to the men's names and "Sara" to the women's. Some even changed their last names. The German consulate in La Paz did all it could to make their lives impossible. Those who wanted to renew their passports would show up at the legation, and their passports would be stamped with the red "J" even if they had entered Bolivia without it.

The German community detested Hochschild, Blum and Grünebaum, not only because they were Jewish but because they had more power and money than they did. They knew that Moritz had contacts at the Palacio Quemado, and that he made friends with all of Bolivia's presidents, who would rise to and fall from power in a matter of months, mainly due to military pressure. He even used the familiar form of address with most of them. They were also aware that the Peruvian head of state, Manuel Prado, and his wife, Clorinda Málaga, were very fond of him and Germaine. One afternoon, Moritz and the engineer Soux, a miner friend of his who lived in Potosí, were leaving a meeting at the National Bank. Moritz proposed they go for a stroll to enjoy the winter sunlight. As they walked, they observed how quickly the Jewish community was consolidating itself. The main street was full of Jewish businesses, such as Optalvis Opticians, and Foto Linares Studio, whose owner, upon recognizing them, came out to greet them and even asked to have his picture taken with them. They also walked past the Bolivian-Jewish school.

"Did you know, Soux, that this school was built by my people through sheer grit, and that PhDs in physics and medical doctors teach mathematics and other subjects to our children?" Moritz said proudly. "The government, unfortunately, doesn't recognize their university diplomas," he added, his face changing.

"How courageous of them . . ."

"And those who don't speak Spanish work as truck drivers, construction workers and plumbers on building sites. They built the Sucre Palace Hotel and stayed on to work as waiters, to the delight of the oligarchs, who prefer to be served by whites rather than mestizos. And the women work as laundresses or maids in hotels or in landowners' houses," he added. "And as we're Jews," he smiled, "others work as hawkers, buying things at a certain price and selling them at a greater one, going from house to house offering things and accepting credit from their clients. They've even imposed the practice of paying on credit. It's mostly the Polish Jews who do this kind of work."

"Their ability to adapt is remarkable."

Continuing on their walk, they saw the façade of the central post office graffitied with swastikas, a plethora of offences, and Nazi propaganda such as "Get out *Jude*," "Long live Hitler," "Death to the Jews," "All Saras are whores, all Israels are faggots," and "Job stealers."

"It's the Brownshirts! They do it to turn the Bolivians against us. Tomorrow I'll instruct the mail workers to paint the walls again."

They stopped to have tea and pastries at the Club de La Paz, a café frequented by the city's high society. Many people came up to greet them when they entered; then they sat down at a table.

"It's infuriating that these fascists celebrated our imprisonment. They also did so at their club in Cochabamba, with a picture of the Führer hanging in the main hall."

"They're shameless, these people... What's the situation with Germans in Bolivia?"

"It's a pity that pro-Nazi families founded the brewery and the paper mill, which are apparently quite profitable. The worst thing is that the owner of the mill controls most of the paper imports, and he can afford to restrict paper sales to the opposition press. He and the German community even subsidize the pro-Nazi newspapers, such as *Stürmer* and *La Calle*, where they publish news from German press agencies. Augusto Cespedes writes for *La Calle*, and despite being a famous writer, he's willing to sell his pen to the highest bidder."

"That's why they call him a shady character. I don't read him out of principle. He once said: 'I'm a friend of my enemies' enemies.'"

"The man is dangerous because he's talented. And they've accused the director of the *Rundschau von Illimani*, a weekly published in German, of being a traitor. The German community is doing everything possible to get the government to shut down the newspaper. Fortunately, so far they haven't succeeded. But the one that really gets to me is the German ambassador, Wendler. That fool is the leader of the Auslands-Organisation, the foreign branch of the National Socialist German Workers Party. They work in secret because they're aware of Busch's support for Jewish immigration."

"How many of them are there?"

"Only a few, compared to us," he assured him, sighing. "Right now in Bolivia there are one hundred and seventy active militants backed by about a thousand Germans. They even got German uniforms made for themselves! They wrote an 'Anti-Semitic Manifesto,' which was circulated anonymously throughout the country. They're so sure—just as we are—that Hitler will start a war that they're starting to care less and less whether the government knows what they're up to. Their headquarters are in the same building as the German embassy. They meet there once a week with the excuse of catching up, but all they do is conspire against us. Wendler has also bought several politicians who publicly protest against the immigration decree and complain about the disproportionate number of Jews in Bolivia. They accuse them of taking away their jobs, and they say so many have arrived that they just roam around the streets—which is true, particularly in Cochabamba."

"But are they taking their jobs?"

"Very few of them, since they prefer to have their own businesses. Wendler has also bought some journalists. The pro-Nazis jump at the chance to publish editorials against us, with headlines such as 'The Imperialist Jews of Wall Street,' or 'The Conspiracy of Zion.'"

"Just ignore them."

"I recently read that they're accusing us of being leftists involved in an international conspiracy linked to communists and Bolsheviks. They say Bolivians regret having their country inundated with big-nosed, physically unattractive Jewish immigrants who are avaricious and unwilling to adapt. They say the streets reek of Jews, and they repeat, in this Catholic country, the eternal refrain that they are the murderers of Jesus."

"They also publish offensive caricatures. I recommend that you don't pay any attention to it, though."

"The German government bought them off with a cheap airplane, which I will never board even though it bears the flag of Lloyd Aéro Boliviano. They feel very safe in Bolivia because during the Chaco

War, German pilots transported wounded soldiers and provisions while they trained the locals."

"It's a pity that they flee from them but end up running into them again here."

"My people's biggest fear is that if war is declared, they'll retaliate against them."

"It's possible," he said, nodding.

"These Nazis have never taken their sights off Bolivia. They see it as a small gold mine. They're interested in its strategic position and in its wealth of mineral deposits; they also say there might be oil and gas."

They left the Club de La Paz, walking past the Tesla cinema where a show was about to begin. Night had fallen. They heard shouting at the theater door. They came closer and saw some young men dressed in brown shirts insulting and beating another group of young people with sticks. The girls began to scream, asking for help, while the boys defended themselves with their fists. The scene caught the attention of the municipal police, who were stationed just around the corner at city hall. Moritz and the engineer ran over to help and the Brownshirts fled upon seeing them. They had beaten up some Jewish students, who recognized Hochschild when he approached them. Some of the victims were suffering from head wounds and complaining of pain in different parts of their bodies. More than anything, though, they were terrified, especially the girls, who were weeping.

"Get home as quickly as possible, boys," Moritz said after removing his handkerchief from his pocket to wipe one of their wounds. "I'd like to speak with you. I'll be expecting you tomorrow morning in my office. Damned Nazis!" he exclaimed indignantly.

The next day they went to see him. He recommended, gravely, that they arm themselves so as to protect their people from "those abusers." Their mothers protested vehemently when they were told, but they were left with no choice after the attack. They decided to go out in groups of five or six to make the rounds every night, thereby protecting their people in public places such as cinemas and theaters, and allowing them to feel safe while out in the streets. When the Brownshirts saw that they were armed, they decided not to attack them again.

In August of that year something unexpected happened. President Busch found himself feeling depressed in his office at the Palacio

Quemado. His mother had died a few days before. He lived in the residence with his relatives, who served as bodyguards because he didn't trust anyone. While they were celebrating a relative's birthday in the main hall, a letter arrived from one of his brothers-in-law. It gave an account of the poor attendance at the funeral of the leader's mother in Cochabamba. Busch's father hadn't been able to attend because he had to travel to Germany. This depressed him even more. He also felt he lacked the support of the people of Cochabamba. Busch always carried a Colt pistol in his pocket, and he pulled it out and shouted: "The presidency ends here!" He tried to shoot himself. His aides-de-camp grabbed his arms, but the shot went off anyway, shattering the window into a thousand pieces. Then he said to his brothers-in-law: "Let's kill ourselves, all three of us!" They were stunned and begged him to calm down. "He really is crazy," one of them thought. Busch put the gun away, sat down and tried to calm himself. Minutes later, he shot himself in the right temple, falling face down on the desk in a pool of blood. He didn't die. They took him to the hospital to remove the bullet, but it proved impossible. He died the next day, leaving the population stunned. They held a vigil for him in the main hall of the Palacio Quemado, during which they bestowed upon him the highest honors. People lined up for hours to pay their last respects. The Jewish community attended all the funeral rites and sent numerous bouquets of flowers. Crowds of people came. Moritz wasn't surprised that the president committed suicide; he knew the man had never been in his right mind. He was grateful, though, for everything he had done to help his people immigrate.

"Send a bouquet of flowers, the biggest one you can find," Moritz instructed his secretary. "I'll write a note expressing my condolences."

With Busch's death, the decree against the miners was annulled and never implemented. His successor, Carlos Quintanilla, did not change the immigration policy, thanks to the influence of Hochschild, who spent hours extolling what the previous government had achieved for immigrants.

Chapter 3
Bolivia, 1939–1940

It didn't take long for the ship's passengers to realize that the captain of the Tiberius was a fifth-rate Italian pirate who had overloaded the boat with Jews who didn't have visas. He had gotten rich off of the bribes he had accepted over the past two years. Boris recalled all the money he had had to pay the travel agency and was outraged. "If we had bribed the captain, we would have been able to travel without any problems . . . but it we hadn't bought the tickets, they wouldn't have given us the visas . . . those crooks . . . there's not one person who hasn't found a way to take advantage of our situation," he thought.

The majority of the ship's passengers were Jewish refugees from a variety of European countries. Boris and Isaac recognized several people whom they had traveled with on the train, and they became friends. The journey on the Tiberius seemed eternal, even more so because they were heading toward the unknown, which awakened feelings of insecurity and anxiety. Were they afraid? Of course they were, although they didn't let it show. It was difficult because, on top of everything, they had been deceived. Instead of being given the cabin they had paid for, they were assigned to a huge room with three-tiered bunks shared by some thirty-odd men of all ages. The women were quartered in similar fashion in another room; like the men, they refrained from complaining. The bathrooms were also shared. They had to line up to wash themselves as best they could. They ate poorly: the food was bland and the portions meager. They were fed, almost every day, the same vegetable soup with fish, a piece of bread, and a pitcher of water to share. Eating beef or chicken was an unimaginable luxury. Most had to turn a blind eye to the notion of kosher food. In fact, they behaved quite stoically, and no complaints were uttered about the difficult situation. The waters of the Atlantic Ocean were very rough, though, so most of the passengers became seasick. Panic would suddenly seize the young men whenever some fool told stories about the sinking of the Titanic or the recent case of the St. Louis, a ship full of Jewish German refugees whose visas, upon their arrival in Cuba, were declared false. Despite being docked in Havana for weeks, the president of Cuba denied entry to more than 936 passengers. And even though they were only ninety miles off the coast of the United States, the US government didn't take them in either, despite the fervent efforts of the American Jewish Distribution Committee. It turned out to be a brazenly shady deal. The ship's captain was forced to return to Europe with the passengers, and many later died. When Boris and Isaac heard this, they checked their passports to make sure their visas were real, and they were overcome with fear at not having a transit visa for Chile. Boris told his friend: "The consul stamped the passport in front of my eyes when I went to pick up the documents." And regarding the Chilean transit visa he said: "The worst they can do is escort us to the Bolivian border, which we have a visa for . . . but it would be truly terrible if they wanted to put us on a boat going back . . ."

There was a group of Jews who did nothing but discourage the refugees headed to Bolivia, telling them it was like an African country, only with savage Indians instead of black people.

Little by little they began to discover what sort of people were traveling alongside them. They were a sundry group: from orthodox Jews who looked like rabbis to others who were so Europeanized that they didn't even appear to be Jewish. Among the travelers were Zionists, atheists, intellectuals, academics, wealthy and refined people as well as poor and humble people. There were socialist and communist political refugees who were persecuted and considered enemies by the Nazis, as well as Spanish Republicans and Latin Americans who had fought in the Spanish Civil War and were fleeing as a result of Franco's victory. They also observed that there were four German families who said next to nothing and only consorted discreetly among themselves. Boris and Isaac deduced that they were members of the Nazi Party who were also fleeing.

"It's disgraceful that these Nazis are trying to blend in among us to escape," said Isaac.

"It proves that war is imminent," Boris replied.

The passengers were very well informed about everything that went on in Europe, thanks to the fact that some of them had brought portable radios. Any news was relayed immediately to their fellow travelers. They speculated day and night about the German occupation of Austria and Czechoslovakia and the annexation of the Sudetenland, concluding that this would continue since the Führer's delusions of grandeur were such that he believed he was the reincarnation of Napoleon. Mussolini, meanwhile, was intent on creating the second Roman Empire. The Spanish passengers were outraged by the German bombing of Spain in support of the fight against communism. Given this panorama, they could do nothing but thank God for being alive, even though their future was uncertain.

Arriving in Panama filled them with hope because they saw the mainland and felt that they would soon reach their destination. Black boys approached them in small boats, offering tropical fruit for sale. They took advantage of the opportunity and bought pineapples and bananas, which they had never seen before, for next to nothing. They were advised to choose the greenest ones so that they would last during the trip. They also amused themselves watching some of the passengers throw coins into the sea while the boys dove down like fish to retrieve them, keeping them as a reward. They also noticed that the Italian sailors were smuggling tobacco, alcohol, and pearl necklaces.

Many people boarded the ship in Panama; they were mainly Latinos and a few Americans, mostly mining engineers. It was there that they began to hear the Spanish language spoken, and they made an effort to learn it. They even became friends with a Chilean crew member, whom they paid to give them Spanish lessons.

Isaac, who spoke Hebrew, became friends with some of their fellow Jewish passengers, and Boris later got to know them too. They noticed, however, that there was racism even amongst the Jews themselves. The German speaking Jews, or the *Yekkes*, only socialized with each other and looked down on the Yiddish speaking Jews from eastern Europe. This group felt superior because they came from countries such as Germany, Austria, Lithuania and Hungary, which they considered to be more cultured. They dressed as occidentals and passed themselves off as members of the European, non-Jewish bourgeoisie. They only presented themselves as Jews to those who recognized them as such; otherwise, they would say they were from their country of origin, which was most often Germany. They even added two "n's" to the last names that ended with one so as to pass for Europeans.

They called the Polish Jews *Polacken* and Jews from the east *Ostjuden*, because they generally wore caftans and the women wore handkerchiefs tied around their necks instead of hats. They were considered provincial, uneducated and lower class.

"Does it bother you that they ignore us and look down on us as 'Jewish riff-raff'?" Isaac asked Boris.

"It's actually hard to believe that in these times of adversity our own people discriminate against us because we're from Poland," he responded.

"Nobody brushes you aside because of the way you look; you could be Nordic."

"They know I'm Polish all the same."

Regardless, the young men ignored them and killed timed playing poker, chess and holding ping-pong tournaments. Their self-esteem was so high that they took the competition very seriously and began to win at everything, which made the others stop looking down on them. "The bad thing about being Jewish is that we have always been segregated, we have to stand out in everything we do in order to earn respect . . . even in a simple game."

Boris passed the time playing bridge with a group of Jews who played obsessively, without pause. "If you play bridge, any society in the world will open its doors to you," one of them told him. He found this surprising. They discovered a group of intellectuals with whom they began to exchange novels. And their chests would tighten when suddenly, at dinner time, they heard a fellow Jew play the violin. They would recall, nostalgically, everything they had been forced to leave behind. Boris looked again and again at the photo of Varinia and remembered that special, passionate, and unforgettable night of love. He missed her deeply, just as he missed his family. In moments of extreme sadness, he would pray to the Black Madonna, who had become a kind of good luck charm for him. He thought that as long as he had God and the heavenly court in his words, thoughts and heart, he would never be abandoned. He recalled his mother's words about prayer: "Pray and you will be heard."

On the Sabbath, under the direction of a rabbi, those of Jewish faith put on the kippah, lit the candles of the menorah, placed a veil over their heads and read the sacred texts of the Torah. They prayed and sang hymns, such as the Pesuke de-Zimra, rocking back and forth. They also said afternoon and evening prayers such as Mincha and Maariv. And when they felt happy they sang the Hatikvah (Hymn of Hope), united in their faith.

When they were a few miles north of the Chilean coast, on a pitch-black night amidst the rough, cold waters of the Pacific, they heard an explosion. The terrified passengers came out of their rooms in their pajamas, stumbling aimlessly around the ship, to the point of stepping on and colliding with each other. Boris and Isaac, also in pajamas, ran to put on life jackets, which others were already fighting over.

"The ship is burning!" a woman cried.

This frightened the passengers even more, and they continued stumbling over each other. Then they heard a deafening alarm and whistles being blown by crew members who pleaded for calm amidst the screams and cries of women looking for their relatives. Suddenly the lights went out and they found themselves in darkness. The people who had crowded into the corridors stampeded onto the deck; some fell and were trampled on. Once on deck, they heard a passenger wail: "The ship is sinking!" This cry further increased the terror, and people began to run to the lifeboats, clambering to get into them. The crew members ordered them to form two rows: one for women, children and the elderly, and the other for men. And amidst the whistles, shouts, and shoves, they began to board passengers into the lifeboats. Because they were young and male, Boris and Isaac were among the last in line.

"We're screwed," Isaac said to Boris. "We're damned fools. We fled from the Nazi dogs to drown to death in the middle of this horrendous ocean!"

"Shut up, don't be pessimistic, idiot . . . be brave . . . have some guts! God and my Black Madonna are protecting us! Have faith!"

"Screw your gods. No one can save us from this."

"You're a moron, an idiot! Instead of saying stupid things, pray, Isaac, pray . . ."

The Jews suddenly began to pray, and this gave them a certain amount of tranquility and hope. Women and children said goodbye to their husbands, fathers, and older sons as they boarded the lifeboats. Families began to separate. Within a few hours, most passengers had managed to get in the lifeboats. Meanwhile, the Italian sailors were doing all that was humanly possible to put out the fire with extinguishers, even breaking some containers full of water to pour onto the fire.

The only ones who stayed behind were those who burned to death from the explosion in the engine room and those who were trampled in the stampede. Their relatives didn't want to leave them, but after sending several doctors from among the crew to reconfirm that they had died, the captain ordered that the bodies be left behind.

Once Boris and Isaac got into a lifeboat and started sailing on the high seas, Boris exclaimed:

"And . . . the painting?"

"What do you care about the painting?"

"But it's our life insurance!"

"We are our life insurance. Forget about it . . . it's too late!"

"But my mother gave it to me . . ."

"Let it go. I already had to let go of the ring my mother gave me."

They were sure that they wouldn't survive because they hadn't been able to put on anything warm and were shaking from the cold, they had no food, and they were in the middle of an immense ocean. Miraculously, a cargo ship from the Chilean Navy appeared—it was responding to the SOS call that the captain of the Tiberius had managed to send. They were filled with hope upon seeing it.

They suddenly saw the Tiberius turn into a ball of fire that lit up the sky and heard a deafening explosion. The survivors looked on in astonishment as the ship sank little by little, vertically, amid the wails and sobs of the refugees who watched as their dead relatives sank along with it. Nearly thirty people lost their lives. It was later discovered that the shipwreck was caused by a short circuit that had gotten out of control. Upon witnessing this scene, Boris thought for a moment of the Kandinsky painting sinking with the ship. He reflected and said to himself: "You're an idiot to think of a painting when these poor people have lost their loved ones . . . forgive me, God."

The young men made sure that their pouches were in place and thanked God for Isaac's mother. They had managed to save their documents, money, family photographs and a couple of jewels their mothers had given them, because they slept with all this tied around their waists for fear of being robbed.

The commodore of the Chilean ship instructed his crew to help the survivors aboard and to accommodate them as best they could. The young men were allocated a space where food, containers, and crates were stored, and they were provided with blankets, coffee and hot chocolate.

The families stayed together and, despite the exhaustion, no one could sleep a wink. Most of the survivors, especially those who had lost family members, were crying. Others said: "We're alive and we must thank Jehovah."

Dawn broke, and in the distance they saw a hill surrounded by fog with a few lights that twinkled like stars, illuminating the city. The boat docked at a makeshift port. They had arrived in Arica, a small, inhospitable city on the coast in the middle of a hot, arid desert, without even a palm tree; all it could boast of was a headland. They learned that it had previously been Peruvian territory, won by Chile in the War of the Pacific of 1879. They also learned that Bolivia had lost a lot of territory in that same conflict, including large mineral reserves and access to the sea. But for them it was dry land, and that meant freedom and gave them hope. The survivors thanked God, feeling that they were blessed because they had been saved twice: first from the Nazis, then from the shipwreck.

They disembarked and went to the immigration office, a storehouse in which employees sat at small tables with typewriters, stamps and forms. They were simple men, unshaven and dirty, who looked as though they had slept in their clothes and, moreover, were not very eager to work.

Even though the Tiberius had sunk, these men showed no regard for the survivors. They made them line up and show not only their documents with the transit visa to another country, but also their money to make sure that they would leave the country, since Chile had stopped granting visas to Jews—although not to German families, which confirmed the suspicions of the majority. This piece of gossip went down very badly among them. But what passports could they present if their documents had sunk with the ship?

The pirate-captain of the Tiberius was sorely shaken and unable to do anything; he stood in stark contrast to the Chilean commodore, a tall, gray-haired man in his sixties, with the signature white beard of a sailor, impeccably dressed in the dark-blue uniform of the Chilean Navy. He appeared to be of English ancestry, and he inspired respect and exuded authority.

Annoyed with the civilian immigration authorities, he defended the survivors, whom he took to be Jewish. He went to the office of the chief of immigration and requested that he facilitate their admission to the country and grant them asylum visas. The official was reluctant to do so, and the commodore flew into a rage.

"But . . . how dare you ask for their documents?" he snapped. "Perhaps you don't see that these survivors have lost not only their families but everything they had?"

"Yes, Commodore, we will consult Santiago and give them asylum visas."

"Do not consult anyone!" he exclaimed, raising his voice again. "I will assume responsibility before the immigration authorities in the capital and I will personally take charge of their case. What's your name?"

"Well . . . it's . . . Ricardo Soto. I'll follow your orders, Commodore," he replied, terrified.

In a way, this was the best thing that could have happened to many of the refugees because they had boarded the Tiberius clandestinely. The majority, trembling and wrapped in blankets, approached the commodore one by one to thank him. News of the shipwreck was published on the front page of the only newspaper in town, as well as in the international press.

The young men discussed in hushed tones whether it would be convenient for them to stay in Chile, but they decided not to change their plans and the authorities gave them a transit visa. They noticed that the German families remained in Chile.

With the money they had saved, they went to buy clothes and then to the train station to buy tickets to La Paz. The train departed four times a week, so they bought tickets for the next day. Then they went to look for a place to spend the night, finding accommodation in a shabby but clean hotel. They took advantage of the remainder of their time that day to walk around Arica.

They were truly surprised to find that the Cathedral of San Marcos, the customs office, and the government house had been designed and built by the legendary Gustave Eiffel. A French Jew who had allegedly taken refuge from his debts in Chile, Eiffel had also designed the Church of Guayacán in the city of Coquimbo, as well as the Malleco Viaduct. A year after his work in Chile, he moved to Paris and built the world's most famous tower, which bears his name. This discovery encouraged them, making them think that there was some culture even in this faraway place.

The next day, Boris and Isaac arrived early at the train station, where they and other survivors boarded the train that would take nine hours to reach La Paz. During the journey they did nothing but talk about the shipwreck.

As the train rolled on, they were astonished by the aridness of the Altiplano and the majesty of the snowy Andean mountains in the background. They were also shocked by the indigenous people they saw; they were moved to see them impoverished and neglected, herding sheep, llamas, vicuñas and alpacas. The women worked alongside the men, carrying their babies on their backs with brightly colored *aguayos*. These were the only flashes of color in the desert plateau landscape. The closer they got to their destination, the more unwell Isaac felt due to the lack of oxygen; this was not the case with Boris. By the time they reached the border at an altitude of more than four thousand meters, Isaac felt like he was dying. He was as white as a sheet, could barely breathe, and was suffering from tachycardia and a headache so strong he thought his head was about to explode. "It's altitude sickness," the waiters on the train explained. He asked them for help and paid for an oxygen tube and some aspirin, which brought him some relief.

They finally arrived in La Paz and saw that the city lay in a hollow surrounded by ocher, gray, and reddish mountains. In the background loomed Illimani, a perennially snow-covered mountain that looked like a giant condor with its wings spread wide. "The mountains are spectacular," they all said in unison. The train station was a faithful copy of a nineteenth-century French station, and when they saw it they felt more at home.

Since bad news travels fast, the Jewish Youth Organization of La Paz had already heard about the shipwreck and taken charge of going door to door to raise funds for housing, food and clothing for the survivors. They were waiting for them at the train station, and this show of support made them feel safe. Boris was very concerned about his friend.

"We need a doctor, please," Boris pleaded, his half-unconscious friend's arm around his shoulder. Isaac was in a worse state than he had been after the shipwreck. He was as pale as marble. Immediately a Jewish doctor approached them and examined him.

"Don't be afraid, my boy. It's a typical case of altitude sickness, or *soroche*, which doesn't affect everyone. Look at you—you're cool as a cucumber. Your friend should rest thoroughly for a few days, try to eat as little as possible, drink coca tea and take aspirin for the headache."

They took them, along with other survivors, to the Dörfler Guesthouse, in the middle-class neighborhood of Miraflores. They gave them a shared room with two other young people. Others went to the Newmann and still others to the Europa. They also accommodated many men in the police barracks of La Paz.

The first thing Boris did was send telegrams to both of their families and to Varinia, letting them know that they had survived the shipwreck and telling them to leave Poland as soon as possible, and that he would explain the details later in a letter.

The Israelite Community, the Israelite Circle (founded by Polish and Romanian Jews), Maccabi, and the Jewish Community Organization all collaborated laudably. The young men had never imagined that there could be such a large and well-organized Jewish community in La Paz. Moritz, whom everyone spoke of, was behind it all. "In Poland I heard talk of Hochschild helping our people emigrate from Europe, and here he is overseeing our reception," said Boris. "That man is involved in everything. We've fallen into good hands," he continued, feeling relieved by Isaac's restful silence.

The community of Jewish immigrants was quite heterogeneous. Its members came from several countries, practiced diverse professions and trades, and were of different social classes and ages. There was everything from Austrian and German Jews with noble ancestry to peasants. They adhered to different religious creeds and ideologies, from the most extreme orthodoxy to atheism, from Zionism to communism. The common denominator was that none of them had a penny to their name. There were so many of them that several associations had been created. They formed the Bolivian Jewish Pro-Palestine Committee, which would later advocate for voting in favor of the foundation of the State of Israel, which the Andean country did. From the committee emerged the Bolivian-Israelite Cultural Institute. They also formed the El Cóndor Association of Boy Scouts, and the Federation of Free Austrians, an association affiliated with the World Movement of Austrian Youth based in London, which was very conservative and advocated for a free and independent Austria. They also founded the Amistad Club, made up of a handful of leftists, inspired by the Non-Aggression Pact between the Soviet Union and the Nazis. Then, with the aim of bringing together all groups of German Jews, the Union of Free Germans in Bolivia (UALB) was founded, which adhered to the communist tendencies of the Latin American Committee of Free Germans (CLAL). The Polish Democratic Association was created, which advocated for a free Poland. There was even a group of women Zionists who joined the Women's International Zionist Organization (WIZO) and ran a charitable organization. A colony of thirty families of Polish Jews was formed in Samaipata, in the department of Santa Cruz, but it did not prosper due to a lack of support from the Jewish community.

While Boris waited for Isaac's altitude sickness to pass, he went to the post office every day to send telegrams and letters to his girlfriend and their families. He even rented a mailbox to receive correspondences. When Isaac felt better, the first thing they did was go to see the city: it left them speechless. La Paz was three thousand six hundred meters above sea level and served as the political capital of Bolivia since the seat of government was located there, even though Sucre was the official capital. It certainly didn't seem to be a tiny village, as Dr. Kominsky had scornfully warned them. Although it was a small city, it was stately, well maintained, and much larger than many Polish cities. It had green parks and plazas with monuments, and a boulevard full of trees and benches called La Alameda, along which people strolled and flaunted their European clothing. Women used parasols to protect themselves from the sun and men wore suits and hats. They were struck, however, but the fact that La Alameda was fenced in and indigenous people were not allowed to enter.

"How racist the society of La Paz is!" Boris exclaimed.

"It's terrible," Isaac agreed. "The more indigenous people there are in a country, the more discriminatory the upper class is."

They also saw that the trams, buses, taxies and automobiles in the streets were imported from the United States and Europe. The city boasted extraordinary monuments built during the Spanish colonial era of the seventeenth and eighteenth centuries, particularly Andean baroque churches with silver-plated altars or wooden altars covered in gold leaf, surrounded by enormous paintings depicting religious motifs. Isaac was horrified by all the iconography, the majority of which was in the style of tenebrism. Boris, on the contrary, exclaimed: "How happy I am to have landed in this Catholic country!" When they entered the Basilica of San Francisco, in the "Indian neighborhood," which the high society of La Paz did not deign to enter so as not to rub shoulders with the Aymaras, Boris knelt and thanked God and his Black Madonna for having survived the shipwreck. He thought: "God, if you've allowed us to live, it's for a reason . . . help us during our time in this beautiful city." He also prayed for his family and for Varinia.

While exploring the city they also saw eighteenth-century mansions whose balconies were covered with red geraniums in the middle of winter. This was the flower of La Paz, so named because it remained in bloom all year long. The houses were so large that they took up almost an entire block; they stretched from one street corner to the next and each had three inner courtyards. The landowners entered through the front door on the main street, and the indigenous workers entered through the back door, bringing food from their employers' farms. They also visited neoclassical monuments such as the cathedral, and saw mansions in residential neighborhoods, such as Sopocachi, that were faithful copies of French neoclassical palaces. They were pleased because everything turned out to be better than they had expected.

They turned as red as tomatoes because at that altitude the sun burns rather than tans the skin, so they decided to buy wide-brimmed hats for their future outings. The weather was typical of mountainous climates: in the middle of winter, it was boiling hot during the day and as cold as the Antarctic during the night, which forced them to cover themselves from head to toe. The sky remained cloudless and as blue as the sea, and the blinding sun warmed the city at that altitude.

The following day they visited the makeshift synagogue in the Israelite Circle, from whose ceiling hung the Star of David. Isaac was moved, and he prayed. There they met some fellow Jews whom Isaac spoke to in Hebrew. The Jewish community even had its own cemetery, where the deceased were placed in coffins underground and not just wrapped in shrouds like they were back home. The young men were pleased because everything they saw turned out to be much better than they had hoped.

"If the Nazis invade Poland, Varinia and I could live happily in this blessed country," said Boris, feeling content.

"La Paz has truly been a revelation," Isaac agreed.

Although Bolivia was a large and diverse country, the gap between rich and poor was abominable, even more so because ninety percent of the inhabitants were indigenous people living in extreme poverty and ignorance. They were practically slaves, living at the mercy of the whims of an exploitative minority.

They weren't even allowed to enter certain places; they were mostly confined to the "Indian neighborhood," which was mainly a market, filled with *aparapitas* carrying huge bundles on their backs as if they were pack animals.

After getting to know the city, and once Isaac was feeling better, they went to look for work, not just because they were running out of money but because they could request visas for their relatives if they had an offer of employment. They preferred not to go to the agricultural colonies because they were both chemical engineers, and they decided to consult some fellow Jews who met almost every night at the Blue Danube Café. They were told that no one would hire them, not simply because they didn't speak Spanish but because the chemical industry in Bolivia was practically nonexistent. They came to the conclusion, therefore, that they would have to go to the jungle.

They were assigned to work in the subtropical region of Nor Yungas, in a colony for Jewish refugees called Buena Tierra. The situation was just as the Bolivian consul in Poland had said. They obtained their offer of employment letters and went immediately to the Ministry of Agriculture, Irrigation, Colonization and Immigration, under the direction of the writer Alcides Arguedas, where a National Department of Immigration had also been created. There they were registered as agrarian migrants and Boris filled out forms to request visas for his parents and siblings. Isaac did not, despite Boris's insistence. "It wouldn't hurt . . . you never know what might happen," he told him. They were informed that they needed to work for at least a year before their relatives would be granted visas. Boris thought: "No problem, I'll wait."

"This is our life insurance," he said.

"This is shit!" Isaac responded. "To get anything done in this country, even legal procedures, you need to pay extra. These wretched public employees are semi-illiterate and accepting bribes is probably the only thing they're good at," he complained.

"These poor men must earn next to nothing, which is why they live off of bribes. Forget about it. Just give them some small change and that's it."

"I'm not giving a cent to those wretches."

"The good this is that our situation is completely legal, and I hope my father agrees to come soon. Blessed be Bolivia!"

A few days later they got on a bus and set off for Buena Tierra, a colony near Coroico, the capital of Nor Yungas. It was a town surrounded by natural beauty, full of exotic vegetation and with a subtropical and humid climate. It was the last "finger" of the Amazon. They reached the deserted snowy peak—an altitude of four thousand eight hundred meters and encompassed by snow-covered mountains—by way of a winding dirt road that skirted cliffs of up to five hundred meters. Isaac began to feel ill again due to altitude sickness, and he took a couple of aspirin. On the way, the driver threw pieces of bread to the dogs that were wandering around, as well as to some black birds with white spots called *allkamaris*, saying that feeding them would bring them good luck on their journey. They were terrified by the road, which was so narrow and muddy that the bus kept sliding toward the edge, forcing them to peer over the cliffs. When they suddenly felt as though the vehicle were half suspended in the air, they stopped looking out the window. Both were sweating like racehorses and Boris was almost at the point of praying out loud. The driver, roaring with laughter, told them by way of some tourists who served as interpreters that this was the "road of death," which scared them even more. He told them it had been built by Paraguayan prisoners during the Chaco War, and that people said they had made it extremely narrow on purpose as revenge for their enslavement, so that the Bolivians would fall over the precipice and die. And so it was: people died every day. There was only enough space for one vehicle to pass. As a result, the transit authorities arranged hours to "go down" to Yungas as well as to "go up" to La Paz. In spite of the danger of this infernal route, it was in frequent use because the Yungas supplied coca leaf to indigenous people all over the country, as well as fruit to the city of La Paz.

When they began to descend into the subtropical region, Isaac started to feel better and they both calmed down. The landscape was extraordinary: mountains lush with vegetation, a waterfall of almost three hundred meters, which they called the "Bridal Veil," monkeys swinging from one tree to another, and trees from whose branches fell oranges, mandarins and bananas.

"This must be the closest thing to the paradise of Adam and Eve," Boris said. "I imagined Africa as being like this. Who would have known that the earthly paradise existed in Bolivia? I had only heard of the Andes and the Altiplano, never of this deep green jungle."

"This is the end of the world, and we're in the middle of a wild jungle."

"Could you be a bit more positive, brother?"

Isaac was silent.

They stopped and went down to where some indigenous women were selling food, and they bought sweet corn with cheese.

75

"But . . . what is this!" cried Isaac, startled, trying to free himself from something that had fallen on top of him and provoking a chorus of shy laughter from the natives. It was a small, friendly monkey rummaging through his pockets to see if he could find anything to take. And he did, in effect, extracting a coin that Isaac never saw again. After the initial shock had passed, he grinned.

After traveling for ten hours, they finally arrived at the Achachicala Crossing on the way to Caranavi, their final destination. It had a warehouse with agricultural and construction materials belonging to the Charobamba hacienda. Several Aymaras were waiting for them there with mules, two of which they mounted and others on which they loaded their luggage. They climbed the hill, which was teeming with vegetation and insects, by way of a path illuminated by a kerosene lamp. They suddenly saw all kinds of snakes and tarantulas the size of their hands, and their terror provoked laughter among the Aymaras.

"This place is the end of the world!" Isaac muttered to his friend. "And on top of that, these damned mosquitoes won't stop biting me."

"Stop complaining, brother," Boris replied. "We'll be there soon."

After almost an hour, they arrived at the old Charobamba hacienda, where they were received by Dr. Blumberg; his wife; their two teenage daughters, Misha and Ruth; an Argentine agronomist; and several Jewish men who worked there. The doctor served as a sort of patriarch of the plantation, on which two hundred settlers lived.

The arrival of the young men was something to celebrate, as the people there lived in absolute solitude and isolation. In order to offer them a warm welcome, they sacrificed some lambs, which they shared with the community.

"These damned insects are going to drive us crazy!" Boris and Isaac complained, scratching their entire bodies.

Dr. Blumberg immediately provided them with a homemade ointment that was a mixture of clay and repellent. And his wife gave them a few servings of "English salt," a powder mixed with water that they were told to drink daily.

They dined on the terrace of the main hacienda house, where Dr. Blumberg and his family lived. The young men thought the dinner was delicious. After they had finished eating, they were shown to a small furnished house for singles, built by the Jews themselves. It had a couple of rooms, a kitchen, a bathroom, running water, and a terrace, but the shower was communal and outside. The houses were modest, but clean and perfectly habitable, despite the adversity of the terrain. A diesel engine supplied the plantation with electricity and light. They slept like logs inside their mosquito nets, and the next morning they woke up to the sound of some birds, called *uchis*, pecking at the windows of their room, and the song of the *kewis*, which sounded like a dreadfully cacophonous choir. They ignored them and continued resting. After they got up they went to the hacienda house to say good morning to Dr. Blumberg, whose wife offered them breakfast. The house was old, made of adobe, stucco and colonial tiles; it was impeccably clean and well maintained. "We cannot live in filth, especially not in this climate," he said. Then the doctor and the engineer in charge of administering the plantation showed them around. The crops were grown on terraces because of the steep slope of the hills. This was an effective sowing technique they had learned from the indigenous people. They saw rows of coffee trees, as well as fruit trees with avocados, grapefruit, tangerines, oranges, bananas, and loquats. They saw other trees such as ceiba, cinchona, *siquili*, laurel, and walnut, around which wild turkeys wandered and birds flew. The birds were hated because they ate the best fruit, which then couldn't be sold. They also saw hummingbirds, woodpeckers, *parabas*, and parrots, which would suddenly take flight in flocks. All this was accompanied by the perpetual murmur of waterfalls in the background. They also saw small bushes with coffee beans and a large quantity of coca plants. They imagined that Shangri-La, the mythical place of the Himalayas, must be just like the wild paradise they were gazing at. And even though everything was quite primitive, they felt at ease. Isaac suddenly realized how much better he was feeling and was glad; it was because they were at an altitude of one thousand six hundred meters.

"What's this?" Boris asked.

"It's the sacred leaf of the Indians. They chew it to stave off hunger and to give them energy. It's what we sell the most of because we supply the mines of Oruro and Potosí," Dr. Blumberg said. "Try it— it's harmless. Of course if it's produced in large quantities it becomes cocaine, which is an alkaloid that also serves as an aesthetic."

The young men tasted it and found it so sour that they ended up spitting it out; the Aymaras laughed, covering their mouths with their hands.

"Why are there so many black people in Yungas?" Isaac asked Dr. Blumberg as they walked.

"From the little I know, during the colonial era the Spaniards brought ships full of Africans to work in the mines. But they didn't adapt to the cold or the altitude of Potosí, so they started dying by the dozens, mainly from pneumonia and polycythemia. The slaves learned that there was an area similar to where they came from, which is right here. Many escaped and came walking here along the Inca Trail, settling in Chicaloma and Mururata. They formed a colony where they work the land and live to this day. In the final years of the colonial era, the Spaniards brought them to work in the haciendas as servants and on the plantations as slaves. Some landowners gave them plots of land in exchange for unpaid labor, so their families could support themselves and exchange produce in the village on Sundays. It's strange, but there's even a king."

"A king!"

"I know this because we've gone to meet him. His name is King Don Bonifacio I."

"And how do they know he's a king if they were brought as slaves?" asked Boris.

"He was recognized by his fellow Africans while he was bathing in a river. They saw that his torso was tattooed with figures that only members of the royalty are allowed to display. They told their employers and decided to work an extra half hour a day so that he didn't have to work. He told them that his ancestors were abducted from a Kongo tribe in Senegal and brought over with the last contingent of slaves in 1820, five years before Bolivian independence. They were brought to these lands and worked in the hacienda of the Marquis de Pinedo. Seven years ago, Prince Boniface I was crowned king. And as slaves often do here, in Brazil and elsewhere, the king adopted the surname of his employer: Pinedo. They say it was a very moving ceremony. We didn't live here yet, otherwise we would have loved to attend, because many black women come to see me and bring their sick children for me to examine and treat. I recommend attending their annual Festival of Tocaña, which takes place this weekend."

And so they did. The following Saturday the young men got a group of settlers together, including Dr. Blumberg's daughters, and they went down to Achachicala Crossing on foot. From there they took a bus to the village of Coroico to see the celebration.

They arrived at the plaza and saw that there was a large Afro-Bolivian community. Some black women were wearing the same clothing as the Bolivian natives: *polleras*, Manila shawls, and Borsalino hats, which the Spaniards had made fashionable during the colonial era. They were surprised to see indigenous women with curly rather than straight hair. The celebration was bursting with music, rhythm and cadence, and everyone was dancing.

"Which one is the king?" several people asked.

The natives pointed to him, and as it turned out, he was the king of the party, too. He was leading the dance, with everyone following him. He was loved and respected by all because he lived exactly like them, in complete austerity.

The men played the *raca-racas* and bass drums, which they made themselves from tree bark, and which they beat with sticks from coffee trees. They danced to the rhythm of Saya Negra, Caporales, Zemba and Mauchi. The female dancers wore native dress, but white in color and made of cotton, as well as sandals. Their blouses were embroidered with various colors and inlaid with lace on the chest, back, and arms. The male dancers wore trousers and white shirts and hats with a cord that hung down their backs. The music was so catchy that the settlers joined in. With bottles of beer in hand, they began to dance awkwardly, not that they cared; they just wanted to have fun. They knew they would never be able to have the rhythm and grace of the locals. Boris and Misha danced with their arms around each other and holding hands. They stayed together throughout the party.

When night fell they decided to head back because they noticed that the Afro-Bolivians were beginning their Macumba rituals. They took a bus back to the crossing, where several Aymaras were waiting for them with donkeys to climb the hill. They arrived back home delighted and couldn't stop talking about the festival for days.

Dr. Blumberg was the physician for Charobamba and the entire region of Buena Vista. Everyone went to see him, and since he received a salary from SOCOBO, he didn't charge a penny. Out of gratitude, many Aymaras and Afro-Bolivians brought him chickens and other animals, which he refused to accept. He told them: "I'm here to take care of you." The natives were peaceful and respected the new settlers. Their children even played with the children of the refugees.

Blumberg converted an old caretaker's house into a doctor's office. He had white tiles placed on the walls up to the ceiling, a ceramic floor and toilets put in, and stretchers, glass medicine cabinets, and medical equipment brought in from La Paz. The office was a kind of refrigerator in the middle of the jungle. It was modest but impeccably clean, since it was disinfected daily with bleach. There he cared for the sick—mostly injured workers, pregnant mothers, and those who had contracted tropical diseases such as yellow fever, dengue, malaria or leishmaniasis. When a Jewish baby was born, the mother gave birth there, and he would circumcise the boys in a ceremony in which the locals also participated. They would comment under their breath: "This custom of the gringos is . . ." In the main hacienda house he had a sort of study, where he conducted research on tropical diseases with the plan of writing a book on them one day, which he would illustrate personally. For this purpose, he even had a microscope brought over from Germany.

Mrs. Trude Blumberg looked after their daughters. She also took care of the food, the kitchen, and the cleaning of the hacienda house with the help of several Aymara women who received a salary and daily meals. There were a few classrooms in Charobamba, with two teachers who taught reading and writing in Spanish as well as other subjects to children and teenagers. The teachers, who were Bolivian, had been hired by SOCOBO, and they also gave private lessons to the adults. Boris and Isaac studied in the evenings. The settlers were well organized and very hard working. They spoke to each other in Hebrew, German, and above all Yiddish.

It was a luxury for the plantation to have two chemical engineers, but their professions were of no use there. The administration gave them a few chickens and ducks to raise and paid them a salary with which they bought food at the grocery store subsidized by SOCOBO. They were able to save the rest, which pleased them. The hacienda also had a bakery, a shoe store, a carpenter's shop, a sawmill, and a mechanic's workshop, all operated by the settlers.

The young men worked the land, but as they had never done this before, the Aymaras taught them how. They were made responsible for some tools and they carried out their work with youthful speed and enthusiasm. They spent their time growing citrus fruits, coffee, cocoa, bananas, papayas and coca. They also took care of the chickens and ducks, and sold their eggs. The only problem was the mosquito bites, which drove them crazy.

"These damned mosquitoes!" they would mutter over and over again.

They were constantly scratching their bodies, opening up wounds that later became infected. They were advised to wear long sleeves and pants as they worked, and to continuously apply the ointment. They did this, but then they had to endure the infernal heat. When the rainy season arrived, which resembled the monsoons of India, they would stand beneath the falling water to cool themselves down. Every evening they listened religiously to the National Radio, and then later tuned into the BBC in London. The few of them who understood English would translate the news. After dinner, Mrs. Blumberg would put on a gramophone and play music by Bach, Beethoven, Strauss or Chopin. This touched their very souls, making them long for their loved ones and their homeland, and they would use this time to write letters to each and every one of them. They sent the letters to the offices of SOCOBO in La Paz, from where they would be sent off to Europe. They had no way of knowing whether they arrived or not. They also didn't receive any letters from their families. On weekends they would organize theater performances or dance mazurkas or Viennese waltzes, thereby reliving memories of their past. The young men of Buena Tierra bought mules so that they could go to the nearby haciendas of Polo-Polo and Santa Rosa, where they formed many friendships and some of them even found partners and got married. They celebrated the Sabbath, Passover—during which time they would read passages from the Torah—and more than one Bar Mitzvah, where they would eat food very similar to what they were used to back home, such as jachnun, hummus, falafel, and shakshuka. The new settlers also organized festivities for Rosh-Hashana and Yom-Kippur.

One morning when Isaac was doing his daily work, he began to feel unwell, suffering from chills and nausea. He went to the bathroom where he vomited and had uncontrollable diarrhea. When he began to work again, Boris noticed that he was pale and shivering. "What's wrong, brother? Are you feeling bad?" Isaac didn't respond, and he collapsed right there, falling like a stone. Boris asked a worker for help, and the two of them carried Isaac to the infirmary where they found Dr. Blumberg, who examined him after they laid him on a stretcher. He had such a high fever that he had lost consciousness.

"He has a severe case of malaria, with a fever of forty-two degrees," the doctor said gravely.

"And what's the treatment?" asked Boris, his voice trembling.

"We don't have the malaria vaccine. The ones sent by the Ministry of Health were expired. I've seen cases like this, and we can only try to cure it with homemade remedies to lower the fever and pray for him to be saved."

"Pray for him to be saved . . .?"

"Yes, my boy. We will do everything humanly possible to help him recover."

It wasn't an easy thing to hear. Boris begged the doctor to take care of his friend. "We will both take care of him," he replied. After Blumberg had given his instructions, Boris was unable to sleep for hours, placing cold compresses on Isaac's forehead, armpits, neck and groin to help lower the fever. He checked the fever incessantly, but the thermometer reading remained the same. Isaac suddenly began shaking and raving deliriously in Polish about his family and his country. And his skin and eyes turned sallow, which increased his friend's anxiety even more.

Misha acted as though she were a certified nurse. She seemed to be the reincarnation of Isabel Zendal or Florence Nightingale. She was just a teenager, but she had clearly inherited her father's vocation. Despite being sixteen years old, she was determined and smart, with a direct gaze. She said little. Her honey-colored eyes shone with a special brightness, and she wore her hair, which was the same color, in a ponytail because of the heat. Physically, she appeared fragile because she was extremely thin and looked as though she would break at any moment, but she had extraordinary fortitude and willpower. She took charge of bringing ice from the main house throughout the day, washing the dressings, carrying buckets of boiling water and helping Boris in whatever he needed. She brought him food, but Boris refused to eat. His stomach was in knots. Never in his life had he been so afraid. He was so terrified of what might happen to Isaac that he built an altar with the picture of his Black Madonna, lit two candles, and prayed fervently: "Please help him, God . . . I have no one but him in this suffocating, lonely jungle. What on earth are we doing here? Black Madonna, although we are of different religions, please save him because we are the same: we are countrymen . . . please save him, Mother. I brought him here, and I'm responsible for him. What if something happens to him? What would I do with him? How could I face his mother? Black

Madonna, Queen Mother, give me the courage and serenity I need to handle this horrible situation."

He spoke to young Misha in German. She became his companion to such an extent that her mother would call her constantly to remind her she was spending too much time in the office. Misha, however, didn't pay any attention to her. She felt useful and liked being with him. She told him she planned to study medicine like her father. The doctor came in throughout the day to check on Isaac, but the situation remained unchanged. Everyone on the plantation was very worried. A procession of people came to ask how he was, since they were all fond of him. Boris didn't sleep a wink for three whole days; he was desperate because his friend's fever wouldn't go down. He became a wreck of a human being. Those who came to see them couldn't tell which one was the sick man. He didn't eat, he didn't shave, he didn't bathe, and he didn't even change his clothes. Blumberg told him to go rest and wash, but he didn't pay any attention to him. When he suddenly fell asleep in his chair, Misha and the doctor took over for him.

On the third day the fever began to fall and, in a fit of joy, Boris embraced Misha and gave her a heartfelt kissed. He sent her to inform her father, who immediately appeared in the infirmary. Boris thought: "God puts us through trials, but never too grave," and he knelt in prayer to thank Him, the Black Madonna, and the heavenly court.

"This is a miracle," said Dr. Blumberg. "Especially because, on top of it all, he has jaundice; see how he's yellow all over. I was afraid he would go into cardiac arrest. Very few have survived this illness."

"This is a gift from God," said Boris with tears in his eyes. "This is further proof that our Lord exists and makes miracles happen. He heard my prayers."

Isaac was able to withstand the disease because he was a strong young man and had always been well fed. He lost a lot of weight, though, and he developed severe anemia. He recovered gradually with the support of his friend and Misha, who never left their side. The three of them spent hours together. "If you could only imagine how Misha helped us . . . she will be a great doctor one day!" This filled her with pride, especially since it was coming from Boris, whom she admired.

One night, the two best friends were swinging in the hammocks that hung at the entrance of the cabin, and they began to talk. In the background they heard the sound of the waterfall, the song of crickets, and the cry of monkeys, and they saw the flickering light of fireflies.

"I don't want to stay any longer in this green hell or in Bolivia. It's like Africa, only with indigenous people. I almost died of this damned malaria, I can't stand the mosquitoes, and I can't tolerate the altitude of La Paz, where I can barely walk because I feel tired immediately. Everything that's happened to me here has been one misfortune after the next. We barely made it off that pirate ship alive. We're chemical engineers and we're working as farmers. And . . . I miss my family, my homeland . . . let's get out of here, brother . . . I'm asking you to leave this place . . . I feel like an involuntary refugee."

"Are you serious?" his friend asked, wide-eyed.

"I've never been more serious in my life, brother. I beg you to understand me."

Boris said nothing and got up from the hammock. Both were silent for a few minutes, which felt like an eternity.

"I've been thinking about it too, and I don't want to stay in Charobamba either, but I do want to stay in Bolivia because, frankly, I believe it would be extremely risky to go back to Poland."

"How can you know that, seeing as we live in complete isolation and hardly understand the BBC news?"

"I saw it with my own eyes when we went through Czechoslovakia and Austria. What makes you think that nothing like that could happen in Poland? Our country has always been coveted by its powerful neighbors: the Russians and the Germans. During the Great War, the Russian area of Poland was invaded by Germany and Austria, and in 1920 it was attacked by the Bolsheviks. Before that, it was invaded by the Swedes. Why wouldn't it happen now?"

Isaac didn't know what to say.

"So . . . what have you decided?"

"Let's leave this place."

The next day they went to meet with Dr. Blumberg to let him know their decision. He acquiesced, but with great sadness, since he recognized the large contribution they had made to the planation. The news devastated Misha because she had become very fond of them. The doctor offered to recommend them for work on a plantation in Caiconi, which was located in Miraflores, about fifteen minutes from the city of La Paz. This gave Boris hope, as he was very anxious about his future.

The day of their departure arrived; it was a moving farewell. Misha wept silently, recalling the intense embrace and kiss Boris had given her. When they said goodbye, he hugged her in the same fashion and told her: "I'll never forget you, my dear Misha . . . thank you . . . thank you so much for helping me and staying by my side." She embraced him with all her heart, trying to hide her tears.

The young men spent three months in Charobamba, and they saw their time there as an experience. They returned to La Paz the same way they had left it. Isaac, as they entered the high-altitude zone, became even sicker than last time because the malaria had left him weak. The young men returned to the Dörfler Guesthouse. The first thing Boris did was go to the post office to see if any letters had arrived for them. And they had! They discovered that the letters took more than a month to arrive. They were happy to hear that their families were fine, though they missed them dearly. Boris received letters from everyone except his father, which didn't surprise him, though it hurt. His girlfriend reiterated her unconditional love and told him that she prayed to God every day that he would return soon to Warsaw so they could get married and raise a family. "How naïve she is . . . I don't know what world she lives in." Olga told him that his father hadn't changed his mind about emigrating, but that he asked about his son. She said the mood had become tenser and rumors were going around about an imminent Nazi invasion. Sonitzya wrote that all she did was miss him and cry over him, and that his friends kept calling to complain about how he left without saying goodbye and to ask if there was any news. Sergei told him that life was very boring without his company, and that every day he would hear of another friend who had paid a fortune to emigrate and that by now it was almost impossible to leave Warsaw.

The young men went to Sagárnaga Street, adjacent to the Basilica of San Francisco, to buy some gifts for their families. Boris bought vicuña shawls embroidered with figures of llamas for Olga, Sonitzya, and Varinia, as well as hats with Aymara motifs for his father and brother. He also bought his girlfriend a gold ring with Tiwanaku motifs. Then they went to the train station to buy Isaac's ticket to Arica; from there, he would take a boat back to Warsaw. The next day, before dawn, Boris went to say goodbye to his friend with a heavy heart. They embraced each other so affectionately that they both broke down into tears. Their hearts were as sad as the dawn.

"Thank you for saving my life, brother," Isaac said.

"If I have a brother in life, it's you," Boris replied.

"Please forgive me for leaving you."

"Who knows? Maybe I'll be on the next boat after you . . ."

"Hopefully . . ."

The train left, taking Isaac with it. Boris had rarely felt so alone; he especially missed Varinia, his partner, but he swallowed his sadness. He thought: "I can't throw it all away after three months . . . I'll give myself some more time, even more so because of what Mom says."

After Isaac left, Boris went to the Caiconi farm to look for work, and with Dr. Blumberg's recommendation he was hired immediately. This place aimed to be a "model farm." After working with shovels and picks in the tropics, the job felt like child's play to him. They grew legumes to supply the city of La Paz and the interior of the country.

The following day he went to register his work permit at the immigration office and to find out how the family visa process was going; it hadn't advanced at all. There, however, he received the best news they could have possibly given him. The Bolivian state was going to buy land in Chimoré, north of Yungas, so the government had issued a decree stating it was not advisable to keep the families of immigrants living apart. This meant that his relatives could obtain a visa immediately. The sole condition was that they work the land.

He immediately reinitiated the application process, slipping a large bill to the chief immigration officer for good measure. The documents were sent as quickly as possible to the Ministry of Foreign Affairs, where they instructed the consulate in Warsaw to grant visas to the Kominsky family. Boris then headed to the Official Gazette, bought a copy of the decree, then went to the post office and sent off a telegram informing his family of the new law; he attached a copy of the decree. He begged his family to take the necessary steps immediately. He went back to the immigration office every day, and even though he had bribed them, the officials kept telling him to "come back tomorrow." When he returned the following day, they would say the same thing. The refrain of "come back tomorrow" became a nightmare, but he returned every day, regardless. It was exhausting. And later he wondered: "Maybe the bribe I gave them was too low? I'll triple it." And he did so, but without success. The little he could save he gave to these corrupt civil servants. He also went to the Ministry of Foreign Affairs to check if the application had been delivered by the immigration office, but he didn't make any headway there either. No one would tell him anything, despite the bribes he slipped to the bosses and employees, and after so many hours of sitting there waiting, without any answer, at the risk of losing his job. The business of issuing visas was lucrative for employees of both public agencies. They told him he would have to bribe the highest authorities, the minister and the assistant secretary general. He acquiesced, handing over large amounts, but how could he know if they actually received the money? They told him that the visa had to have a "determined recipient." It did, but they still wouldn't issue it. They also informed him the parliamentarians were requesting that a cap be put on visas. He went to the parliament building and pleaded his case, but to no avail. "It's a shame that this country forces you to become corrupt, and the worst of it all is that it doesn't work for anything," he said to himself. "But I'll keep insisting, and at some point they'll listen to me. Unfortunately, these things are a matter of influence, and we're just refugees here. We don't know anyone other than our own people."

Boris was lucky, and his family and Varinia continued to write to him. She never mentioned the possibility of a German occupation, though. Was it that she was too young? Or that she didn't want to see reality? Her letters filled him with hope because they were suffused with love, which was what he needed most. She never took off the chain with the cross he had given to her. "It's a symbol of our eternal love," she said. She also said that she had told her parents about their future marriage. They were delighted, she wrote, but his future father-in-law had been surprised that he had left Warsaw without asking for her hand or bidding them farewell. She had explained to them that it was because of the need to emigrate as quickly as possible. She also narrated her plans for their future together down to the minutest detail, and this filled him with hope.

Boris also received letters from his family, which he would read over and over again, and then respond to immediately. He insisted that they go to the Bolivian consulate in Warsaw and apply for the visas. He said they would live happily in Bolivia, where there were very few doctors, so their father wouldn't have any trouble finding work. He also wrote that La Paz was a much more modern and beautiful city than he'd been told. He said the climate was so dry that Olga wouldn't have any asthma problems. He also told them about his experience in the jungle and about his new job. He told them how happy he was—even if it wasn't true—since he wanted them to emigrate. He said he loved them and missed dearly, as he did Isaac. One day after work he stopped by the post office and found a letter from his father, which shocked him. He opened it immediately and began to read it right then and there. His father wrote that people were saying it was only a matter of days before the Germans invaded Poland, and he acknowledged, implicitly, that his son had been right. He said he felt responsible for the future of the family, but that he was sure that nothing would happen to them because they were Polish. Boris held the letter to his chest and wept inconsolably. "Why? Why?" he cried, in the middle of the street. He arrived at the guesthouse and reread the letter. It made him so angry that picked up the chair beside the small desk in the room where he lived and hurled it against the door, breaking it, not caring who heard. His pain was so intense that nothing else mattered. He collapsed against the wall and thought: "What if something happens to them? What if their Polish nationality counts for nothing? What if they don't let them leave? How can I be sure that their visas are being processed if every day the immigration officers here tell me to come back later, even though I've bribed them countless times? Have they applied for the visas with the decree I sent them? How scared they must be, and here I am, unable to comfort them . . . my darling twin sister, my mother with her cursed asthma, Sergei, who's younger than I am, and Dad, who's so intelligent but who acted like a fool . . . and to think how I always admired him, but now I hate him . . . at least I can be sure that nothing will happen to Varinia because she's Polish through and through. Did I do the right thing in leaving them? Maybe I acted selfishly, thinking only of myself. Maybe I should have gone with Isaac, at least we would all be together . . . Black Madonna, give me the courage to bear this sadness . . . help me to calm down . . . I'm so confused . . ." He went to the nearest church to pray. His profound faith had the power to soothe even the greatest suffering. What he liked about La Paz was how close everything was, which made it an easy and comfortable city to live in. In the evenings, to stave off loneliness and to meet people, he would dine at cafés such as the Vienna, the Blue Danube, Eli's, Maxims, or Pigalle, which were all within his budget. There he met well-respected people with whom he engaged in long conversations.

Most of these places were run by fellow Jews. He thought: "If we always socialize with other immigrants, we'll never be able to meet Bolivians." When he wanted to eat something special, he would buy canned goods at Lebensmittelgeschäft Brückner & Krill, return to the guesthouse, make himself a sandwich, and stay up late, reading. To console himself, he would say: "When you read a book, you're never alone." Often, when he didn't have any new books, he would reread the same ones. Later he learned that Osmaru bookstore lent novels, and he went there frequently. He also bought books in Spanish to improve his command of the language, and he took classes at a language school in the evenings, as did many immigrants. He also read the local newspapers and the weekly *Jüdische Wochenschau*, which was published in Buenos Aires and contained news of Jewish immigrants in Bolivia. His Spanish was improving considerably.

To keep informed, he bought a radio on which he listened to the BBC news from London, but mostly to classical music. He was able to understand some of the news, despite his poor English, because he found English similar to German. He made sure never to miss the daily broadcast of the National Radio, which allowed him to remain up-to-date on what was happening in Europe and in the community. He also never missed a concert. Music made him feel more nostalgic than anything else, but at the same it, it also reminded him of happy times in his beloved Poland.

On weekends he usually went to the Maccabi sports center, where he would play basketball, table tennis, and billiards. He joined a group of young men and women his age, and went out with them on weekends to the Paris, Bolivar or Miraflores cinemas. He also went on excursions organized by fellow Jews to Lake Titicaca, Sorata, or to a villa they rented in Obrajes. And sometimes he went out to have a few drinks with his friends at the seedy Kleinkunstbühne cabaret where women (some of them Jewish) danced half-naked. Since he didn't have enough money to buy new clothes in the well-known Vienna-Paris House, where the oligarchs shopped when they weren't traveling, he bought second-hand European suits sold by his people at Casa Wera. He paid for brand new button-down shirts at Opus Shirts, however, because he didn't like wearing used ones. Since he was so handsome, the women in the Jewish community who had daughters would invite him over to try to hook him, and he would go. He made it clear, however, that he was only interested in friendship, which would stir their passion even more. His friends told him that the best way to learn a language was "horizontally," with a Bolivian girlfriend, but he remained unconditionally faithful to Varinia. He knew that the high society of La Paz was very closed and would never permit Bolivian women, and he was sure that no family would accept a Polish immigrant, least of all one of Jewish ancestry. They despised Jews and made fun of Poles. While most of his friends went to the synagogue, where they celebrated the Sabbath every week, reciting Selichot to become closer to God and the Jewish community, Boris never missed the Catholic Sunday Mass at the Church of La Merced, where he received Communion without fail. On one occasion, a seminarian played some religious music on the organ that Boris recognized. He had heard it at St. Martin's. The music touched his very soul, and he wept. Since most of the Poles were communist political refugees, there were only a few Polish Catholics who attended Mass. Usually, after Mass, they would go eat meat empanadas called *salteñas* at Eli´s, a speciality from La Paz that Boris quickly took a liking to.

Even though he had a relatively well-organized and active life and was generally in the company of others, Boris felt very lonely. As a foreigner, without his family, without a home, without an identity, surrounded by circumstantial acquaintances, he suffered from a kind a nostalgia that only refugees, expatriates and exiles understand. "My head is here, but my heart is there . . . everyone I love is so far away, and I have no other way of consoling myself except through their letters."

The only thing he was sure of was that he would never find a friend as loyal as Isaac.

Chapter 4
Warsaw, 1939–1940

Isaac arrived in Arica and stayed a few nights in a squalid hotel, which was the only place he could find. There were cockroaches everywhere. "Insects are following me, damn it!" he thought. He was so disgusted that he didn't even go underneath the covers; he slept on top, covering himself with a coat. The next day he boarded a ship much like the Tiberius, which made him shudder. The big difference was that there were very few passengers, and not one other Jew. Because of his low budget, he had to share a cabin with two other young men, whom he introduced himself to and shook hands with. When he opened his suitcase to hang his clothes, he suddenly noticed that something was moving. He couldn't believe his eyes.

"Cockroaches! How disgusting, cockroaches!" one of his roommates cried.

Dozens of the bugs began to crawl out of the suitcase, darting over the bed and the cabin with astonishing speed. Isaac tried to kill them with a sweater he took out of his suitcase, but it was impossible because the vermin were pouring out from that very same garment. He squashed them with his shoes while his roommates panicked and screamed like little girls.

"These damned Jews, they even bring cockroaches with them!" one of them shouted. The two of them left the small room in a hurry.

Isaac killed them with his feet, his hands, his coat, and with anything else he had at hand, but they kept multiplying. He spent a long time crushing them and eventually got rid of them all. He had to clean every last corner of the room, getting rid of even the faintest trace.

His roommates asked to switch cabins, so Isaac stayed there alone, which suited him fine since the young men had insulted him. For the first time in his life, he experienced discrimination personally. He thought: "Am I going back to my country to be treated like this?" And he asked himself over and over again whether returning to Warsaw was the right thing to do. He didn't dare ask to change cabins because he didn't want to prolong the awful cockroach situation. He was also afraid that his former roommates would file a complaint against him. Despite the fact that he cleaned and disinfected everything, the cabin filled him with revulsion. He was so disgusted that he decided to wash all his clothes and clean his suitcase to the point of exhaustion. He was traumatized and repeatedly dreamed that the vermin were crawling all over his body, and that his bed was surrounded by water because the ship was sinking, and he could neither rid himself of them nor save himself from drowning. He would later wake up covered in sweat, go to the bathroom, wash his face and, in an effort to distract himself, read a book until he fell asleep again.

His ex-roommates didn't say a word to him throughout the three-week trip; he managed to develop a friendship, though, with some girls from Switzerland.

He arrived in Warsaw in the middle of autumn. He decided not to tell anyone he was coming. He rang the doorbell of his mother's apartment and one of his sisters opened the door. Upon seeing him, her face turned pale, and she cried: "Isaac is back . . . Isaac returned!" She embraced him with all her strength. Then his mother and his other sister came running, and they wrapped their arms around him and kissed him. They were all in tears. Isaac felt happy for the first time in a long time. He ate his favorite food, slept in his bed, and was surrounded by his loved ones. They stayed up until dawn listening to his experiences in Bolivia, which left them speechless.

The next day he went to see Boris's parents to deliver a letter and the presents their son had sent them. Dr. Kominsky didn't mask his surprise.

"Why didn't my son come back with you?" he asked.

"Because he decided to stay a while longer to try his luck," Isaac said.

"To try his luck . . . and why did you come back?"

"Because I couldn't get used to the way of life or the altitude," Isaac answered, intimidated. "Boris stayed to process your visas," he continued, without daring to ask whether they had applied for them. The doctor was stunned.

Isaac went to see Varinia the following day, and he brought her the shawl and an envelope with a letter and the ring. She said: "How can he be so far . . . and so close," and she wept.

The invasion was a foregone conclusion; on the fateful day of September 1, 1939, Germany invaded Poland. The world trembled. Every newspaper on the planet published front-page stories announcing the outbreak of the Second World War, a continuation of the Great War. The Germans had borne a grudge since their defeat, especially because they were forced to sign the humiliating

Treaty of Versailles. They blindly supported Hitler because of his natural leadership abilities and his extraordinary oratory skill. The rest of the world saw him as an ambitious extremist who wasn't in his right mind.

The Kominsky family heard on a local radio broadcast that Poland was surrounded by the army of the Third Reich. They were under attack from the air by the Luftwaffe, on land by Panzerwaffe, and from the sea by frigates. The Polish army, meanwhile, had to defend itself with poor and obsolete armaments: horses pulling wagons loaded with men firing machine guns, and lancers mounted on horseback. The defense was heroic but powerless to stop the Wehrmacht. The Poles dropped like flies.

The Warsaw radio, along with other radio stations, played the Polish national anthem day and night to reaffirm the patriotism of the population. They also played the Eroica and Chopin's polonaises to boost morale. They never played the Funeral March, though, so as not to dishearten the Poles. On the third day of the invasion, France and Great Britain declared war on Germany. The Poles thanked God and said: "We're not alone anymore." The Varsovians lived in terror of the impending attack on the capital, and they talked about it day and night. Olga and Sonitzya were so afraid that they didn't leave the house; when they did, it was to buy food, which was becoming scarce even on the black market. The doctor, on the other hand, spent night and day at the hospital trying to save wounded soldiers and civilians. He even slept at the hospital. He was the most sought-after man in Warsaw. Sergei continued attending class, saying that every day he didn't go was a day wasted.

Seventeen days later, the Red Army occupied eastern Poland, whose army no longer had the soldiers or weapons to fight back. On the morning of September 23, the Germans invaded Warsaw. Olga and Sonitzya were knitting clothing for children from the church when they heard the whistling of bombs dropping, followed by their immediate detonation and the destruction of the city. They stood up and ran to the window, from which they saw people running around in all directions.

"The Germans are attacking us!" the crowd began to scream.

Men, women with children, and elderly people began running around aimlessly to protect themselves, inciting more panic and chaos amidst the terrifying sound of sirens and gunshots. At that moment a message was broadcast on the radio urging the population to take cover. Olga and Sonitzya left everything and ran down to the basement of the building. They bumped into their neighbors on the way, some of whom were in such a hurry that they fell down the steps. They finally arrived at the shelter, a long, dark, cold and humid room, with a broken pipe that dripped into a puddle on the floor, and walls with the paint peeling off. There was no light aside from a candle the neighbor had brought. They sat on the ground, waiting for the bombing to stop and for the sound of sirens, which became a symbol of death and destruction, to cease. Olga and Sonitzya, their arms around each other, did nothing but pray, and many of the others joined in. They couldn't stop worrying about Sergei and Dr. Kominsky. They had reason to hope that the Third Reich wouldn't bomb the hospital, since it was needed to cure the wounded, but they feared for Sergei, who had gone to the university.

"I begged Sergei not to go to school," his mother said, and they wept silently.

Warsaw began to crumble in a matter of minutes. Its inhabitants listened to the sound of the Panzer convoys making the ground and the buildings shake and shattering the windowpanes. They also heard low-flying planes drop cascades of bombs and fire machine guns at the army and civilians. The buildings began to fall, creating clouds of black smoke that made it impossible to see even a meter ahead. The traditional houses with wooden beams went up in flames like matchboxes. The city was reduced to rubble, the streets everywhere full of holes. Warsaw darkened in broad daylight, taking on a grayish color that blocked even the rays of the autumn sun. There was a fire on every corner, and the black smoke made the city darker still. Even the trees began to burn. Not a single building remained undamaged. The walls were gone, displaying furniture that had not fallen into the streets. Everything one could imagine was lying amidst the rubble: corpses and scattered, blood-covered bodies pleading for help; dead and agonizing dogs; shattered glass; balconies that had fallen off; broken flowerpots and tiles; window frames that had been blown out; broken street lamps; electric wires strewn in the streets; pieces of furniture; torn curtains; overturned park benches; crushed and abandoned cars. The gates of the zoo had collapsed and animals had begun to run wild around Warsaw, adding to the chaos. The Nazis shot and killed them. The smell of charred metal, burnt rubber and gunpowder spread through the city, poisoning the inhabitants. The roads were blocked by the trucks and tanks of the German army.

94

Hours later the marching of Nazi soldiers was heard, and the Poles shuddered.

Around midnight, when the bombing stopped, Olga, accompanied by a neighbor, decided to go up to the apartment to see if Sergei had returned. They arrived there by the light of the candle, opened the door, called out softly, and looked everywhere, but they didn't find him. They tried calling the university as well as one of his friends, but the lines were cut. In the meantime, they filled the bathtub with water because they imagined that would most likely be shut off soon too. They looked around the apartment and found that, miraculously, it hadn't suffered much damage, except for the broken windows; not one remained intact, and the windowsill on the balcony facing Mila Street was chipped. They also saw that most of the stucco plaster on the neoclassical building had come off, with barely a trace of it remaining.

"All I can do now is go look for him at the university," Olga said.

"That would be suicide," the neighbor told her. "All you can do is wait for him to return."

Olga grabbed some coats and blankets and they went to see how the neighbor's apartment had held up; it was in a similar state. Then they returned to the basement. They spent the entire night there, fearing that the attacks would begin again. They did. No one slept a wink that night.

The next day, when they stopped hearing the whistling of bombs, people starting to venture up to their apartments even though they could still hear the sound of machine guns in the distance. Olga and Sonitzya went into their apartment and Sergei wasn't there. Sonitzya burst into tears as her mother embraced her.

"We haven't just lost Boris, we also know nothing about Sergei or Dad," Sonitzya said.

"Never say that again! Your bother is safe and sound in Bolivia, a glorious country, at some point we'll hear from Sergei, and your father is safe in the hospital. Have faith."

They spent the entire morning covering the windows with cardboard, and they had a bit of bread with butter and some coffee heated on a small kerosene burner. They were very cold and didn't have any wood for the stove, so they walked around the house with their coats on even though it was September.

The hours passed and they still had no word from Sergei. They suddenly heard someone unlock the front door. They got up, ran, and found the doctor. They hugged him and told him that Sergei was missing.

"Thank God you're alive! But Sergei's disappearance is very worrying," the doctor said. "I'll go look for him at the university right now. I had to escape from the hospital because I wanted to come see how you were, and I've barely slept the last two nights. The amount of wounded men coming in, whether Polish or German, is endless. And the dead are left all over the place to rot. With my doctor's pass and this stained apron, the Germans will let me through."

The doctor got into his car and saw that he was almost out of gasoline. "I'll go as far as I can," he thought, and headed toward the university. As he passed by the wounded, he told himself: "I can't do anything for them right now." He shuddered and closed his eyes for a moment.

It wasn't easy to make his way through the rubble and the people running around screaming, looking for their dead and wounded relatives. The tanks drove through the streets, and when the doctor saw them coming he had to move aside; otherwise, they would have barreled straight over him.

After a half hour of navigating through this and hearing shots and explosions all around him, the doctor arrived at the university and saw that a section of the building was in ruins. For the first time in his life he felt his heart stop. "My son!" he cried. He parked the car on the side of the road and ran to see what was left of the building. There were wounded men and women in agony, crying out for help. There were also corpses. He began to search for his son or any familiar face. Then he began shouting in desperation: "Sergei Kominsky . . . who has seen Sergei Kominsky?" No one answered him. "Damned Nazis, how many young and innocent people have they killed?" he wondered indignantly. He felt mixed emotions since he needed to attend to some young men who were agonizing, but at the same time he needed to look for his son. He helped as much as he could, making tourniquets out of the clothing of the wounded and trying to save them; most of them, however, were beyond hope. He spent several hours yelling his son's name, just as others looking for their relatives did, but to no avail. Disheartened, he went back to his car and headed home. He arrived feeling devastated, but he didn't lose his composure. Olga and Sonitzya had been praying out loud the entire time he was gone, and when they saw him arrive alone, they began to weep.

"Our only hope is that they took him to a hospital," he said to console them. He sat down in a chair. "I'm going back to work now. If I hear any news about Sergei, I'll let you know. In the meantime, don't go out for any reason."

Even though they were terrified, they didn't listen to him. They both tied handkerchiefs around their heads, put their coats on, and went out to look for him. They were met by a phantasmagoric scene, with the never-ending sound of bullets whistling by and explosions going off in the background. They soon managed to make out, amidst the rubble, bloody corpses being devoured by rats, and others covered with flies. They also saw abandoned battle tanks and overturned artillery trains, as well as people looting shops. Whenever they saw tanks or troops marching down the street or standing guard on the corners, they hid and tried to take the back streets. They noticed, though, that the invaders were beginning to take control of the city.

"This is very dangerous, we have to go back," Olga exclaimed.

"Yes, Mother, let's go back. I'm really scared."

They returned to the apartment, where they did nothing but pray and wait for news of Sergei.

Meanwhile, the doctor had returned to hospital and begun looking for his son, peering into the faces of the wounded one by one and calling out Sergei's name loudly, without any reply. The hospital was full of wounded men and women, many of them lying on the floor. It was almost impossible to walk. Kominsky instructed his assistants to ask for help from volunteers over the radio, mainly to rescue the wounded in the streets.

All of a sudden, the head of the SS, Hans Frank, arrived with great pomp at the Szpital Zachodni, accompanied by several military men. Upon seeing him, all of the soldiers stood at attention, raised their arms and shouted: "Sieg Heil!" He demanded a meeting with the medical authorities, and they all sat around a table.

"I have come to order you to give top priority to the treatment of German soldiers," he spat.

"I'll leave that in the hands of the doctors," said the chief administrator, giving the floor to Dr. Kominsky, the chief surgeon.

"The wounded will be taken care of according to the gravity of their injuries, and we will prioritize those who have a chance of survival over the rest, regardless of nationality," the doctor asserted with authority. "Moreover, if you have doctors and nurses, we would appreciate you sending them to this hospital as soon as possible, because our medical team is not sufficient. We also ask that you provide us with medicine and supplies, please."

Frank flew into a rage and cried: "Have you forgotten that I am the German King of Poland?"

They were speechless.

"I order you to fire this citizen," he told the chief administrator.

"Excuse me, but Dr. Kominsky is the head of the medical corps and chief surgeon, and we desperately need him here. I'm sorry, but I will not fire him," the chief administrator answered firmly.

"Don't you realize that the SS is in charge here?"

"I'm sorry."

This enraged the Nazi even more.

"You will pay for this!" he cried, slamming the door as he left.

After leaving the meeting, Frank ordered two soldiers to keep an eye on Kominsky.

That evening, with the excuse that he had to rest, the doctor dodged the guards, took a vehicle from the hospital and went to other hospitals and small clinics to look for his son, but he didn't find him. He finally mustered up the courage to go to the morgue, which looked like a butcher's shop filled with rotting meat. There were no names or lists, just hundreds of dead bodies piled up. He made his way through that hell, looking for his son, but he didn't find him. This filled him with hope. "What suffering one goes through for one's children," he thought, and returned to the hospital. It was almost morning.

Two days later, there was a knock at the door of the Kominsky family apartment. Mother and daughter ran to open it. They found a simple, slightly overweight man with a kind face. He removed his cap as he greeted them, and handed them a note that read: "Stanislao saved my life, but I'm injured. I'm at his house, please come and get me. Sergei." They didn't know how to thank him. "May God bless you," they said over and over again. He told them he would have liked to inform them earlier, but it was very dangerous for him to leave and the telephone lines in his area were cut. Then he left. Olga phoned her husband at the hospital, and he immediately went to rescue Sergei in an ambulance. It turned out that on the day the center of Warsaw was bombed, the students had stampeded out of the classrooms, and Sergei had stumbled and been trampled on, nearly dying. The owner of the café opposite the faculty and his wife, who knew him, had dragged him and a young woman to their place and taken care of them.

Marek arrived at Stanislao's café as quickly as possible and found it was closed. He knocked on the door, and the owners opened. The doctor couldn't thank them enough. He went up to the second floor to the small and modest apartment where the couple lived. He went in and saw Sergei, who had recently gained consciousness. He had been in a vegetative state for two days. His father examined him, assessing his injuries: his body was bruised all over, he had suffered a concussion, had two broken ribs, and his kidney and liver were injured—but they hadn't ruptured, otherwise he would have suffered an internal hemorrhage. "Of all the things that could have happened to you, this certainly isn't the worst; besides, you're alive, my dear son," he said, embracing him. Sergei's eyes filled with tears because, for the first time in his life, he felt his father's affection.

"I don't know how to thank you for saving my son, for giving him back to me."

"He's a wonderful boy, and very well-mannered," Stanislao said. "He used to come to the café often with his friends."

They put him on a stretcher and took him straight home. The doctor thought: "He just needs to rest, and he'll be better cared for at home." When they saw him come in, Olga and Sonitzya received him with kisses and tears in their eyes. The doctor gave them instructions and returned to the hospital. On the way, he picked up more of the wounded who were lying in the streets and thought: "Damn this war, damn these Nazi dogs!"

When the German army occupied Poland and the Red Army occupied the Northeast, the invaders divided up the country, which disappeared from the map. No one could stop them. The Polish people were crucified, condemned. The provisional government capitulated and Frank, whom they called "The Butcher of Poland," was put in charge. He became the head of the *Generalgouvernement*, a sort of Polish state administered and militarized by the Germans. He installed his office in a medieval castle, a national heritage site. It was an open secret, though, that the person entrusted with the elimination of the Jews was the head of the SS and the Nazi police and Himmler's right-hand man, Heydrich, nicknamed "Torquemada."

A curfew was imposed in occupied Warsaw, and people were only allowed out of doors from eight in the morning until four in the afternoon. Anyone who didn't comply was executed. The trams only ran intermittently, so citizens had to run errands on foot. The Nazis asked to see their documents at every corner. Pretty young women took care not to go out alone or at night because even though the Third Reich had forbidden the Germans to have sex with Jewish women, they raped them all the same.

Once the Nazis had taken complete control of Warsaw, they forced the citizens to collect the rubble and rebuild the decimated and ghostly city in which fifty thousand civilians who had not even participated in the battle had been killed. There were no more coffins in which to place the dead, nor was there space in Powazki Cemetery. The bodies had to be buried in common graves and makeshift cemeteries. The women walked through the streets in mourning, and the citizens wandered around with their heads down, their faces expressionless and their eyes unseeing, without speaking a word to anyone, afraid of everything and nothing. The bishop held a service for the fallen, mentioning the German soldiers as well.

The Nazis even stole their national artistic treasures. They seized castles from the aristocrats and appropriated and exploited their raw materials. The Polish flag no longer flew; it was replaced by the Nazi one. The Gestapo took over the radio, replacing the Polish national anthem and classical music with the German anthem. They also heard German marches and folk music being blasted through the streets and squares. The formerly beautiful, cultured and monarchical Warsaw ceased to exist. Arts and culture were no longer enjoyed, not even in small groups, because the people were morally and physically destroyed, and no one had a penny. People no longer listened to the great Chopin or danced mazurkas, even when they celebrated a marriage or a baptism in secret. Only as a rare exception did they attend Sunday Mass. There was a shortage of light, water, gas, and, worst of all, food. They were given ration cards for three hundred calories a day. The line-ups for a little lard, bran bread, or canned milk were endless. The Nazis ordered the cans to be sold open so that they couldn't be resold on the black market.

One afternoon, while Olga and her daughter were talking, Sonitzya said:

"Mother, I'm sick of waiting in line in the square with buckets to get a little more water under the mocking eyes of those Nazi swine!"

"Be patient, my daughter. We're at war. Don't even think about looking at them, especially not when they ask to see your documents, and always cover yourself when you go out and tie a handkerchief around your head. Don't let yourself be seen."

While they were mending some socks, the doorbell rang. They opened the door apprehensively because they weren't expecting anyone. It was Varinia. They received her with open arms since they were very fond of her. They invited her in for a cup of coffee, and they sat down in the living room to talk.

"Have you heard from Boris?"

"Not a word since the war broke out."

"Me neither. I've sent several letters, but only God knows if they arrived."

"It's the same with us. We want to tell him that we're alive and well, but it's impossible. They say the post office is controlled by the Gestapo, and that all correspondence is intercepted by them."

"I've written him several letters to tell him some big news, but only God knows if he received them."

"And . . . what's the news?"

"The news is that . . . I'm pregnant."

They jumped up instantaneously to kiss her, and she was happy because she had been worried about how they would take the news, since she wasn't married to Boris.

"Varinia, this is wonderful! The arrival of a baby in the world is a very important event in life . . . but . . . Poland is occupied, the world is at war, and it'll be next to impossible for Boris to return to Warsaw."

"I know. All that worries me, but it won't stop our child from being born. I'm going to call him Boris, like his father, if he's a boy."

"I'm going to be an aunt!" Sonitzya chimed in.

"And I'm going to be a grandmother! Blessed be the Lord!"

"And what do your parents say?"

"The same as you. We're all happy, but we have the same fears."

"You have all our support, dear Varinia."

"Thank you, God bless you!"

"I'll start knitting clothes for the baby right now. What joy!"

Olga was worried, and she bit her lower lip. At that moment Sergei, now fully recovered, arrived home in an agitated state. They told him he was going to be an uncle, and he said: "Finally, some good news in the midst of this hell!" He embraced Varinia.

"If you hear anything from Boris, please let me know."

"Please do the same for us."

"Let's not lose touch, especially since we want to know how you and the baby are."

"Now more than ever."

They said goodbye to her at the door and continued discussing the big news amongst themselves.

"But . . . Boris and Varinia aren't married," Sonitzya said.

"At this point . . . that's the least of our worries."

Then Sergei said: "Now going back to sad reality, I have to tell you what's happening. It's outrageous! What they're doing to the Jews and Poles is inconceivable. They're dismissing them from their jobs and sending them to Danzig, Lublin, Nisko and Lodz, which they've turned into labor camps for Polish prisoners of war, but where there are actually more Polish Jews, whom they force to work as slaves. They're also doing the same thing in Piotrków Trybunalski, which they've turned into a ghetto. But the worst thing is what I found out today. In the Jewish neighborhood of Warsaw they're building walls to make a ghetto right in the middle of the city, and they're forcing our people to build them at gunpoint."

"My darling Sergei, they've been creating ghettos for Jews throughout history," Olga said.

"That's no consolation, Mother. Those damned Nazis have sent them there so that they can take possession of their homes. But the worst of it is the rumor going around that they execute Jews summarily in the labor camps, just for being Jews. They say hundreds of Polish Jews have been murdered in Ostrów Mazowiecka. It's equally terrifying that the Nazis murdered non-Jewish partisans who rebelled in the district of Wawer."

"How terrible! That's why, as I keep repeating over and over again, you must never tell anyone that your father is Jewish; it would be the end of us. For the Nazis, if you have three Jewish grandparents, you are a Jew. If you have two and aren't married to a Jew and don't practice the Jewish faith, you are considered a *Mischling*, but they'll persecute you anyway. It's terrible to hear that they're also after the Poles," Olga said.

"Mother, I'm scared, I'm so scared," Sonitzya cried, running to hug her. "I've heard that many people, mostly Jews, are fleeing at night, even on foot, to the border. Do you think we'd still be able to escape?"

"Don't be afraid, Sonitzya, don't be afraid . . . have faith . . . your father is sure that nothing will happen to us, especially since he's a doctor and is very well respected at the hospital. Besides, they need him desperately during this horrible time of war. As you've seen, he's even had to stay overnight at the hospital many times. If we flee, we'd be admitting your father's ancestry. And besides, at this point, where could we go?"

"I'll write to Boris so that he can send us visas and we can go to Bolivia," said Sonitzya, beginning to sneeze.

"Don't be naïve, sister. It's too late," Sergei said. "The letters are no longer being delivered and by now we won't be able to get out of Poland. The borders are closed, they're even patrolled by tanks."

"We have to thank God for your father's salary, it's the only thing keeping us alive. Otherwise, we'd have nothing to eat," Olga added.

Despite the chaos of war, Sergei, his classmates and their professors found a way to continue their classes. Since the university had been destroyed, the professors came up with the idea of holding classes in a small theater in Warsaw that remained intact. They had to act in secret because the Nazis only allowed German-language primary school classes to continue. "The only thing in the world that can save us, in spite of this horrible war, is knowledge," the professors said in encouragement. And the students attended class. When they weren't studying, the young people volunteered to help rebuild the university lecture halls.

One gray morning like any other, amidst the still ubiquitous rubble, Sergei was walking to class when he was approached by a man who appeared to have been waiting for him. Like Sergei, he was wearing a gray coat with the lapels turned up and a short-brimmed hat. His skin was greenish white, as if he suffered from tuberculosis; he had thin lips, drooping eyes, and a hump that he tried to hide.

"You there, young man. Show me your documents!" the man in civilian dress demanded arrogantly. He said he was a member of the Gestapo.

Sergei, like everyone else, never left the house without his documents because he was frequently asked to show them, and he handed them over without saying a word. After checking them carefully, the man said:

"So, you're Polish."

"That's right, sir." His hands and forehead began to perspire and he felt short of breath.

"The SS has informed me that you are a Jewish dog, and I order you to accompany me to the Gestapo headquarters where they will have you pull your pants down to confirm that you are circumcised!"

"No, sir, I assure you I'm not. I'm Polish and Catholic. My entire family has been baptized; we go to Mass every Sunday and take part in all the ecclesiastic celebrations. My mother even teaches catechism classes. I swear by the Holy Catholic Church and the rosary hanging around my neck that I'm a Catholic. If you'd like, we can go to St. Martin's Church where even Father Peter, or the other clergymen, can confirm what I'm saying. Let's go, come with me to the church, where the priests will vouch for me. Do you believe that I, as a Catholic, would lie, when it's a sin to lie? Besides, my father is Dr. Kominsky, a Polish Catholic and chief surgeon at Warsaw General Hospital, known and respected by all, and all this time he's been treating and saving the lives of wounded Nazi soldiers. He's even saved many of them from death."

"Catholic converts, but Jews by race, by blood! Why do you have a Russian name, then? Listen, Jewish trash, all of Warsaw knows that your family converted to Catholicism to protect yourselves."

"That's not true, I swear!" He joined his hands together as if in prayer and bowed his head.

"All of you dirty Semites humiliate yourselves by praying for your lives. Look, boy, I'll let you go for now, but if you want to remain free, you'll have to come once a week, every Monday, just like today, at the same time and to the same place, to inform on Jewish families. Otherwise, you and your family will be sent to the Jewish ghetto . . . and then to who knows where."

Sergei was left stunned and shaking like a leaf. His heart was beating so hard that he could hear it. He was sweating, and he took out his handkerchief to wipe his forehead and hands. He had never been so afraid. He felt the need to go to St. Martin's instead of to class. On the way there, he thought: "How could that pathetic, disgusting man know that we have Jewish ancestry? I could swear he was Jewish. Of course he was Jewish! People say that they can save themselves by turning in other Jews. Dad acquired a new identity when he converted, but that was almost thirty years ago. Someone has betrayed us, just as they expect me to betray others. What am I going to do? Could what this cruel, sinister man said be true? How can I know if he's from the SS if he didn't show me any credentials? He wasn't wearing a uniform, either, but that isn't so strange, seeing as that's how spying is done."

When he arrived at the church, which was empty because it was very early, he crossed himself and knelt down on one of the first benches. He took the rosary, which he always wore, from around his neck, and began to recite the prayers of Our Father, Ave Maria, and Gloria. He was so afraid that tears poured down his cheeks. He suddenly stopped praying and decided to speak to God and the Virgin Mary in silence.

"God, my Father, Virgin, Queen Mother, why have I been put in this horrible predicament? Why do I have to go through this? What should I do? Betray those of my blood to save my family? How did that man know we have Jewish ancestry? Someone must have betrayed us the same way he wants me to betray others . . . the whole community knows one another, even though Dad never wanted to be linked to them . . . God, this is the worst punishment I could have been dealt: to betray my friends. We all know who the converts are, beginning with Dad. It would be of an unspeakable cruelty. But . . . what if they take us to the ghetto? How can I be the one responsible for the fate of Mom, Dad, and Sonitzya, for their lives? People say that no one comes out of there alive, that they disappear forever. Everything is so uncertain, so confusing, so elusive . . . I'd rather die than denounce someone . . . can such evil exist? Why didn't we listen to Boris? It was because of Dad's damned stubbornness; he thought he was untouchable. How come I didn't stand up to Dad? I was so weak. Oh, my God! Hear me, help me see this clearly. Show me the way. Give me a sign, any sign, and I'll understand. I'll stay alert every second to hear your voice."

Sergei couldn't take it anymore, and he began to cry again, burying his face in his arms, which were folded on the bench. Father Peter suddenly appeared. He was a tall, thin man in his fifties, beginning to gray. He was wearing a cassock. When Sergei felt him draw near, he tried to hide his tears by wiping them away.

"Sergei, what are you doing here so early? Has something happened? Tell me, why are you crying?" He sat down beside him on the bench. "It's nothing, Father . . . it's the war," Sergei responded, without daring to tell him what had happened.

Father Peter read him a passage about hope from the Bible and blessed him, and Sergei left feeling comforted. Then he went to school to try to distract himself, but he couldn't get that sordid man's threats out of his mind.

That week he spent the nights lying awake. Sonitzya noticed he was acting strangely, and late one night, when she heard him walking around the apartment, she even got up and offered to make him a cup of tea. She tried to speak to him, but he didn't want to talk.

A week went by and Sergei plucked up his courage. He put on a dark coat and a hat so as to pass unperceived, left the apartment slightly early, and took a different route to class. He was walking more quickly than usual so he could catch the tram, but he noticed that he was being followed. He didn't turn around so as not to reveal his face, but his height, broad shoulders and blond hair made him easily recognizable. He suddenly felt someone pull him by the arm, and he felt his heart stop. It was the man from last week. He almost fainted from fear and turned white as a ghost.

"Did you think you could escape from me, you damned Jew?" the man hissed. "Speak! Confess! Tell me who the converted Jews are." He was wearing a knuckleduster, and he punched Sergei in the stomach, causing him to double over and fall to the ground.

"I don't know, I swear I don't know. I'm not Jewish," he said, stuttering because of the pain.

"You're lying, you wretch . . ." He began to kick him as he lay on the ground, and passersby began to back away.

"I swear, I don't know. I have no idea."

"Give me names! Otherwise, the Einsatzgruppen will raid your apartment and take your whole family to the ghetto."

"You're the Jew, you damned informer! You're the one who betrays others of your race to save yourself," he shouted, plucking up his courage.

Sergei's remark left the man speechless; he left him lying there and vanished. Even though Sergei was much bigger and stronger than the man, he hadn't dared to defend himself, and he was upset and in pain. He thought: "This is serious, this horrible man is capable of ordering them to raid our apartment because he knows where we live." He got up, fixed himself as best he could, and noticed that he had a cut just above his eyebrow that was bleeding. He wiped it with his handkerchief. He didn't go back home, though, not even to drink a glass of water, because he didn't want anyone to know what had happened. He didn't know who to turn to. It suddenly occurred to him to go see Isaac, his brother's best friend, who was very close to the family. He took the first tram to Boris's loyal friend's apartment. As usual, representatives of the Gestapo dressed in civilian clothing asked for his papers along the way, and he presented them, trying to seem as natural as possible. His physical appearance helped him. He arrived and walked up several flights of stairs because the elevator was broken. He rang the doorbell several times. Eventually a short, fat, poorly dressed and unfriendly looking lady answered the door. He had never seen her before.

"Good morning. I'd like to see Isaac Levi, please," Sergei asked politely.

"For your information, young man, the Levi family no longer lives here," the lady replied. "We are the owners of this apartment."

"And where have they moved to?"

"To the ghetto, where they belong."

"The ghetto?"

"And if you're looking for him, you must be Jewish too."

"No, ma'am. I'm Polish and Catholic. We're classmates."

"You're lying! You're all Jews! Dirty Jews!"

All of a sudden the woman pulled out a whistle that was hanging around her neck, underneath her blouse, and began to blow on it wildly. She shouted: "A Jew, there's a Jew here, catch him!" Sergei starting running, stumbling down the steps three at a time. When he reached the door he fell flat on his face. Once in the street, he started to walk slowly so as not to attract attention, and he got on the first tram he saw without even knowing where it was headed. He got off in a distant neighborhood, started walked, and began to cry again. He thought: "This is inconceivable. Isaac came back from Bolivia, where he was far away but alive, only to end up in a ghetto . . . how is he coping, how are his mother and sisters, how can I find out? Now I understand why he stopped visiting us a few weeks ago. I thought it was because of the war. God . . . this is the end. And Boris? He's far away and alone, but he's safe and sound. He was smarter than the rest of us, although we haven't heard from him for ages. But how can we hear from him if letters no longer reach their destination? And us . . . my family? And me? Living day by day since that damned traitor threatened me . . . and now this news, on top of everything. The only thing I know for sure is that you have to be a bastard to be an informer."

Night had already fallen. Every inch of Sergei's body ached, but his heart ached even more. He felt ill. He was freezing and his appetite was gone. He arrived at the apartment and found his mother, Sonitzya and, by chance, his father. They were all in the living room listening to classical music. The doctor was reading and the women were knitting clothes to sell. Olga noticed that her son's face was the color of marble and his coat was torn.

"Son, what happened?" she asked him.

"Nothing, Mom . . . nothing," Sergei lied.

"But why do you look like that? What happened to your forehead?"

"Nothing, Mother." He kissed her on the cheek. "I went to see Isaac, and he and his entire family have been taken to ghetto. A German family is in his apartment now."

"God protect us," his mother said.

"What happened to your forehead? You have a cut and dried blood," his father asked him.

"Nothing, Father." He kissed him as well.

"I want to examine you."

"No, Father! I'm fine."

"Come here."

Sergei had no choice but to obey, and he drew closer. "It's just a scratch," he said.

"I have to give you stitches," the doctor said. "You need to rest, and take special care of your head. Did the Nazis apprehend you?"

"No, Father—I tripped on the street."

His father cleaned the wound with hydrogen peroxide, because there was no alcohol in all of Warsaw. He gave him a few stitches and an analgesic.

"Now go have dinner and then go to bed," he said.

Dr. Kominsky didn't want to hear about anything that put him and his family at risk. He didn't even ask for details about Sergei's visit to Isaac's house. His mind was blocked; he was blinded, unable to see reality clearly. Sonitzya was deeply upset because she was very close to Isaac's family. She had even had feelings for him at one point.

Sergei couldn't sleep that night. He tossed and turned in bed, wondering what to do. In his moments of greatest despair, he clasped the rosary in his hands and prayed. He finally fell asleep in that position.

Chapter 5
Warsaw, 1940–1942

Despite the conflagration, the Kominskys continued with their daily lives. Sonitzya gave piano lessons to German children, although she kept this a secret from her family. She thought they were the only ones who could pay since the Poles didn't have any money, and she needed to contribute to the household. Olga went to St. Martin's every day to teach catechism and help the priests with whatever needed to be done. She became a kind of honorary administrator of the parish. Sergei attended class, though without books, because the Nazis had ordered that the few books remaining after the invasion be burned. He was still traumatized by that "damned Jewish traitor," whom he didn't dare to tell anyone about. Fortunately, he didn't see him again, but he still felt that he was living under threat. The Kominsky family always carried some coins around in their pockets, which the doctor gave them in case they came across any food, socks, thread, or wool. Whenever they saw people lining up they would join the line to buy whatever there was, since they could exchange it later. One Sunday evening the doctor and a group of Polish colleagues took a break and went for a drink at one of the few bars still operating in Warsaw, although somewhat covertly. They left the bar a couple of hours later feeling relaxed and relatively calm. Suddenly an SS patrol—under the command of the already well-known and feared Hans Frank—approached them.

"Show me your documents," the Nazi officer demanded.

They all took out and presented their documents.

"Are any of you Jews?" he asked arrogantly.

No one said a word. Dr. Kominsky broke the silence:

"We are doctors at Warsaw General Hospital, and we were taking a break."

"I asked if there are any Jews among you!" he bellowed.

There was a disconcerting silence. As if by tacit agreement, they began to discreetly separate themselves, bit by bit, from Kominsky.

"Are you a Jew?"

"No, I'm not a Jew. I'm Polish and Catholic."

"I recognize you. Have we met before?"

"I don't believe so, Officer."

"Alright, you can go now."

Marek turned around and saw no one. They had left him alone. He stood there stunned for a few seconds, motionless, his mind in shock at his colleagues' behavior. When he finally reacted, the Nazi patrol officer had left and he was alone in the cold, empty street. He shivered, crossing his arms to cover himself, and thought: "If your own colleagues, whom you've worked with for years and whom you see every day, have abandoned you . . . then they know you're Jewish! Treacherous Poles! They didn't hesitate to betray you to save their own skin . . . well . . . indirectly, because they ran away like thieves . . . they do know you're Jewish, even though they've never said it. That means many people must know . . . and . . . how you've helped them! You made them your surgical assistants, you taught them everything you learned in the Soviet Union . . . you even recommended some of them for government positions, just to help them out . . . and the saddest thing of all is that you became friends with them, close friends, just like their wives became friends with Olga. Friendship is worth nothing when your life is in danger. To save themselves or for money or a crust of bread, anyone can denounce you and your family. At least that's what has been happening. Why did you think you would be free? Now the Kominskys are in danger . . . how stupid you were not to listen to Boris."

For the first time in his life, the doctor felt stupid and naïve. He was so frightened that he returned home immediately. He took the first tram and arrived at his apartment, where he found Olga mending used clothing for both their children and the children of St. Martin's. Sergei and Sonitzya were there with her.

"I exchanged a few rolls of thread for a can of beans," she told her husband. "But what's wrong, Marek? Why are you so pale? And why do you smell like you've been drinking? But . . . where have you come home from? Where were you?"

"I have to tell you something," he told them. She put her sewing aside, and the children put their books down.

He told them what had happened. So as not to make things worse, his wife didn't tell him that Boris had been right after all.

"So, what do you suggest we do?" asked Olga. "Because the only thing I know for sure is that if someone finds out about our situation, they'll send us all to the ghetto."

"Don't be so negative, Olga," her husband snapped back. "All I ask is that you don't make us more fearful than we already are. I'll go to the Bolivian consulate tomorrow to request visas."

A deep silence fell. Tears began to well up in Sonitzya's eyes, and she took refuge in her mother's arms.

"Marek . . . don't be naïve. None of the consulates are granting visas anymore, not to anyone; the Gestapo has forbidden it."

"So what should we do? Could we take refuge in an embassy?"

"Listen to me, Marek. All the embassies in Warsaw are closed off with barbed wire and guarded by Nazis tanks so that Jews can't enter."

"Do you think that Mrs. Müller might give us away because we had to let her go, because we couldn't afford to keep her on any longer?"

"I don't know. Nothing surprises me anymore these days."

The doctor went to his office to see if he could find the only proof of his Jewish origin: the menorah his father had given him. He hid it behind the books and returned to the living room.

"I want to tell you all something that happened to me with a man who said he was from the Gestapo," Sergei said.

"That day you got hurt?" his mother asked.

"Yes."

The story terrified everyone even more.

"And has that man returned to threaten you again?" his father asked.

"No, thank God," his son replied.

"And why didn't you tell me about that man?"

"Because you wouldn't have wanted to hear it. Father, forgive me, but you've never wanted to accept your Jewish origin, you've always shielded yourself behind Polish documents. The Nazis' main goal, besides occupying territories, is to hunt Jews, and everyone knows it."

"Go to bed, everyone. We'll decided what to do tomorrow."

Sonitzya was so scared that she went to curl up in the armchair in her parents' room. They were all terrified, but nobody dared to say it. They were still awake when, around four in the morning, they heard the sound of a patrol in the street. They all stampeded to the living room window to see what was happening. There were a couple of motorbikes and a truck full of armed soldiers who were jumping down to the street at full speed. All of a sudden they heard rifle butts banging on the front door of the building.

111

"It's Hans Frank himself . . . the man who asked to see our documents when we left the bar!" exclaimed Marek. "The Nazis are coming for us! That abominable man recognized me! Put your coats on, leave everything else, and we'll go hide in the apartment opposite ours."

"No, Father!" Sergei said vehemently. "Even if Polish people live there, the Nazis will search floor by floor. Let's go out through my room and down the back stairs."

Dazed and terrified, they put on the first thing they could find over their pajamas: shoes, coats, and the women tied handkerchiefs around their heads and wrapped themselves in the vicuña shawls Boris had sent them from Bolivia. Sergei opened the window to make sure the coast was clear. And while they heard the Nazis raiding the building floor by floor and people running out into the hallways screaming, Sergei and his father helped Sonitzya and her mother down the fire escape.

"Hurry up!" said Marek. "Don't worry about the height . . . don't look down. Concentrate on what you're doing and hold on tightly."

They finally reached the street and heard a couple of soldiers approaching. They ducked behind a parked car. It was a very cold night and an icy wind was blowing, but they didn't feel it; on the contrary, they were sweating from head to toe. From where they were hiding, Sergei could see the soldiers looking at the fire escape and talking. They suddenly began to blow their whistles, probably to tell their comrades that the family had fled down the back stairs. They thought it was the end. The doctor, however, told them not to move. Olga and her children were trembling to the point that their teeth were chattering. Sonitzya couldn't stop sneezing. The soldiers whistled and whistled, but their comrades didn't hear them because they were focused on the raid. Finally, the Nazis decided to go back to the main door of the building, which was on the next street over, and the family ran along a parallel street. "Let's go to St. Martin's," Olga said. They ran and ran until they were exhausted. Olga and Sonitzya, on the point of collapsing, were helped along by Sergei and his father, who took them by the arm. From one moment to the next, Olga began to gasp for air and lose her voice, which made them all even more nervous. Her husband rubbed her back, trying to soothe her. They all prayed to God for Olga not to have an asthma attack. Whenever they saw Nazi soldiers at the street corners they dodged them and hid, and when they saw they were out of danger they kept running. It took them almost an hour to reach the church. When they finally arrived, they saw from a distance that, as always, there was a Gestapo patrol stationed in front of the parish because the Nazis doubted the Church's loyalty to the regime. In the middle of a poorly lit street, they hid underneath some cars parked a block away. Olga, Sonitzya and Sergei were trembling like leaves and praying; the doctor, on the other hand, was monitoring the situation. Suddenly Olga said: "Wait for me here, I'll come back for you." She plucked up her courage and went alone to ring the doorbell of the church. The soldiers immediately approached her.

"Show me your documents," one of the officers demanded.

"Since when do you ask me for my documents if you know me and know that I work here?" Olga asked in a defiant tone, even though she was scared to death. She felt an asthma attack coming on, and she tried disguise it. "Besides, I've got the flu."

"Oh right, it's true!" one of the soldiers said after shining a flashlight in her face.

"But why are you coming to the church so early?"

"Because I'm behind on my work. These abusive clerics even make me sweep the courtyard," she lied.

Olga rang the doorbell again because no one was coming to open the door. After what seemed like an eternity, Father Peter finally came to the door, wearing a coat; he immediately sensed that something strange was going on and invited Olga inside. He greeted the guard coldly, even though they knew each other. Father Peter and Olga went into the church lobby.

"Father Peter," she said tearfully, choking as her asthma attack erupted. "They raided our building looking for us, but we managed to escape through the back door, and I beg you to give us asylum. My family are hiding under a green car in front of the bakery. Forgive me for taking the liberty of coming here without asking. I know it's complicated for the clergy, but please, Father Peter, we didn't have anywhere else to go."

"This is the house of God, and we will figure it out. For now, rest, calm down and try to breathe. We need to figure out how to get your family here before dawn, because they could be discovered then," the priest said. "Wait for me here."

She entrusted herself to God and prayed over and over again for the priest to rescue her family. She tried to forget about the asthma attack. The priest was gone for a few minutes, but it seemed like forever to Olga.

"Listen to me, Olga: at six in the morning the soldiers change guard, and they'll be distracted. I'll take the car out of the garage on the street beside the church, which they never patrol, I'll go find your family, and I'll hide them in the trunk. At exactly six o'clock, go to sweep the church entranceway, take out the garbage, even sweep the sidewalk to distract the guards, and . . . keep calm. God will be with us. Have faith."

"I'll do whatever you say, Father Peter. Thank you . . . thank you so much."

The priest took the car out of the garage beside the church, pushing it so that no one would hear when he turned it on. As the car rolled down the street, he jumped in swiftly, started the engine, and drove very slowly to look for the Kominskys. Right at six o'clock he saw the guards changing shifts, and he also saw Olga sweeping the parish entrance to make sure no one noticed what he was doing. At that moment the priest parked behind the green car, opened the door very carefully, got out, and called to them very gently. They recognized him immediately. He told them to get in the trunk. Sonitzya and Sergei managed to do so, but there wasn't enough room for Marek. "I'll come back for you," Father Peter assured him. His children didn't want to be separated from him, but the priest told them that they'd see each other again in a few minutes. Father Peter put the car in reverse and took a parallel street back to the side gate, and drove the vehicle in. He opened the trunk and helped Sergei and Sonitzya get out. Minutes later Olga appeared; she embraced her children and asked about her husband. Father Peter told her that he would go get him now, and he left immediately. Olga took her children by the hand and quietly led them into the church. They thanked God for saving them and prayed to be reunited with the doctor as soon as possible.

The priest performed the same maneuvers and went to look for the doctor. He arrived at the same place, but he couldn't find him. He looked under and around the car several times, but didn't see him. Suddenly he saw that the guards patrolling St. Martin's had arrested him. One of them had noticed something moving in front of the bakery; he had gone to see what was going on and found the doctor hiding under the green car. The cleric observed him from afar and saw that he had his hands behind his head and was being interrogated. Father Peter crossed himself and entrusted himself to God. He approached the guards courageously.

"Why are you arresting this man?" the priest asked. "Don't you know that Dr. Kominsky is the chief surgeon at Szpital Zachodni?"

"Father, we're already fed up with you priests because you're against the Third Reich," said the highest-ranking officer among them. "This citizen doesn't have his papers."

"But Dr. Kominsky is Polish. I can attest to it. I asked him to come urgently to attend to a priest who is very sick."

"Then why did he hide underneath a car?"

"Probably because he didn't have his papers with him."

"Indeed," confirmed the doctor, his hands still behind his head. "I left in a rush and I forgot to bring my documents."

"The fact remains that we need to take him because the regime detains all people without papers."

"Then take me in his place."

"Don't play the hero, Father." He let out a forced guffaw.

"And . . . where are you taking him?"

"I refuse to let you take me," the doctor exclaimed. "I need to attend to a patient. It's an emergency."

"Yes, the poor man is very ill . . . he's dying . . ."

The Nazis kicked the doctor in the stomach, forced him into a van, and took him to an unknown place. Father Peter stood there, shaken. He thought: "At least I saved three." He didn't have the nerve to return to St. Martin's to give the family the terrible news, but he had no choice. He went in and found Olga and her children praying.

"And my husband? Where is he?" Olga asked, with tears in her eyes.

"Well . . . my dear Olga. I couldn't bring him. The guards in front discovered him and arrested him on the grounds that he had no documents. They took him despite my efforts to stop them."

"They took him. But . . . where?"

"I don't know. I'll do everything I can to find out. We'll be able to get him out because it was only a matter of his not having his documents with him. I will ask the cardinal to help us."

A profound silence reigned, broken by Sonitzya, who let out a cry of anguish and ran to her mother's arms. "And now . . . what will we do without Dad?" she said between sobs.

The doctor remained calm in the van, although every now and then a shiver went through him as he recalled the gravity of the situation. He cracked his knuckles over and over again and didn't say a word.

What could he say to these low-ranked soldiers now that he'd fallen into their net?

Twenty minutes later they arrived at the Gestapo headquarters. The sun was rising. According to the rumors, "once you go in, you never come out" of that place. At the gate of the barracks hung the flag despised by all who opposed the regime: the red and white one with a black swastika. The barracks were guarded by tanks and armed soldiers, and the high walls were lined with barbed wire. Guards armed with machine guns manned the two corner towers. When he went inside, the doctor felt so lost that he closed his eyes and prayed: "Jehovah . . . I know I shouldn't invoke your name, but protect me . . . shelter me, my God . . ." For the first time in his life, he entrusted himself to God. He recalled, for a moment, that the revolution of 1917 promoted an atheist form of communism that was averse to Christianity, and Sunday Mass was replaced by unions. Not that it mattered to him. He thought: "Whom should I invoke, then?" His hands were sweating. They opened a huge gate and entered a sort of citadel full of soldiers, trucks, cannons, and crates. They took him to a building next to the main one, which seemed to have offices. Prodding him with rifle butts, they dragged him out of the vehicle and pushed him down to the basement. It was a filthy place with blood-covered walls. They brought him to a storage room where there were a dozen or so single men, without their families, who had been taken prisoner that night. A few Polish Jews recognized him, and they greeted each other. No one asked him why he was there. They imaged that he must be of Jewish ancestry. He, however, discovered that they were political prisoners, partisans arrested for organizing a resistance movement. They'd been captured after someone informed on them, they said. A few of them were wounded, and the doctor examined them, but he couldn't treat them because he had no medical equipment. "It's nothing serious," he assured them. All of a sudden a couple of guards came in and shouted: "Kominsky, come." The doctor's stomach knotted. The soldiers took him to a small, windowless room with a table, a couple of chairs, and a light bulb hanging from the ceiling. The doctor felt faint. He waited there alone for about ten minutes, then Frank appeared and ordered him to sit down.

"So you're not Jewish?" the officer asked. "Then what was this menorah doing in your house?" He placed it on the table.

116

"It was a gift from a patient I treated for a long time who didn't have money to pay," the doctor said while the Nazi put it away.

"You're lying, you're a liar, you filthy Jew, you smell like shit! And all those books on Marxism? You're also a communist! Is that why your Polish colleagues left you outside the bar?" He slapped him, causing his glasses to fall and break.

"That's not true. I'm Polish, and I'm a Catholic."

The doctor felt disoriented without his glasses—he could barely see without them—and he bent down to look for them. While he was on the ground, the officer stood up and kicked him. The doctor cried out in pain.

"You know what, Doctor? For being a liar, you'll have to make do without glasses," he said. He stomped on them, smashing them to pieces, and left the room.

The guards dragged Marek back to the storage room. They opened the door and threw him on the ground. The prisoners all thought the guards would come for them next. They helped him up immediately, but they couldn't do anything for him. "My glasses, my glasses," Marek moaned. A few hours later a squad of soldiers came to take the political prisoners; they left with their hands behind their heads. They were thrown in a truck and taken, as was later known, to a forest near Palmiry, twenty-eight kilometers outside of Warsaw. They were made to dig their own graves, and then, in broad daylight, they were executed.

Father Peter went personally to speak with the cardinal in Dr. Kominsky's favor, reminding him that Olga, whom the prelate knew, volunteered at St. Martin's. "I must be frank, Father. I can't do anything because, as you know, we've broken off relations with the Nazis precisely because they have accused the church of harboring Jews, Poles and political prisoners."

The priest came away disheartened, left with the difficult task of telling Olga and her children the truth. She replied, "Then it's up to me to go ask where they took him." She crossed the street and asked the guards where they had taken the doctor because there was a priest he needed to attend to. They got annoyed and told her to go away. She didn't give up, and she went to all the police stations with Father Peter, but they were turned away from each one. They eventually mustered up the courage to go to the Gestapo headquarters. They were stopped at a security checkpoint a block away and told that they weren't allowed to get any closer to the building; Father Peter's presence did nothing to sway them. They even went to the hospital in the hope of finding him there, but to no avail. Then they went to Olga's parents' house to tell them what had happened. Her father, who was a civil servant and knew some Nazis personally, offered to do everything possible to discover the whereabouts of the prestigious doctor.

After several miserable days of looking for him, Olga collapsed into tears. She arrived at the parish completely broken and confessed the sad state of affairs to her children. They hugged each other and cried together. "Is this Dad's end?" asked Sergei. "No, son. The last thing we lose is hope. We'll find him. Let's pray, let's pray for him."

Several days after the raid, Olga's parents went to see the apartment and found that a German family was living there. They had no choice but to go and tell their daughter and grandchildren. All of them broke into tears, and then Olga said, mustering courage she didn't even know she had: "We don't know where Marek is, and we've lost our life's work . . . but I still have you, and you have me. Boris is in Bolivia, alone, but he's free, and that's what matters. The difficult thing is how let him know we're safe if we can't write to him. We have to leave all this in the hands of our Lord Jesus Christ. We have to accept that this is his will, and thank him for every day we're alive."

Olga's parents called her daily to let her know about the inquiries and arrangements they were making to find out what had happened to their son-in-law. They even bribed the Nazis, but it didn't get them anywhere. They also went to visit them, bringing clothing and food. They told Olga: "Daughter, thank God that you and your children are being protected, because in Warsaw not a single Jew has been able to escape; this is a witch hunt."

From one day to the next, however, they stopped going to visit them for fear that the Gestapo would follow them and discover where their daughter and grandchildren were. They also feared arousing the suspicions of the Nazis stationed in front of the church. Furthermore, when speaking to Olga's father, a Nazi remarked: "You've been asking an awful lot of questions about that Kominsky fellow . . . are you by chance linked to the Jews in some way?"

Since they had lost everything, the priests invited the Kominsky family to stay in the parish on the condition that they didn't say a word to anyone and that they didn't leave, not even to go to the corner to buy bread. In gratitude, Olga gave them a gold ring, the only piece of jewelry she was wearing on the day of the raid, so that they could trade it for food. The clergymen accepted it. She was filled with rage when she thought about how she had had to leave her jewelry box behind that night, because the four jewels she kept there would have proved useful.

At first the three of them slept in one room and thanked God and each and every one of the priests continuously for allowing them to stay there. Nevertheless, they felt imprisoned and as if they were walking on eggshells. Olga forbade them to complain, especially in front of the priests. "Being here means being alive . . . being outside means disappearing, so do everything they ask of you graciously," she said with a furrowed brow.

Every morning at seven they listened to Mass behind a screen so that the women who attended at that hour wouldn't see them. Olga and Sonitzya always wore a veil of black lace on their heads, and the three of them received Communion. The priests didn't give sermons, except on Sundays, because they feared being heard by members of the new regime; they had started to see unfamiliar faces at Mass.

The family, now reduced to three, did whatever work they were asked to do. Olga stopped attending reception so as not to be recognized, and she devoted herself to bureaucratic matters with the help of her daughter. The two of them also helped out in the kitchen, even though there was already a housekeeper. Mother and daughter mended the tablecloths, napkins, cassocks, and clothing of the priests, which incensed Sonitzya. She would say: "Mending priests' underpants and undershirts is degrading," and she would pass them over to her mother. Her mother would reply: "Remember, my dear daughter, that clergymen take vows of poverty." Sergei was in charge of cleaning the church and tending the garden. He began work at six o'clock every morning.

Everyone helped with the housework. There was very little food, but they managed. They received it from the archbishopric and they made do with the quotas assigned to the priests. Father Peter was in frequent contact with Olga's parents to see if there was any news of the doctor, but the answer was always negative.

The Kominskys were so Catholic that they accepted their new life with stoicism, saying that these new circumstances were God's will, which they must accept. After a few days, Sergei was moved to a tiny bedroom, which gave the three of them more privacy.

After dinner, the priests, Olga and her children would sit and listen to the BBC news in London, just as everyone else in the world probably did. They never missed the weekly opinion program "Association of Talents." They listened, horrified, to updates on the evolution of the war, on how the Germans were invading and occupying more and more countries. It was their only contact with the world.

Varinia, since she was pregnant, stopped attending dance classes. She was so depressed by Boris's absence that she no longer danced at all. She missed him desperately; her love for him was imprinted on her heart like a tattoo. All she had to console herself with were memories. But . . . what good were memories? Nevertheless, she tried to recall every detail of that night they had made love, but it proved difficult because she realized that the passion she felt had made her close her eyes while they were making love. She reproached herself: "I will never make love with my eyes closed again." She wanted the image of her boyfriend's passionate gaze and pliant body to be etched in her mind forever. She wanted to relive the feeling of love. She closed her eyes and placed the tips of her fingers on her lips, desiring to feel his kisses. She wanted to feel that sweet taste on her mouth again, wanted it to linger forever. "How did I not kiss him more!" She began to caress her body, trying to imagine those moist, secret places, reserved for him alone, where he had kissed, caressed, and penetrated her.

She would lie in bed all day, trying to read. To stave off loneliness, she played cards with her mother and sister. She also got together with her neighbors, the sisters Ewa and Maryla Bielik, who were dear friends of hers. They had grown up together and gone to the same school. They would stay up till dawn pouring their hearts out. They filled her with the hope and strength she needed to endure the pregnancy and Boris's absence. They were Polish, with German ancestry on their father's side. Their father had become rich off of some land he owned outside of Warsaw, on which he raised livestock.

Every night at dinner time Varinia and her parents listened religiously to the program "BBC News at Home" in English, a language they understood. She thought: "At least we're able to listen to the news, even though it's terrifying; otherwise, we'd be talking about the same thing: the difficulty of getting food, the servants robbing food, and the scarcity of everything." Her father had forbidden them, however, to criticize the Nazis: "The walls have ears . . . and the servants do, too." She began to feel a certain degree of resentment toward her father, which made her distance herself from him. She saw how linked he was to the Nazis—he and her mother even attended their social events, which she found shameful—and she couldn't forgive him for not helping her find out what had happened to the Kominskys. Later she would ask God to forgive her for feeling this way.

Eight months of Varinia's pregnancy passed, and as she hadn't heard from her boyfriend or the Kominskys, she decided to go to the family apartment. It was a sunny morning, and the Nazis asked her for her papers at every corner, strutting about in front of her as if they owned Warsaw—which, in fact, they did.

When she asked about the Kominsky's whereabouts, the German woman shouted at her and said: "I don't know, and you'd better leave now or else I'll call the Gestapo!" She slammed the door in her face, just as she'd done to Olga's parents.

Varinia was left trembling and immediately thought: "They were sent to the labor camps. God help us. Or have they fled to Bolivia? They would have told me because I'm carrying their son's child. But what if they didn't have time? Boris is far away, but safe, thank God. Cursed Nazis!" She began to cry over the situation in which she found herself: she was a single mother. And now . . . where could she find the Kominskys?

She walked away frowning, biting her lip, engrossed in thought. "Where . . . where can I find them?" she said to herself. She tried to calm down and thought: "Maybe they're staying with friends." She went to Isaac's house and had the same experience as Sergei. Then she went to the homes of Polish and Catholic friends they had in common, but no one would open the door to her. Finally, one of their friends leaned out of a first-floor window and said: "I don't know where the Kominskys are, but I beg you not to come back here again because the Gestapo have us all on file, even us Poles, as if we were Jews. Goodbye." And she closed the window. These words devastated Varinia because she had considered the girl who said them a friend. "In war, there are no friends," she thought. She didn't know what to do or where to turn.

It finally occurred to her to go see Father Peter. He received her in the lobby and didn't even offer her a seat. For the safety of the family, he was obliged to lie to her. He told her he knew nothing of her friends, and even less of Boris. He later asked for God's forgiveness for having said that.

This left her destroyed. She returned home and decided to talk to her parents. While they were all having coffee in the study after dinner, she told them about the painful day she had had and asked her father to help her find out about the Kominsky family's whereabouts.

"Forgive me, Daughter. If it were Boris, I would, but I don't want to ruin my good relationship with the Nazis. That would cause them to connect us to the Jews, which would be very risky," he said with astonishing coldness.

"Father . . . but . . . how can you cut yourself off from the family of my future husband, of your grandchild?"

"One day you'll thank me . . ."

"And Boris! You say you would have helped him just because he's not here!"

"Don't raise your voice! I swear to you that we will never end up in the ghetto or in a labor camp because we don't have Jewish ancestry and, as you well know, I am related to the Polish nobility by blood. Besides, everyone sees us take Communion at Sunday Mass. I'm sorry to say it, but all of Warsaw knew that the Kominskys were Jewish converts."

"Olga didn't have a drop of Jewish blood; she was Polish."

He stiffened.

"In any case, don't worry, nothing will happen to us because I also have contacts in the Nazi administration. We've come to an agreement which allows me to continue running my business importing glass and crystals."

"I can't believe it! How can you associate with those murderers!"

"Business is business in both war and peace."

"And you, Mother . . . say something!"

Her mother remained as mute as a portrait.

Varinia, passionate as usual, stood up, went to her bedroom, and shut herself up in her room. She couldn't understand her father's opportunism. Was it for the good of the family? Was it the price one had to pay to stay alive and have something to eat? But who could associate with the Nazis? They were invaders, the persecutors and murderers of Jews and Poles, the very essence of cruelty.

She threw herself on the bed, inconsolable. Her parents opportunistic attitude outraged her. She felt lonely and misunderstood, and she began to weep silently, with the photograph of her boyfriend in one hand and the chain he had given her in the other.

All of a sudden she felt liquid between her legs, and she called out for the maid. At the same time, she started to feel contractions that were stronger than usual. The maid saw her lying there and ran to get her parents. They came into the room, and her father said: "It's time!" Her mother said: "But it hasn't been nine months yet!" Her father rushed to the phone, and a few minutes later the doctor arrived. They wanted the baby to be born at home rather than at the hospital, which they said was full of diseases because of all the wounded.

After eight hours of pushing, howls, sweat, blood, prayers, and running to get boiled water, towels, sheets and bandages, the much longed-for baby was born. It was a boy, and just as Varinia wished, he was named after his father: Boris. When she held him in her arms, she cried, feeling happy for the first time in a very long time. She went down on her knees to thank God for the healthy boy who, according to her, looked exactly like his father. It was the best thing that had happened to her since the war had broken out. It improved her life considerably. Now she had someone to take care of, and she did so devotedly, with the help of her mother and sister. Even her relationship with her parents improved, because they were delighted with the baby. It filled her with sadness, though, that she couldn't find the Kominskys to show them the child. "I can't believe that his grandparents on his father's side don't know they have a grandson," she said. The baby became the center of attention. The Bielik sisters were enchanted by the newborn, especially Ewa, who came to see him every day.

What caused her the most distress, however, was that although she wrote to her boyfriend every day, she had no way of knowing whether he received her letters. "How can he not know about something so momentous in our lives . . . our tiny child, who will unite us forever!" Then she thought: "At least I have his son."

Time went by, and all her plans and illusions began to vanish. The only thing she could do was go to check the mailbox daily, although the post was becoming more irregular with each passing day. She refused to accept the fact that letters from Bolivia were no longer being delivered. Stubborn as a mule, she would say: "Those damned Nazis aren't going to beat me." And without telling anyone, she would go to the post office to send off letters written in pen and India ink, smudged by tears, in the hopes that at least one of them would reach him.

On one occasion, she slipped a bill to the woman at the post office to make sure that at least one would be sent. She even let her read the letter and showed her her son, whom she'd brought in the car. This letter said the same thing as all the others: that she'd given birth to little Boris, that she loved him, and that she was planning for their future together. It was all she could say, because she certainly couldn't tell him that the Kominskys had disappeared or describe the horrors that were occurring. In the depths of her heart, though, she knew that the letters she wrote would never reach their addressee.

Olga's parents phoned Olga every day at first, and then once a week. They lived in such a state of paranoia that they even feared their calls to the church would be traced. All of a sudden they stopped calling, and this worried Olga greatly. When two weeks had passed, she asked Father Peter to go see if they were all right. He found their apartment occupied by a German family, which once again confirmed the "Germanization" of Polish territory. This news devastated Olga. She kept blaming herself for her parents' fate. She said to herself: "They were discovered because they came to see us so often, or else someone informed on them." She cried until she began to choke and suffered another asthma attack, which kept her bedridden for several days.

She thought continuously about the fate of her parents and her husband. She said to herself: "I'd rather be told they're in a labor camp, or even dead, than not know how they are . . . forgive me, God, but not knowing where they are is much more painful. Is there anything worse than having a loved one missing? Nothing destroys one's spirit more than the lack of information. We'll always wonder what became of them, especially because of what people say they do to Jews and Poles."

Olga spent most nights lying awake, crying, with her handkerchief in one hand and a crucifix in the other. She thought about her childhood with her parents, and how profoundly happy she and her husband had been when their children were born.

She had fallen in love with him because they were so different. For Olga, being with Marek meant entering a new and fascinating world. In their intimate moments, the first thing she would do was gently remove his glasses and ask him to look her in the eye as they made love. She was dazzled by his brilliance. In her view, the most attractive thing about a man was his intelligence; otherwise, she would be bored to tears. Her love for him was so strong that she used to say doctors were the closest thing to God, because it was in their hands to save lives. This made her husband walk with his head held high.

Seeing their sadness, the priests would read them passages from the Bible to strengthen their faith, but in spite of their efforts, they began to lose it. They resented God, mainly because they knew nothing about Marek or Olga's parents. All they knew about Varinia was that, when she was about to have the baby, she had come to ask Father Peter about them, and he had said they weren't there in order to protect them.

One night, while Olga and her children were sitting together in her room, Sonitzya exploded:

"Mother! I can't bear this confinement any longer, it's like living in prison! We haven't left the walls of this church for more than two years! I have to wear this horrible clothing that's patched and too big for me; I don't have even one pair of stockings that isn't darned, and I have to wash the few pairs I have with lye soap—that is, when we even have that. We don't have enough toilet paper, so we have to use newspaper instead, and we have to brush our teeth with baking soda because there's no toothpaste. And there's barely enough food . . ."

"Shut your mouth Sonitzya! And lower your voice! Outside of these walls we would also have had to live like this, or worse," her mother said vehemently. "What do you want, for them to send us to the labor camps to do God knows what? You should be thanking God every second that we're here. Please, Sonitzya, grow up. We're in the middle of a war."

"I'm sorry, Mother, forgive me."

"I understand how you feel, dear." She wrapped her arms around her and stroked her hair. "Pray, my little Sonitzya, pray."

"Mother . . . I do nothing but pray, but there's no word from Dad, and the priests don't do anything about it. No one does anything. What good are prayers? I'm tired of praying. If only we were in Krakow."

"In Krakow?"

"I heard the priests say that in Krakow there's a movement called the Catholic Youth Resistance, and they say there's a seminarian named Karol Wojtyla, a member of the anti-German group, who risks his life to shelter Jews and help them escape. If the priests at St. Martin's were like him, then . . ."

125

"Your father will show up sooner or later. Don't lose your faith in prayer. For now, let's leave it in God's hands. Remember that God's timing is perfect."

"They don't go looking for him because they're not related to him."

"Sonitzya, don't ever say that again! If they heard you, they'd kick us out of here."

"Everyone knows that the Catholic and Lutheran Churches don't do a thing for the Jews," Sergio chimed in, tense and on edge. "They say the only ones who help our people are socialists and radicals, not Polish nationalists, who hate us."

"They've done a lot for us. Does it seem like little to you that they allow us to live here, risking their own safety?" his mother replied.

"That's just it. They do it for you because you're Polish and you volunteered here for years, but the Vatican is so mute that it seems as if it were allied with the Nazis. Their silence is unmistakable, and their lack of action is sinful. Even the BBC tacitly criticizes them! Pius XII's role in all this is shameful, and deep down the Catholics hate us."

"That's not true," his mother said calmly. "And I advise you, Sergei, to speak not with gall but from your heart, and remember that the Vatican is neutral. Most likely, the Holy See doesn't want to confront the Nazis for fear of being invaded and destroyed."

"Mother, the Catholic Church is very powerful, and no one will lay a finger on them. It's beyond belief that the Church declared that Mussolini was 'sent from heaven.' That's a betrayal of the Catholics!" Olga was petrified.

"Yes, it's shameful," she said, her voice trembling.

"Mother, did you hear the sermon on Sunday? Father John stood at the pulpit and raved against socialism and communism and implied that the Jews are left-wing, as if he were trying to ingratiate himself with the fascists. They're afraid of the Nazis and want to be on good terms with them, but there's nothing more dangerous than politicizing religion. The extraordinary thing is that these priests have started doing just that in their sermons, and unfortunately, 'intelligence' isn't exactly in abundance in the parish."

"I can't deny that. But I can assure you that Pius XI issued the encyclical, albeit late, 'With Profound Concern,' which warned against the deification of race and the state, and proclaimed the right to practice religion freely."

"Hot air, nothing but hot air! He didn't even mention anti-Semitism or the persecution of the Jews. Even Father Peter, the most open-minded of the priests here, recognizes that. Besides . . . what was the use of the encyclical on racism if the current pope didn't enact it? This pope and the previous one knew about the pogroms, raids, murders, and disappearances in Germany, and I can assure you that they know what's happening here in Poland, and they've done nothing to save our people, the Poles, or even the Catholics in Germany, whatever their ideology, and that's a cardinal sin. And the worst of it is that, if even the 'all-powerful' Catholic Church won't speak out against the murderers, who will?" he said angrily. "The pope's mission is to defend not only his followers but all who are unjustly persecuted. Pius XII has always been tied to Germany, and he has a de facto alliance with the Nazis. He was an apostolic nuncio in Germany and he prefers to ingratiate himself with the fascists. The Church looks more like a political institution than a religious one. It's even known that Germany's Catholic bishops opposed Nazism, but Pacelli ordered them to revise their attitude toward National Socialism because he sympathized with the Third Reich. It's an unspeakable disgrace!" he cried.

"Don't yell, son . . . for the love of God!" his mother begged. "It's not that I want to defend the clergy, but the priests told me that Pacelli wrote a letter of resignation before a notary in case he is taken prisoner by the Third Reich, so he's not as connected to them as you say. And how dare you speak about the Church that way, when it's thanks to them that we're alive? You're being ungrateful, and that is indeed a sin."

"Mother, I'm sorry . . . but there are none so blind as those who will not see."

"You know, because Father Peter told us, that the Vatican has sheltered thousands of Jews in monasteries and convents."

"Yes, but there were still raids by the Gestapo for the *Judenaktion*, and some were deported while others were executed."

"Don't be unjust, son. Priests have performed heroic acts that not even rabbis have done, as far as I know. Father Peter told us that a German priest was sent to a labor camp for praying for the Jews in public. Another example is a priest by the name of Grüber who, with a group of priests, set up an office to help persecuted Christians as well as thousands of Jews escape. The Nazis sent him to a labor camp as well," she said, taking deep breaths to stay calm. "My son, all I'm asking is that you don't criticize the Church because it could cost us our lives. For the love of God, don't provoke the priests, who've been extraordinarily kind and generous to us."

"But try to be realistic and stop trying to defend the indefensible . . . I'm sick of it!" he said. "I'll ask Father Peter to obtain fake papers for me, Spanish or Swiss, which are neutral countries, and I'll go look for Dad myself."

"But . . . have you gone crazy? Son, my dear Sergei, it looks like your father isn't coming back, and I'm not willing to lose you too."

"If these priests don't have the courage to look for Dad, then I'll do it."

"Son, for the love of God, don't say that!" she said. She felt like she was choking and began to have an asthma attack.

"You're an idiot for scaring Mom!" Sonitzya exclaimed, getting up to assist her mother.

"I'm sorry, please forgive me," said Sergei. "I didn't want to upset Mom."

Once again, no one slept a wink that night.

Sonitzya was as attractive as her twin brother, and sensuality oozed even from her pores. The priests couldn't stop looking at her, but she was so ingenuous that she didn't even notice. This infuriated Sergei, who as dying of jealously. He tried to make sure that she was never left alone with them. Whenever they spoke to her, an unconscious protective instinct would rise up inside of him. He thought: "Living with so many men produces too much intimacy." He went so far as to think that the priests were in love with her.

She had the poise and grace of a queen and a perfect figure, although she was very thin because she had lost weight. She had an unblemished complexion, blue eyes like the rest of the family, a delicate nose, naturally carmine-colored lips, and a cleft-chin, just like her twin brother, which they had inherited from their father. Blond bangs grazed her forehead, and she usually pulled her short hair back in a ponytail. She was even more beautiful than her mother, and no one could deny her—albeit distant—White Russian ancestry.

The only thing she found consolation in was playing the piano. In the afternoons she would lock herself in the nursery and play, to the irritation of everyone, because she would repeat the same sections over and over again with all her heart and soul. Her mother, a gifted pianist, begged her not to play with such fury. Some evenings, when she was in a peaceful mood, she would play duets with her mother as if they were concert pianists: pieces by Mozart, sonatas by Schubert, Brahms, and their compatriot Chopin, whose compositions they knew by heart. The music rang throughout the parish. Her playing grated on Sergei's nerves, but he couldn't tell her that. The next day, at breakfast, the priests would tell her how the music touched their hearts and lulled them to sleep, which further aggravated Sergei. He thought: "Damn these sexually repressed priests, all they do is lust after my sister . . ." Olga had never noticed anything untoward; the possibility hadn't even crossed her mind. Sergei began to feel ill will toward them and stopped speaking to them; he even stopped speaking altogether. He performed his duties more and more poorly. The only one who understood him was Father Peter, whom he considered a friend. The prelates took his silence to mean that he was going through a bad time, and they left him alone.

After a few days, Sergei told Father Peter that he wanted to go look for his father and asked him to obtain fake documents for him. The prelate replied that it was very risky, but that he understood his desire to discover what had happened to his father as well as his grandparents.

Father Peter called the Swiss consul in Warsaw because he knew him personally and because Sergei spoke German, which meant he could pass for a Swiss German. The consul asked him to come meet him discreetly at a bus stop at noon. The prelate told him about the Kominsky family's situation, and the diplomat agree to give him a safe conduct pass that would allow Sergei to travel around Warsaw, but not a passport. He begged him to ask Sergei to use it as little as possible and to not tell a soul, because he received hundreds of requests daily. He also made it clear that he was only granting the favor because of his regard for Father Peter, and he asked for Sergei's details and a photograph. The priest thanked him profusely. He returned to St. Martin's and the priests took Sergei's picture right away; Father Peter delivered it that afternoon, and Sergei received the document that very night. The cleric thought: "It's better than nothing . . . we couldn't do anything for his father, and that left me with a great sense of guilt. Thank you, God."

Sergei felt as free as a bird and wanted to leave St. Martin's as soon as possible, but they didn't let him. His need to leave the parish had become an obsession. He felt suffocated, depressed, with no desire to pray and even less to attend Mass. He thought: "I'll finally get out of this prison. You have to be very holy or very stupid to be a priest, or even worse a monk: to be locked up for your whole life . . . what punishment!"

Father Peter suggested that, for his own safety, he should wear a cassock, and Sergei had no choice but to agree. He found one of more or less his size and asked the priest: "Do you think I'll be able to walk in this long skirt?"

"You'll get used to it, just as we have," the prelate replied. Sergei smiled for the first time in a long time. Father Peter offered to accompany him, which made Sergei feel safer. And like two priests, they went out to find out what had happened to Marek.

When he stepped into the streets of Warsaw, Sergei felt alive again. He stopped, looked up at the sky, stretched out his arms and smiled again. Father Peter watched him and understood his sense of imprisonment, but he didn't say anything. He asked the prelate if they could go on foot, and he walked with such enthusiasm that it seemed as though he had been imprisoned for his entire life. All of a sudden he stopped to close his eyes and breathe deeply, but he opened them quickly again so as not to miss anything around him. What there was to see, though, was disheartening: his Warsaw had been disfigured and dominated by the enemy. He saw that many apartment buildings had been confiscated for the new government's offices. The Germans had yet to begin rebuilding the city; they had dealt only with the urgent matters of light, water and phone lines.

They went first to the Gestapo headquarters, but they wouldn't even let them near the main entrance. Father Peter told him that the same thing had happened to him right after his father had disappeared. Sergei felt discouraged, but he didn't give up.

They went next to Szpital Zachodni, where Sergei stayed waiting outside. Father Peter asked the doctors if they knew anything about Marek. No one had heard from the doctor, and they began asking the priest if he knew what had happened to the prestigious surgeon. "The hospital isn't the same without him," one of his colleagues said. Next they went to the homes of some of Kominsky's doctor friends, but the answer was the same. Sergei was very discouraged. Father Peter told him: "Son, hope is the last thing you lose." Sergei thought: "If he only knew how many times I've heard that empty phrase . . . to me, hope is just a word . . . God dammit!"

The following day they got up early and headed to Okopowa Street. There were two entrances. One, for the Jews, consisted of a drawbridge that crossed a wide street. The other one, the main entrance, had a sign hanging above it that read: "Entry to the Jewish quarter is prohibited." They opted for this entrance and went inside the walled neighborhood, the most densely populated ghetto in Europe.

The priest approached a man who appeared to be the highest-ranking official and asked if they could go to inspect a Catholic church that had been enclosed in the ghetto. He showed him a fake letter from the archbishopric, as well as their documents. The Colonel wrote their names down and allowed them to enter because they had been instructed to maintain good relations with members of the Church. He had them searched from head to toe in case they had brought food, jewelry, or money to give to those living inside the ghetto. They found nothing. Savvy Father Peter asked that they be provided with entry and exit passes. Entering the ghetto wasn't difficult, but leaving it was impossible. The disagreeable officer gave them the passes.

They walked past dozens of guards and walls lined with barbed wire. They made their way over to a hut beside the entrance that served as an office; it was run by Jewish *kapos* under Nazi supervision who served as intermediaries. The Jews saw these kapos as dirty traitors, opportunists who did the Nazis' dirty work, such as beating, abusing, or denouncing their fellow Jews in exchange for certain privileges. For these men, however, it was a means of survival. Sergei and Father Peter asked about Marek; the kapos were disinclined to help, but Father Peter raised his voice and bellowed: "I have orders from the archbishopric to find Dr. Kominsky." Intimidated by this show of authority, the man who appeared to be in charge opened the record books without even asking to see their documents. He pretended to look for the name, then told them to look for it themselves and left. "Disloyal sons of bitches who sell out their own people . . . they'll burn in hell for this," Sergei muttered indignantly. "That's why they hate us, because of the indecent acts our people are willing to perform for small rewards." "Calm down, boy, keep your thoughts to yourself," his companion replied under his breath.

Father Peter and Sergei divided up the work. Sergei looked for his parents' last name and Father Peter looked for those of Olga's parents and Isaac's family. They also looked under possible dates of entry. They spent the entire morning reviewing a stack of notebooks, many of which were missing or out of order; each one contained an infinite number of names, but they weren't able to find the ones they were looking for. This upset Sergei once again.

"Why are two Catholics looking for a Jew?" asked a kapo who approached them.

"He's not a Jew, he's Polish and Catholic, but he might have ended up here by mistake. We're looking for him because he's an exceptional surgeon, and we need him to operate urgently on one of the priests from our order," the prelate replied. Sergei was surprised by the priest's ability to respond to any question; he thought he was the best liar in the world, and very courageous.

"Look, sir," Sergei chimed in. "Since we can't find him in the notebooks, what do you suggest we do?"

"Listen, Fathers, thousands of Jews arrive here every day, and another thousand are taken from here to the labor camps. They might have taken him, or maybe he never arrived here. I recommend asking the rabbis and the people in the streets. And remember that you need to leave before six o'clock in the evening, otherwise I'll have to put you in the detention center," the kapo threatened them.

"What are the labor camps like?" Sergei asked.

"We don't know and we're forbidden to speak about them," he replied.

"Is it true that those who go there never return? Have you ever seen someone who was sent there return to the ghetto?" Sergei insisted.

"We are forbidden to talk about that!" the kapo replied angrily.

"We'll leave before six. Thank you very much," Father Peter said. They said goodbye and shook his hand, much to the kapo's surprise.

"Don't be discouraged," Father Peter told Sergei. "Let's keep looking."

They began walking and saw that Schultz, the textile manufacturing company, had employed thousands of Jews to make uniforms for the German army. "They opened the factory here so that the Jews don't leave," said the priest. They continued walking a few more blocks and were surprised to see that the trams were running. They saw that the ghetto had turned into a dark, grimy, vile-smelling neighborhood whose streets were full of garbage and whose buildings hadn't been repaired after the invasion. It looked like a neighborhood of beggars, where emaciated children, women, and old people roamed the streets like zombies. As they walked, hungry, sick, and ragged children swarmed around them, tugging at their cassocks and begging for food or whatever else they might have.

They continued walking and saw that some people had set up small businesses to survive, making bands with the Star of David on them, selling used books, or trading objects such as jewelry and clothes for food, the most valuable of all things. They saw the naked, emaciated corpses of adults and children lying in the streets, with spots on their skin and black scabs on their lips, covered with flies. They were rotting. It looked as though no one was coming to claim them. "They have typhus, don't go near them," a woman warned them. "It's because of hunger and the filth," said Father Peter. Just then they saw a group of Jews walking toward them, wearing gloves and holding handkerchiefs over their mouths. They covered the dead with newspaper, picked up the bodies, threw them in some wheelbarrows, and took them away. Hundreds of them died of starvation. The Judenräte, by order of the SS, gave out ration cards for four hundred calories per day. They also died from the cold, from an endless number of diseases, and many of them, even entire families, committed suicide rather than handing themselves over to the enemy, just as at Masada. They considered it the last right they had: to take their own lives.

Father Peter and Sergei saw a building and went up to the first floor. It was in utter disarray and stank like a sewer. There were four or five families living in each apartment; there were Polish Jews as well as Jews of different nationalities who had been transferred to the ghetto. They lived in that tenement filled with fear, perpetual uncertainty and latent anguish. Entire families shared one room and slept on the floor; there were long line-ups for the washroom, as well as for the kitchen. Babies cried and women complained or fought over a crust of bread. They also noticed that the SS had rationed light, gas, and water, and if they needed water they had to go out into the street with a bucket and line up for hours on end at the water fountain on the corner.

They approached a man and asked if he knew Dr. Kominsky. He looked at them as if they were lepers and replied: "Here we're no longer anything or anyone." They approached a woman, but she wouldn't even answer them. They left the building and began asking passersby about Marek, but their responses were all negative. Suddenly Sergei recognized a friend from university who was waiting in a line-up that spanned two blocks.

"Leo, Leo, do you remember me?" he asked shyly. "It's Sergei Kominsky."

"Ah, yes. When did you become a priest?" Leo asked.

"That doesn't matter. Have you seen my father, Dr. Kominsky?"

"I haven't even seen my own parents for months, and I have no idea where yours might be. I've been living in this shithole for six months."

"Do you have any idea whom I could ask?"

"No. But you should get out of here," Leo told them. "The Nazis come in all of a sudden to conduct raids, and they kill people at random, even parents in front of their children, and vice versa."

Father Peter and Sergei, however, continued their terrifying search. They went to several synagogues that had burned down and were left in ruins, and there was no one there who could explain what had happened. One person told them: "Our people were locked up inside and burnt alive." They shuddered. They asked to speak to the rabbis and were told: "They took them away because of their age. No one knows where." They went to the Catholic Church, but it had been demolished. Then they went to the hospital, which was located just in front of the Umschlagplatz. They found the ruins of what had been a medical center. They went inside and were overwhelmed by a nauseating stench. There were dozens of people, near death, lying on stretchers and on the floor. An elderly, tall, and plucky Jewish woman told them: "Get out of here, this place is infected with every disease you can imagine."

"I'm looking for my father," Sergei said. "Do you know Dr. Marek Kominsky? He was the chief surgeon at Warsaw General Hospital."

"Listen, boy," the nurse replied. I've been working in this place of rot and death for more than two years, and I've never heard that name. Now please go."

Her words devastated Sergei. He began to wander around aimlessly, just like the moribund residents of the ghetto.

It was almost six o'clock and they had to leave. Father Peter took him by the arm and said: "We'll come back to look for him, but for now, walk quickly." Before they left the ghetto a woman approached them and handed them a note. She said: "This was written by my twelve-year-old daughter." They read it as they walked toward the exit:

FEAR
Today the ghetto knows a different fear.
Close in its grip, Death wields an icy scythe.

An evil sickness spreads a terror in its wake,
The victims of its shadow weep and writhe.
Today a father's heartbeat tells his fright.
And mothers bend their heads into their hands.
Now children choke and die with typhus here,
A bitter tax is taken from their hands.
My heart still beats inside my breast.
While friends depart for other worlds.
Perhaps it's better—who can say?—
Than watching this, to die today?
No, no, my God, we want to live!
Not watch our numbers melt away.
We want to have a better world.
We want to work—we must not die!

They were both stunned by the poem. They arrived at the checkpoint right before six. They showed their exit passes and began walking home. It had been the worst walk of Sergei's life. He was completely demoralized and didn't say a word. His gaze was blank and his heart was empty. Everything looked gray to him, just like his soul. Father Peter tried to raise his spirits by telling him they wouldn't let their guard down and would continue the search. Nothing, however, consoled him.

When they arrived at the church he immediately went to see Olga and Sonitzya in their bedroom and embraced them with all his strength.

"Mother, we didn't find Dad," Sergei said.

"Let's not lose hope," Olga replied.

"We went to the ghetto, which is something from another world, a living nightmare, phantasmagorical, something that's never been seen or imagined before. Could Dad have spent time in that hell? Could he have been sent to a labor camp?"

"Try to stay positive, dear son. Remember that your father will always be needed because he's a doctor. In wars, doctors are the most valuable people, even for the enemy."

"I hope God is listening to you, Mother. How can they be forced to experience that agony and humiliation just because they are of another race? Can such evil exist in man? Can man grow to hate his fellow man to such a degree? Why do our people surrender like cattle, with biblical humility, and not fight for their lives?"

135

"What choice do they have if they have guns pointed at their heads? What would you do? What would we do? I don't even want to think about it. That's why, my darling Sergei, you should thank God that we're alive and protected . . . and pray, pray for the Jews and Poles not to suffer."

"Not to suffer more than they already have? Mother, how can I pray if they keep sending our people to labor camps, which I find doubtful, or killing them without pity? Only God can decide who lives and who dies. I don't want to attend Mass either because it's very repetitive and I can't stand the priests anymore. I feel profoundly wronged. The pope and the Catholic Church are the worst sinners of all, and they'll have to bear of burden of thousands of deaths on their conscience!"

"But . . . how dare you question God? Our Lord will hear our prayers sooner or later, even if for now he responds with silence, for reasons neither you nor I can understand."

"Well, right now he appears to be deaf! My faith dwindles day by day. Mother . . . now you're taking away my right to think freely!"

Chapter 6
Bolivia, 1942–1943

"Not having heard from Varinia or my parents for more than three years has caused me terrible pain . . . intense grief . . . and all because of this goddamn war," bewailed Boris, driven to despair, to the point of kicking doors and walls. He hadn't received a single letter since the war began. To find moments of relative peace, he would go, rosary in hand, to the Catholic church down the road, and he would pray to God and his Black Madonna, asking them to protect his family and friends. All he could do was entrust them to God's keeping. "At least my faith gives me the strength to face this horrible situation . . . what else can I do?" He went continually to the Ministry of Agriculture, Irrigation, Colonization and Immigration, and the answer was always the same: "Visas are no longer being granted." He knew it was pointless to go, but he went all the same, without knowing why. He also went frequently to the post office, which was equally futile.

The other refugees had also stopped hearing from their relatives and friends. They relied on newspapers, and the hour of the BBC news was sacred. They lamented that more of their family members and friends hadn't been able to emigrate. Many had stayed in Europe due to lack of money, indecision, doubts about leaving other loved ones behind, fear of leaving the fruits of a life's work, or fear of starting a new life and leaping into the unknown. The immigrants thanked Jehovah for saving their lives. The Jewish community in Bolivia did nothing but discuss the war and speculate about what was happening. The first person who heard the smallest bit of news would pass it along immediately.

Global public opinion found it hard to believe that the world was still at war. They learned through the press that a large number of European countries had fallen under the power of the Third Reich. France, Germany's historic enemy, continued to fight alongside the Allies, and many Frenchmen volunteered to go to the front.

De Gaulle, who had fled to Britain after accusing Pétain of being a traitor, served as the leader of Free France, with Churchill's consent. He called on his compatriots to join the French Resistance, which became unified by the charismatic political leader Jean Moulin.

Mussolini entered the war because he shared Hitler's views; he wanted Italy to become a world power and had aspirations of expansionism. Churchill asked for support from Franco's Spain, but Spain preferred to remain neutral because it had just come out of a civil war during which a million Spaniards had been killed.

In 1941, Japan, one of the Axis powers, a country that was waging war with China and was as racist as the Nazis, attacked Pearl Harbor in Hawaii as well as the Philippines. The United States joined the war alongside the Allies, and Churchill could breathe a bit more easily. The Axis powers trembled, and at the same timed began to attack European colonies in the Far East. The United States started the Pacific War, during which they occupied island after island as well as the countries occupied by Japan. The Soviet Union, a member of the Allies, was attacked twice by Germany, but without success. The Germans never imagined that the "invincible" Red Army had the largest number of tanks on the planet and as many planes as all the armies in the world combined. The Germans also had to confront another great enemy: winter. Millions of soldiers died of hunger, hypothermia, and exhaustion. Their defeat at Stalingrad marked the beginning of the end of the war. Meanwhile, the battle in North Africa ended with the Allied victory. Rommel begged Hitler to end the war, but he refused; this was another milestone signaling the beginning of the defeat of the Axis powers.

Boris received a promotion and was appointed head of the small office of the Miraflores estate. He was put in charge of sales, distribution, marketing, and accounting for the plantation. One afternoon while he was doing the books in the hacienda's small office, someone knocked on the door. He got up to open it and founded himself face to face with none other than Misha, whom he recognized immediately.

"Misha . . . but . . . how wonderful to see you!" They embraced one another affectionately. "But . . . this is a gift from God . . . how you've grown . . . how beautiful you are! You cut your hair, and your eyes are bigger and more beautiful than ever! When I left, you were just a girl, and now you're a full-grown woman . . . even though you're still as thin as a rake!"

"Oh . . . Boris! I'm so happy to see you . . ."

"Tell me, how are your parents and your sister?"

"My parents are still at Buena Vista, and my sister lives here with me. We're both studying at the university."

"Look, it's just about the end of the work day, let's go . . . I'll take you out for dinner . . . I'll take you anywhere you want to celebrate our reunion. Have you noticed that we're speaking in Spanish now?"

"Yes, now we know how!"

Boris grabbed his coat and they took a taxi to the city center. They started walking through the streets to see which restaurant she would like best. They ended up at the Wiener, which was one of Boris's favorites. She felt like a princess because she never went to such expensive places. Luckily, she was wearing her nicest outfit—a two-piece suit and a charming hat. The waiter showed them to their table and brought them the menu. She took her hat off delicately.

"Tell me about your life, beautiful Misha . . ."

"Well, I'm studying biochemistry at university, because I wasn't admitted to the medical program, which was what I really wanted to do. My sister is studying pharmacy, so we make a good team."

"And . . . why didn't they accept you?"

"They said our high school diplomas weren't recognized by the Ministry of Education. We took the exams and passed them, but they still didn't accept us. They also said that medicine is a career for men, since only men can stand so much work."

"How ridiculous! It's their loss . . . not yours. And do you like your program?"

"Very much. But when I graduate, I'll study medicine."

"Good for you. You've always been a fighter."

"Do you remember when we almost lost Isaac? I've rarely been so afraid . . . I thought he was dying."

"And you were extraordinarily helpful, an indefatigable companion. I'll never forget it."

"I saw you were suffering, and I suffered along with you."

As they were having dinner and chatting in those cozy surroundings, beside the fireplace, he noticed that she was smiling with both her mouth and her eyes. He found this captivating. They felt as if they'd known each other all their lives.

"And . . . how are things at Buena Vista?"

"It's growing rapidly, even though refugees are no longer coming because it's impossible to emigrate from Europe. Its richness knows no bounds! If a seed falls to the ground a few months later you see a tree shooting up quickly, before you even know it."

"I had to escape from the jungle. Isaac and I couldn't stand it."

"And . . . how is Isaac?"

"He went back to Poland, and I haven't heard from him or my family since."

"I'm sorry . . . I'm truly sorry. This war is destroying even those of us who live far away."

They finished their dinner and Boris offered to accompany her home.

"No!" she replied firmly. "We'll say goodbye here."

"Are you sure? It's dark, and it's not a good idea for you to walk alone. I want to see you again, Misha."

"I'll call you at work," she said.

"If you like . . . would you like to go to a matinee this weekend? They're showing the film *Gone with the Wind*, and I don't want to miss it. We can go to Eli's afterward. What do you think?"

"I'd love to. I'll call you," she said, and she wrote down his phone number.

"So now it's fashionable for young ladies to call men?"

"I'm a university woman!" she said laughing.

They said goodbye at the restaurant entrance, much to Boris's surprise. He told her: "Don't forget to call me."

The weekend arrived and Misha phoned, which pleased him greatly.

"What do you think if we meet at the Paris cinema at ten fifteen in the morning?"

"Great. I'll buy the tickets and I'll be waiting for you at the door."

And so they met there. As they greeted each other, he gave her an affectionate kiss on the cheek and offered to buy her a hot dog, but she refused.

"Hello, Misha!" the vendor greeted her.

She barely acknowledged him. It was Mr. Loewenthal, who sold sausages with black bread and spicy mustard on the street. His wife stood on the corner with a kerosene stove, where she boiled them in a pot. They were the precursors of Bolivian *embutidos* and they were very popular with the people of La Paz. They bought popcorn and went in to see the movie, which moved Misha deeply. When the film was over they went to the Jewish-owned Eli's to eat *salteñas*, which they loved. There they saw many members of the Jewish community who usually met there on Sundays. They had a wonderful time chatting together.

Later in the afternoon, Misha told Boris that she needed to go home because she had to study. He, of course, wanted to accompany her, but she refused.

"But . . . why don't you want me to go with you?"

"Because . . . it's too much of a bother for you. I'll go on my own."

"What's wrong, Misha? Tell me what's wrong!"

"Let me go alone. Go on now."

He took her by the arms and asked her firmly:

"What are you hiding from me?"

"It's . . . it's that . . . we live in a tenement . . ."

"What's wrong with that? I live in a boarding house. Everyone lives where they can . . . And you are both students and everyone is poor. I used to be too. Please, let me go with you."

"If you want to . . . but don't be disappointed."

Misha pouted and spoke little during the walk. They walked to the intersection of Sucre and Bolívar, where all the old colonial mansions were, each one spanning almost an entire block, with four inner courtyards. They were all very rundown. The building had two entrances, one on each street. They went in the one on Bolívar Street, and he saw that it was indeed a tenement. Dozens of families lived there, mostly Jewish ones, and well as bus and taxi drivers.

The Loewenthal family had installed a sausage factory whose products they sold to a shop on Colón Street, as well as on street corners. The most popular place was on the corner of the Paris cinema, in Plaza Murillo. There was a man who repaired cars with Klim milk cans. Another had a small textile factory. One woman, the wife of a prestigious lawyer who didn't speak a word of Spanish, sold jams to the grocery stores. She told him that Mr. Katz, who was sunbathing, played the organ and worked as an organ grinder to make a bit of extra money, and he transported his instrument by bicycle when he had to perform somewhere. From Monday to Friday he dressed like a beggar, but on the weekends he wore a shiny, threadbare tuxedo and a crooked bowler hat that he would take off to receive tips in when he played at the Israelite Circle. "That man is a complete nutjob; I've seen him speak to the police in Plaza Murillo in German, and the officers spoke back to him in Aymara, as if they understood each other." "It would be best to stay away from him," Boris said.

There was also a certain Walter Kohn who lived there, a miserable man who would later collaborate with the infamous Claudio San Román, a torturer during the revolution of 1952. They visited the second courtyard next, where the Sapirstein family had installed the first laundry service in La Paz, called Record. All the oligarchs sent their white clothes there to be washed. Some women were washing and scrubbing clothes on wooden boards, and then they hung them up to dry, taking advantage of the afternoon sun. Others were ironing dry clothes with charcoal irons and cornstarch, leaving them impeccable. The success of this laundry business prompted a certain Mr. Sorsky to open the first dry and steam cleaning service, on Comercio Street, where the Clique sent their garments and three-piece suits to be cleaned. The residents of the tenement, most of whom were German speaking, sent their young children to the Bolivian Israelite School, whose intake grew year by year. They had a synagogue right there. The older children, however, attended the Ayacucho School, or the Ingavi, which was on Diaz Romero Street, in Miraflores. It was founded by the Jewish community and later became a nursing home.

"As you can see, this is a real tenement. People work and live right here."

"And why are you ashamed of that? Work is dignified, no matter what it is, and if they have no other place to do it, it shouldn't bother you."

"Even the prostitutes?"

"Well, we'll have to think philosophically about that case . . ." he said, and they smiled at each other. "They're refugees, just like the rest of us. Some have had better luck than others. It would be worse if they did nothing at all and begged in the streets, giving immigrants a bad name and turning the locals against us."

"You know what, Boris? I'm the daughter of a doctor, and in Europe, being a doctor is a very honorable profession," she said with tears in her eyes.

"Listen to me, my dear Misha. Times have changed. We're in the middle of a war, and the repercussions are felt even here. We have to survive, and we all do what we can. As long as no one disrespects you or your sister, you should stay here."

"Sometimes, on the weekends or on holidays, our people share food with the mestizos, or *cholos*, as they call them, but we don't like to take part because the Bolivians always end up getting drunk."

"You're right not to. You're both young and pretty, and you need to take care of yourselves."

Misha took him to see her room. It had two beds separated by a bedside table with a lamp, two desks with chairs, and a window through which sunlight was streaming. It was impeccably clean and tidy. It had a hardwood floor, which was unusual. It also had a private bathroom, and there was a kitchen with a small refrigerator in the hallway.

"This is a respectable place, thanks to you and your sister. Don't be embarrassed about all the rest . . ." He took her in his arms, and she shed a few more tears.

"Thank you, my dear Boris, thank you for understanding . . ."

"There's nothing to thank me for. I've spent a wonderful day with you, Misha . . . I'd like to see you again."

"Me too. Call me. You can reach me by calling the laundry lady's phone number."

That Sunday, Boris decided to attend evening Mass at seven o'clock at the Church of La Merced. He saw a young woman he knew there, a Bolivian girl who did nothing to disguise her attraction to him. They had become friends while taking a course called "Deepening Our Understanding of the Gospel." She was a typical high society girl from La Paz, the daughter of an idle, landowning oligarch who lived off of his inherited estate and the labor of the *pongos*, the indigenous men who worked the land.

One afternoon, she asked him to come visit her at her house. She later told him that her mother had scolded her at the top of her lungs: "I forbid you to speak to him, he must be one of those Jews who are taking over Bolivia." She had retorted: "If he were Jewish, he wouldn't go to Mass." That silenced her. Boris put it out of his mind. A few days later, while Boris was at work, Moritz Hochschild turned up unexpectedly. The workers gawked at him when they saw him arrive, as he had become a legendary figure. Boris always went to work in a suit and tie, and when he saw Moritz come in he looked down at the suit he had on; it was a relatively good one. Something he had learned from his mother sprung to mind: "People treat you according to how you look," and he thought to himself: "I'm going to impress this man." All the men working on the farm came to greet him reverentially. He shook hands with each and every one of them. Then Boris greeted him and struck up a conversation in German. His self-confidence and smart appearance pleased the mogul.

"Are you a German Jew?"

"I'm a Polish-Catholic Jew who grew up in Poland. I learned German at school."

143

"And you've learned it well. I've heard about you, and I know you've been managing the estate for the past three years with great efficiency. Would you mind showing me the books?"

"I'd be delighted to, Herr Hochschild."

They went into the modest office where Boris worked alongside an accountant, and he explained in German how he kept the books. Hochschild could see that Boris managed the hacienda with efficiency, ingenuity, and integrity. "This boy is young, very intelligent, and good-willed," he thought.

"Would you like to come work for me?"

"It would be an honor, sir. But who will take over the management of the estate?"

"We'll find someone soon enough. I'll see you in my office on El Prado at eight o'clock tomorrow morning."

"Hochschild has heard of me," he thought. This made him feel proud of his work, and he gave thanks to God. He also saw it as a great challenge to work for a man as successful as Hochschild.

The day after that first encounter, Boris put on his best suit and presented himself at eight o'clock sharp at the elegant office complex of Mauricio Hochschild. He was made to wait twenty minutes because Hochschild was in a meeting. While he waited nervously, he thought about what he was going to say to the "Baron," a workaholic who would work while he slept if he could. When he finally went into his office, he was dazzled. For a moment, he felt like he was in another country. The desk, tables, and chairs were made of mahogany and had been imported from Europe. Even the walls were lined with wood, and mineral samples decorated the shelves. The curtains were silk and the rugs were Persian.

"Come in, young man." He shook his hand and invited him to have a seat. They began to converse in German.

"Tell me about yourself. Did you go to university?"

"Yes, sir. I'm a chemical engineer with a degree from the University of Warsaw."

"And do you have work experience?"

"Yes. I worked in a laboratory making pharmaceutical products."

At that moment a senior executive and friend of Hochschild's, Dr. Adolf Blum, entered the office. He was a lawyer who had studied at the University of Heidelberg. Hochschild introduced them to one other, and Blum took a seat.

"As you know, I'm the owner and administrator of several mines in Bolivia that are part of the Mauricio Hochschild SAMI (Sociedad Anónima Minera Industrial) Company. At present, I'm looking for a young man to supervise the quality control of the minerals we export, because I don't want to have complaints from buyers. And I think you, as a chemical engineer, are a perfect match for the job. We have a laboratory in Potosí."

"Does that mean I'll have to go live in Potosí?"

"No, Boris. It's a very cold, arid place that's four thousand two hundred meters above sea level, and you'd be desperate to escape from there after a while. You have too much potential for that. I just need you to go there every so often to check on things. I also need you to travel to Oruro, Tupiza, and Arequipa, in Peru, where we have offices, so that you can make sure the quality of the metal we buy fully meets the standards of our buyers. If you have any questions or need anything you can always contact Dr. Blum."

At that moment they called the secretary. She was an elderly and well-dressed lady, one of those upper-class women who had been widowed and left penniless after the Chaco War, like many others, and she depended on her job to make ends meet. Hochschild gave her instructions, and she asked a few employees to set up a desk in a large room shared by several clerks. Meanwhile, Moritz took Boris on a tour of the office complex and introduced him to the executives. The majority were Jewish, which made him feel at home. Many of them were surprised that he didn't speak Hebrew.

There were roughly two hundred Jews employed by Hochschild in his mines and offices, even though many of them didn't speak Spanish or know anything about the industry. He hired them on intuition, and if they didn't fit in the area he'd assigned them to, he simply switched them to another one. Boris couldn't believe what was happening to him; he was thrilled. When he sat down at his new desk he thought: "This is the best thing that has happened to me since I arrived in Bolivia. A new world is opening up before my eyes, and I no longer have to inventory lettuce, potatoes and tomatoes, or buy fertilizer, or suffer when it rains and the sowing is ruined. And when there's a drought, I don't have to go find water wherever I can so that we don't lose the crops, because that's the climate of La Paz, typical of mountainous terrain. I need to call Misha to tell her! . . . she has become my partner, although just in a platonic sense, unfortunately, but a friend nonetheless. I've been so lonely these past few years . . . it's as if my family and Varinia no longer existed . . . and what if they no longer do, in reality? God, don't let me think like that . . ." Boris and Misha went out for dinner that night to celebrate his new job.

Moritz was away for a few weeks because he had to take a trip around Latin America and the United States to see how his businesses were going.

Boris worked at the same pace as Hochschild and many other employees in the company: from sunrise to sunset. He would arrive at the boarding house exhausted and fall asleep with a book open and the radio on, tuned in to El Cóndor, which broadcast live concerts, operettas and opera arias sung by his people, under the direction of Hugo Landesmann.

Misha didn't usually go out with him during the week because she had to study; weekends were a different story. On Saturday mornings, Boris played sports with his friends, and at night he would take her to the Municipal Theater, where they never missed the concerts of the National Symphony Orchestra directed by fellow Jew Erich Eisner and comprised almost entirely of Jewish musicians. They also went to the Israelite Circle, out for dinner, or to the cinema. And on Sundays they would go out of the city with others from the community to Obrajes, a rural area south of the city. They also went along on trips to Lake Titicaca. On one occasion they saw their fellow Jew Liselotte Susz swim across the cold Strait of Tiquina. She was the first woman to cross it, and they were very proud. Never, though, did Boris go back to the Yungas, despite Misha's many requests. That place brought back bad memories of what he had lived through with Isaac. The two of them were the talk of the Jewish community and a source of vexation to the mothers who wanted to set Boris up with their daughters.

Boris was sent on a business trip to Potosí. On the train, he read some chronicles that recounted how the Spaniards had taken gold and silver from there, at the expense of the lives of millions of indigenous people. Spain made an empire and won wars with the silver extracted from the famous Cerro Rico, which turned the city into an "El Dorado" for centuries. According to the legend, there was enough silver to build a bridge from the tip of the mountain to the port of Seville. He read that between 1550 and 1650, Potosí was the most important city on the planet, with the same number of inhabitants as London and even more than Paris. The residents included everyone from pirates to mercenaries to ruined Spaniards with suspect titles of nobility, some even boasting kinship to royalty. It was baptized by Charles V as the "Imperial Villa," and ruled by the Viceroy Hurtado de Menoza. The wealth of Potosí was so great that certain parts of horse saddles (which they brought from Chile and Argentina), as well as the spurs, were made of silver. The people of Potosí and the thousands of foreigners who decided to settle in the Imperial Villa lived like kings and had everything imported from Europe and Asia. The city became a little "Andean Paris," packed with nouveau riche. There were around thirty churches with silver or gold leaf altars, and the ecclesiastical ornaments were also made of gold and incrusted with precious stones. There were all kinds of theaters, a small bullfighting ring, casinos, restaurants, fashion houses, seedy bars, and brothels.

Its inhabitants lived in palaces with hand-carved furniture; damask curtains; Persian and Turkish rigs; Flemish tapestries; Bohemian and Venetian lamps and crystal; Chinese porcelain and decorations; Russian tablecloths; and cutlery, plates, and tea and coffee sets all made of pure silver by indigenous silversmiths.

The women wore brocade and shantung dresses embroidered with gold and silver thread; necklaces, rings, and bracelets with diamonds and rubies from India; baroque pearls from the China Seas; and sapphires from Cambodia and Thailand set in filigree by the natives, which proved to be a luxury very rarely seen.

When he was about to arrive in the city he saw the famous Cerro Rico, which made a strong impression on him. It was the richest mountain in the history of the world. He then saw, however, that despite its tremendous mining wealth, the city hadn't advanced at all. "The Bolivians are sitting on a silver throne, but all that reigns here is appalling poverty." The only people in the streets were the miners who had aged prematurely as a result of spending their lives in the depths of the mountain extracting minerals, the same fate their ancestors had met and to which their descendants were condemned. It was the poorest and most neglected mining town in Bolivia, quite unlike Oruro, which was prosperous, and where there was more money than cobblestone since most of the equipment retailers and mineral traders lived there. Some members of high society even resided in Oruro. And what had become of Potosí? It was now a neglected, inhospitable city, mired in poverty, haunted by tormented spirits.

Boris went to the M. Hochschild & Cia. Laboratory every day, at the foot of Cerro Rico. He spent hours reviewing samples of all kinds of minerals next to a stove. In his free time he bundled himself up and visited the city and the churches, whose art and design offered some of the best examples of colonial-era style. He was surprised to find paintings from the schools of Titian and Bitti. He visited the Casa de la Moneda, where silver *macuquina* coins were minted for the Spanish Empire. He also went to the Santa Teresa Convent, where the Spanish aristocrats sent their daughters to a "living death." "Is there a worse punishment for a human being than a cloister? It's like a jail . . ." he thought. They would send them there by ship, never to see their families again, with considerable donations for the Church: precious jewels, gold and silver cutlery, Murano and Bohemian glass, and dresses embroidered with gold and silver thread that they would never wear because they were made to take vows of poverty.

When Boris returned to La Paz, the first thing he did was call Misha, and they went out for dinner; he wanted to share his impressions of Potosí with her.

His standard of living improved considerably because he was earning a much higher salary. He bought new clothes and moved to an apartment on Ingavi Street, relatively close to the office. He bought a bed, a stove, a refrigerator, and little by little he furnished the place with the help of Misha, who finally fell into his arms, but not into his bed. "If I sleep with him, he'll leave me," the shrewd Misha thought. They kissed and embraced tirelessly, like teenagers. They were happy and enjoyed each other's company. He had to confess to her, however, that he had left a girlfriend in Warsaw. She didn't mind because she knew he couldn't return to his country as long as the war lasted. She thought: "For now, I'm his only reality . . . and that's what counts." He felt very attracted to her, but he couldn't stop thinking about Varinia. Whenever he looked up at the full moon, which lit up the La Paz nights like the sun, he inevitably thought of her. He said to himself: "Every time I see the moon as full as it was that night, I feel that I still love her . . ."

He became very close friends with a Jewish man who kept telling him: "Live in the moment, you can't do anything for her right now. Your girlfriend is in Poland, and you're in Bolivia . . . be practical."

Hochschild finally returned from his trip and met with Blum, the managers, and Boris. Boris gave him his report, stating that in the samples he had selected at random, he hadn't noticed anything irregular.

"Do you have plans for dinner?" Moritz asked Boris and Blum.

"No," responded Boris, his face lighting up.

"Well then, come dine with me."

"Thank you very much, Mr. Hochschild."

"Unfortunately, I have a family engagement tonight," Blum said.

At eight o'clock that evening, the secretary summoned Boris to Hochschild's office, and they went out for dinner. A black Mercedes Benz with a chauffeur impeccably dressed in a cap and white gloves was waiting for them below. He drove them to the brand-new Club de La Paz, recently built in Art Deco style. After climbing the huge steps covered with red carpet, they entered the establishment and were greeted with great courtesy by all of the waiters. The head waiter brought them to the table that was always reserved for him. Moritz drank a couple of gins—unlike Boris, who was not much of a drinker and wanted to remain lucid for the conversation. A pianist played on a Steinway in the background. Boris knew that Moritz loved to tell stories, especially after a few drinks, so he didn't hesitate to ask him about the first thing that came to mind.

"Herr Hochschild, how do you like living in Bolivia?"

"This is a wonderful country that has always filled me with great satisfaction. I love it so much that my headquarters are in La Paz . . . . Besides, to be honest, this is the center of the mining world. I've generally been welcomed by everyone, although I've also had problems, but I've put those behind me. All I know is that the Left, the ones behind those lampoons that have fortunately ceased, hate me and my colleagues. I've given lectures and written newspaper articles against the Germans and the war. I've stated that the communist, fascist, and Nazi revolutions are effects, not causes. I've done nothing but defend our people and attack Nazism. They accuse me of being a fascist because I own mines, but I'm simply a non-practicing liberal."

"A capitalist, you could say."

"Yes, perhaps. The interesting thing about Bolivia is its strategic location; it's in the heart of South America. I've always dreamed, just like Simón Bolívar, of a united Latin America. A utopia that neither the Liberator nor anyone else has been able to bring to fruition. I also have the hope that if the indigenous people stopped chewing coca leaves, they would become better workers."

"But that, Herr Hochschild, is an ancestral custom, impossible to eradicate."

"It's true, but it's a shame to see them become so stupefied. I also have plans to build a power plant that uses the waters of Lake Titicaca, which Bolivia shares with Peru. It's a titanic project of the greatest interest for this country, more so than for its neighbor, but, of course, there's no money for it, especially since the Chaco War with Paraguay, which cost Bolivia lives and territory and left it broke."

"And . . . is there anti-Semitism in Bolivia?"

"I think the Bolivians have come to love our people because they've seen how we have contributed to the development of the country with new and more modern working methods. A testament to this appreciation is the fact that last year the mayor of La Paz invited the Jewish community to march in the parade commemorating the anniversary of the department of La Paz, as well as Bolivian Independence Day. In addition, highly respected intellectuals publish articles in our defense. Cases of anti-Semitism, in reality, are exceptional and isolated, except for the MNR, which, when it was founded a few years ago, adopted the Nazi Party platform and declared themselves anti-Jewish. In the case of the Bolivian Socialist Falange, its leader, Únzaga de la Vega, an orthodox Catholic, declared his anti-Semitism openly. But I don't pay any attention to those emerging parties. Bolivians are possessive of their country. No one can criticize Bolivia except them, especially when it comes to politics. And they don't like our people meddling in their internal affairs. The Bolivians have never organized a pogrom, nor do I think it would ever cross their minds to do so. The Clique, comprised of miners, landowners, bankers and merchants, are Catholic, very conservative, and, without a doubt, racist and classist. They don't like to associate with immigrants, and even less with refugees. They're not mestizos, they're criollos—descendants of Spaniards born in South America, some of whom even have aristocratic titles, especially in the city of Sucre, where they think they're the crème de la crème of society. The upper class is so exclusive that they also don't mix with Yugoslavs or Arabs, whom they contemptuously call 'Turks,' or with diplomats, because, according to them, as Bolivia is a faraway country in the process of development, only people of no importance are sent here. I've even heard them say: 'Even though they're white, they're not from our class . . . in their own countries

150

they must be nobodies.' I heard that at a carnival party the oligarchs mocked our people, putting on masks with big noses and ears and wearing signs covered with dollar signs that said 'Jew.'"

"And the middle class?"

"Those things don't happen with them because they love socializing with our people, something they can't do with the exclusive and contemptuous haut monde of Bolivia. They like having their children play with the children of the 'gringos' in the parks or on the street. They even appreciate our people because we give them jobs in our stores and warehouses. The indigenous people don't accept us, however, because we're white and they associate us with the oligarchs and worry that we'll mistreat them."

"And what does the community do to integrate?"

"Nothing, since they send their children to the Israelite School and always socialize amongst themselves. They want their children to marry other Jews, an atavistic custom known by all. An absolute stupidity!"

"And have you ever felt rejected?"

"Never; it's quite the other way around. The upper class usually invites me, but I'm not interested in socializing with them. I'd rather spend my time with my mining colleagues, with other men of my trade, with my employees, the Jewish community, and politicians. You must understand that one has to protect 'the shop,'" he said, smiling from ear to ear. "And the only guarantee of that is to have good relations with the current government. I don't really get along with the landowning Clique. They exploit the indigenous people, whom they call *pongos*, treating them like slaves to be sold, bought, and rented out. They own not only their lives but their families. They enact the *jus primae noctis* with their daughters, which is why the countryside is teeming with light-skinned villagers with western features. It breaks my heart to see the extreme poverty and the marked difference between them and the criollos. Those people act like colonizers and see themselves as foreigners in their own country. They say they're Bolivian when it suits them, since they have access to unpaid labor, which allows them to live like kings. But otherwise they're so pretentious that they speak to each other in English and French and think of nothing but their European ancestors," he said bitterly and ordered another gin and tonic. "Am I boring you?"

"Not at all, Herr Hochschild. Tell me more. And . . . what has Bolivia's stance on the war been?"

151

"In the first year of the war, Bolivia sold tin to the United States and Great Britain at a special 'war rate,' for next to nothing. In reality, Bolivia probably subsidized the Allies for the sake of democracy and the free world, and they created a buffer stock that allows them to control market prices to this day, which I consider dangerous. Although Bolivia increased its production, this damaged the country's economy. One month after the attack on Pearl Harbor, during the government of General Peñaranda, Bolivia broke off relations with Germany and Japan and joined the Allies. Although I met with him several times to explain the importance of my Jewish settlement project, he stopped the immigration of our people and canceled the colonization contracts with Jewish agencies."

"That was devastating for me."

"Don't lose too much sleep over it, my boy, because war had already broken out and those abominable Nazis wouldn't have let your family or any of our people leave the occupied countries.

"There was the famous Nazi Putsch, a plot I'll tell you about," he said, lighting a cigar. "A certain Jenjins, who was secretary of the US embassy in La Paz, showed the Bolivian chancellery a letter signed by Belmonte, the attaché of the Bolivian legation in Germany. The letter was addressed to the German ambassador here, that is, to Herr Wendler. It announced the intention of staging a coup against Peñaranda and installing a pro-Nazi government, thereby extending the reach of Nazi ideology and establishing a satellite in the heart of Latin America. Bolivia was the ideal place. This was the detonator that set President Peñaranda off. Fortunately, he took the opportunity to expel the ambassador, a nasty man, leader of the Nazi group. When the people of La Paz found out, they raided the German embassy, hurling the furniture into the streets and taking everything they could."

"I heard about that and I can't deny that it made me happy."

"They even threw out teachers from the German School, although curiously enough, not the director, a certain Eric Fischer. They also expelled the owners of INTI Pharmaceuticals, the Schilling brothers and a man by the name of Flossbach, among others. The government put them on a military plane and sent them to the United States; the US administration has them locked up in detention centers in Texas and elsewhere. They've also detained about a hundred thousand Japanese, many of whom were born in the United States and are citizens. They're not treated as slaves, but they don't

152

live in liberty. Returning to the putsch, it was later discovered that British intelligence had forged the letter. Isn't it fantastic? Those Englishmen never let an opportunity pass them by. Later, the government shut down *La Calle* newspaper, which was blatantly anti-Semitic, as well as the *Inti* and the *Busch*. Anyway, I'll stop boring you," he said, taking a deep breath. "Now tell me about yourself. Tell me about your family. Why did you come here alone?"

Boris's face darkened, and he lowered his eyes.

"I begged my father to emigrate, but he refused, knowing full well that the war was coming and that they were persecuting our people in Germany. My mother and siblings stayed in Warsaw because they didn't dare to leave him alone, I think. I haven't heard from them since the war broke out. I keep writing to them and I go to the post office almost every day to see if there are any letters from them, but there never are. Checking the mail has become an obsession of mine. I've also written to my girlfriend and my priest friends at St. Martin's Church, but I've received no reply from them either."

"Son, the postal service died when the war broke out. I must confess that I also begged my family to come, but no one agreed. They thought Bolivia would be like an African country, and they preferred to stay where they were."

"I'm completely desperate. I don't know what to do. And now I'll ask you, Don Mauricio: do you know of any way I could find out about my family and my girlfriend?"

"Look, boy. I have to go to Germany in a couple of days. First of all, I want to see how my family is, and second, I want to see how Planitz & Co., a small company run by my younger brother Heinrich, is getting by. Their office in Cologne represents my interests in Europe, and I haven't heard from them in a long time. Come with me and we can look for our families," he said with his usual pragmatism.

"Are you serious? I'd need to go to Poland, though."

"Let's go, then! I've never been so serious. I became an Argentinian citizen for safety reasons, which saves me from many difficult situations because the Argentinian government is neutral and has even shown sympathy for the Nazis. That's why I travel with an Argentinian passport. I'll get you a passport with another name, and we'll go to Europe together. We shouldn't be afraid because we're Jewish. No one will recognize us or question our passports. At least in my case, the border guards have never questioned me, and I even use my real last name."

153

"Yes, but there's a war going on now, and Poland is occupied."

"True. The most important thing is to have courage. Be brave and be prepared to hear good or bad news."

Boris fell silent, lost in thought. He stared vacantly for a moment.

"It would be worse to do nothing," he said.

"We'll leave as soon as I've taken care of a few things here and you get your documents. But I repeat, son . . . don't get your hopes up. You have to be prepared for anything. We're going off into the unknown. And don't worry about the expenses. Paying for one is the same as paying for two, and relieving woes is what money's good for."

"I don't know how to thank you. I'll be grateful to you for the rest of my life. May God bless you, now and always."

Hochschild, who was agnostic, didn't know what to say. Finally, they both went home.

Boris couldn't fall asleep that night. He was very afraid. He was terrified of not finding his family, but he told himself: "Never lose faith." He prayed fervently.

Since Hochschild always got what he wanted, he was able to obtain an Argentinian diplomatic passport for Boris. Was there anything he couldn't get? A couple of days later he told Boris:

"You're Ricardo Santiesteban now, the First Secretary of the Argentinian Ministry of Foreign Affairs, and you're on vacation." He handed him the document. "I'm your distant uncle, and you are accompanying me to see my company in Cologne. We depart for New York the day after tomorrow on Panagra, and we'll cross the Atlantic by plane as well. We can't afford to lose three weeks by boat. Wear your best clothes, son. Appearance is everything. Not for a single day will we take off our tics, waistcoats, or hats," he added with his characteristic confidence.

Boris spent almost his entire savings on several white shirts, a pair of suits and waistcoats, ties, a raincoat, and a short-brimmed hat. He also went discreetly to ask his Jewish friends for the names and surnames of their family members so he could look for them. He didn't explain why so as not to get their hopes up, but since they knew he worked for Hochschild they were hopeful nevertheless.

Shortly before leaving, he invited Misha to his house and told her that he was going to Europe to look for his family and Varinia.

"Listen to me, Boris," she said, rattled, her face red. "You're lucky to have this opportunity to go and look for your family, especially under your boss's protection. But . . . if you find your ex-girlfriend . . . will you bring her to Bolivia?"

"Yes . . . if they let her leave."

"Then . . . you've been deceiving me, using me all this time?"

"No, Misha. Don't take it like that. I told you from the beginning that I had left a girlfriend in Warsaw, and I never imagined I'd have the chance to go look for her. Please understand."

"You know what? I hate you . . . I never want to see you again . . ."

"Don't be childish, Misha. Don't make things any more complicated than they already are."

She slammed the door and left without saying goodbye. "Women are going to drive me crazy," he thought.

On November 1, 1943, the night before they left, Moritz and Boris attended the commemoration of the fifth anniversary of the pogrom against the Jews in Germany. The ceremony was organized by the Jewish community at the Municipal Theater, and even the president of the Republic was in attendance.

Chapter 7
Europe, winter of 1943

The day of the journey arrived. It took them four days to reach
Europe. Their destination: Berlin. They stopped over in New York,
staying in the suite that Moritz rented year-round at the Waldorf
Astoria, where they treated him like royalty because, on top of it all,
he gave out substantial tips. It was a two-bedroom apartment. He
showed Boris the paintings hanging in his living room: a Tintoretto,
a Holbein, and a chiaroscuro portrait from the school of Rembrandt.
That night they went down to the hotel restaurant to have dinner
and saw Patiño, who rented several floors at the hotel for his offices.
He was having dinner with a couple of executives. Moritz went over
to greet them reluctantly, and he introduced Boris. The magnate was
impeccably dressed, but he was significantly overweight.
"What brings you to New York, Moritz?"
"We're on our way to Berlin."
"But . . . Europe is in the middle of a war . . . and the Jews. . . ."
"Really, Simón? I hadn't heard! A good evening to you all."
"I told you Patiño was tiresome," he told Boris. Boris was so anxious
that he enjoyed neither his dinner nor the city of skyscrapers; all he
could think about was what the future had in store for him. They
crossed the Atlantic and finally landed in Berlin. They arrived
exhausted, but when they saw how strict the Nazi control was, their
adrenaline rose and their fatigue vanished. The airport was covered
with Nazi flags of all sizes and packed with members of the Gestapo
and SS officers. It was a terrifying sight. There were also soldiers
from the army; these men hated the officers because they had been
installed by the regime, displacing them. The soldiers were sent to
the front as cannon fodder. Upon entering Germany, Moritz and
Boris were interrogated in true Nazi style. While the Nazis were
questioning them, Moritz looked down at his huge, heavy, Vacheron
Constantin gold pocket watch and interrupted them, asking what the
best hotel in Berlin was. This confused them, and they let them in,
stamping their passports. Their elegant and distinguished appearance
also helped make a good impression, as did their ability to speak the
language perfectly. They took a taxi to the hotel recommended by
the immigration officials. Hochschild rented a suite with two

bedrooms and a living room. They were so tired from the trip and the tension that they asked for their dinner to be brought to the suite. They had to pay extra because of the scarcity of food. The dinner was elegantly presented, served on Meissen porcelain dishes and silver-plated trays, but the food was definitely insufficient. They slept through the night, and as soon as they got up they left the hotel and took the train to Cologne, the city on the Rhine. They stayed at the hotel where Moritz always stayed: the Dom Hotel Cologne, located right in front of the gothic cathedral, on the banks of the Rhine and close to the train station. It was the best in the area. The terrace that overlooked the small street he loved had become a Nazi hang-out. They would sit there drinking coffee or beer, talking loudly, ogling young women and asking to see their papers to strike up a conversation. The city was entirely changed. The streets were almost empty and people walked fearfully, bundled from head to toe as it was the middle of winter. After they had lunch, Moritz and Boris headed to Planitz & Co. on foot. Krause, the engineer, opened the door. He was working alone in an office that spanned an entire floor. He was a large, smart and very friendly man in his fifties. After greeting each other politely, they sat down and Hochschild cut right to the chase.

"I've come to find out about my brother Heinrich and my sister Rosa."

"Herr Hochschild, we've sent many letters to your offices in various countries; I can show you the copies right now." He got up from his desk to get them. "Last year, the Nazis raided this office and took us all prisoner. We were all set free, except for your brother, and we haven't heard from him since. We've gone regularly to ask for information regarding his whereabouts, and they hit us with rifle butts, warning us that if we kept asking about Jews they'll start taking us for Jews."

Moritz's face turned greenish.

"Where do you think he might be?"

"They say the Jews are being taken to labor camps."

"And . . . what are those places like?"

"All we know is that they're labor camps. We Germans are ashamed of the Nazis, of our own people. Herr Hochschild, excuse me for being so frank, but they take them away and no one ever hears from them again. It's a one-way trip; no one even receives letters from them afterward, at least that's what we've been told."

157

"And the others who worked here?"

"They resigned and left because there wasn't any work to do once communication with the Latin American offices got cut off. I decided to stay here, and I've taken the liberty of using the office to finish up some work that was left to do for the company, as well as my personal affairs, in the hopes that at some point you would return and the war would end. I even wrote to ask for your permission, promising to pay the monthly utility bills, which I have up until today, but I didn't hear back from you."

"It's no problem at all, Herr Krause, you're welcome to stay here. And how might we find out about my sister Rosa?"

"You could go to Biblis, her town. Your brother also complained about not hearing from her. He attributed her silence to the fact that the mail within Germany is being intercepted. And the telephone lines in the villages aren't working."

"And do you think there's any way we can find out about my brother Heinrich? I have money to exchange for information."

"We can go to the police station tomorrow and bribe the Nazis to see if they'll tell us anything. But let me take care of everything, please. Neither of you should say a word."

"Very well. We'll see you at the hotel at eight o'clock tomorrow morning."

Moritz, who was generally a controlled and calm man, felt unwell and turned pale. Boris didn't know what to say or how to comfort him. Moritz was experiencing mixed emotions; his conscience was clean, though, because he had done everything possible to convince his family to go to Bolivia. He recalled how he had gone to Biblis in 1935 to urge his sister and relatives to emigrate, but no one had listened to him.

The next day they went to the police station. It was a *petit palais*. The taxi driver told them, in a mocking, cynical tone, that it had been confiscated from a rich Jewish family. The Nazis had good taste. Once they got out of the vehicle, the engineer repeated: "I'm ashamed of the Third Reich."

As in any public office, people had been coming and going since early morning. Upon entering, Krause greeted everyone by raising his arm and saying "Heil Hitler" so naturally that he seemed to belong to the party. Moritz and Boris were stunned and said nothing. The office was full of soldiers, some low-ranking ones who were guarding the station, and others from the secret police. They sat down on a bench against the wall and Boris's hands began to sweat; he tried to hide this by drying them on his pants. Meanwhile, the engineer went to find the assistant to the head of the Gestapo in Cologne, whom he found sitting at a desk. He approached the man; he was wearing a uniform like all the rest, only with more awards and decorations, which he seemed to be proud of. He was a particularly terror-inspiring Nazi: tall, unfriendly looking, with several scars on his face and neck and with the arrogance that comes with power. His uniform was impeccable, however, and his boots shone. The engineer very covertly slipped him a thousand dollars, which Moritz had given him, and asked if they could step into the hallway to talk. The Nazi sprang to his feet; dollars were extremely valuable on the black market since the Reichsmark was worth less every day. They went out to a hall where some stairs led to the third floor and had a chat. Krause, as if he were an expert in this sort of thing, showed him twenty wads of hundred-dollar bills wrapped in newspaper; the Nazi's eyes bulged.

"I need information about Heinrich and Rosa Hochschild," he told him, stone-faced, as they climbed the stairs. "I'll give you the money when you've got it. When should I come back?"

"I'll meet you tonight at eight at the bar on the corner of this street, in the square. It's the only place open at that time."

"No tricks," he warned firmly.

The engineer signaled to Hochschild and Boris that it was time to go, and without saying a word they stood up and followed him out. Before hailing a taxi, he told them: "We need to meet him tonight at a bar in the square on the corner."

The day seemed to go on forever. They went to the office, had a coffee, and talked about the fate of the Cologne office. Moritz told Krause that he'd rather have him using it than the Nazis. Then they went to have lunch at the hotel restaurant. Hochschild was so nervous that he drank too much. A hundred images raced through Boris's mind. He was terrified that something similar had happened to his family, and he didn't say a word a lunch. In the afternoon, Boris went to look for a Catholic church, where he knelt and recited the Rosary with heartfelt devotion. Finally it was time, and Krause came to pick them up in his car. They arrived at the bar fifteen minutes early, and Boris and Moritz stayed waiting in the car. The engineer went into the bar, lit a cigarette, sat down at a table, and waited for the police officer. Eight fifteen came and went, then eight thirty, then suddenly eight armed officers stormed into the bar, demanding to see everyone's documents. Krause immediately thought: "The policeman tricked us! He wants to steal our money." But once the Gestapo left, the police officer came in dressed as a civilian and sat down at the small table beside the engineer without saying a word. Krause told him: "Let's go outside, to the car." He put some money on the table and the police officer followed him out. When he saw them leaving, Moritz got behind the wheel and stopped at the entrance to the bar. They climbed in; now they had him. Krause immediately repeated the question.

"What do you know about the Hochschild family?"

"Auschwitz, Poland."

"What's in that place?"

"It's a labor camp."

"Are they alive?"

"I don't know."

"How can we find out?"

"It's impossible to find out. Give me my money."

Krause gave him an envelope with the money, and the Nazi began to count it anxiously.

"That's all?" he asked with chilling cynicism.

"That's what we agreed upon, no more, no less," Krause shouted angrily. "You saw the twenty wads of bills, but you haven't given me all the information I asked for."

"Auschwitz is a one-way trip. No one comes back from there, just empty trains to take more Jews."

"If you can tell me whether they're alive or not, I'll give you another wad."

"I'd have to lie to you. No one knows. There's talk of the Final Solution, the *Endlösung der Judenfrage*, which means getting rid of all those who aren't Aryan in the labor camps."

"Getting rid of . . . how?"

"I don't know. I swear I don't know. Give me more money!"

The engineer gave him another wad. Moritz thought about what the man said: "That damned bastard is telling the truth." At that moment the Nazi asked to get out of the car. They left him there.

"Poland?" Boris burst out, unable to control himself. "It's not possible! My girlfriend and my entire family live there!" he cried out in despair, turning paler than he already was and burying his face in his hands. "And . . . Auschwitz? I've never heard of the place."

Krause took a deep breath. He looked nervous. Moritz told him: "You've done an extraordinary job, Herr Krause." He said nothing in response, and they continued on their way to the Dom Hotel Cologne, the back part of which was being rebuilt because it had been bombed. They went straight to the dining room, where the clients were mostly Nazis in uniform accompanied by women, some very pretty and others heavily made-up but not so attractive. Only Nazis could afford to go out for dinner in those days. They ordered; the dinner menu was the same for everyone. They could barely eat.

"A one-way ticket . . . to get rid of non-Aryans," Moritz said in a tremulous voice, which was very unusual for him. "Do you think, Herr Krause, that Auschwitz is a labor camp, like the Nazi said, or are we being naïve?"

"There's no way to know for sure. I've tried to find out because there are hardly any Jews left in Germany. They say there are three camps here: one in Dachau, another in Buchenwald, and another in Sachsenhausen, where they've imprisoned German and Austrian Jews, according to their German relatives and neighbors. It's an open secret, though, that no one has ever returned. And they say there are other camps in Poland."

Boris felt a knot in his stomach and was unable to continue eating.

"What can we find out about Auschwitz? I've never heard of it before," Moritz asked.

"Neither have I, and I'm Polish," said Boris.

"To be honest, I think we know as much as we possibly can, and that's only because of the fortune you gave me, Herr Hochschild, to hand over to the Nazi. The only thing you can do is hope they are there and that this perverse war ends soon. I promise to do everything within my power to find out what happened to them, but I don't recommend that you continue your search because you're risking your lives, especially because you're Jews, even though you have foreign passports. If they catch you, they won't hesitate to take you prisoner. I've heard of such cases, and it's my duty to warn you. Leave Germany. There's no point in staying here. I'm sorry to put it so crudely."

"I'm not leaving without going to Biblis. We'll leave tomorrow morning, via Frankfurt," Moritz said.

"I don't think you should go alone, though. I'll accompany you, Herr Hochschild."

161

"Thank you. Thank you very much. Please come by the hotel tomorrow at eight in the morning."

The next day, Krause went to meet them punctually. All three were elegantly dressed, wearing cashmere scarves, hats, and classic Burberry raincoats. They bought tickets at the station and headed to Frankfurt, where it was snowing and bitterly cold. When they arrived, they hired a taxi to take them to Biblis, a small town of eight thousand inhabitants that was less than an hour away. Out of precaution, no one said a word.

They arrived at the farm, which was in a small village on the left bank of the Rhine. They got out of the taxi, which waited for them, and saw that the hundred-year-old house was abandoned and the main entrance was sealed off. There was a sign across the door that read "Property of the Government of the Third Reich." They walked through mud and snow toward the back of the house and saw that the livestock was no longer there. The second hand iron tools that Moritz's father used to sell were also gone.

They went around to the modest house at the back, knocked on the door, and found old Franz—the caretaker who had lived there forever—and his wife. He didn't recognize Hochschild at first, but once he had introduced himself, he quickly took off his hat, bowed to him and said: "Moritz, my boy . . . you're alive!" They embraced warmly, and Franz and his wife were deeply moved. His remark had put everyone on edge.

The caretaker told Moritz that after Kristallnacht, the town of Biblis, where many Jews lived, had fallen into disgrace. The Nazis began to raid homes and apprehend the Jews. Some were able to escape while others were arrested. The SS broke into the house, stole money and jewelry, and took Rosa away in a truck, along with some neighbors. "They didn't even have time to put their coats on," said old Franz, distraught.

Moritz felt his legs giving way beneath him.

"And . . . my other relatives, who lived near here?" he asked in a tremulous voice.

"They were also taken away. They were forced into a truck. I saw it with my own eyes. A few days later they came to take the livestock, not leaving even one behind. They took all the chickens, eggs, ducks and geese. I've gone to the police to ask about my little Rosa, but they won't tell me a thing. On the contrary—they kicked me out, screaming at me, warning me never to come back. We've taken the liberty of staying here because we had no place to go and we live on the crops that we grow in secret. By now, my boy, we're afraid and hungry."

Moritz turned even paler upon hearing this, and they all entered the house through the back door that led to the kitchen. Franz told him: "Fortunately, they haven't taken over the main house; many houses have been occupied by the authorities of the Third Reich." They opened the blinds to let some light in. They walked around the house and saw that it was abandoned, but not destroyed. It seemed to be haunted by suffering spirits. It was just as they had left it, except for the sheets Franz had covered the furniture and paintings with. There was so much dust that the visitors' shoes left footprints on the floor. After examining the house from top to bottom, Moritz took only a few photographs of his family. He thought: "I hope to get it all back after the war . . . these are just things, just money." Then he told them, heartbroken: "Okay, let's go." He said a sad farewell to Franz and his wife, handing them some money, and asking Franz to please stay on as caretaker. On the way back, no one said a word.

Moritz felt broken and drained. He thought about his childhood and his adolescence in the country, where he had been both happy and sad. He recalled how, once he had begun to earn his own money, he had brought his father a fine, expensive leather jacket from London. That same afternoon his father had gone to the village store to resell it. When he came back, he showed Moritz the money and said: "Now I have more money." His son was left speechless and thought: "What an ungrateful, miserly man."

They arrived at the station and took the first train back to Cologne, on which they ate deer from the Black Forest for lunch. They sat at a table in the corner so that they could speak freely.

"Tomorrow we're off to Warsaw. We need to look for Boris's family," Hochschild said. "Tell me, Herr Krause, what do you think will happen next in this war? I ask this despite the fact that I'm ashamed to have German blood, and that this was once the country in which I grew up, studied and fell in love."

"It's hard to say. All I know is based on hearsay and inference. People don't talk much about the war because we live under a regime of terror and the propaganda machine is scrupulously maintained by that pernicious Goebbels fellow, a lame dwarf who's skilled at lying. All I can tell you is that one has to be either very ambitious or very reckless to attack the Soviet Union. The Russians, unless they reach a stalemate, will win. One also has to be very audacious to confront the United States, even though it's thousands of kilometers from here. They are countries with immense military strength and manpower. This war has become Hitler's obsession. I can only say that hopefully the Allies put an end to this nightmare soon, and I hope that the sacrosanct rallying cry of the 'Thousand-Year Reich' turns out to be merely an empty slogan," he said, lighting a cigarette. "And Hitler?"

"I must confess that no one even imagined that an insignificant corporal would end up having undisputed leadership over the German people, making them become deranged. Hitler is nothing more than an accident of history . . . a disastrous accident that we hope will soon be toppled." He began to smoke incessantly. "He appeared at the right time and place, in a Germany defeated, worn out, bankrupt, destroyed, unemployed and demoralized after its defeat in the Great War, and without a leader. He has proven to be a kind a savior to my compatriots, since recovering a country's pride by promoting nationalism is an effective method of social control. And he's done it. The Führer not only kills those whom he considers enemies, but he has also sacrificed the German people. How many millions of my compatriots have died at the front? And those of us who have not gone to fight suffer from lack of food and live in fear. The worst of it all is that the man isn't crazy, he's in possession of all his faculties."

Moritz and Boris looked at each other, stunned.

"And who is leading the war?"

"Right now? People say it's Hitler himself, because after the defeat of Operation Barbarossa and Stalingrad, he dismissed his generals and decided to run things himself."

They finished lunch and the train arrived in Cologne. They thanked Krause for all the help and information he had provided them with. Before leaving, however, Hochschild gave him six Bolivian passports with visas in case he was able to locate his family members when the war was over. When he saw this, Boris thought: "No wonder Moritz has built an empire . . . he thinks of everything . . ." They said goodbye and returned to the hotel. They hardly ate anything for dinner because they were both quite shaken. Then they went up to the suite and sat in the living room. Hochschild paid a fortune for a bottle of whiskey and began to smoke a cigar. Staring vacantly, his heart broken, he tried to drown his sorrows. Full of bitterness, he began to tell his companion:

"You know what, my boy? All my efforts to get my family out of Germany were in vain. I saw it coming when they began to issue decrees against our people. But like everyone else, they thought nothing would ever happen to them because they're German Jews, born and raised in Germany, and they considered this country their home. My parents are no longer living. My sister Hazel is safe because she went with her husband to live in South Africa; they have a son named Michael. Julius lives in Switzerland; my other brother, Sali, who worked with me in Chile, started up his own mining company in South America. And Rosa, my favorite . . . why she didn't listen to me?"

"At least you have a clear conscience because you did everything you could," Boris said, trying to comfort him. "They were the ones who chose not to leave Germany."

"Boris, I think I've lost my brother and sister. Those damned Nazis took them from me! Why didn't I have more children? The truth is that I have no family, no family life. That's why I love Bolivia. I have my company there, and my people are my family. You won't believe it, but I've never visited Israel, and I should, because I have relatives there," he said, downing drink after drink. "My personal life has been a disaster. Although I'm always surrounded by people, I'm lonely . . . very lonely. After my wife died, I entrusted Gerardo to the governesses, and they spoiled him. It's also my fault, because I gave him things instead of the attention he deserved. Now he's studying abroad and shows little interest in the company. He probably does it to annoy me, because he knows I'll leave it to him—to whom else? When he goes to Bolivia, he occasionally shows up at the office, and the employees, my own people, do nothing but flatter him, which makes me angry. Years after Käthe died, I met Germaine, the love of my life. We fell madly in love and got married. It was wonderful, and on top of it all, she made love like Aphrodite. I needed a mother for my son. I know she did all she could to be one, but she and Gerardo didn't get along well. I don't know if Germaine was a real mother to him, or if maybe she was the mother I wanted her to be. Her biggest fault was that she was insanely jealous of anyone I paid attention to. She was very possessive, which was one of the reasons why we divorced. I never tire of saying that I should never have taken her away from my cousin. That's why they say: relationships that begin badly, end badly."

"And where is she now?"

"In Switzerland. She devotes her time to charities, and I still send her money for an orphanage in Lugano. I hope to go back to her one day. I loved her, and I think I still love her. I've never stopped thinking about her. Do you know something, my boy? You love whomever you think about. And since our divorce, not a day goes by when I don't think about her."

"Why don't you go see her now that we're in Europe?"

"It's not the time. Besides, we came for something else. My biggest fear is to end up alone. Money isn't everything. I need a woman by my side, someone to grow old with . . ." he said, slurring his words by this point. "Loneliness is bad company. . . ."

"You have plenty of time to rebuild your life, either with her or with another woman."

"The truth is, I wish I were with Germaine . . ."

Hochschild's eyes closed, and he fell asleep on the couch, spilling the glass of whiskey on the carpet. Boris went over to him, took the glass from his hand, put his arm around his shoulder, led him to his bed, took off his shoes, and covered him, fully clothed, with the feather duvet. Then he went to his room, where he spent another night lying awake. He prayed incessantly, his rosary in his hand. "God, you are my only consolation. Give me the courage to bear whatever news I receive about my family and Varinia, whom I still love as much as ever."

Very early the next morning, they took the train to Warsaw. The trip took an entire day. At the border, which was patrolled by dozens of soldiers armed with machine guns, hung a giant flag with a swastika. It took several hours to cross the border because they made them get off the train and pass through immigration. Once their passports had been stamped, they reboarded the train in Polish territory. Boris was nervous, but Moritz (sly old fox that he was) once again asked the officials: "What's the best hotel in Warsaw?" He was such an upright and generous man that he wasn't afraid of anyone, probably because he knew that as long as he did good, everything would turn out for the best. Nevertheless, they were intimidated by the tight security at the Polish border. The Nazis wanted to show that the country was under their control, and they succeeded. The train continued toward the capital. Since it was the middle of winter, night fell early. With the little light remaining from the gloomy day, Boris looked out over the Polish countryside and felt moved, although it pained him to see his country thus oppressed. He was back in his beloved Poland, and he gave thanks to God. He did nothing but pray. Hochschild thought: "This boy has great inner strength, and his faith helps him . . . a man who prays is a good man . . . I wish I had his faith . . . to believe in someone, whoever he is . . . one has to have faith in something in order to keep living." Moritz was so distraught that he didn't say a word; he couldn't read either, but he tried not to let his suffering show. He lit one cigarette after the next. They arrived in Warsaw at night. Boris could barely contain his emotion. He recognized the station immediately, although it was as heavily guarded as the border. He was trembling with fear, but he tried to hide it. They didn't speak. They took a taxi to the best hotel in Warsaw, the Waltz. They had agreed to only discuss essential matters because they assumed that the taxi drivers were Nazi spies. On the way there, Boris saw that Warsaw was completely changed. It was gray, dull, dirty, with very little light; the streets were empty, in ruins, full of holes, flanked by colorless buildings that hadn't been rebuilt. The trams were practically empty, and there were guards on the corners and patrols making the rounds. His eyes rested on a low-lit bar where young women were coming and going, laughing loudly, their arms wrapped around Nazi soliders. He heard the agonizing howl of a dog echo through the streets. He was outraged to see that the main square, Pilsudski, had been renamed Adolf Hitler Platz. When they arrived at the Waltz their spirits rose slightly, because at least there was a bit more light. A porter picked up their suitcases and took them to a suite on the top floor. Boris didn't even unpack. He told Moritz:

"I need to go to my house right away. I'm extremely worried and anxious."

"I'll go with you. It's time to take action, not to worry."

Hochschild picked up the phone and ordered a taxi, and they went down to the lobby. The car was there waiting for them. "We're going to 255 Mila Street," Boris said. He could hear his heart beating, which reminded him of the palpitations he experienced due to the altitude whenever he went jogging in Bolivia. When they were about to arrive at the apartment, he asked the taxi driver about the high walls closing off part of the street. "Haven't you heard of the Warsaw ghetto?" he replied.

167

Boris realized that the rest of the long street on which he had lived had become part of the ghetto. He thought: "Oh God, our apartment was nearly made part of it." The taxi stopped in front of the building were Boris had lived. He felt very cold. They knocked on the door and after a long wait a very grumpy doorwoman came to the door. She greeted them in German.

"Good evening. I'd like to go up to the Kominsky family apartment."

"No family with that name lives here," the woman shouted.

"You must be mistaken. The Kominsky family lives on the third floor, apartment A," Boris replied. He was beginning to get a bad feeling.

"No, young man. You'd better leave if you don't want me to call the Gestapo."

"One moment please, ma'am," Moritz said. "We would like to visit the Kominsky family who live on the third floor." He slipped her a handful of dollar bills.

"Ok, but be quick about it; otherwise, the Nazis could hang me. . . ."

"Do any Nazis living here?"

"No, sir."

The elevator no longer worked and Boris leaped up the stairs two at a time. He rang the doorbell of his apartment and a woman answered. It was the same woman who had opened to door to Varinia years earlier.

"What do you want?" she asked, opening the door slightly with the chain still locked.

"I'm looking for the Kominsky family."

"That family doesn't live here."

"And . . . where do they live?"

"I don't know, young man. Poland is under German control. Don't you know that German resettlement has been put in effect since the occupation? And even if I knew where they were, I wouldn't tell you, because we are forbidden from supplying information. Now leave or I'll call the police."

"But if you tell us where they are, we'll give you a handsome reward," Hochschild assured her, while Boris tried to peer inside his house. He recognized a few pieces of furniture.

"We'll give you whatever you want!" Boris cried desperately. Moritz took him by the arm in an effort to calm him.

168

"Please," Hochschild said, handing her a wad of dollar bills, which she accepted.

"We are the new owners of this apartment. I don't know what happened to the family that lived here before. Now go away and never come back, otherwise I'll blow my whistle and the Nazis will be here in a flash."

Boris knocked on the door opposite and a German man came out; this surprised him as well because his friends the Franks used to live there. The woman began to yell:

"Throw them out! They must be Jews!"

As they left, they asked the doorwoman about the whereabouts of the Kominsky family. She said she didn't know anything and didn't refer them to anyone who might know either. They left in a new taxi and, fearing for their safety, they began to speak Spanish. They decided that it would be better to speak this language in front of others and at the hotel.

"Don't despair, boy, don't get discouraged. We'll keep looking for them."

When they arrived at the Waltz, Boris said: "Now I'm the one who needs a drink." He took a swig of whiskey, which made him shudder. After several more, he fell asleep.

The next day they got up early and continued their search. Boris had a splitting headache because the whiskey turned out to be of poor quality. They took a taxi to Varinia's house, which was in the richest district of Warsaw.

As they passed by the train station they saw a group of men, women, children and elderly people walking with their heads down. They were all bundled in heavy clothes as dark as the day. They wore a thick band with the Star of David on their arms, another sewn on their chests, and they were surrounded by armed soldiers. They were carrying small leather suitcases that contained, no doubt, their most valuable possessions. Moritz and Boris couldn't believe their eyes. Boris imagined that the Exodus must have looked like this. When the Nazis saw the taxi, they whistled at them, ordering them to deviate.

"They are probably Jews who were in hiding and who are now being taken prisoner," said the taxi driver. "That's the order of the day here."

Boris wanted to get out of the car to see if could find a familiar face, but Moritz stopped him and told him firmly in Spanish: "Do you want us to end up like them? Calm down, boy." The taxi continued on the road to Varinia's house and dropped them off there. They saw a Nazi flag flying from the second-floor balcony, and they didn't dare to ring the doorbell.

"What should we do?" Hochschild asked.

"A Nazi must be living there," Boris replied. "Let's go see the neighbors, the Bielik family. They are Polish and very good friends of Varinia's."

They went up to the house and timidly rang the doorbell. They waited a long time, until Ewa eventually appeared at the garden gate. She recognized Boris immediately.

"Boris, how wonderful to see you!" she said excitedly. "We stopped hearing from you."

"How wonderful to see a familiar face! This is Herr Hochschild."

"I'm sorry for not inviting you in, but we live in terror."

"Don't worry."

"Do you know where Varinia is?"

Ewa fell silent for a moment.

"The Nazis took their house and sent them away."

"Where to? But . . . they're not Jewish!"

"The Gestapo apprehends Jews and non-Jews. Varinia's father, as you know, ran a glass importing company that brought him a lot of money. The Nazis learned of this and appropriated the business to rebuild Warsaw after the bombing, although as you can see, the city is still in ruins. One day a Gestapo truck came and took the whole family; they even shot and killed the dog. We saw it all from the bathroom window. No one knows where they were taken, and we can't ask either because we might end up meeting the same fate. You can't imagine how sorry I am. She was our best friend. I need to tell you something . . ." she said, placing her hands over his, which were gripping the bars of the wrought iron fence tightly.

"Varinia has a son . . . he's your son, his name is Boris, just like you."

"A son . . .?" He felt as though his heart were about to burst. He turned as white as a ghost and thought he was going to faint.

A deafening silence fell, echoing through the deserted street.

"He looks exactly like you. He's the most beautiful child we've ever seen. A lovely boy, blond with blue eyes just like yours."

"And . . . what happened to him? Did they take him too?"

"Yes. When they raided the house, she refused to let him go and they tore him from her arms."

"They took him?"

"Yes. People say that white, blond Polish children are taken from their mothers and passed off as Aryan children."

Boris closed his eyes, lowered his head, and began to cry. Moritz put his arm over his shoulder.

"And where can we go to find out where the child, Varinia and the Kominsky family are?" asked Hochschild calmly. Boris was beside himself.

"To the Gestapo headquarters, but no one's allowed in. It's a house of horrors."

"A son, a son! How am I just learning of this now?" said Boris, sobbing like a child as he leaned against the tall black fence. "How have I not met my own son? How come I didn't know about his birth? Do you think he's alive? That he and Varinia are still alive? And my family?"

"Calm down, son," Moritz said.

"Varinia stopped receiving letters from you when the war broke out. She wrote to you many times to tell you about your son, I know that for a fact. The war began just a few months after you left, and your son was born on March 30, 1940."

"When and where was he baptized? Do you have a picture of him?"

"I don't, but the church required a photograph to baptize him."

"And when was he baptized?" Hochschild asked.

"Shortly after he was born, and in absolute secrecy, at St. Martin's Church. This is all more painful for me than you can imagine. Please, you need to go now, and don't tell anyone you came here or that we spoke, because we're forbidden from saying anything. This is a reign of terror."

"Goodbye . . . goodbye, Ewa, and thank you."

She turned around and quickly went back inside. They stood there in silence for a few moments. "A son . . . a son . . . Varinia and I were going to get married," Boris said, drowning in tears. "I did everything for them to emigrate to Bolivia . . . I did all the legal paperwork . . . I bribed whomever I had to, but it was impossible to bring them. . . ."

"Don't lose hope, my dear Boris. Have faith—I know you have it in abundance. Leave it in God's hands. We'll continue our search. I swear we'll go see whomever we have to, and we'll spend all the money that's needed. We'll bribe whomever we have to."

171

Moritz hailed a taxi on the street and said: "To St. Martin's Church." Fifteen minutes later they got out in front of the main door of the parish. They rang the doorbell and a lady appeared. Boris, struggling to express himself physically and spiritually, said:

"We're looking for Father Peter."

"Father Peter no longer lives here."

"Then please call someone we can speak to. Tell the prelates that it's Boris Kominsky."

"Oh, yes. Come in, please. I'll call Bishop John."

They went into the parish sitting room and waited several minutes for the ecclesiastical authority, who appeared shortly.

"Bishop, I'm Boris Kominsky. I didn't know you had been ordained a bishop," and he bent down to kiss his ring while the prelate gave him his blessing.

"But of course I remember you, my son," he said, giving him a hug. "Please, sit down."

"This is Herr Hochschild." They shook hands in greeting, and the bishop ushered them into his office.

"I know you've been in Bolivia these past few years."

"Yes, Bishop John. I've come to find out about my family. And . . . I know I have a son who was baptized here."

"Yes, you have a son, a beautiful son . . . that terrible day . . ." He put his elbows on the desk and buried his face in his hands.

"What terrible day?"

"A few months ago, the Gestapo raided St. Martin's, which was supposed to have immunity, and they took your mother, your brother and sister, and two priests, Father Peter and Father Patrick."

"What? My family was here?"

"Yes, except for your father."

"What happened to him?"

"The day they raided your house, your family came to take refuge in the church, and everyone made it in except your father, whom the Nazis took away."

"Where to?"

"We weren't able to find out, despite all our efforts. Sergei and Father Peter even went to the ghetto, to hospitals, and to the homes of his doctor friends, but they couldn't find him."

"And my mother and siblings?"

"They lived here for a few years in hiding. But it seems that someone informed against them, and the Nazis raided the parish and took them all away, accusing them of conspiracy against the state."
Silence fell, and Boris's hair stood on end.
"Where did they take them?"
"We don't know, and we'll never know. I've spoken with the nuncio who intervened on behalf of the two priests and Olga, Sergei, and Sonitzya. We informed him that they were working as volunteers in the parish, and he sent letters and held meetings with the higher-ups of the SS, which I also attended. The nuncio even obtained a letter from the Vatican secretary of state himself, but we received no response. They say no to everything. I personally insisted on meeting with them, but they always come up with an excuse at the last minute. Even when I run into them at a concert, I ask them again and they say they don't know anything. I swear on the Holy Catholic Church that I will keep insisting that they tell us what happened to your family and our priests, and I will continue sending letters and requesting the Vatican's support. We assume they were sent to the labor camps. You don't know how sorry I am, my dear Boris."
"And where are the labor camps?" Moritz interjected.
"There are twenty scattered throughout Europe. In Poland there are six labor camps, the largest of which is Auschwitz-Birkenau. There's also Pawiak Prison."
"Krause mentioned that place," Boris said, looking at Hochschild.
"And where is it? Could we go there?" he asked naively.
"Nobody knows where it is. And . . . don't even think about going there. You can't even get close to it because they'll kill you or imprison you right there," he said, frowning. "We're at war, my son."
"And what are the labor camps like?"
"Nobody knows. The SS maintains total secrecy about them. I couldn't even tell the Holy Father himself what they're like, because I don't know and there are no witnesses. All I know is that those who go don't come back. Boris, all you can do is hold fast to the will of our Lord."
"How can we find out where they are?" the visitors asked in unison.
"At the Gestapo headquarters, but it's impossible to access."
"Have you heard of the Final Solution?"
"No."
"They say it's a euphemism used by the Nazis to get rid of the Jews."

"I wouldn't be surprised . . . nothing surprises me anymore . . . God help us . . . our only hope is that with the United States joining the war on the Allies' side, this nightmare will be over soon. The Axis powers are trembling. We're not just living through a world war; there's another war going on in Poland. There's a resistance movement made up of Poles and Jews to combat the Nazis, but it's a suicide mission. Warsaw has become a guerrilla war camp, where more Poles than Nazis are dying. There are even priests who give them Communion and Extreme Unction before they go to fight because they know the chances of them surviving are slim. And the worst thing of all is that there are Poles and Jews who collaborate with the Germans. Our own people! There's always an informer, a traitor willing to sell himself to the enemy . . . without these men, there wouldn't be so much violence or so many victims. And on top of it all, the Russians are performing summary executions. As you've no doubt seen, the city has been disfigured. There are so many fallen Poles that no one even reclaims the bodies anymore; they lie there clogging the sewers, covered with flies, and are devoured by hungry dogs. The Nazis leave them there to, as they put it, 'teach a lesson' to the Polish people. I've even heard that Jews hide in the sewers and live in those disgusting labyrinths that they come to know like the back of their hands. It's terrible."

"And my son?"

"Father Peter baptized him here in the parish in absolute secrecy. We have the record and a photograph, though."

"A photograph? Ewa was right," thought Boris. The bishop asked someone to bring the file. Boris felt as if his heart would burst from him chest, and his underarms, face, and hands were sweating. He held the file in his hands and read that his son had been baptized with the name of Boris, his name, and his godparents were Varinia's parents. He saw the picture and wept bitterly. He kissed it over and over again. "He looks so tiny here . . . I wonder how he is now . . . is he talking yet? Does he ask about me?"

"Take it with you, Boris."

"Thank you, thank you very much."

Moritz thought: "Unfortunately, all babies look alike at that age."

"Do you know anything about the place where they take all the blond, white, blue-eyed Polish children to give them to Aryan families for adoption? At least that's what Ewa told us."

"I don't know a thing. This is the first I hear of it."

"And where might I find out about these families?" Boris asked as he handed him a list of the relatives of his Jewish acquaintances in Bolivia, much to Hochschild's surprise.

"Boris, if we haven't been able to discover the whereabouts of our priests and your family, we can hardly find out anything about these people. I'm sorry. But leave the list with me, and I'll search for them once the war is over."

Hochschild gave the bishop twenty Bolivian passports with visas, and an envelope full of money.

"This is for the Kominsky family," he said. "And the rest of them are for the people on the list. When they return, they'll just need to attach a photograph and stamp it."

"Thank you very much. This will save them."

The bishop was impressed by Hochschild's manner. They stood up and said goodbye, leaving their business cards with their addresses and telephone numbers in Bolivia with the bishop. They went next to Isaac's apartment, but received there the same response they had at the Kominsky apartment.

They returned to the hotel and when they asked for the key to their suite, they were given an anonymous, typewritten note that read: "Leave now or you will suffer the same fate." They were petrified. They went up to their rooms and Boris threw himself on the sofa. He was a wreck.

Boris wanted the earth to swallow him. He didn't want to hear about anything or anyone. He was destroyed. He sat down in an armchair and covered his eyes with his hand.

"I've lost everything, everyone I loved," he said, crying liked a baby. "Why did I ever leave? Maybe it would have been better for me to stay . . . I would have met my son, helped Varinia and accompanied my family. The informant in Cologne talked about the Final Solution, which is to destroy our people . . ."

"I know, son, that nothing I can say will make things better, but don't think about it like that. Think that they're in the labor camps, and as long as they're alive, there's hope. Think about why they stayed. It was their choice, just as it was yours to leave. We're alive, we're alive by the grace of God and thanks to Bolivia, that blessed country. Life is a gift from God; we only live once, so we must live the best way possible. Listen to me, we can't do anything other than what it is in our power to do, and all of this is a damned nightmare which we need to escape from as soon as possible, especially because these damned sons of bitches know we're here and have even taken to threatening us," he said, his face red with rage. "Boy, this is war, and Poland is under the control of a perverse enemy who is against us and against everyone who is not Aryan, an absurd concept created by a bunch of abominable people with delusions of grandeur who are trained to kill and hate. Have faith, boy. This damned war is going to end sooner than you or I imagine, and we have to think optimistically about being reunited with our families, just like the prisoners returned to their families after the Great War."

"I'm sorry, Moritz . . . but who wants to live without their loved ones, without those they love and are loved by . . . and to think, I would have started my own family . . ." He took out the photo of his son and held it to his heart. "You know what? I'm going to enlist in the resistance movement."

"But, boy . . . have you lost your mind? Didn't you hear the bishop say it's a suicide mission? Listen to me, Boris. Don't make such an important decision in a moment of despair. Don't let the frustration and the desire for revenge lead you to make the wrong decision. Joining the fight against the enemy won't help you find your family. I know you're in unspeakable pain, but it's not all over yet. Don't go looking for death while you're still alive; you're alive and that's what matters. Don't give in to despair . . . no one knows what the future holds, who says you won't find your family and happiness after the war, no one knows . . ."

"I'm sorry. I'm being selfish because you're in the same situation and I'm only thinking about myself. Excuse me. I need to be alone. I'm going to find the nearest church."

Boris left the hotel and went to a chapel, where he remained for more than an hour. When he returned, Hochschild breathed a sigh of relief because he was worried he wouldn't come back. Early the next morning, they left for Bolivia.

Chapter 8
Bolivia, early 1944

Boris and Moritz arrived in La Paz, and there wasn't a single member of the Jewish community who didn't ask them about the state of the war. Boris's friends asked him for news of their relatives, and he had to tell them the truth: all they had been able to do was leave Bolivian passports with visas for their relatives for after the war. If they heard from them, they should contact the bishop at St. Martin's Church in Warsaw.

Boris spent a few days mulling over whether or not he should call Misha. After hearing that he had come back, however, she went to see him at the office, and he greeted her warmly. He invited her over for dinner at his apartment and told her about his painful experience, weeping. After hearing his story, she embraced him with all her strength and said, her eyes also full of tears: "You never know, my dear Boris . . . give it time . . . this damned war will end soon . . . we're still alive . . . God bless Bolivia and the Bolivians. I want you to know that you can count on me for whatever you need."

She was as confused as he was; she didn't know what state her relationship with Boris was in, because they hadn't parted on good terms. She didn't dare ask about "them," either, because she saw how upset he was. Although Misha offered her company during these difficult times, Boris told her that he would call her when he felt up to it. He thanked her for her support and later took her home in the second-hand Studebaker he had bought. When he said goodbye to her, he thought: "I know that, apart from Moritz, she's the only person I have close to me . . . but I need to heal before getting involved with her again."

In 1944, Bolivia was governed by Gualberto Villarroel, who had overthrown President Peñaranda in a coup d'état with the help of an emerging party called the Revolutionary Nationalist Movement (MNR). The new head of state had risen to prominence during the Chaco War and was a member of a secret military lodge called *Razón de Patria* (RADEPA). His was a fascist, pro-Nazi government, with its eye on the Tin Barons, particularly Hochschild, because he was Jewish and because he openly declared his allegiance to the Allies, as did all Jews in Bolivia.

177

The government allowed its supporters to graffiti swastikas and slurs against the Jews on the walls. Some supporters even wrote an anti-Jewish newspaper serial. And on two separate occasions they shut down the *Rundschau von Illimani* newspaper and arrested its director. This man, a defender of the Jews, publicly supported the petition by a Bolivian envoy to the World Jewish Congress for the creation of a Jewish state in Palestine.

President Villarroel, thirty-five years old and flat faced, was a weak, unremarkable man, dominated by a couple of henchmen who also belonged to RADEPA: Escóbar and Eguino. Captain Escóbar, chief of the La Paz police, was a short, stocky man with bulging eyes; a falsetto voice; a shiny face; thin, colorless lips; and child-like hands. Major Jorge Eguino was the general director of the police; he was darker skinned and had a malicious look about him. They were known as the "Tiny Kings" of Bolivia. Escóbar's office was on Ayacucho Street, next to the Palacio Quemado, and it had a secret door behind a bookcase that led to the very same palace. These men, therefore, were able to come and go as they pleased. Their power terrified the Bolivian people, and its extent surpassed that of the president of the republic himself. Under the pretense of raising the country's moral standards, the secret military lodge carried out acts of violence and repression.

One night in May of 1944, when Moritz was in the study of the mansion he rented in Sopocachi, reading company reports and sipping whiskey while reclining in a bergère armchair by the fireplace, the police raided his house. The butler, who was impeccably dressed and even wore white gloves, opened the door and was knocked to the ground by a rifle butt. They shoved the maids out of the way, sending their caps flying through the air. Without offering any explanation, they took him prisoner for a second time, amidst the screams and sobs of the maids, who immediately phoned the company managers. When they called them, they learned that Adolf had just been arrested as well. They also called Boris, who immediately contacted Dr. Gerhard Goldberg, the second vice-president of the group. He picked him up and they went to the police station, a dirty and foul-smelling place, just like all the government detention centers—although this one was probably the worst. Boris, already an expert in the art of bribery, brought a wad of bills to try to set up a meeting with whoever was in charge. After handing some bills over to the guards, they entered the office of the dreaded chief of police, Captain Escóbar, on whose desk lay files filled with documents and photographs. The desk also had two telephones and two chairs in front of it. On the wall—as in all public offices—hung a huge portrait of the charming President Villarroel. Escóbar neither stood up nor shook their hands when they entered. It seemed as though he had just removed his feet from the desk, because the office was also foul-smelling.

"Could you tell me what charges have been laid against the executives?" Goldberg asked firmly.

"They've been arrested for conspiracy against the government."

"Conspiracy? Impossible. What plot are you referring to? We want to see them," said Boris.

"Visit them? Don't even bother asking, young man. The Palacio Quemado has ordered that they remain in isolation."

"And . . . Mr. Blum? He has a wife and children . . . couldn't his family see him, even for a few minutes?"

"Gentlemen, don't insist, otherwise you'll be sent to join them."

"Tell me how much you want, and I'll get it for you."

"I said don't insist, dammit! Get out of my office you dirty coup-plotting Jews!"

Boris and Goldberg turned pale and left quickly.

They went back to Goldberg's house and met with the other directors, the lawyers, and Adolf's wife to analyze the situation. She, white as a sheet, said: "At what point did this switch from a headache to a migraine?" There was no such conspiracy: it was just a pretext. They phoned Gerardo in the United States to let him know, since he would have heard it from friends or in the news anyway, and they told him not to worry because they'd have his father out in no time. They said it was probably all a misunderstanding, and it wasn't worth him coming back to Bolivia and interrupting his studies. They also called Aramayo's house on Arce Avenue to ask if he had also been arrested and were told that he was in Paris. They told his relatives to advise him not to return because the government was arresting whomever they pleased. They stayed up all night trying to find someone to turn to, but they found no one. They didn't have any influential contacts in the government. They were terrified because the government had attacked some politicians a month earlier, leaving them severely wounded. What shocked them most, however, was that the RADEPA militant had rejected the bribe.

179

The next day Boris went to Escóbar's home, bribing each and every one of his bodyguards to get close to him. He managed to speak to him as he was getting into his jeep. After slipping him a wad of dollar bills under a newspaper, without anyone seeing, he said:

"All I ask is for you to tell me where they are."

"Boy, if you give me more, I'll tell you."

Boris took out another stack and handed it over surreptitiously.

"They're in my office."

"Then let me speak to my boss for a few seconds."

"No way! It'll cost me my head. Besides, your 'little boss' will most probably be sentenced to death for plotting a coup. Now get out of here! I wouldn't let you see them even if you gave me your house."

Boris was petrified. "Moritz, sentenced to death on a whim of this government of murderers?" he thought. He met again with the directors, lawyers and Blum's wife to tell them that they wouldn't let them see them for all the money in the world.

Blum's distraught wife and children, as well as Hochschild's butler, went to leave blankets, food, cigarettes, and clothing for them. They never imagined that this would become their daily routine. Boris sometimes went along too. They had no way of knowing whether what they brought would reach them, but they continued going all the same. The Jewish community found out what had happened, and they brought food, books, cards, and whatever else they could think of. Sometimes there was even a line-up. The government didn't budge. They even paid for some slanderous leaflets to be published saying that they had been arrested for "conspiracy, worker exploitation and tax evasion." They were used as scapegoats to stoke fear. Rumors that the tycoon would be sentenced to death began to spread, and Boris became desperate because he had come to appreciate Moritz deeply and was very grateful to him. "He's like the father I never had . . ." he thought, and he went to church and prayed for them. His continuous efforts to speak with Escóbar and Eguino were unsuccessful. He thought: "What if they killed them and made them disappear . . . how would we know? What really amazes me is these two henchmen's reluctance to accept money . . . I imagine it's because there must be spies among their own bodyguards, and they might lose the trust of the president and the lodge members . . . but there's always a way to bribe these bastards . . ."

They informed him, by way of an anonymous telephone call, that there was an order from the Palacio Quemado forbidding him from going anywhere near the police precincts or the authorities; if he did so, it was at his own risk. Boris remembered having received the same threat in Warsaw, and he got scared and decided not to approach them. Moritz and Adolf had been locked up there because the police chiefs wanted to keep a close watch on them, since they knew they were rich and could pay off whomever they wanted. Meanwhile, the detainees kept track of the days they had been detained by writing them on the wall, like inmates, because the policemen had taken their watches. The cell was two and a half by three and a half meters and scattered with straw, like a stable. There were two mattresses lying on the floor, stained and bloody, with a blanket on each one. The walls were peeling and moldy, covered with blood stains, obscene drawings, and all the swear words in the dictionary. They were blackened with soot, as if there had been a fire. They weren't allowed to wash themselves, and when they noticed they were beginning to stink they began to despair. They weren't young, either; both were in their fifties. Everything exasperated them and got on their nerves, but they had no choice but to bear it all stoically: the disgusting place in which they were forced to stay, their unjust and inexplicable detention, the lack of communication with their loved ones, and their uncertain future. What could they do? There was no money or influential contacts to turn to. All they could do was wait for Goldberg, Boris, their office employees and their friends to get them out of this hell. Whenever a guard passed by, Moritz would say: "Let us speak to our relatives . . . if you let us see them we'll make it worth your while . . . we swear." The guards, however, would walk right by without even appearing to hear them. Everything they tried was to no avail, which terrified them all the more.

"Here, where you can bribe anyone because the people are unscrupulous and earn next to nothing, for them not to accept anything . . . it's very strange . . . every man has his price, even when he says otherwise," Hochschild said.

"Do you think they'll kill us?" Adolf asked.

"I don't think they can be that stupid."

They were allowed to relieve themselves once in the morning and once at night in a bathroom for the soldiers from the barracks. They were given a revolting soup that gave them stomach aches and diarrhea. For these emergencies, they had to use kerosene cans, which were left in the cell for days. It reeked like a sewer. They were deeply ashamed of being forced to relieve themselves in front of each other, as well as of being seen in this dirty, smelly, and depressed state. They were never given the clothes, food or blankets that their relatives and fellow Jews had left for them. They knew that these things had been brought, though, because they saw the guards wearing some of their clothes. One day Adolf saw a policeman walk by wearing his cashmere tweed blazer. On another occasion, Hochschild saw another guard wrapped in a feather comforter whose cover he recognized because he used to sleep under it. These men also ate their food right in front of them. Once, all of a sudden, they threw them a couple of books written in German; they treasured them, reading them over and over. The books had a double use because they could tear out some pages and place them underneath their shirts to keep warm. Receiving the books and seeing their belongings consoled them, as it assured them that their friends and relatives knew they were there and cared for them. The guards didn't beat them because they weren't hiding anything; the supposed conspiracy was nonexistent. But they did torture them psychologically at night, when they were sleeping. The guards would bang on the bars of their cell with cans and cry: "You're going to be shot tomorrow!" The policemen drank heavily at night and threw parties with indigenous prostitutes, blasting *chichería* music on the radio. They had wild, debauched orgies. Escóbar would come by daily to make sure his captives were still there. "They're my prisoners . . . I have two millionaires in my custody," he would say proudly.

If Moritz and Adolf hadn't been put in the same cell, they would have lost their minds from the isolation and loneliness. They did nothing but talk. They recounted the stories of their lives, going all the way back to their first memories. They formed a deep, unconditional friendship and a bond that would last a lifetime; they became like brothers. They asked each other over and over again whether they had made the right choice in emigrating to a country like Bolivia, where a military coup could take power at any time and run the country as if it were their own barracks.

"And on top of it all, this despicable fascist government hates Jews," Moritz lamented. "I've made money . . . a lot of it . . . but what's the use if they have us locked up in this disgusting hovel crawling with rats? By a government that makes false accusations against us, laying charges that they don't even understand? Adolf . . . you would know if I were plotting something . . . or if I hadn't paid taxes. We're always

182

especially careful to do so. It's true that we established a holding company in Buenos Aires, and then in Panama, to protect some of our profits. But that's completely legal. You know all my secrets . . . the biggest of which is the passports, which fortunately no one found out about. What kills me is that they've arrested you too, just because you work for me. It's an unspeakably dirty trick . . . I'm sorry, I'm so deeply sorry, dear Adolf."

"Don't feel guilty on my account. We know that this is just a pretext for getting hold of your assets."

"That's probably true. Do you think they'll kill us like they've been threatening to since they locked us up?"

"It would be too obvious . . . I don't think they would be so stupid, because everyone knows that we're here. Don't even think about that."

They both broke down suddenly, but fortunately, not at the same time. One night Moritz grabbed the bars of their cell like a monkey and began to howl: "Fucking thief, give me my comforter! While you're there all wrapped up, we're here freezing to death!" The police officer heard him out, then went up to him and smacked his fingers with a truncheon, yelling: "Tomorrow you'll go without food, dammit, for disrespecting authority!" Moritz got up immediately and pulled Hochschild away from the bars as he doubled over in pain.

Such aggression caused them to loathe their situation even more. They hated the government, the country, life, and even themselves, but they tried not to sink into despair.

"Thank God we're together," Adolf said. "We must accept the situation and resign ourselves, it's all we can do right now."

"Accept it? After everything I've done for the Aymaras? I've given thousands of them jobs, and even better than that, I've taught them to fish, helping them open their own mineral-trading businesses. And this is how their compatriots repay me? They don't give a damn about the Indians," he shouted angrily. "These government big shots don't even recognize what we've done for their people. What's this socialism they keep talking about? What's this nationalism they keep referring to? It's all just lip service."

They spent forty-five days in complete isolation, a period of intense tension for their families, friends, and employees, until all of a sudden, without any explanation, Goldberg and Blum's wife received a telephone call informing them that the men were being released. They were asked to come pick them up. When they heard the news, they exclaimed: "They're alive!" Their greatest fear was that they had been killed. Goldberg called and asked Boris if he could pick them up; he arrived in a matter of minutes and they were off like lightning. They were made to sign some documents written in cryptic language for Moritz and Adolf's release; they didn't even read them. When they finally saw the prisoners, they were stunned: they had lost several kilos, their faces were gaunt, and their skin was green and lifeless. Their beards were long and their hair was dirty, as were their threadbare clothes, the same they had been wearing the day they were arrested. They smelled awful. Mrs. Blum threw herself into her husband's arms, stoically controlling her tears so as not to give the henchmen the satisfaction of seeing her cry. Boris gave his boss, whom he considered a great friend, a warm hug, as if he were his father. Moritz felt his affection, which he so badly needed, and was moved. They got into the car and, struck by the silence of the recently-freed men, Goldberg said: "You don't have to tell us anything right now, if you don't want to. The time for that will come." And, indeed, they didn't say a word. They dropped off Adolf and his wife at their home, and the two men hugged each other warmly as they said goodbye. "If I have a brother in this world, it's you," Moritz told him. Then they went to Hochschild's house. He was still silent, distracted, lost in thought. The only words he uttered were to invite them in. The staff gave him an affectionate welcome; the maids even shed tears. The freed man didn't smile; he only thanked them. They went into the study, the owner of the house's favorite room, and amidst the deafening silence he offered a drink to those who were there, saying: "*L'Chaim!*" They raised their glasses, looking each other in the eye. And that was all Moritz said. He later sat down in his bergère armchair next to the fireplace, which was lit, and didn't say a word. Boris and Goldberg didn't know what to say, much less what to ask him. They had a drink and Goldberg called Hochschild's family doctor to ask him to examine him, and they left; it's not as if the owner of the house had asked them to stay longer. He remained watching the flames flicker in the fireplace in silence. He went over what he had experienced in his head, and his hair stood on end. He recalled his forty-five days and forty-four nights in captivity. "Sentenced to death once . . . and twice sent to prison," he thought. "And why? Why did the dictatorships of Busch and Villarroel treat me so mercilessly?" While he was waiting for the doctor to arrive, he said to his butler: "Bring me my robe." He took off what he was wearing, put on his robe, and threw his clothes into the fire, to the astonishment of the staff. "Am I going crazy?"

Before the doctor arrived, Hochschild stepped underneath the steaming hot shower jet. He shaved because he was repulsed by himself and didn't want the doctor to see him in that state. It was the best shower of his life. Although he felt quite weak, he scrubbed himself as hard as he could with some sponges. He had never felt so grateful for hot water, clean towels, the spotlessly clean bathroom, the luxury in which he lived, the clothes he had, and the number of employees he had to administer to his every need. As he washed himself he thought: "What luxury I live in . . . but I've earned it all by the sweat of my brow." His house was a mansion with furniture imported from England and France. Silk brocade curtains cascaded onto the mahogany floor. The lamps were from Bohemia, the rugs were Persian, the porcelain from Sèvres. The Bolivian silverware collection was of the highest quality, with everyday and ornamental cutlery hand-made by the best indigenous silversmiths. Curiously enough, he didn't have any paintings by great European painters like those that adorned the walls of his New York apartment.

The doctor arrived and went up to the second floor to examine Moritz. He told him to go in for some tests, but found him, overall, to be in relatively good health. The only injuries he had sustained were broken knuckles on the index and ring fingers of his left hand. Regarding this, the doctor told him: "They have already healed, so don't worry, but you should go to physiotherapy to help with the rehabilitation process." Then he said: "Herr Hochschild, the only urgent thing I recommend is that you go to the dentist as soon as possible. The lack of cleaning must have caused severed cavities."

Moritz stayed home for several days. A mass of people came to see him, but he didn't want to see anyone save a few of his closest colleagues. When he saw them, they embraced each other warmly.

A few days later, when he was feeling better, he called a meeting with his managers. On a Friday morning, he gathered them in the dining room, which served as a meeting room, and with his characteristic frankness, albeit somewhat diminished, he said:

"My dear friends. I would rather not tell you what I have lived through because I don't even want to think about it. I would like to tell you that I am going to Chile for an indefinite period of time. I need to leave Bolivia; it's a country that has betrayed me. We have suffered a punishment we did not deserve, at the whim of a repressive government, for reasons we are still unaware of. All of the mystique surrounding this country I loved so much has vanished because of the injustice inflicted upon me and Adolf. Tomorrow I'll go with Adolf to the Chilean consulate to ask the consul for a visa. Fortunately, we know each other, and he'll make sure all is settled for me to depart on a Monday morning flight."

Moritz said nothing more. Everyone understood. He wasn't even interested in hearing about the affairs of his companies. He just wanted to leave as soon as possible.

That evening, the police appeared at his house, making an ostentatious show of their power. He calmly let them in.

"Dr. Hochschild, we have been ordered to confiscate your passport," a thug with smallpox scars on his face told him.

"For what reason?"

"I only have orders to inform you that tomorrow at six o'clock in the evening the minister of government will receive you in his office."

Moritz had no choice but to hand over his passport. He was worried. "This nightmare never ends . . . they couldn't have guessed that I plan to leave the country . . . these scoundrels . . . they must have bugged my telephone," he thought. He called Adolf and filled him in on what had happened so that he and the managers were aware of the new situation. He was able to sleep that night because the doctor had left him some tranquilizers. He used to sleep like a baby, but since his arrest this was no longer the case.

The next day Adolf went to pick Hochschild up and accompany him to the Ministry of Government. At the end of the meeting, which lasted almost two and a half hours, the minister, Lieutenant Colonel Pacheco, reiterated:

"So, it's not true that you want to withdraw your capital from Bolivia?"

"Absolutely not. On the contrary, I plan to invest even more capital in Bolivian mining and agriculture. I must also reiterate that I am one of the main contributors to the Bolivian state, and I have never avoided paying taxes to the Treasury. I have demonstrated this on several occasions. Moreover, I support the new revolutionary government," he lied without batting an eyelash.

Adolf was startled to hear this final statement, and he did his best to hide his surprise.

"Then, taking your word, I offer you my highest assurances of protection," he said and ordered his right-hand man, Escóbar, to hand over Hochschild's passport.

"Excuse me, Mr. Minister, but I have it locked up in the safe at the detention center. I'll bring it to his residence myself tomorrow," he said.

"Always making things difficult for me . . . bastards," thought Hochschild. The next day, a Sunday, he received his passport from Escóbar; it had an exit stamp, which was required by the Bolivian authorities. Once Moritz had the document in his hands, Adolf came to pick him up in his car, and they went to the Chilean consulate to obtain the visa. The consulate was located in the neighborhood of Obrajes, a sparsely populated area in the south of the city. The consul received them warmly and stamped the passport immediately. Then they both left.

The hours passed and Hochschild didn't arrive home. He had told his service staff that he would return in an hour and had asked them to light the fireplace in the bedroom because he planned to go straight to bed when he got back; he was still feeling quite fragile. Adolf's wife called several times to ask about her husband and the butler's response was the same: "They haven't arrived yet." The butler called Dr. Goldberg, a lucid, direct, and discreet man whose physical appearance allowed him to pass unnoticed, and filled him in on the situation. Around three o'clock in the morning, Goldberg called Boris, who put on the first thing he could find, got in his car, and went to look for them at the places they frequented, such as the Club de La Paz, the Israelite Circle, Aramayo's house, and several restaurants, but he didn't find them. Finally, it occurred to him to go to the Chilean consulate, on Zalles Avenue, and he was surprised to see Adolf's car parked out front. He imagined they had remained there talking in the diplomatic legation. He looked for a pay phone and called Blum's wife and Goldberg, who felt slightly relieved but nonetheless surprised, because Hochschild was supposed to take the first flight out the next morning.

Dawn broke, and they still hadn't turned up. They began to panic. They called Boris again, and he returned to the consulate, where he found Blum's car in the same place. He got out of his Studebaker and rang the doorbell. The consul himself came to the door and told him that they had left the previous evening. Boris showed him Blum's car, and both men were disconcerted.

187

Goldberg summoned everyone to his apartment to try to analyze the bizarre situation. Meanwhile, the news spread. On El Prado Boulevard, everyone was talking about the disappearance of the mining magnates. La Paz was a very small city, and everything soon became public knowledge. People, mostly from the Jewish community, began to call Moritz's house over and over again. The staff members were instructed to say: "No one knows anything." Reporters even went to the company headquarters to interview the executives, but they refused to comment.

The following day, photographs of Blum's car were published in the newspapers alongside the title: "Where are Tin Baron Hochschild and his chief executive Blum?"

Misha heard the news and called Boris to ask about his boss; he told her he would call her back and set up a time to meet so he could tell her everything in person. "We can't rule out anything at this point." She understood immediately. A couple of days later, when Boris mentioned to the committee that he was going to have dinner with Misha, Goldberg begged him to wait until they had found Hochschild and Blum. Boris was frustrated, but he understood, and he called her to explain the situation. She thought: "He'll say anything to avoid seeing me. I need to accept that he doesn't love me."

President Villarroel, who had been placed in his high position by RADEPA, summoned Detective Luis Adrián, head of the National Department of Investigation (DNI), to find the magnates. The DNI was an apolitical entity, created for the purpose of collaborating with the League of Nations during the bloody war. The agent was of virile appearance, tall and heavyset, and despite his apparent wish to go unnoticed, he made quite an impression. He wore coats or raincoats with the collar turned up, a short-brimmed hat, sunglasses (even at night), and he always had a lit cigarette in his mouth. Oddly enough, he never wore a watch, which everyone but him found incomprehensible. He seemed to have been influenced by Humphrey Bogart's style in *Casablanca*, which was in vogue. Adrián went to the Palacio Quemado accompanied by an FBI agent, an American called Dean.

He discovered that the Nazis were using Bolivians to obtain information about tin production, a sensitive matter because Bolivia was the only country that supplied them with the mineral during the war. The agent's role was to prevent any sabotage or interference in production or shipping. The North American country and the Allies urgently needed Bolivian tin, for which Hochschild was key. Dean thought that the disappearance could be a German plot, since he was also Jewish. Villarroel asked them to find the executives as soon as possible, and they agreed that Dean would act solely as an adviser. After the meeting, Adrián returned to his office on the third floor of a nineteenth-century house on Jenaro Sanjinez Street, a few blocks from the Palacio Quemado, and instructed his team to begin the search. He ordered three teams of two to patrol the city exits: El Alto, Yungas, and the south. He thought: "It would be disastrous if they've taken them to El Alto, because they can reach the border from there; if they've taken them to the tropics they can hide them in the jungle and it will be impossible to find them; hopefully they took them to the south, because it's a dead end, although I doubt they would be so stupid."

He went with an assistant to see Blum's car, which was still parked outside the consulate, and they went to speak to the neighbors. He interviewed a woman, Mrs. Soligno, who lived in front of the legation and had witnessed the event. She told them that when the executives were getting into the vehicle, they were intercepted by two cars waiting on the corner. One stopped in front of them and the other behind, blocking Adolf's car. Armed men forced them to get out at gunpoint, put blankets over their heads, and forced them into a car, which headed south. She managed to make out that one car was black and the other green, with a license plate ending in eighteen, and that the men were carrying pipes. Remarkably, she continued looking out at the street, which had very little traffic, and saw that about ten or fifteen minutes later the same cars went by but without any passengers. She had been able to note down the green car's license plate number: 2818. Adrián thanked her, said goodbye, and immediately remarked to his assistant: "They've been kidnapped, her testimony is irrefutable proof."

Goldberg found out through a company employee that a friend of his was in charge of the investigation; they had fought in the Chaco War together. He asked to be put in touch with Adrián. When they met, the agent told him:

"It's a case of kidnapping."

"What?" the executive exclaimed, his eyes bulging. "Well . . . we'll have to wait for a phone call or some kind of message, and to have money ready in briefcases. We'll pay whatever's necessary! We have to get them back."

"But first we need to make sure that they're alive."

"Of course. Don't think for a second that we'll hand over a single cent without proof that they're alive. I'd be eternally grateful if you could let us know as soon as you know anything, even the smallest detail. Please notify me immediately, no matter what time it is."

"I'll keep you up-to-date on everything. Please do the same. We'll be in touch."

The first ones to learn what had happened were the media. Every day they published news articles, editorials, and opinion pieces in which they speculated and conjectured, especially *El Diario*, which was funded by the government and published what they were told to. They said all sorts of things, even contradictory ones. They wrote that Hochschild and Blum had been arrested again; that they had fled incognito because they were conspiring to topple Villarroel's government; or that Hochschild's company had gone bankrupt, and they had escaped with all the money. Such contradictory statements only served to confuse public opinion. When Goldberg and Boris read the latest headlines, they oscillated between rage and nervous laughter. Boris said, "But their capital is invested in Bolivia, idiots . . ."

The news spread and was published in the world press via agencies. An American morning paper published a story with the headline: "Wall Street Trembles: Mining Magnate Kidnapped." When Patiño read this, he said: "Thank God my heart prevents me from living in Bolivia." The minister of government issued a press release stating that state security was deploying all its forces to discover the miners' whereabouts. Boris, behaving as if he were Moritz's son, offered to help in any way he could. Goldberg appreciated his courage and youthful energy, and made him his right-hand man. The first thing they did was go to the National Bank of Bolivia to obtain the money to pay the ransom. They asked the manager of the institution to provide them with lower denomination bills. They also asked to be protected by the bank security guards while they were taking out such an amount. They took the money out of the back door in a duffle bag provided by the bank itself. Under Goldberg's direction, they decided to meet daily at his apartment on Sánchez Lima Street. They organized a committee, whose members swore to maintain the utmost secrecy. Their main aim was to pressure the government to speed up the search. Goldberg and Boris went from embassy to embassy to ask their representatives to visit Villarroel. They also phoned the company's managers and lawyers in Chile to ask them to come to La Paz and request an audience with the head of state. The presidents of the Israelite Circle, the International Red Cross, and other Jewish associations also met with the committee to express their solidarity, and Goldberg advised them to meet with the head of state.

Goldberg's wife went to Mrs. Blum's house every day to keep her company. They sat by the telephone for hours, knitting or embroidering as they waited for a phone call or a note, some kind of message from the kidnappers. The minutes passed, the hours piled up, but there was no word from the kidnappers. The two women, who had known each other before, now began to form a deep friendship.

Several days later, the investigators received a telephone call from the Palacio Quemado claiming that the missing men had appeared in New York. The morning paper *El Diario* published the story; *La Razón* did not, and they later verified with the committee that the story was false. Goldberg told the director of *La Razón*: "Impossible, we would have known . . . they would have said goodbye and left instructions . . . this is getting more and more complicated by the minute because the government is lying."

After hearing this bizarre story, the head of investigations went to Panagra, where he looked over the flights and dates. He came to the simple conclusion that it was impossible for them to have arrived in New York in such a short period of time, especially since the airline didn't have any flights to the United States scheduled for those dates. Luis, distrustful of the government's statements, continued with the investigation. That night he went with one of his detectives to inspect the southern area of La Paz, where the neighborhood of Obrajes was located, and he saw a boy climbing the wall of a house. He stopped and interrogated him.

"Hey! What are you doing? Are you trying to rob that house? Get down from there immediately, dammit! You little brat . . ."

The young man was trembling and he spoke quickly, stuttering. He told them that he lived in the area, and that he had recently seen armed men in uniforms going in and out of the abandoned house. It looked as though they were planning a coup d'état, but they left two days ago. They made the boy part of their team because he knew the

191

area. He felt very important. He talked so much that they nicknamed him "the Mute." "The only condition we'll need to place on your collaboration is that you cannot speak, and least of all about this subject," the chief said, making everyone laugh. They made him swear not to say a word to anyone.

The next day Adrián sent "the Mute" and a couple of agents to inspect the house. They jumped over the wall and found, in the trash, the wrapper of a Havana cigar, which Hochschild always carried in his pocket, crumbs from relatively fresh bread, and banana and orange peels. They had found the house where the kidnapped men were being held, and it was barely a kilometer away from the place they had been attacked! The detectives were shocked to discover that it had been rented by Major Eguino. They still had to figure out, however, where they had been taken. Luis went to fill Goldberg in. The committee decided to publish a reward announcement in the newspapers:

A REWARD OF ONE MILLION BOLIVIANOS IS BEING OFFERED TO THE PERSON WHO DISCOVERS THE WHEREABOUTS OF SEÑOR MAURICIO HOCHSCHILD AND SEÑOR ADOLFO BLUM AND RETURNS THEM TO THEIR RESPECTIVE HOMES IN LA PAZ.

The company, which occupied the entire second floor of a modern building in La Paz, set up an office to receive reports. Goldberg, Boris, and an agent from Adrián's team responsible for coordinating the ransom were placed in charge. A mass of people came in, telling all kinds of stories. Most of them were anonymous reports about where they could be found, ranging from claims that they were being held on a hill to claims that they had been seen dead. At first they believed them, or wanted to believe them, and Adrián's agents went immediately to the places to search for clues. They never brought the ransom money for fear of being caught in a trap and robbed. Everything, however, turned out to be false. "These stories are enough to drive the sanest man insane," Boris said. At the end of each day he would go to Mass to pray for his friends to be set free, and he lost sleep over their uncertain situation. Goldberg wasn't sleeping well either. Every day that went by left him a little thinner, paler, more haggard looking, with larger bags under his eyes and more wrinkles on his face. He was aging at an alarming rate. "This uncertainty is going to give me a heart attack," he told Boris. Boris said in reply: "Don't even joke about that, Doctor."

Adrián, whose agents had infiltrated the Calama Police Regiment (the central police barracks), learned from one of them that a van with armed guards left every day for an unknown destination carrying food for around twenty people. The chief ordered them to follow the vehicle. His spies informed him that it stopped on Catavi Street, located in a marginalized neighborhood in Miraflores, close to Caiconi, a seedy red-light district. They saw the food being left at a house just steps away from Las Concebidas Convent. Adrián and another agent went there that same night, and while they were hiding behind some bushes, they saw Escóbar and Eguino enter. They approached the house and were able to hear:

"You Jewish usurpers, you sons of bitches, go out and do your business," someone shouted.

The victims relieved themselves outside, even though there was a bathroom inside the house. Then someone shouted:

"Alright, you dogs, backs against the wall!"

Moritz wet his pants, becoming dizzy and feeling as though he were about to faint, and Adolf felt his blood freeze. "Goodbye, brother, goodbye . . ." he whispered. They shut their eyes tightly at the same time and heard the sound of the rifles being cocked.

"Ready!"

Then they heard shots. They looked at themselves, at their bodies, which remained standing and unscathed. They wanted to embrace each other, but they restrained themselves. The shots had been aimed into the air. Forced laughter followed. Tears began to fall from Adolf's eyes, and he felt like his legs weren't responding. One of the henchmen approached them and shouted:

"Get a move on, gringos! Back to your room, goddammit!" He prodded them with rifle butts.

Barely able to walk, they were escorted back into the house. Adrián said softly: "These damned dogs have just put them through a mock execution." The kidnapped men didn't know if it was better to fight for their lives or hope for death, since what they were living through was worse than hell. They were locked in a windowless room that looked like a depot, with two dirty mattresses on the floor. They were forced to hand over their shoes and pants so that they wouldn't escape. As a result, they spent all day in their underwear, freezing, full of fear and uncertainty. Although they were kept together, they were forbidden from speaking to each other. They could only talk when the two guards who were watching them dozed off inside the same disgusting room. They couldn't take their weapons because they were handcuffed.

"This is the worst form of punishment," Moritz whispered. "What have we done to deserve this treatment again? They made us suffer for forty-five days in that filthy prison, we hadn't even fully recovered from that, and now they kidnap us. If they want money, I'll give it to them. I'll give them whatever they want. At this point I couldn't care less about money, it doesn't matter one bit, it's only good for these kinds of situations anyway, especially if it can save us. You know, brother, I've never been so afraid in all my life. This is an endless war of nerves. I'm exhausted. They have to be truly evil to put us through that mock execution for a third time . . . I imagine they'll kill us for real at some point . . . do you think they're getting us ready?"

"I don't think so, brother. It's pure cruelty," replied Adolf, with tears in his eyes. "I feel like I'm dying, little by little . . . I'm closer to death with every passing minute. God has forgotten about us. I'm destroyed, too. The only good thing about all this shit is that we're together."

At that moment the guard woke up, and they stopped talking. The next day, Escóbar approached them and said arrogantly to Moritz:

"Hey, Jew, tell Goldberg to transfer two million to an account for me and I'll let you go."

"Tell me the account number and I'll instruct him to do it immediately."

"You fell for it, you bastard!" He let out a shrill guffaw.

Adrián had confirmed that the men behind the kidnapping, responsible for both its plotting and its execution, were the police chiefs, and that the house in the neighborhood to the south had been rented by Eguino. Luis went to fill Goldberg in on all this, and Goldberg exclaimed:

"It's not possible! I can't believe those morons are the ones who kidnapped our friends, when they had just let them go!"

"It's precisely because they just released them," said Adrián. "It's because they want their money. It's a kidnapping for ransom. It's become a business. They must have made them confess how much money they have in prison, then they released them without providing any explanation so they could kidnap them."

"Bastards!"

He then met with President Villarroel and informed him that he had evidence implicating Escóbar and Eguino. The president let out a shrill laugh and said:

"Impossible! They can't have been foolish enough to rent a house under their own names for a kidnapping."

"They're that stupid, indeed," he replied. "They think they can do whatever they want with impunity, and they don't even realize they're leaving behind obvious tracks."

"All I can say, Mr. Adrián, is that I'm getting desperate; they're pressuring me from all sides. The ambassadors, even the nuncio who delivers messages from the Vatican itself, keep threatening me with their hypocritical lectures; Hochschild's lawyers come here to intimidate me; even the institutions are demanding that I find them. I can't even sleep anymore. Do doing everything possible to find them; if you don't, it could mean the end of my government." They said goodbye, and the detective left. As he went down the palace steps, he thought: "How can I make the president understand that the police chiefs, his friends from the lodge, are the criminals behind this?"

The head of state summoned the Tiny Kings and ordered them to find the kidnapped men. He told them he had evidence, although he didn't dare to say against whom, because even he was afraid of them. Unlike the kidnappers, he was not a murderer. Escóbar and Eguino, feeling threatened, moved Hochschild and Blum to the house of one of the police officers involved, in Riosinho Park. Meanwhile, the investigator's agents continued watched the house on Catavi Street. Two nights later, when Luis himself was on duty, he saw the kidnapped men being taken into the house on Catavi Street. He was sure it was them, because when they were forced out of the car in the street (the house had no garage), the blanket covering Hochschild's head fell down. "They're alive," he thought, breathing a sigh of relief. He went to Goldberg's house immediately to assure him he had seen them and that they were alive. The news relieved everyone. The agent told him to demand "proof of life" if they phoned to ask for a ransom.

When they saw they were at risk of getting caught, the kidnappers gathered the lodge members together, and Escóbar addressed them: "We must get rid of these parasites who are ruining the Bolivian economy. The people of Bolivia are determined to free themselves from these men for the common good, and they wouldn't hesitate to sweep them away from the path toward economic freedom and the progress of the people." After voting by secret ballot, the Great Council decided to shoot them. The chiefs instructed a couple of soldiers to dig two graves in the Altiplano, at a site on the way to Chacaltaya, near a newly built ski resort.

The next day, one of the soldiers who had spent the entire night digging the graves lost his nerve and told some friends from the regiment about his dubious deeds. His comrades laughed, and one of them said: "You're crazy, brother, they've made you dig for the buried treasure of the Incas!" As informers inevitably abound, this man went to tell his superior what he had heard, and the officer sent him ipso facto to the border, threatening to kill him if he dared to tell anyone else. In addition to this, the infiltrators went to get drunk with some police officers at a bowling alley next to the Calama Regiment headquarters. A lieutenant who had had too much to drink confessed disappointedly that Escobar was behind the kidnapping, and that he was angry with him because he hadn't paid him his cut for participating in the plot.

Carlos Víctor Aramayo received anonymous telephone calls every day telling him that his "days were numbered," and this kept him awake at night. The henchmen from the Tiny Kings' gang raided the apartment of the director of *La Razón* in search of the tycoon. He became frightened and decided to leave the country to avoid meeting the same fate as his friend Moritz, about whom he was extremely worried. Claiming that he had to travel to France for business, he requested an exit stamp, but Escobar himself denied it. He told Goldberg what had happened, and he told Adrián, who immediately arranged for two agents to protect him day and night. Aramayo was so scared that he asked to meet with the agent.

Since Aramayo didn't want anyone to see him, his nephew, Luis Felipe Aramayo, went on behalf of the Tin Baron to the Basilica of San Francisco to meet with Adrián. They sat down on a bench inside the enormous church to speak discreetly.

"Mr. Aramayo, I recommend that your uncle dress very casually, pack the bare necessities in a small suitcase, and take the train that goes to Quechisla. He should not change trains in Tupiza, but continue on to Villazón. Tell him to get off there, walk four kilometers, and cross the Argentinian border on foot. He needs to leave Bolivia as covertly as possible. You can arrange for a car to wait for him there, or he can take another train. If they ask to see the exit stamp, tell him to bribe whomever he has to. It's the only way to save his life. I'll assign a couple of agents to accompany him. Another alternative is to seek asylum at an embassy on the grounds of persecution. I could serve as an intermediary in that case."

"If he decides to cross the border, I'll go with him," affirmed the young man.

"Good idea. It's better to leave the country at once, because seeking asylum at an embassy would delay his departure, and the government might deny his right to leave, which would leave him stuck there until God knows when."

"I can't thank you enough."

"Let me know what he decides to do."

The millionaire received the message, and he stayed in hiding at a friend's house as he mulled over his options.

Dean went to the Departmental Transit Office with the license plate number that the witness to the kidnapping had given, and he discovered that the vehicle was registered under the chief of police's name. It was the car that Escobar drove.

Adrián and his team watched the house on Catavi Street twenty-four hours a day from a munitions dump on a nearby hill. They saw two vans leave the house, heading south. The agents in charge of surveillance in that part of the city saw the same vehicles go by and confirmed that they were headed toward Valle de las Ánimas, in Palca. Half an hour later, they saw the vehicles go by without any passengers. History was repeating itself. "It's impossible to miss them because this place is more deserted than the Sahara," the agents reported immediately to their superior.

The Tiny Kings realized they were being watched and decided, by vote, not to execute the hostages. Meanwhile, Adrián went to tell Goldberg that his friends had been taken to a hut in Palca. When Boris heard this, he said firmly:

"I want to go rescue them before they kill them."

"Absolutely not, Mr. Kominsky! It would be too dangerous; those people are armed. This needs to be negotiated, money must be given in exchange for the men, but first we need to make sure they're alive."

"Wouldn't it be better to carry out an armed operation?"

"No, because there could be a confrontation. They might take advantage of the attack to execute the men and place the blame on me."

It was already common knowledge that the Tiny Kings were the culprits. Villarroel called Adrián and suggested that he organize an armed attack to retrieve the victims. Adrián refused because of the risk that the kidnappers would execute the men.

"Mr. President, I know how to resolve this. Declare publicly that Escóbar and Eguino have found them, and blame my office for doing a bad monitoring job. I don't care about the consequences for me; at the end of the day, the lives of two men and the prestige of your government are at stake, and this way an international scandal will be avoided. It doesn't matter if the criminals come off as heroes."

Villarroel called the Tiny Kings and, in order to have witnesses, he confronted them in the presence of the ministers of defense and government.

"Adrián has shown me proof that you are behind the kidnapping of the mining magnates. Therefore, I order you to release them, because they are key players in the sale of minerals to the Allies. These men are worth a fortune," he added.

The Tiny Kings denied their involvement and reminded the head of state that he owed his presidency to them. The president kicked them out of his office, yelling. His ministers were astounded by the president's authoritative manner.

That night, Adrián went to Palca with some of his agents. They hid in a cornfield and saw some guards sitting around a bonfire. They approached them silently and heard them talking about the terrible conditions in which Hochschild and Blum were being kept. They could see the house in which they were being held hostage from there. "They're still alive, and that's what matters," Adrián said, feeling relieved. The guards discovered them and fired at them with a machine pistol. Seeing that they had little choice, the Tiny Kings decided to release the men. That same night they phoned Goldberg's house; fortunately, he was home. They asked for the ransom, and the executive told them firmly:

"I'll only give you the money if Hochschild authorizes it. I demand to speak with both of them. And don't play any games. If they aren't delivered alive, you won't see a cent. Put them on the line."

"Moritz, are you okay?" Goldberg asked.

"Yes. Give them the money. They're demanding unmarked bills."

"The bills are unmarked. Adolf's wife wants to speak with him. Tell them to put him on the phone."

"Are you alright, my love?" Blum's wife asked.

"Yes, darling. I love you so much."

"Me too," she said, her eyes filling with tears.

They snatched the phone away from Adolf and hung up. Boris reiterated his offer to make the exchange. "Thank you, my boy," said Goldberg, because he knew that the moment of the attack and that of paying the ransom were the most dangerous, although he didn't tell him. They phoned Adrián, and he told Boris:

"Mr. Kominsky, follow the instructions given by these thugs down to the letter, and don't look at anything other than what's right in front of you."

"What if they kill them along the way and take the money?" Boris asked.

"They won't. They're risking their necks and they want the money. Have faith, boy. By this point, we're in a situation we can no longer control," Goldberg added.

The agents saw the vans go by with people in them, leaving Palca, and they informed their boss. In the meantime, the Tiny Kings left the men locked in a repair shop in the plaza, breaking the vans' headlights. With youthful valor, Boris took the briefcases and went to Alexander Plaza at the agreed upon time, in the neighborhood of Miraflores. He was trembling and perspiring. Boris arrived at midnight, the agreed upon time, and parked his Studebaker. He left the money beneath some benches in the plaza. He never learned how much; only a few people knew the amount. He knew he was being watched, and he didn't look around. He went straight to the repair shop and found the corrugated iron door half open. He entered stealthily and Moritz recognized him.

"Boris, we're over here."

"You're unharmed! Thank God . . ."

The three of them embraced warmly, and Moritz and Adolf thanked Boris with tears streaming down their cheeks. He saw that they had become shadows of human beings. They had lost weight, their hair was gray, and their beards were long. They had become old in only two weeks. They looked withered, but Boris didn't comment on this. He told them: "Keep your eyes on where you're going." They walked several meters and got into the car quickly. He first dropped Adolf off at his house, where his wife and children were waiting on the ground floor. They got out of the car and Adolf ran to kiss and hug them with tears in his eyes. Then his wife embraced Hochschild and, without knowing what else to say, they said goodbye. Next, Boris took his boss to his mansion, and Moritz invited him in.

"Boris, I love you like a son," he said, his voice choked with emotion. "I can't express how grateful I am for the risk you took in rescuing us," he said, deeply moved. "My life has been in danger for a long time. I've been imprisoned twice, and now kidnapped. I've escaped from death by the skin of my teeth. I've been threatened and mistreated without doing anything to deserve it, so I'm leaving Bolivia for good. I used to love this country, but now I don't want to have anything to do with it. I'm leaving as soon as possible, even if I have to go in secret, and I'm never coming back. I'll go look for Germaine in Geneva and ask her to marry me again."

"I don't blame you, Moritz. I think I'm destined to lose those I love . . ."

"You'll never lose me. I'm going to Chile, and I'll send instructions from there, so you can come whenever you like."

Boris phoned Adrián to tell him that he had delivered the money and that they were both safe. Adrián took a deep breath and thought: "Mission accomplished." He immediately sent four agents to guard their residences. They also called Moritz's son Gerardo, and Aramayo's house, asking the butler to tell Carlos Víctor that his friends had been released.

Adrián returned home and noticed that his house had been broken into. He leaped up the steps two at the time, opened the door, and saw all his things in a mess on the floor. After looking around, he realized that all that was missing were the reports written for the president on the case he had been in charge of. He received a phone call asking him to go to the palace at once. He arrived there and presented himself, but was told that no one had called him. He left and was beginning to walk home when he was hit on the head from behind and knocked unconscious. They picked him up and took him as a prisoner to the Calama Regiment headquarters. He woke up inside a cell on a filthy mattress with his head and hair wet. He imagined they had thrown water on him to wake him up. They tortured him, making him swallow enormous quantities of castor oil, beating him with a braided leather whip and threatening to kill him. The torturers wanted him to confess who the traitors who had informed on them were. "I figured it out myself, with the help of my team," he cried. He neither gave up nor betrayed his people. The

Tiny Kings wanted to have him executed because he knew too much, but by orders of the president of the republic, they refrained.

Adrián's team found out that he had been taken prisoner, and they bribed a guard to give them the key to unlock the cell. They planned to help him escape at noon the next day. The same guard, however, didn't hesitate to inform Escóbar of the agents' plans. The Tiny King decided to make the most of the situation and came up with a plan to kill him: while Adrián was running away, he would be shot in the back, but before that he would publicly declare his release. The hour of the escape arrived, but Luis Adrián remained in his cell. Was it intuition? A bad feeling? Mistrust? Self-preservation? Suddenly another group of soldiers arrived to announce his release, and they found him alive and well, sitting on the damp mattress. They inspected the padlock, saw that it had not been opened, and let him go. What was it that saved the head of the DNI? It's simple: he wasn't wearing a watch.

Moritz's decision to leave Bolivia for good was a crushing blow to everyone. He left the country after having lived there for more than twenty years. He was sixty-three years old. His friends and employees begged him to reconsider his decision, but to no avail. All he wanted was to leave as soon as possible. The company was placed under the direction of Blum and Goldberg.

Boris was devastated. He had no choice, however, but to accept his departure. Moritz was like a father, even closer to him than his own father, of whom he'd had no news for the past five years since the global conflagration was still raging. "You're like a son to me," Moritz told him when they said goodbye. "And you, Moritz, are like a father. I still don't know if mine is alive or dead because of this cruel war."

The Chilean government put a plane at his disposal, and he flew to New York, where he stayed at the Ritz Carlton Hotel. Then he went to live in Chile.

When Moritz left, Boris felt alone again, just as he had during his first few years in Bolivia.

Chapter 9
Auschwitz-Birkenau, 1943–1944

One autumn afternoon, when the daylight was fading and everything looked gray, the Nazis raided St. Martin's Church and took the Kominsky family, Father Peter, and another priest. They weren't even allowed to bring a small suitcase with clothing in it; all they managed to take were their coats and the shawls Boris had sent from Bolivia, which were hanging in a closet. They shoved them roughly and made them—even Olga and Sonitzya—put their hands behind their heads like criminals. They were unable to put up a fight, and Bishop John wasn't there to intervene on their behalf. They forced them into a truck and took them to the Umschlagplatz railway station, adjacent to the Warsaw ghetto. Everyone was surprised to see two Catholic priests in cassocks, because the rest of the people there were Jews and Poles wearing coats, hats, and gloves. They were surrounded by armed guards with dogs, waiting for a train to take them to an unknown place. Rumor had it that they were being sent to a labor camp, and everyone was very afraid. The SS announced by loudspeakers: "We're going to relocate you." They all wandered around like ghosts, their faces contorted and their gaze bewildered, amidst the general murmur thudding dully in the background. Women tried to feed their children with pieces of stale bread they had hidden in their pockets and some milk they kept in bottles. That night, the victims tried to sleep in the open air on the station floor, but the cold and uncertainly made sleeping impossible. Disoriented children wailed as they searched for their parents, while kind women did their best to comfort them. Some people rested against their little leather suitcases, others against bundles of clothes. Olga and Sonitzya felt no hunger because their stomachs were in knots. Sonitzya, who couldn't stop crying, never left her mother's side, nor Sergei's. They hugged each other to stay warm. Olga kept coughing, and her children rubbed her back. The priests, Peter and Patrick, walked around to warm up.

"What have we done?" Sonitzya asked her mother.

"They found out that we have Jewish blood."

"But you don't!"

"You and Sergei do, though."

202

"And the priests?"

"They're being punished for protecting us. Someone must have denounced us. I always feared this fateful day would come. We were too lucky to still be alive after they raided the apartment and your father disappeared."

"Why doesn't Father John come to look for us?"

"They've probably taken him too."

"Or maybe he's a coward! How could he not come to demand the return of the priests from his parish?"

The victims weren't allowed to ask where they were being taken. They accepted everything submissively. They had to obey. Many had lost hope because they had heard that the labor camps were a one-way trip, and that those who rebelled or tried to flee were executed immediately. Only one thing was certain: their fate was sealed.

Around four o'clock in the morning, a freight train arrived, the kind used for transporting livestock, and the guards forced the prisoners to board by beating them. Sergei and Father Peter helped Olga and Sonitzya, and Father Patrick aided a young family with two children, one of whom was still nursing. They closed the doors, which had latches wrapped in barbed wire. In the upper part there was a small window with iron bars; it was the only place through which air entered. The car was overcrowded and the victims, barely able to breathe, were forced to stand. Sergei saw the small window and pushed through the crowd so his mother could move to the front and breathe in the air.

There were approximately a hundred people in the car. The floor was covered in straw, and there was a kind of small barrel full of urine and excrement where people could relieve themselves. The foul smell was unbearable, so they began to breathe through their mouths.

A whistle blew, startling everyone, and the train departed. Olga began to cough uncontrollably, and they switched roles: Sonitzya began to take care of her, praying without pause, from memory, clutching the rosary she always wore around her neck. "God, don't abandon us . . . protect us, take care of my mother . . ." They were both dizzy from lack of air. Sonitzya rubbed Olga's chest while Sergei rubbed her back, trying to help her breathe better. At one point, they began to give her mouth to mouth resuscitation because she was choking.

A few hours into the journey, a rabbi began to pray, reciting prayers such as the Mincha, Maariv, and Shema Yisrael as he rocked back and forth, trying to comfort them. Many joined in to block out reality. The car was so crowded that the passengers began to suffocate, not just for lack of air but also because of the heat. They perspired to the point that their clothes clung to their bodies, their hair became wet and dirty, their skin sticky. People began taking their clothes off; the women were left in their petticoats and the men in undershirts and underpants. They were incredibly thirsty, but there was no water. That was the worst of all. An elderly couple began to lose consciousness. Suddenly someone shouted: "We need a doctor!" There was only a nurse among the passengers, and she pushed her way over to assist them. She examined them as best she could and saw that they were dead. She only told the rabbi so as not to stir panic. Several men helped to carry them to the back of the car, beside the barrel. "No one deserves to die like this, amidst all this excrement," the rabbi thought as he gave them his blessing. Sergei thought: "This is the train of death."

Olga couldn't stop coughing. She coughed so much that the pain in her back became unbearable. Suddenly, the young woman with the tiny baby began to scream: "My baby . . . my baby's not moving!" Father Patrick went up to her. The tiny girl had died, suffocating from the lack of oxygen and from hunger, probably because the mother had stopped producing milk to feed her due to the lack of water and the stress. When he confirmed she was no longer breathing, the mother began to wail. He gave her the last rights and baptized her in silence. Confused and inconsolable, the mother didn't object to the Catholic priest's blessing. Then the rabbi came and also gave her his blessing.

They suddenly heard the chilling blow of the train whistle, which sounded like a woman shrieking. The train stopped to pick up water. The victims held their hands out the small window, begging for water, but they were ignored. Once the water was loaded, the whistle blew again and the train left. For many, it was the slowest train they had ever taken in their lives. Nothing mattered anymore; they had reached the point of urinating where they stood. Elderly people began to faint and wet themselves, but they remained standing, supported by the human mass.

The journey lasted until dawn. Finally, the train stopped at Auschwitz-Birkenau. The Nazis had built a railway line to the camp.

Many were nearly dead by the time they arrived. The doors were opened, and to feel the air was like coming back to life; the air, though, was heavy and thick, and they could feel the ash accumulating on their faces and hands. They began to get off the train, aided by Ukrainians and Jewish kapos wearing striped prisoners' uniforms with the Star of David sewed on, hats of the same material, and holding batons. Music by Wagner was being played through a speaker. Jews were particularly sensitive to music, and those of the Third Reich used this to their advantage.

The station was surrounded by barbed wire, soldiers armed with machine guns, and growling German Shepherds and Dobermanns baring their teeth. Their suitcases and the few items they had brought with them were taken away and thrown aside. "How can a labor camp be like this?" Sonitzya whispered to her mother, who didn't answer because she couldn't stop coughing. Sergei put his mother's arm over his shoulder to help her walk, and Sonitzya took her other arm. Women were carrying their young children in their arms, trying to wake them up. Were they dead? When the Nazis saw the priests, they said: "Step to the side." Everyone obeyed in silence.

Some of the elderly people, either dead or dying, remained lying in the train, next to the dead couple. An old lady was hugging one of them—probably her husband—and crying. An officer wearing a white apron climbed into the car and saw the elderly people dying of dehydration and lack of air. He shot them in cold blood, along with the woman, to shut her up. The victims had been traveling beside passengers who had died standing up, and no one had noticed.

The Nazi shouted to the kapos to take away the dead. The bodies were lifted by the arms and legs, thrown into wheelbarrows, and hauled away.

Suddenly a captain shouted through a megaphone: "Women in one line and men in another!" Sergei and Sonitzya were very worried about their mother's health. He kissed and embraced them with all his strength, telling his sister: "Take care of Mom, don't leave her alone for even a moment." Suddenly he felt a rifle butt in his back, which knocked him to the ground. "Stop whining, you Jewish dog! Get in the line fast if you don't want to be shot!" Sergei stood as best he could and went to the men's line. Everyone was crying. Once the line had formed, some doctors began to inspect them. One of these men was Josef Mengele, who on that very ramp, with a small gesture, determined who would live and who would die. When they saw children with Aryan features—and there were many of them—they would separate them from their mothers, giving rise to screams and tears from the whole family. When Sonitzya arrived with Olga, who was nearly unconscious from coughing so much, she dared to say: "I can't be separated from my mother, she's sick." Mengele touched Sonitzya's jaw with a baton and said: "You go with her." "Thank you, thank you very much," she replied. Sonitzya put her mother's arm over her shoulder and led her away, practically dragging her. The guards pushed them from behind as they walked. Sonitzya glanced at her mother and saw that she looked withered. She thanked God they had not been separated. Did she know where she was going?

Auschwitz was in Oswiecim, a town in Poland. The SS, or Schutzstaffel, had decided to give it that name for strategic purposes, so that no one could find the place or discover anything about it. The Nazis preferred to be stationed there; otherwise, they were sent to certain death on the front. It was an old military barracks with dozens of stables and soldiers' blocks, a citadel with a theater, canteen, grocery store, sports club, and a brothel. Many different languages could be heard. There were Jews from all the countries of Europe, as well as homosexuals, Gypsies, Slavs, Jehovah's Witnesses—considered *Untermenschen*—Russian soldiers, political prisoners, and Poles.

Varinia had been sent there just a few months earlier. Her journey had been much the same as that of Olga and Sonitzya. She cried the whole way because she had been forced to leave her son Boris and she couldn't find her parents or her sister. She felt alone, very alone, and confused, because when they raided her house they had taken her parents and sister in one truck and her in another. Again and again, her hands wet with perspiration, she clutched the cross her boyfriend had given her in the hopes that she would feel protected. She prayed without pause.

When she arrived at the camp, she got off the train, helped by a willing kapo. He found her so beautiful that he said:

"Tell them that you know how to do any kind of manual labor."

"Where are we?" she asked.

"In Auschwitz. Be quiet."

When she saw the SS tearing children from their mothers' arms, she thanked God that she had left her son behind. "Everything happens for a reason. My boy is safe. Thank you, Blessed Lord. Thanks to you, he was left in Ewa's care, and I know she'll take care of him as if he were her own son." When they saw how tall, big, and strong she was, she was immediately selected to work. After leading the women to their assigned place, they took the jewelry they had on. Varinia was no exception, and they yanked off the chain with the cross and the ring with Tiwanaku motifs that meant so much to her. They were the only material things she had left from Boris. She felt that she needed to have something tangible from him. They made them undress and took them to some pools of cold, dirty water so they could wash themselves. When they got out, they sprayed them with disinfectant, a white powder kept in cans similar to those used for kerosene. Then they gave them striped dresses, similar to the uniforms worn by the kapos, and wooden shoes that were either too small or too big. Next, they shaved their heads, "so they wouldn't get lice." The guards inserted their fingers into the vagina and anus of each and every one of the victims to make sure they weren't hiding any jewelry. They found that three women had hidden diamonds and pieces of gold in tiny plastic containers. Upon discovering them, they beat them and immediately separated them from the rest. Then they tattooed a number of the left forearm of each prisoner.

The Nazi women were led by the chief of surveillance, Maria Mandl. She was an ignorant prostitute (which made her all the more dangerous), like the majority of her comrades, with the eyes of a billy goat. Aside from her professional role, she was the "Madame" of the camp whores. She was large and strong, fat as a cow, like the majority of the female guards, with breasts like grapefruits, wide hips, and a Nazi uniform so tight the buttons always looked as though they were about to burst.

All the female guards were very servile and obliging toward the SS, who would screw them whenever they felt like it in exchange for a drink, a piece of bread, or nothing at all. Orgies took place in Block Twenty-Four, where the brothel was located. There were also lesbians and pedophiles among them.

After the physical inspection, the female guards made the victims line up like soldiers in the central square, prodding them with rifle butts. They counted them, and Mandl appeared. In a hoarse, loud voice, she explained the rules of the game. Varinia, like nearly all the rest of them, couldn't stop shaking from fear and the cold. Before sending them to the barracks, Mandl shouted out, laughing: "I have surprise for you." They made the three women who had hidden jewels and precious metals climb onto some stools: their hands were tied behind their backs, and they placed a thick rope around their necks. Suddenly a female guard kicked the stools out from under them, and the women were hanged to death. "Let them serve as a warning to you!" the Madame cried, letting out a forced laugh. A woman suddenly let out a scream from the depths of her soul. The guard approached her and killed her with one shot. She was someone's sister. Upon seeing this, Varinia closed her eyes and bit her lip so hard it started to bleed, staining her uniform. She wanted to scream, but a fellow prisoner next to her said: "Unless you want to end up like them, be quiet."

After the hangings, Mandl ordered the prisoners to go to the barracks. Each block housed about seven hundred women, all crowded together. The bathroom had a few sinks (with very little water) that were originally horse troughs, and some barrels cut down the middle served as toilets. That night they ordered them to leave the barracks to eat, and they gave them cold, watery soup with onions and potato skin. "Not even a dog would eat this disgusting thing," Varinia whispered to her new Polish friend named Miriam. They were so hungry, though, that they devoured the soup. Varinia was very cold, especially her head, and she prayed continuously for her son, her beloved Boris, and her family. Like everyone else, she fell asleep from sheer exhaustion and stress. The next day, before dawn, they awoke to the sound of a whistle, which frightened them. They had slept in the same clothes, and they were all scratching themselves. The barracks was full of lice. They made them form a line and they counted them. No one was missing. They lined up in front of several desks behind which Jewish kapos were sitting, and were asked, one by one, what they knew how to do. When Varinia was about to speak, the kapo who had helped her get off the train said: "This one will go to the clothes shed." What did this man want? It was the second time he appeared by her side at a crucial moment. Thanks to him, she was assigned to a relatively good place in Auschwitz, near Birkenau. It was the best thing that could happen to a prisoner; otherwise, they were made to dig pits or tunnels, build barricades, work in the coal mines, as stonemasons, wash filthy latrines or, if they were lucky, work in factories such as Bavarian Motor Works (BMW) or IG Farben. These were private companies that paid the SS next to nothing in exchange for Jewish slave labor. Four hundred thousand Jews worked in the arms industry. It was an ideal situation for the Nazis because it was unpaid labor and, by isolating them, they made sure their military secrets wouldn't be revealed.

Alongside a group of fellow prisoners, Varinia entered a huge shed used for storing clothes confiscated from the prisoners. There were mountains of shoes, and her task was to look for pairs. There were so many that she didn't know where to start. She spent the entire day in this occupation. At times she thought that she was going crazy, but the Jews found ways to make the work easier. They only looked for pairs that were in good condition, and they separated them by gender, age, color, and style of heel. They also organized the clothing in a similar way. She learned that everything would be sent to the German people. She noticed that there were some black chimneys emitting black smoke, and that the air was thick with ash, and she didn't understand why. According to the SS, it came from a tire factory. It was impossible to see clearly beyond a certain distance. Everything looked opaque and gray, like her heart.

Varinia got scabies, and her body became covered with sores because the lice made her scratch herself incessantly. Her fellow prisoners died daily of typhus, dysentery, pneumonia, black fever, and the beatings ordered by Mandl and the SS. Often, they couldn't hold their diarrhea, and they had to relieve themselves in the containers they ate from so the kapos and the SS wouldn't notice. They later had to wash these, although they never managed to clean them entirely. They drank their own urine to cure colds, and they also applied it to wounds.

One night, driven to desperation from so much scratching, Varinia left the barracks to go to the infirmary and came across the kapo who had his eye on her. He approached her.

"What's your name, beautiful?" he asked cockily. "Even without your hair you're still beautiful. You have a phenomenal body!"

"Um . . ."

"Answer me quickly, it's thanks to me that you're alive and working in the shoe shed! If you don't do what I tell you, I'll make them send you to work in the latrines!" He grabbed her arms. She tried to push him away, but she couldn't.

"Stop it, bitch, now you'll finally be mine," he said, opening his slimy, lustful mouth and putting it over hers.

Varinia jerked her head back and bit his ear, but he slapped her so hard that she fell to the ground, her mouth and nose bleeding. He took her by the arms and, despite her kicking, dragged her into a dark corridor. He put her back against the wall and showed her a sharp knife.

"If you say a word, I'll slit your throat," he whispered in her ear, panting as he held the knife to her jugular. She began to tremble like a leaf, her teeth chattering and her heart racing.

"Take off your panties," he ordered as he tore off the top part of her striped dress.

He lifted her skirt, turned her around, and penetrated her from behind with such force that she let out a silent cry of pain and impotence. Then, seeing that there was no one around, he threw her to the ground and ripped off what was left of her dress. She began to writhe on her back like a cat until he picked up a stone and hit her in the face. She was dazed, and the kapo penetrated her again and again while he bit her breasts, licked her body, and thrust his tongue in her mouth. When he finished ejaculating and pulled out of her, covered in sweat, she began to vomit.

"And on top of it all you throw up, you bloody whore!" he said, mocking her. "Choke on your vomit, because you won't live much longer!" Before he left, he kicked her as she lay on the ground. "You'll never get to Kanada!" he spit. (The Poles called a sector of the camp by that name because they imagined that country to be the richest and most beautiful place on the planet.)

She lay helpless on the floor, trying to move. She realized suddenly that blood was dripping from her vagina and mouth. She got up slowly, tried to put her clothes back on, and walked, half fainting, to the infirmary. As soon as she arrived, she was greeted by a young German sergeant, the doctor on duty. The infirmary was a pigsty and smelled of goat. It was just as filthy, or even more filthy, than the barracks. There were victims there dying—or already dead—from typhus, dysentery, scurvy, infections, the cold, hunger, tuberculosis, depression, and exhaustion. There were several rooms with rotting straw mattresses shared by the living and the dead and covered in excrement, urine, and blood. Feces dripped from the upper bunks, where women suffering from dysentery lay, to the lower ones, where there was always someone lying sick. The bodies of the deceased were picked up every day by the kapos, who piled them onto a wheelbarrow and took them to an unknown place. "Why even come to the infirmary if everyone winds up dead?" she thought.

"I have scabies," she said, trying to conceal her tears.

"This is more than scabies," he told her, noticing her beautiful, big blue eyes with long lashes, despite her shaved head.

"What happened to you, girl?"

"I have scabies."

"But you're bleeding all over the place."

"I have scabies and I'm covered in lice."

"We don't give out medication; we only give it to those who are very sick. But in your case . . . I'll make an exception. Take this antiseptic ointment. It'll help you."

"Thank you very much," she said, crossing herself.

"Are you Jewish?"

"I'm Polish."

He thought: "This girl has just been raped." She walked back to her barracks and saw the kapo who had assaulted her on the corner, leaning against the wall and smoking a cigarette. She began shaking again and kept her eyes down. She arrived at the barracks and collapsed on the floor. Her fellow inmates came to her aid immediately. Sara, the leader of the barracks, an older woman who was tough as iron, looked at her and said: "She's been raped." Miriam and some others took out some rags and a bucket of water they had hidden. They cleaned her, applied the antiseptic ointment, and dressed her in the striped uniform, underpants and coat of a woman who had died minutes before. They saw that she had lost three teeth from the left side of her mouth.

"Nazi bastard," a woman exclaimed.

"It was a kapo," she said.

"Girls, it was a kapo!" Sara exclaimed, although it didn't surprise them because it had happened before. "I already told you. Don't even think about going anywhere alone, especially at night. Pigs, bastards! They're as bad as the Nazis."

That night, as was to be expected, Varinia was unable to fall asleep. It felt like the longest night of her life. Her body and soul ached, and she could do nothing but weep silently. Miriam, who slept next to her, heard her sobs and stoked her hair, saying: "Cry, it'll do you go, let it go."

She couldn't even speak; her thoughts whirled through her head like a surging river. "How disgusting! . . .what a revolting man. Abusive bastard! He had his eye on me from the start, but I never imagined he would do something like that. Just the thought of his penis inside me, his slimy mouth licking me, his grubby hands on my breasts, my vagina, my buttocks, and then hitting me. And to top it all off, he left me without teeth! No! I'm revolted by my own body. I hate myself. I'm dirty and sticky, covered in that disgusting pig's dry semen," she thought. The smell of her body reminded her of what she had suffered. "My armpits, my vagina, and my feet stink, and so do these clothes. My hands are always dirty and covered in sores, and I have to cut my black fingernails with my teeth, although they fall off on their own because I'm so weak. My feet are destroyed by these wooden shoes that, even though I exchanged them for my size with another prisoner, give me calluses and blisters that never heal and constantly ooze and bleed. I'm a walking wound. My body is covered in black dirt that's impossible to scrub off. I'm covered in scars from scratching so much because of the lice we have to live with. And now I have scabies . . . how disgusting! I've even lost the hair in my armpits, my pubic area, and my legs, and the hair on my head barely grows. They say it's due to malnutrition. Thank God they shaved us; otherwise, without being able to wash our hair, ours heads would be a thick layer of filthy grease, a nest of lice and spiders. We work and sleep in the same clothes, which we've never washed. The only way to wash them would be to put them on wet, and then I'd get pneumonia. Many other prisoners have died that way. So I wash my dress one part at a time, with a rag." She remembered the fragrance of soap in her house; it had been such a long time since she'd used it, and she became so distraught that she began to feel disoriented. "Everything reeks. It's been months since I bathed or brushed my teeth. The sinks and latrines are revolting. We have to wash ourselves bit by bit in filthy bowls with dirty, murky, freezing water. And we're forced to relieve ourselves in front of everyone, and it's all left there, and some poor fellow prisoners are forced to clean it. My body feels battered. I can touch each and every one of my bones: my collarbone, my hips, my ribs . . . my cheekbones stick out . . . my stomach is concave, I don't even have breasts anymore. I look like a sagging, walking corpse. I must have lost about ten kilos in just a few months. I still get my period, but it's lighter every time, luckily. They say it's because of the lack of food. I use a rag that I wash in muddy puddles, there's mud everywhere. I've never seen so much mud. This entire shithole is a swamp . . . a swamp of shit! We're all emaciated, famished, exhausted, and we barely have the strength to work. Our faces are ashen, greenish, the color people turn when they're about to die. Even our lips are colorless." The sound of some women coughing in the barracks interrupted her thoughts. It was like coming back into a world in which life and death walk hand in hand, one dragged along by the other. "We live surrounded by lice—they're the ones who transmit typhus—and everything feeds into a vicious cycle of infection, disease, and death. It's all one unbearable pandemic. And licentiousness abounds. I've seen women fondling each other, others having sex, and others masturbating. They say it's the only pleasure to be had in this place. Many of them have already started relationships, and they even fight over each other. I don't judge them; it's the least of these evils. The worst thing, aside from the fear and uncertainty, is hunger, which is an unspeakable affliction. I'm always hungry, so very hungry. It wakes me up at night. It gives me cramps, stomach aches, and my guts rumble day and night. I dream about food. I'd give anything to work in the kitchen so I could eat a bit more, even if they hit me. The hunger is so bad that most of the fights that break out are over food. I gobble up that disgusting soup in a matter of minutes. And I need to save the bread they give us at midday for the night, because they only feed us twice a day. I chew every bite ten times, and extremely slowly; they say that'll make you feel fuller. I'm always thirsty, but you can't drink the water because it's contaminated and makes you sick. I cherish my tiny bottle of clean water, from which I only take small sips. I can only wash myself properly and drink more water when it snows. The cold is so bad that I had to exchange my piece of bread for a handkerchief to cover my head. I put newspaper under my blouse and socks to keep warm. They say the inks warms you up. Does Boris know we have a son who's identical to him and who bears his name? I never heard from him. Bastard . . . piece of shit . . . I bet he sleeps with dozens of women, telling them a bunch of lies to get them into bed, just like he did with me! Is he married now? Does he have a new family? He must be living like a king in Bolivia, while I'm here, mired in slovenliness, living in this shithole, going through hell and dying little by little . . . he has no idea about all this, he doesn't care . . . he forgot about me . . . I know that he forgot about me . . . he abandoned me and our son . . . I never received a single letter from him . . . not one word . . . he never figured out a way to let me know how he was . . . and I, like a fool, went on writing and writing mountains of letters, like an idiot . . . I hate him with all my soul . . . I hate him! The only thing I love is my little Boris . . . his love is unconditional . . . he, at least, is mine . . . God, please take care of my son . . . thanks to you

213

he's in Ewa's care . . . the best care possible . . . and if I don't survive, let him live . . . and let him know who his parents were, and how much we loved him . . . how I suffered the day he was born, but I'd go through it all again just to have him with me . . . and Boris, too . . . whom I still love, in the end . . . I don't think I'll ever love anyone like I love him . . . I think I'll die loving him . . ." Varinia let her tears flow freely. "In this dump there's no sense of time. I never know the date, neither the month nor the day. All I know is that they brought us here at the end of 1943, in the middle of winter. All I know is whether it's day or night, whether it's cold or hot. I've even become a thief. A little while ago I saw one of my bunk-mates in the throes of death. When I woke up the next day, she was lying dead beside me. It was hard to figure out whether she was dead, because there's not much difference between the living and the dead. I had slept beside the corpse of a fellow prisoner, and I even stole her piece of bread and eating utensils. The worst of it is that I didn't regret it or feel ashamed. I was able to exchange her pot and spoon for two rations of bread on the black market, which is run for the most part by the kapos. Bastards! I hate them as much as the Nazis! Everything is worth something, from a button to a piece of wire for sewing. Am I becoming a bad person? What do I care? We all behave the same way. It's about doing whatever it takes to survive. When we see someone on the verge of death, we begin to prowl around them like hungry wolves, wanting to be the first to grab whatever they have. And when they die, we all fight to see what we can get. They end up naked, and the kapos come and take them away in their wheelbarrows. I've never felt so lonely and helpless. I'm totally and utterly alone. Thank God I've found Miriam, who's like a sister to me. Only one reality exists here: death at the hands of these abominable men, who have taken on the role of God. If killing is permitted, anything goes. We live waiting. Waiting for what?"

Not a day went by without one of her fellow prisoners waking up dead; many of them couldn't get up to go work because of the swelling in their abdomens, or malnutrition, or depression. She tried not to become too close to anyone. Whoever didn't show up for work was executed by the Madame without qualms. Maybe the victims unconsciously yearned for this fate because death was preferable. They all had death in their eyes and considered it a form of emancipation. It wasn't uncommon to hear of suicides, women who had slit their wrists with cans or barbed wire, or had thrown

214

themselves into the electric fence. She tried not to lose hope; she knew she had to triumph over this, not just for her herself, but for her son. Most of the time, however, she was overcome by dejection, sadness, and fear, especially when she saw the smoke rising from the chambers.

"To live, you have to have hope, but there's none here. We're just another number. I'm 394985. How tiny we are in the face of death . . . what power it has over us! We've gotten used to living with it. How could we not when, on top of it all, it's an open secret that the black smoke billowing from those chimneys, the smoke that pollutes the air with ash and the smell of meat, is generated by burning human flesh and hair? The smell is so strong that it never goes away. The kapos say there are gas chambers where they kill children, the elderly, pregnant women, the sick, even entire families, whose bodies they later cremate, because that way they save bullets that are needed on the front, and there's no place to bury them. They say that in summers past the camp reeked because of all the buried bodies. I'm sure they'll end up killing us once we can no longer work. We'd be naïve to think otherwise. No one talks about it, but I have no doubt that the thought that a loved one could have been sent to the chambers, and that they will be too, has crossed everyone's mind. This isn't a labor camp; it's an extermination camp. But it's not I who should be ashamed of living in this shit, it's these Nazi bastards who should be. Our bodies and faces are disfigured, and our hearts are broken. Our eyes no longer see; they only stare. I've become a heartless woman. This is a living cemetery, where we wander around like corpses because we live in the world of the dead and those of us who are still alive are nearer to death than to life. My life, our lives, belong to them, and they do what they want with them. Why do these bastards have control over our lives? Will I manage to survive? I have to. The others keep saying that we need to hold on, that the war will be over soon, that we shouldn't let ourselves die, if only to spite the Nazis who want us to disappear. The motto is to resist, to have the willpower to resist. We must survive, even if it means living in the midst of this terror. We must exercise the patience and the willpower needed to endure. I have to live to get my son back, to find Boris and my family. I say this to myself over and over again. But . . . there's no body or soul that could stand this nightmare."

The women chose either to cry or to remain silent. The occasional scream could be heard in the middle of the night. Miriam woke

Varinia tenderly when she cried out in her sleep, repeating the name of her two Borises. She told her: "My dreams are usually the same: a pair of eyes full of hatred, like those of a bull about to charge; the fixed gaze of the dead, accusing me; I'm pushed against a black wall at gunpoint, they shoot me and I fall down dead, they leave my remains as a warning to others, but I'm still alive . . . and I see my Boris and my family who are going far, far away, and they don't even look back at me, or wait for me, and they never come back . . ."

Both the Jewish and the Catholic women in the barracks decided to pray. Varinia told them they were all united by Abraham, the father of three peoples: the Christians, the Jews, and the Muslims. She prayed, as she always did, to God and her Black Madonna, asking them to help her keep faith, which she was on the brink of losing. God felt very far away. She didn't understand how such a benevolent and wonderful being could allow such cruelty to occur. Somewhere between her prayers and her thoughts, she fell asleep around dawn. A chilling whistle woke her a little while later to go to work. She was suffering from terrible vaginal pains, anal hemorrhaging, and bruises on her face, neck and legs.

The kapos' lovers were something like the tsar's secret messengers. Whenever they heard some news, they would go immediately to share it with their fellow prisoners, although they warned them that what they had heard may not be true. They learned that the Axis powers had lost battles in North Africa, and that in June of that year the Allies had landed in Normandy and were increasingly occupying more European territory. This gave them some hope. It was the only thing that kept them going. When they could talk, they speculated and made predictions about when the war would end. They came to the conclusion that Hitler was losing the war, and that gave them the strength to resist.

A couple of months passed and Varinia began to vomit and feel sick. "God, don't let it be typhus or something like that, that would be the end of me, after all that I've done to survive," she thought. She went and told Sara. "Vomiting?" she said. "I'll get Dr. Gisella Perl. She's a Hungarian Jewish doctor everyone esteems and trusts because she helps whomever she can in secret."

Very late that same night, around three o'clock in the morning and despite the curfew, Sara and Miriam risked going to look for her in her barracks. They ran bit by bit, dodging the spotlight. They found her and brought her to see Varinia. With great serenity and

professionalism, she examined her and asked her a few questions.
Then she said:

"My girl, you're pregnant."

"What? Noooooo!" she howled, and Miriam covered her mouth so
as not to wake the others. "Impregnated by that pig!" she exclaimed,
beginning to retch.

"She was raped by a Jewish kapo," Sara interjected.

"They are the ones who most often rape women in the camp," the
doctor confirmed. "My girl, you'll need to abort."

"I can't. I'm Catholic and my religion forbids it."

"Many Catholics have been obliged to do it. I'm sorry to say it, but
if the SS know you're expecting a baby, they'll kill you, because they
won't be able to put you to work anymore. And if they let you live
and the baby is born, that evil Dr. Mengele, who does experiments
on human beings, even living ones, will use your son, and you can't
allow that. His own assistants, doctors like me, have told me about
it all in the strictest confidence."

"I can't do it."

"And your baby? Would you allow him to be destroyed and
eventually killed? Mengele is a monster. He experiments mainly with
twins, with healthy Jews and Gypsies, deformed people like midgets,
people with Down syndrome, and Siamese twins. He opens the twins
up entirely to compare them. Believe what I'm saying, I'm a medical
doctor. He wants to discover the root genetic cause of twins so as to
multiply the Aryan race. He creates mutants. He also bandages up
mothers so they can't breastfeed their children in order to see how
many days they can survive without being fed. He has also thrown
newborn babies into the laundry room furnace to serve as fuel. He
even performs operations without anesthesia to observe the pain
threshold of his patients. He injects substances into children's eyes
so they turn blue. Or he drowns them in buckets of water right after
birth if he feels like it. He's also a sexual pervert."

Varinia wept as the doctor explained all this.

"Do you want something similar to happen to your baby? I've helped
many women have an abortion. I've performed hundreds of
abortions to at least save the mother. I know it's not ethical, but
you're young, you'll get married and have other children later."

"But what if I'm left infertile?"

"You won't be. I'll only use my hands. God will forgive you. Save
yourself, girl, save yourself and your child from a horrible fate!"

"Do it!" Miriam pleaded. "I'm also a Catholic, and faced with what the doctor has said, I would do it too. You have to save yourself to get your son and his father back. We're in the middle of a war!"

"Besides, I don't want to have that bastard's child! God, forgive me . . . I beg you, forgive me . . ."

Dr. Perl, who had been assigned to the infirmary, washed her hands with alcohol she took from a bottle. She instructed Varinia to lie down and spread her legs, and she put a pencil in her mouth to mute her screams. Varinia clasped one of Miriam's hands and one of Sara's, and Dr. Perl carefully, firmly and skillfully extracted the embryo. She withstood the procedure stoically. She lost a lot of blood, and the abortion was more painful than the rape because it hurt her very soul. She asked about the sex of the fetus, but so as not to torment her further, Dr. Perl told her it was impossible to know. She was so devastated that she said: "Now I don't care at all about death. . . this is something I'll have to live with forever, because there's no greater pain than this . . . I killed my own child." She couldn't stop crying. She curled up in a fetal position and asked her loyal friend Miriam to embrace her as she tried to fall asleep.

The next day she went to work just like every other day. She performed her tasks like an automaton, without sense, in silence, her gaze absent and distant. All she could think about was the loss of her baby, and she asked God for forgiveness because she felt guilty. "It's beyond comprehension . . . to be forced to get rid of my own baby, even if he is the child of a scoundrel . . . but he was my own blood . . ." Miriam comforted her by telling her she had no other choice. She felt as though she had suddenly aged many years. She wanted to work to the point of exhaustion and thereby blot out her sin. "The best way to forget is to be busy, even if it's just sorting through these disgusting shoes."

One morning they were told to line up, and a few women were chosen to go work in another sector, Kanada. Varinia was chosen, and when they told her she was going to Kanada, her face lit us. "Kanada!" she thought. "They say it's the best place to work! Could it be true? Kanada, my God . . . Kanada. Black Madonna, I thought you had forgotten me forever."

Kanada was a place set apart, heavily guarded and close the Nazi residences. When she went in, she saw huge, long tables piled with clothes and hundreds of suitcases. The SS knew that the prisoners carried their most valuable possessions with them. The workers were threatened with execution if they stole anything—not that it would have been easy in any case, because the German soldiers didn't let them out of their sight. She later learned that they were brought in to replace some detainees who had been caught stealing zlotys and Reichsmarks. Varinia was struck by the fact that all the women were young, pretty, blond and blue eyed; they even wore handkerchiefs on their heads. They weren't as dirty and they were even allowed to let their hair grow a little. "Now I understand why Kanada is the best place in Auschwitz," she thought. Even though they were fed the same soup, they served it in the evening as well. They let them bathe in a pool with cold water, and although the water was dirty, it was water nonetheless. They were also given a change of clothes, which they were allowed to wash. This meant that they could maintain a certain level of cleanliness. They worked sitting down. She remained living in the same block, though, which fortunately allowed her to be close to Miriam. "I think she's the only person I have in the world," she thought. Her work consisted mainly of inspecting false-bottomed suitcases, where the most valuable objects were found, as well as the folds and lining of dresses, coats, and hats. When they found jewelry or money, they handed it over to the SS, who in turn gave it to some Jewish jewelers. These men inspected the jewels with small magnifying glasses and appraised them. In the suitcases they found gold and silver menorahs of different sizes and with different numbers of branches; tea sets and silverware, some plated in gold; paintings by French impressionists; jewelry boxes with pearl and diamond necklaces, and gold and platinum rings with diamonds, sapphires, and rubies; as well as bracelets, chains and Swiss watches. The furs and clothing were handed over straight away to be sent to Germany. She had never seen so many jewels, valuable objects and money at the same time. There were boxes with jewels and silverware, which the SS confiscated immediately to send back to Germany to finance the war, but they also stole what they could beforehand. The female guards inspected the prisoners from head to toe, not only when they went to the bathroom but also when they left the warehouse in the evening. There were loose women among the guards, as well as lesbians.

One evening while leaving Kanada, Varinia was frisked more thoroughly than normal by one of the guards. This irked her, and she shoved the woman. The guard slapped her, blew her whistle, and detained her with the help of several other guards. At that moment a lieutenant appeared, a tall, young man whom she'd never noticed before, and he intervened.

"What's going on here?" the lieutenant shouted.

"This Jewish bitch pushed me!" the guard responded.

"Why?"

"I don't know."

"Did you catch her stealing something?"

"No . . . I don't have anything," Varinia put in shyly.

"How dare you address me!" shouted the Nazi.

He ordered another guard to frisk her and found nothing.

"Follow me!" the lieutenant commanded.

Varinia felt her heart stop. "God, protect me . . . I shouldn't have pushed her, but I couldn't permit this lewd woman to grab my breasts and crotch whenever she wants, with a smile on her face, even though I always do all I can to avoid it," she thought. The lieutenant took her to his office. Shaking like a leaf, she furrowed her brow and touched the blood spilling from her lower lip. She feared the worst. "If I'm incredibly lucky, they'll send me to clean the latrines . . . if not, they'll kill me . . ."

They walked through a pavilion with a long corridor lined with offices that all looked the same. His office was simple, but clean, and private. There was a portrait of the Führer hanging above the desk, and a flag with the swastika in the corner. In front of the desk were a couple of chairs, and next to it was a table with a water heater, a few cups, a tin of coffee, another of sugar, and several bottles of schnapps. There was also a small leather armchair. She noticed that the office had two doors: one half-open and the other closed. The first one seemed to lead to a room with a bed, and she supposed that the other led to a bathroom. He asked her to take a seat, which left her speechless, and she obeyed without a word. Then he took out a piece of cotton and wiped the blood from her lip himself; she was so intimidated that she didn't dare to look him in the eye. Then he offered her a coffee, which she accepted with a nod. He prepared it himself and handed it to her. When she took a sip, she closed her eyes and thought: "Thank you, God, this coffee with sugar is the best thing that has happened to me since I came to this pigsty." He asked her to remove the handkerchief from her head. She did so, feeling even more intimidated. Her hair, yellow as the sun, had grown a little, and parts of it were bristly while others had begun to curl. She held the cup with both hands and savored every sip slowly, closing her eyes and breathing in deeply. Even though she was still shaking, all her attention was focused on the coffee. It was the best coffee she'd had in her life. He stared at her without uttering a word, taking in her perfect features, her profile like that on a Greek coin. Her beauty was radiant, despite the fact that she had grown extremely thin and was wearing the threadbare clothes of a prisoner.

"What's your name?"

"Varinia."

"How can a Jewish girl be so beautiful and have such blond hair?"

"I'm not Jewish. I'm Polish, and I'm a Catholic."

"You have spirit. I've been watching you work; you're very meticulous and reliable."

She didn't respond.

"From tomorrow on, I want you to come clean my office, bedroom, and bathroom, and to take care of my clothes."

"Yes, as you wish, Lieutenant."

"I want you to be here just before seven o'clock in the morning."

"Yes, sir."

"I'll tell the guard about your new tasks, but you must go to work in Kanada afterward."

"Yes, Lieutenant."

She finished drinking her coffee, and he told her to go. She barely glanced up at him as she left, and on the way back to the barracks she thought: "Since when has there been a friendly Nazi? This miserable man yells at me, and then later he treats me well . . ."

When she arrived at the barracks, she learned that some of her fellow prisoners had been arrested for organizing an underground resistance movement with some of the male prisoners. Four girls who worked at the Krupp factory making explosives were part of a group planning a sabotage operation against the Nazis, because they had learned that there were orders to execute them. Their aim was to blow up the crematoria. Little by little, they had stolen gunpowder and ammunitions, handing them over to the male prisoners so they could make homemade bombs. They did this until they were found out, mercilessly tortured, and made to confess the conspiracy. Two of them died while being tortured.

Varinia wondered over and over again why the lieutenant had given her a cup of coffee instead of punishing her. She was worried that the penalty would come later, and this terrified her. "These Nazis are capable of doing anything," she thought. In fact, no one slept a wink

221

that night; they lay awake worrying about the fate awaiting their fellow prisoners, whom they all loved, among them Roza Robota, a young Jewish leader.

The next day she went to work as she did every day and, minutes before seven o'clock, the guard ordered her to go clean the lieutenant's office. The woman let out a mocking laugh, which confused her. Nevertheless, she wasn't allowed to leave before being frisked. She went to the office and knocked on the door, but no one answered. She decided to go in to do her job and found that the door was unlocked. She began looking around for cleaning tools, but found nothing. She left the office and saw a small room that appeared to be used for storage at the end of the corridor. Next to it was a communal washroom for the officers. She went into the washroom, leaving the door half open so she could hear if anyone was coming, and began to wash one body part at time, as the French usually do. The water felt like balm. "Water, my God, clean, warm water!" she said to herself. She washed herself as best she could, although she only had the same dirty clothes to wear. Nevertheless, she had never felt so clean. Then she went to the tiny storeroom and took out a broom, a bucket, and rags to clean and dust with. She took them to the lieutenant's office and began to clean everything with the utmost care, so that he would have nothing to reproach her for. She made the bed, swept and dusted the small bedroom and office, and cleaned the bathroom. She washed the dirty clothes in the bathroom, hanging them to dry in the shower, and polished his boots. She left everything sparkling and went back to Kanada to continue her work.

That same day they hung the two Jewish women who had survived the torture sessions, in the central square and in front of everyone, for conspiring against the Third Reich. The Nazis achieved their objective because everyone, especially the women, were horrified. They warned them again not to flee, because for each person who did, the SS would execute ten of their fellow prisoners, and no one wanted to have the deaths of innocent people on their conscience. After the hanging, they allowed the women to walk freely through the square to see the executed women "up close." Varinia didn't go near them, and she was overcome with nausea once again. She suddenly felt someone grab her by the arm, and she whirled around, frightened. It was Sergei! They look at each other and, although they said nothing, each felt pity for the other.

222

"It's not possible, my dear Sergei," she said, tears coming to her eyes. "Don't let on that we know each other, otherwise they'll separate us immediately."

"This is the best thing that has happened to me since I came to this hell. But when did you arrive? Did you hear from Boris before you came? Does he know we have a son? Have you seen my family? What happened to Olga, Sonitzya, and your father?"

Overwhelmed with emotion from seeing her, Serge didn't know where to begin.

"When the war broke out, we stopped hearing from him. My mother, sister and I wrote to him to tell him that little Boris had been born, but we never received an answer because, as you know, the mail was being intercepted. I don't know if Boris knows you have a son. I haven't seen anyone from your family or mine for a long time. Have you seen my mother and my sister?"

"No, Sergei. I haven't seen anyone from our past life. I've only made friends with some of the women I've met here. The only thing I found, in Kanada, although I'm not completely sure, is the vicuña shawl Boris sent us from Bolivia, which I wanted with all my heart to keep. They were using it as a rag."

Sergei turned pale.

"And . . . what does that mean?"

"I don't know. Maybe they're in a barracks we don't have access to. This place is so big. Every time I meet people from other barracks I ask them about our families, but no one knows anything."

"My mother arrived on the verge of death because of her asthma, and I begged Sonitzya not to leave her. I saw them go together."

"Where do you work?"

"In a coal mine, just look at my hands and clothes. Tell me about what happened to you, to my nephew . . ."

"By miracle, I was able to leave him with Ewa, my neighbor and dear friend. We . . ."

Suddenly a whistle blew, and they separated without saying another word.

That night, the female prisoners cried more than usual. Two days later, the young men who hadn't been betrayed laid the dynamite and blew up Crematorium III. They killed three SS officers, and twenty-seven men escaped. In retaliation, the SS executed two hundred and fifty Jews chosen at random.

Varinia went every day at the same time to clean the lieutenant's office. When she saw that everyone was going off to their posts, she took the opportunity to wash her clothes alongside his, to wash herself, and to change her uniform. Afterward, she would go back to Kanada to continue her work. The lieutenant stared at her constantly; she noticed this and it made her nervous. And, without even realizing it, she began to seek out his gaze. Despite this, he never said a word to her, nor her to him.

He was a well-built man in his early forties, tall, muscular, and thin, with a perfectly square jaw and, curiously enough, a cleft chin just like Boris's. His features were proportioned and harmonious, his eyes green, his hair light brown and graying at the temples, which gave him an air of distinction. He wore a ring with his family coat of arms on his little finger. The Nazis must have considered him a model Aryan. He was always impeccably dressed in his Nazi uniform, his cap on and his boots shining as he walked around the warehouse. He carried his gloves in one hand, and in the other he held a whip, which he snapped against his legs to instill fear in the prisoners as they worked.

The days passed. Varinia continued her daily routine in silence; she didn't trust anyone. She worked with impeccable precision and efficiency so that they wouldn't kick her out of Kanada. One afternoon, the lieutenant approached her under the pretext of examining a jewel and whispered in her ear: "Come to my office tonight at eight o'clock." She trembled. "What the hell does he want? I don't want to think the worst . . . and going there at night, on top of it all . . . I have to go, dammit, otherwise he'll have me killed," she thought anxiously. She told Miriam that she had to go because he had summoned her. "Be careful . . . be very careful, my dear . . . I'll be waiting for you to come back."

Night fell and the hour arrived; she mustered up her courage and went there running. She was panting when she arrived. The door was ajar. She went in and found him leaning against the wall beside the door, a glass of whiskey in his hand. When he saw her come in, he took her by the arm, cornered her against the wall, and closed the door with his foot. "Don't move, and don't scream," he told her. He was probably twice her age. He put his glass down on the table and, made intrepid by the alcohol, placed his hands on her breasts, fondling her. He touched her buttocks, slid his hand between her thighs until he reached her pubic area, and slipped his finger into her

224

vagina. She was trembling; she closed her eyes and thought: "No, God, not this one too! How stupid I was . . . why else would he have asked me to come?" He clung to Varinia's body so tightly that she could feel his erect member rubbing against her slender body. Suddenly he commanded: "Go to the bedroom." She was shivering, but he was so drunk he didn't even notice. "Take your clothes off." She stood there, naked, timidly covering her breasts with her hands. "Take your panties off and don't cover yourself, I want to see you . . . you're so beautiful, I've wanted you for a long time now," he said. She obeyed. He took off his clothes and led her to the bed by the arm. He threw himself on top of her, biting her and licking her breasts. He opened her legs and penetrated her immediately, which caused her pain because her vagina was dry. He penetrated her again and again. While he took pleasure in Varinia's body, she, her eyes wide as saucers, lay there feeling broken, but there was nothing left to do but endure it. Within seconds, the Nazi ejaculated and collapsed on top of her. She thought she was going to suffocate under the German's weight. Her whole body hurt, but what hurt her the most was the situation she found herself in. He rolled off of her and said: "Get out of here, go quickly." Seeing that he was barely conscious, she took her time washing her vagina and getting dressed. In the corridor she ran into two fellow prisoners from Kanada: Esther and Ruth, two young and very pretty girls in their twenties. They looked at each other without saying a word, then looked away. Varinia thought: "So this is the Nazis' whorehouse! I'm such an idiot! These damned opportunists . . . weren't they forbidden from sleeping with Jews? Not that they care . . ." And with the little strength she had left she ran back to the barracks. When she arrived she found Miriam waiting up for her, and she told her: "The bastard took advantage of me." "That's what I thought, but I didn't want to tell you. I'm so sorry, you can't imagine how sorry I am," her friend replied. "Thank God I'm barely menstruating, so I'm protected." "Kanada is one big orgy for the Nazis." She lay down on the straw bedding, feeling emptier than ever. She tried to fall asleep, but it was virtually impossible.

Sergei worked twelve hours a day in a coal mine. The only advantage was that they were able to eat coal and secretly share bits of it with their fellow prisoners so as to prevent dysentery. But the fateful day arrived. Sergei was young, tall and in better physical condition than his workmates, so they decided to transfer him to another section.

They assigned him to the sector where the gas chambers and crematoria were, where the Sonderkommando kapos were in charge, under the supervision of the SS. The prisoners were replacing Germans who had been unable to withstand the work. Many had become sick or depressed, and some of them even lost their minds. These men were taken to a summer home occupied by the SS a few kilometers from Auschwitz in the hopes that the change of scenery would help them to forget.

Once there, Sergei and his fellow prisoners were made to line up, and the leaders of the Sonderkommando gave them instructions. They were assigned to sleep in a nearby barracks. Among them were Jews of different nationalities, Gypsies, and Russian soldiers who had been taken prisoner. They were all young and relatively stronger than the others. They were horrified by the scenario, but they threatened to kill them if they told anyone about their new work assignment. When Sergei saw the corpses piled one on top of the other and smelled the stench, he was horror-stricken, as were his fellow prisoners. Then he saw the gas chambers and the crematoria and thought: "God . . . this isn't real . . . this can't be happening . . . these mountains of corpses, piled high and thrown away as if they were garbage, like that mountain of shoes. They are babies, children, old people, men, women . . . damned Nazi dogs! A thousand curses on them! This is unforgivable . . . nobody, not even God, will forgive them for this . . . because this will be brought to light . . . and my mother and sister? Oh God! Black Madonna! I hope . . . you wouldn't have allowed them to die in this unspeakable place . . . this is Hitler's apocalypse . . . a diabolical killing machine . . . fucking bastards!" He wept, doubling over and beginning to vomit, although hardly anything came out because of the lack of food. The retching came from deep inside his stomach and his heart. He suddenly felt a rifle butt in his back. "Get up, you filthy Jew!" Sergei stood up. He was taller than his captor, and without saying a word, he looked down at him with contempt, his nostrils flaring.

They were given a kind of mask and some work gloves to prevent infection. The trains kept arriving with thousands of people onboard, most of whom were sent to the chambers. A Nazi would suddenly see a young, pretty girl that he liked, and he would draw her aside, rape her, and send her to be killed. They all walked to the showers, accompanied by music played by a chamber orchestra comprised of fellow Jews. After seeing the looks on the musicians' faces, the victims, naked and covering their private parts with their hands, could imagine the fate that awaited them. In the depths of their hearts they knew that getting on that train was a journey of no return—at least that's what they had observed since the beginning of the war. Once inside, they were locked in, and the most chilling screams anyone has ever heard rang out. Then a soldier climbed to the roof on a ladder and dropped Zyklon B pellets as big as bricks down the vents. Ten or fifteen minutes later, all was silent. They had suffocated to death, each and every one of them. After about half an hour, they opened the doors and Sergei and the others had to remove the corpses before they stiffened. When he went in and saw the pinkish bodies, he felt like he was about to faint; his legs went numb and he began to tremble, so much so that a Nazi shouted at him: "You Jewish pussy, if you don't do your job, you'll end up like them!" He and his new workmates removed the bodies, hauling them as if they were sacks of potatoes, until the room was left empty for the next group. They saw that the walls were stained with blood, and there was vomit and excrement on the floor. The bodies were taken in wheelbarrows to the crematoria, where they were incinerated, or to the pile of corpses, where a tractor with a huge bucket carried them to the vast, deep mass graves, where the bodies were burned. They had begun to do this because in the summer the corpses emitted a foul smell, even when they were buried.

The killing was carried out on an industrial scale. Sergei's group worked into the night, and they were better fed than the others. Sergei was unable to eat, though, let alone sleep, despite the fact that he was starving. He couldn't get the memory of his mother and sister out of his mind. He kept returning to the day they were separated. "God, Black Madonna . . . what became of them?" Despite the exhaustion, no one was able to sleep, and when they did, they had nightmares in which they relived the same scenario. Everyone was in a state of shock, and they were so depressed that they didn't even speak to one other; they were also afraid to talk in case there was an informer amongst them. The cries, screams, and sobs could be heard day and night in that sector, in spite of the Nazis' attempts to silence them. How could they be silenced if the killing machine ran twenty-four hours a day?

That night, the young men heard the SS officers getting drunk and talking loudly in an adjoining house. The Nazis drank constantly, and even when they weren't drunk they still reeked of booze. Upon hearing screams, Sergei got out of bed and saw through a chink in the wall that a couple of Nazis were raping a boy and a girl between ten and twelve years old in the middle of the courtyard. They were howling in panic and pain.

The next day they had to continue with their work. Sergei couldn't find a wheelbarrow, and he had to drag the bodies with a kind of stick given to him by a soldier. He had to put the upper part of stick into the neck of the bodies, which weighed barely thirty kilos, and take them to the pile of corpses. He noticed that many of them had traces of blood on their nails. He imagined that they had scratched the walls of the gas chambers as they clung to life. He tried not to look at their faces and prayed incessantly in an effort to evade reality. He entrusted the souls of the dead to God, offering to make whatever sacrifice he needed to. He felt guilty. "They're already dead, without suffering, fear, or pain," he told himself, trying to ease his conscience. "They're in heaven now, with God and their loved ones."

Sergei observed that the victims' hair, which was piled in a storehouse, was used to make mattresses. He also saw they dumped the ashes from the crematoria into a fertilizer truck. He saw the driver pay a captain; the dead were being sold as fertilizer. He also saw that in another storehouse they were removing the skin from the corpses to make lampshades and extracting the fat from their bodies to make soap. The Nazis forced the prisoners to perform these tasks. That night, Sergei tossed back and forth in bed, overwhelmed and confused by his thoughts. "This could only have been possible with the help of many German civilians. Don't the people who live around here know what's going on? What about the train conductors and truck drivers? Or the people who manage the telephones and telegraphs? The ones who do business with the bodies? I'm sure many Germans know . . . they have to know! Don't they have a friend, a neighbor, or a relative who disappeared and was never heard from again? And what about the companies that have factories here using Jewish slave labor? And the detentions and public arrests of Jews who disappear . . .? How come nobody says anything? Or maybe the Nazis want everyone to know, to continue to spread terror? The most likely thing is that they've all been killed, everyone except Boris." He began to cry. "My father has been missing for four years. And the shawl Varinia told me about? What could that mean? And Boris? In Bolivia, and no news from him since the war began .

. . my God . . . what is this?" Sergei continued to weep, not caring what his fellow prisoners said.

"I'm dying slowly and painfully . . . a victim of this inexplicable and unforgivable horror . . . I feel like I'm on the verge of death . . . I'm more dead than alive, I'm dead even before death because of a situation that defies reason, intelligence, common sense, charity, love of one's neighbor. Something inside me is dying rapidly . . . and time goes by so slowly . . . There's a license to kill here, where we live . . . . I've been a zombie for three days now . . . If I'm able to fall asleep, it's only for a short time, and my own shrieks from my nightmares wake me up. I'm destroyed. I've become a monstrosity. I asked the captain to transfer me to a different sector, and he beat me. No one in their right mind could accept this. After this massacre I can no longer believe in anything or anyone. I have no reason to live, no one to live for . . . I'm not worth anything. I have nothing and no one. It makes no sense to continue living in these conditions . . . no one deserves to live among the dead, not even if it's to save their skin. They say this war is by land, air, and sea, that it spans five continents, and that it looks like it will never end. If it's already gone on for five years, it can go on for another five, or only you, God, know how long. They'll most probably end up killing us all for being Jews, so that we take the truth of this situation with us to the grave."

He suddenly got out of bed and left the barracks, even though it was forbidden. It was a dark night, and he began to walk as if hypnotized, reciting the Lord's Prayer. Transfixed and deranged, he headed toward the electric fence. "Forgive me, Father . . . set me free and receive me into your world, where my loved ones are," he said to himself. He closed his eyes tightly and threw himself against the fence. The light in the area dimmed for a moment. Sergei died, electrocuted, his charred, black body stuck to the fence. Suddenly a whistle was heard and a spotlight illuminated the body. An SS officer said: "Bah . . . another suicide . . . we saved another bullet," and ordered the body to be taken down.

The next day his fellow prisoners threw his burned body onto the pile of corpses to be cremated. One of them shed tears, thinking: "I'll probably be the next one . . . no one can bear this."

Chapter 10
Poland, late 1944

"I'll be waiting for you at the same time tonight," the lieutenant told Varinia very slowly when she reluctantly went up to him to hand him a small cloth jewelry box. He recognized the value of things immediately. He was a connoisseur of fine objects, probably as a result of his family background. She turned even more pale than she already was. "Bastard," she thought. "I've fallen into his clutches and he's going to use me as his sexual slave. Dammit! This is unspeakably shameful. Damn these abusive exploiters. I hate this soldier . . . I hate him . . . bastard. And he's even capable of killing me if I refuse, so I have no choice but to go. God, protect me . . ."

Since orders are orders, she ran over to his office once again that night. The door was ajar and he was standing there as before, leaning against the wall with a glass of whiskey in his hand, his hair disheveled. She closed the door and noticed that the smell of cigarette smoke pervaded the room. She also saw that the German had his shirt half-open, revealing his chest hair. Without saying a word, he signaled her to come closer. She obeyed. He put his glass down on the side table. He took the handkerchief from her head and began, with unexpected gentleness, to slowly undress her. He unbuttoned the upper part of her prisoner's dress, the garment grazing her alabaster white skin. He (less intoxicated than the previous time) noticed that she wasn't wearing a bra. Despite her thinness, her breasts were full and her nipples were like strawberries. Although they were small, they retained their youthful firmness, and this began to drive the German crazy. Her hard nipples seemed to call the man's hands and mouth. Her threadbare underwear covered her intimate parts. She did not dare to look him in the eye because she felt ashamed, as if he were seeing her naked for the first time. He grabbed her by the nape of the neck and said with ironic softness: "Do what I say, do what I want you to do, woman . . . don't think of anything other than giving me pleasure . . ." He lifted her chin firmly with his finger, forcing her to stare into his eyes. With eager desire, he cupped her breasts and, wetting his thumbs with his own saliva, he caressed her nipples rhythmically. Then he pulled her head back and began to kiss her closed eyelids and neck; he placed his teeth gently over her left earlobe and ran his tongue over it, as if he were exploring her. Then he searched for her mouth, licking the corners of her lips and inserting his tongue, which met hers. He kissed her even deeper. He took her hands, interlaced their fingers, and lifted her arms, backing her against the wall. He continued to kiss her without pause, without saying a word. He began to kiss her breasts and nipples with rare passion. She acquiesced in everything. He put no pressure on her. Her breathing became agitated, and she felt moistness between her thighs. She, too, was becoming excited, which confused her. She lost her train of thought and unconsciously let herself go, nearly fainting. She sought out his mouth and found it warm, despite the taste of alcohol and tobacco. Her apprehension began to fade. They kissed endlessly. She felt his tongue and offered her mouth, moving her tongue until their mouths were inundated with saliva. She breathed deeply. When he touched her nipples with his tongue, their first encounter vanished from her mind. She gave herself to him completely, without thinking. He kept his mouth glued to hers. She saw that his eyes remained closed the entire time, and that his nostrils were quivering. Varinia's breathing became more agitated, and she yearned to be penetrated. It was a desire beyond reason, beyond hate, beyond the fact that this man was her captor. She realized this in a fraction of a second, and it excited her even more. "Undress me," she heard. They both moved as if hypnotized. He continued kissing her as they walked, stumbling. She unbuttoned his shirt and took it off. Then she unbuckled his belt, unbuttoned his pants, and pulled them down. All he had on were his underpants now, and she had to take those off as well. He was completely naked, panting intensely. He picked her up, sat down on one of the office chairs, and placed her on top of him. She felt him penetrate her, his firm erection awash in a sea of moisture. She began to move frenetically, clutching the skin of the lieutenant's back. She didn't want to think about a name; thinking of that would break the final barrier. She gave herself over to pleasure. She felt his hands, his fingers, lifting her up in the air. Her buttocks vibrated from the pressure. He thrust into her forcefully. He heard her breathing and searched desperately for her mouth. She kissed him, smothering herself with his mouth. She wanted to say something, to cry out, to beg, but she didn't dare. The silence of the room was enveloped by an animal roar. She knew she was about to come. Then one wave after another shook her, her pelvis and then her entire body trembling in an endless convulsion. She wanted to take in a breath of air, but she couldn't. He separated his lips from hers, and she breathed in. Then she let out an interminable sigh that nearly split her in two . . . All of a sudden, he lifted her off of him and said: "Go now." She picked up her dress, covering her breasts with it, and dressed so quickly that she forgot her handkerchief in the office. She left running.

She arrived at the barracks and lay down in her place next to Miriam.

"You smell like a woman."

"What do you mean?"

"That you smell of sex. Who were you with?"

"The lieutenant."

The next day they saw each other in Kanada. He approached her inconspicuously and said: "You were delicious." She thought: "I'm nothing more than a pleasure-giving machine to this man. I hate him and I hate myself . . . how low I've fallen," and she began to cry, making sure that he couldn't see.

Rumors that the war was coming to an end were intensifying day by day. The kapos passed along everything they heard from the SS. They learned of the Allied landings in Normandy. They also learned, a few months later, after the Resistance uprising, that Paris had been liberated. Vichy France had vanished and the new Free France was established under Charles de Gaulle's leadership. They also learned that Wehrmacht soldiers of the highest rank had planted a bomb to kill the Führer; it had exploded, but, to their great disappointment, it didn't kill him. "Even his generals are turning their backs on him," they commented to one another. "Hitler seems to be a cat with nine lives because he always comes out unscathed," they added. They took all this as proof that Hitler was losing the war, and they were filled with hope. "We have to hold out," said the detainees, " . . . that is, if they don't kill us first."

Meanwhile, the Red Army was rapidly advancing, regaining territory and occupying countries in eastern Europe. Their purpose was clear: to impose the communist ideology and turn these countries into satellite states of the Soviet Union. When they arrived in Poland, they discovered a concentration camp in Majdanek that provided evidence of the atrocities committed against the Jews. They communicated this to the Allies, but no action was taken.

The days went by, and Varinia couldn't stop thinking about the lieutenant, although she did her best to ignore him. "You were delicious," she remembered him saying. "Abuser!" she said to herself. Minutes later, though, she would recall the passion she had experienced with him and glance at him from the corner of her eye. She would see, all of a sudden, that he was staring at her. She noticed that he didn't look at other women, only at her. Varinia started to observe him more closely, through different eyes. He even began to look attractive. He appeared to be a refined, distinguished man, always well-dressed, but he was also ruthless and arrogant, like all the SS officers. She said to herself: "All of these men are vile, abominable abusers, cruel and murderous exploiters." And then she thought: "Why can't I stop thinking about the time we had sex on the chair? He seduced me that time . . . strangely enough, when he touched me, he did so gently, even though he was drunk . . . of course it was only sex, very far from making love. What makes me angry is that I was aroused to the point that my vagina became wet and I was breathing heavily, and I didn't hide it. Is it because of the lack of love? The infinite solitude in which I find myself? I remember the time I made love with Boris; it was extraordinary, but different. He didn't seduce me like the Nazi did. Forgive me, God! How can I think something like that? Boris wasn't as experienced as the Nazi, whom I detest. I love Boris, and I will love him all my life. And from our love, our son was born. And when this cursed war ends, if I survive, the first thing I'll do is go get my son from Ewa's house, and then I'll go to Bolivia with him, and we'll stay there forever. It's strange: what kind of desire can I possibly arouse with this corpse-like, haggard face? I'm missing teeth, I'm as skinny as a street dog, my hair is short and wiry, my skin dry and wrinkled, and my clothes always dirty and tattered from work. I'm one meter eighty tall but I must weight around forty kilos. The lieutenant only likes me because I satisfy his sexual desires, and he must sleep with many other women who work in Kanada, as well as with German prostitutes, who abound here."

Things continued on in the same way in Kanada, with Varinia and the lieutenant unable to take their eyes off each other. They were aware of each other's movements at all times. One afternoon he whispered in her ear: "I'll be waiting for you tonight, but come at midnight." She, as always, did not respond. "God, what will he do to me this time?"

Late that same night, she ran over and knocked on the door. He opened it, and oddly, he was wearing his uniform and was not holding his usual glass of whiskey. He was sober. When he saw her, he pulled her by the arm, closed the door, and handed her a female Nazi uniform. "Put it on immediately and don't ask any questions," he instructed her. As usual, she obeyed. She took off the men's coat she was wearing and put on the white blouse and brownish-green jacket and skirt over her striped dress. They were far too big for her. She also put on some men's boots, which fit her perfectly. He gave her a cap, white gloves, a navy-blue cloak, and a baton identical to the one carried by the Madame and her entourage, which they used to beat whomever they pleased. He also handed her a black tie. As she didn't know how to tie it, he, annoyed and without looking her in the eye, tied it for her as quickly as possible. In the meantime, she listened to the moans of pleasure from women and men in the adjoining offices.

She didn't understand what was going on. Everything happened so quickly. He told her: "Follow me and don't open your mouth." He picked up a briefcase, turned off the light, and they left the office. They walked a couple of blocks. She couldn't believe she was wearing clean clothes. They climbed into a jeep and headed toward the main gate of Auschwitz. She was trembling with fear. Her teeth were chattering. "Don't look, and make sure they see the baton in your hand . . . you look Aryan," he said. With an authoritative and smug look on his face, he handed over some documents. The guard shone a flashlight on them, looking them over for quite some time, while sweat began to drip from her face and armpits. Then the soldier shouted: "Open the gates!" She was so confused that she could do nothing but obey. She didn't dare to move, let alone ask what was going on. She thought: "I'm leaving Auschwitz . . . but this is unbelievable, no one gets out of this death camp alive." She feared the worst. "What's he going to do to me? Will he kill me? God help me, I'm so lost . . . God, don't abandon me . . . I've been through terrible times . . . but I beg you, don't abandon me, I'm so afraid." She wiped her sweat with her gloves. "I shouldn't be afraid of fear, that's what my beloved Boris told me."

She began to recite the Creed with all her soul, repeating it over and over again from memory. She felt extremely hot from the anxiety and all the clothes she had on, but she didn't dare to take off the cloak. The lieutenant turned onto a road with a sign that said Oswiecim. Where was he taking her? All she knew was that it was a town near Auschwitz. She felt a tremendous urge to cry, but she controlled herself. "Will he leave me in the street so I can escape?

No, how naïve I am . . . how stupid . . . Nazis are Nazis through and through," she said. They drove for about ten minutes and arrived in a small, poorly lit village, with a humble main street on which there was a sign that said Hotel. The lieutenant stopped the car in front of it and said: "Let's get out." She breathed a huge sigh of relief. "At least it's a hotel and not some field in the middle of nowhere where he could kill me and leave my body there to be eaten by forest animals and worms. But a hotel . . ." They got out of the car and went in. It was an old hotel, probably the only one in town. It had antique furniture, high ceilings, and dim lighting. At the reception desk he presented his papers, which read Mr. and Mrs. von Deken. "Now this guy passes me off as his wife . . . and to think, I don't even know his name," she thought. They went up to their room; it wasn't luxurious, but it was clean. She was still shaking, and she was sweating so much that her blouse clung to her body.

"You can go have a shower," he said.

She couldn't believe it. She was going to bathe in clean, hot water for the first time in more than a year. She stepped underneath the shower head, so delighted with the running water that she didn't even think about what the Nazi might do to her. He wouldn't do anything worse than what he had done already. She thought only about how wonderful it felt to wash herself with hot water and a soap-like detergent. She washed her body and hair gently, using a sponge full of foam. It was like a miracle. She took such a long time in the shower that the mirror fogged up from the steam. She dried her body with an old but clean towel. She took the opportunity to wash her striped uniform with the same detergent, and she hung it in the shower to dry. The water dripping off it was brown. He knocked on the bathroom door and passed her a beige silk negligee trimmed with lace. She touched the fabric and thought: "It's silk . . . might it have belonged to a very refined Jewish woman? God, make me forget that hell for a few moments." She put it on silently, combed back the little hair she had with her fingers, and came out of the bathroom with her hair wet. Her breasts were visible, as was her pubic area, which was almost hairless, accentuating her mons Veneris and making her even more attractive. He, still dressed, was drinking a glass of wine, smoking a cigarette, and listening to Bach on an RCA Victor record player that was in the room. When he saw her he was so amazed that he stood up from his chair and thought: "This is the most beautiful woman I've ever seen, even though she's lost a few teeth . . . she's a

235

masterpiece of nature . . . Helen of Troy must have looked like this .
. ."

She didn't smile, and she didn't dare to look at him. He took her
hand and kissed it; when he saw the prisoner's number tattooed on
her arm, he shut his eyes. The lieutenant offered her a seat at an
impeccably laid table, which had a floor-length white tablecloth and
a platter of hot food on it. He helped her sit down, offered her a
cigarette, which she accepted but left on the table. She didn't know
how to smoke, but she knew she could exchange it for something on
the black market. She was afraid of him; she had never stopped
fearing him because Nazis were unpredictable. Most of them were
psychopaths, especially the ones at Auschwitz.

On the platter was a fish fillet with sauce and potatoes cooked with
salt and herbs, and on the table were two glasses and a bottle of white
wine. He offered to serve her first, which surprised her. She waited
for him to serve himself, and they began to eat. He thought: "This
woman isn't just any Pole; she has the manners of a queen." Then
he poured her some wine. Varinia was so hungry that she could have
eaten with her hands. The only thing he asked, breaking the silence,
was:

"Are you of aristocratic descent?"

"Yes. My last name is Horodinsky. My paternal grandfather was a
marquis and was related to Polish royalty. But that's all in the past.
In Auschwitz we're all the same, we're all just a number," she replied
without looking at him.

The only thing she was interested in was eating. She began to sweat,
trying to restrain herself from swallowing quickly, but she couldn't
help it and she choked. The lieutenant, seeing that she hadn't drunk
much, picked up her wine glass, extended his arm, and made her take
a sip. The wine dripped from her mouth, down her neck. He dried
her lips with his fingers and stuck his thumb deep into her mouth.
She looked into his eyes for the first time. Varinia, who hadn't drunk
alcohol for such a long time, felt dizzy and relaxed, and thought: "I'm
prostituting myself for a hot shower, a dinner, a bed, clean sheets,
and a room with heating . . . after living in that subhuman camp,
you'd give yourself for anything. I'm not worth a thing, but I don't
care . . . this is paradise . . . it's sex . . . just sex."

After dinner, the lieutenant, burning with desire from the alcohol, as
always, stood up, helped her stand, took her in his arms, and ran a
finger up and down her spine, making her shiver and close her eyes.

Then he kissed her neck, opened her mouth and pushed his tongue deep inside. He slipped off the straps of her negligee, and it slid to the ground. He began to kiss and caress her breasts while he stroked her pubic area and inner labia. She felt her wetness begin to run down her thighs. He put his hand in her vagina and was pleased to find it so lubricated. He began to stroke her in her most sensitive place and inserted two fingers into her vagina, noticing that her inner labia were engorged. She felt faint from pleasure and arched backward. He wiped up some of her vaginal fluid with his forefinger, sucked his fingers, made her taste it, and asked: "Salty?" "No, sweet," she replied. She was as turned on as he was. Was it the effect of the wine? Still standing, locked in an embrace, they made their way to the bed, kissing. She lay down and he undressed, turned off the light, threw himself on top of her, and began kissing her as if he knew her body by heart. At the same time, he stroked the tip of her nipples with his forefinger and thumb. She was so aroused that she began to moan to the point that she became short of breath. Varinia felt like she was drowning from the excitement. Her heart was beating so fast that she could hear it pounding in her ears. He handcuffed her to the bronze bar at the head of the bed. "You're mine," he whispered in her ear. He opened her thighs and penetrated her, slapping her buttocks and legs gently, which excited her even more. She gave herself over to the pleasure of this sweet violence. His member slid in and out as if it were covered in oil. She began to moan with pleasure, feeling as if she were going mad with desire. She spread her legs wider and wider, supporting them on the shoulders or pressing them against the back of the nameless man. They were both covered in sweat. He removed the handcuffs and they rolled around together on the bed. She kissed him as if she had lost her mind. He changed her position, and she took pleasure in everything he did to her. The German inserted two fingers into her vagina, and this gave her so much pleasure that she began to writhe as one orgasm after another rippled through her body. He reveled in seeing her come again and again. "You're multi-orgasmic," he told her. The lieutenant continued to moan with pleasure, and he was suddenly overwhelmed by the desire to come. "I can't take it anymore," he cried, penetrating her again and thrusting until they finished together.

They both collapsed, exhausted. He put his arms around her, and they fell asleep for several hours. After quite some time, accustomed to getting up early and full of energy from the food, she slid quietly out of bed and ate what was left of the dinner, including what the German had left on his plate. She finished everything. To her, it was the most delicious fish she had ever eaten in her whole life. Then she put the dirty dishes in the hallway so the room wouldn't smell of food. She picked up the cigarette, stole two more from him, and put them in the pocket of the uniform he had given her. Then she washed her face. She thought: "If I survive, I'll do nothing but bathe and eat all day, I'll have a pantry with endless amounts of stored food . . . I'll also buy the most elegant, modern, and expensive clothes." Then she thought: "But . . . I could escape, now, while he's sleeping . . . but what if he's just pretending to be asleep? He'll grab me, hit me, and shoot me without a moment's hesitation. His gun is there, in its holster, hanging on the chair. And if I take it, aim it at him, and run away? What if it's not loaded? He would laugh in my face, pick up the phone, and tell the Nazi guards in the hotel lobby to stop me and put me in the gas chamber. I'm nothing other than his lover . . . his prostitute . . . his sex slave." She slipped back into bed, naked, and began to observe the German. He was snoring, which she found funny. She saw that he had a tattoo on the underside of his arm; it was his blood type. She thought: "When the war is over, God willing, they'll all fall . . . with that mark on them, they've dug their own graves." She couldn't sleep anymore. She took the covers off and saw that his member was erect while he slept. She got up and looked out the window; they were in an area with many trees. A few hours later, the German woke up. He looked at her and smiled. She was awake, and she gave him a shy smile as well. "Are you hungry?" he asked. "I'm always hungry," she replied. "Sex makes you hungry. Let's shower and go to the restaurant to have breakfast." They showered together, kissing as the water poured into their mouths. They lathered each other with pleasure. He lifted her up, pressed her against the wall, lifted her leg, penetrated her, and climaxed. She acquiesced in and enjoyed everything. She stepped out of the bathtub wrapped in a large towel. She dried her body delicately, dried him with another towel, and then they both got dressed. They went down to the restaurant and she realized it was Sunday. The buffet was something she could never have imagined. She had coffee with hot milk, croissants with margarine and black current jam, and soft-boiled eggs. "I've never eaten anything so delicious, not even in the expensive hotels in Czechoslovakia where I used to spend the summer with my family," she thought.

They had breakfast in silence because the German didn't say a word and she didn't dare to speak to him. She had to wait for the "Mute" to speak to her before she said anything, just as is done with monarchs. He started flipping through the day's newspaper, although he didn't understand much because it was written in Polish. She was glad he had picked up the paper because that way she could continue eating without him watching her. The lieutenant only said what was strictly necessary. She was well-mannered, as usual, which pleased the German immensely. Who was this man? He was like any other man of Aryan appearance, but he was absolutely captivated by her charms. They finished having breakfast, and she felt like she had eaten too much, so she excused herself and went to the ladies' room where she vomited profusely. He didn't take his eyes off the bathroom door. Varinia straightened herself up as best she could, pinching her cheeks with her fingers so she wouldn't look so pale. She said to herself: "This is my chance to escape, but how . . . he must be armed." Silently, she returned to the table, but he wasn't there. As she searched for him, she heard someone playing the piano, and she went to listen. It was him; he was playing Chopin's Polonaise, Op. 53. The melody moved her, bringing back many memories of her past, of Boris and her family, a time when she was naïve, rash, and happy. Then he played more music by Chopin, which also moved her deeply. He played very well; he was clearly a cultured person. She thanked him with a timorous smile.

"Do you want to take a stroll around the town?"

"Sure."

They left the hotel and she noticed that he was armed, which frightened her. Varinia didn't understand what was going on, and she was unsure whether she should feel safe or unsafe. They walked through the nearly deserted streets. It was the middle of winter. She didn't feel cold; she was used to it. All of a sudden, they turned to look at each other, and they just stood there, staring into each other's eyes. A thousand thoughts flew through her mind, all of them troubled. She didn't understand how she, a prisoner from Auschwitz, could be walking around freely in a town in her own country, with a Nazi whose name she didn't even know. The "Mute" suddenly spoke to her again.

"Are you married? Do you have children?"

"I'm not married, and I have a son I left behind in Warsaw. And you?"

"I'm a widower, and I have two children, a boy and a girl who live with their maternal grandparents in Munich. My wife died while giving birth to our daughter."

"I'm sorry."

"What was the father of your son like?"

"He's the most wonderful man I've ever known. I still have hope that he's alive. He was able to flee to Bolivia before the war. And what was your wife like?"

"She was very much like you."

She swallowed hard, stunned. "So this bastard thinks about his dead wife while he fucks me . . . I shouldn't be surprised . . . nothing surprises me about these damned Nazis." They walked for a long time. She saw a church, and when they passed it she crossed herself, put her palms together with her fingers crossed, and began to pray silently. The German watched her without saying a word. In the distance, she suddenly noticed the black smoke rising from the crematoria and shuddered violently and undisguisedly. He saw this and decided it was time to return to the hotel. He was very courteous as they walked, letting her go first wherever they went. He went straight up to the room, which had been left impeccably clean. He put on some classical music, and when he heard Handel, who for him was German, not English, he closed his eyes. It was one of the few pleasures that lifted his spirit. The lieutenant closed the curtains, undressed, and quickly got into bed. He told her: "Get undressed, Varinia, and come here." She was stunned; it was the first time he had uttered her name. She thought he didn't know it, or that he had forgotten it. She did as she was told while he watched her, taking note of the delicate way she undressed. She slid the clothes off her body and placed them on the chair so they wouldn't become wrinkled. Naked, she slipped into the German's bed as if she had been his lover all her life. Strangely enough, she had begun to stop fearing him in bed; on the contrary, she felt comfortable with him. "We're on equal footing," she thought. "Seduce me," he told her. She threw herself on top of him, interlacing her fingers with his. She offered him her mouth, and he kissed her. She dared to whisper in his ear: "What's your name?" "Nicolaus," he replied. She began to kiss his nipples, sliding her long, slim fingers through his chest hair. Then the German began to kiss every inch of her body while she closed her eyes, enjoying it all, especially when he gently nibbled on her nipples, neck, and earlobes. He reached her pubic area and delicately opened her legs, beginning to kiss her there. Then he penetrated her. He saw that only the whites of her eyes were visible; her eyes had rolled back; she was driven mad with pleasure. She was so aroused that her jugular was throbbing; he could see the thick blue vein underneath her skin. All of a sudden she exploded in an orgasm that shook her from head to toe, and he kept going. He opened his mouth and kissed her without stopping. She followed his lead. He was burning with desire. Suddenly the Nazi turned her around and penetrated her from behind. "Touch yourself, Varinia, touch yourself, so we can finish together," he told her. She began to stroke herself while he thrust into her emphatically and passionately. He continued to penetrate her until he saw she was about to come. "Come . . . come," he told her. He ejaculated, and they finished at the same time, shuddering and sighing. It was as if they were the only two people in the world. They were so exhausted that they fell asleep. They ordered room service for lunch. She ate less and much more calmly. They didn't leave the room for the rest of the day. In a moment of pleasure, he said to her: "Varinia . . . how can you be so delicious in bed . . . how can you give yourself over to sex with such passion . . .?" She didn't know how to respond. He took her from behind, the position that, he had noticed, aroused her the most, and she clung tightly to the metal bars of the antique bed. He penetrated her so deeply that she felt as though she would faint. She evidently couldn't take anymore, and, on her knees, she began to let go of the bars and lose consciousness, dropping down softly on the bed. He pulled out of her to see what had happened. She was unresponsive. The lieutenant said to himself: "*C'est la petite mort* . . . her body can't take anymore . . ." Nicolaus got up, filled a glass with wine left over from lunch, went over to her, turned her over, lifted her neck, and made her drink a little at a time, trying to get her to react. He patted her gently on the face a few times. He waited a few moments for her to react. After what seemed like an eternity, she finally began to regain consciousness.

"What happened?"

"Varinia, I think I went too far. You experienced the 'little death.'"

"What's that?"

"It's when the body becomes overexcited and you faint. Get dressed, we have to get going."

"Can I take I shower?"

"Yes, but be quick."

When she came out of the shower he was already dressed. She put on her prisoner's uniform, then the uniform he had given her. He stared at her the entire time. Once they were ready, they went down to the lobby, where he paid the bill, then they got in the jeep and headed toward the camp. Neither of them said a word, but every so often their eyes met in the dark. When they arrived at Auschwitz, at midnight, she shuddered violently; he saw this and averted his eyes. They were stopped at the entrance gate. The lieutenant presented the falsified documents, and they let them in. They went to the Nazi's office, where she took off the uniform and was left in her striped dress; she put on her old, shabby coat, which she treasured as if it were gold, and slipped the cigarettes into her pockets without him seeing. He gave her a few bars of chocolate, which were worth a fortune in Auschwitz. She accepted them, but she wasn't pleased by the gesture. He also gave her a couple of clean striped dresses and some underwear. She accepted them and thanked him, thinking: "I can't afford to reject anything . . . how shameful . . . it seems like payment." They looked at each other one more time, and then she lowered her eyes, left the room, and started running toward her barracks. The cold chilled her to the bone. She arrived at the pigsty, which was as foul smelling as ever, and found everyone asleep with the lights out, but the room was warm thanks to the amount of people in it. She went over to Miriam, who said:

"But . . . where have you been? Thank God you're alive. I thought I'd never see you again!" They embraced warmly.

"I've become the lieutenant's lover," she said very slowly.

"I knew that . . . my dear . . . but . . . disappearing for two days? You're lucky they didn't call your name on the list."

"He must have arranged that. We left Auschwitz and went to a hotel in the town nearby."

"Be careful, my dear. These men will fuck you for the sake of fucking you, and if you don't please them, they'll kill you and find another one."

"Shhhh . . . I have to survive to find my two Borises and my family. God will forgive me. Miriam, eat these chocolates, and take this dress, it's clean."

"For these marvels, I would become a Nazi's lover too . . . and . . . what's the lieutenant like?"

"I can't explain right now . . . all I can tell you is that he's a god in bed."

"Don't trust a Nazi. Be careful, dear. There's a rumor going around that they're killing people left, right, and center, and that they're destroying the crematoria."

"And what does that mean?"

"I don't know. No one knows. But it's an open secret . . . like everything else here."

Despite the fact that Varinia cautioned her to eat slowly, Miriam gobbled down the chocolates with such speed that she made herself sick; she developed a horrible stomach ache and threw them all up in the end.

The next day, when Varinia got up, she felt a pain in her buttocks that made it difficult to walk. She thought: "What did I do to cause this discomfort? It's from too much sex, it will pass." She went to clean the lieutenant's office and found it locked, which surprised her. Then she went to Kanada and looked around for him, but he wasn't there. She thought: "Perhaps they discovered him? Please, God, don't let that happen because they'll catch me too! What have I gotten myself into? I'm such an idiot! But he forced me to follow him! Shit!"

Two days went by, and the lieutenant still hadn't appeared. Despite her efforts, she couldn't stop thinking about him. She was fascinated by the way in which he possessed her entirely, and how she surrendered herself to the point of losing her identity. The fact that he was the enemy mattered little to her. The lieutenant became a kind of obsession. But whenever she came to her senses, she said to herself: "What do I have in common with this man? This pig used me as a sexual object, as a weekend whore, and then disappeared forever. I should have known it would be like this. I need to forget it all, to put it all in the past, as prostitutes do. They fuck one after another without even remember their faces, let alone their names. I was a whore . . . his whore, and I need to accept it as such. He's my enemy, a Nazi bastard, and he always will be."

Nevertheless, Varinia recalled each and every moment she had spent with him, everything he did to her, how he touched her, kissed her, aroused her, penetrated her . . . and at night, she would caress her body thinking of him. Had she been impressed by the food? By the shower? Did she fear him and want to please him and extol his power over her? Or did she want to be his lover to save herself? As long as she was under his protection, no one would sexually abuse her. Or was she hoping she could turn to him in a moment of dire need? Or had she truly enjoyed their intense sexual relationship? She didn't understand anything. Her spirit was troubled. She thought: "Sex is the greatest thing a human being can experience. But . . . me . . . with that Nazi?"

A week went by, and one morning while she was working in Kanada, she felt someone come to stand in front of her. It was the lieutenant; she was stunned.

"I'll be waiting for you tonight at seven tonight," he said, staring down at her.

She was happy to see him. And she thought: "How can I wash myself and at least clean myself up to be with him . . ."

That night she ran to his office and knocked on the door. He opened it, they looked at each other, and started kissing and touching one another as if they were in love. He carried her to the bed and they began to undress with vertiginous speed so they could feel each other as soon as possible. They began to make love desperately. She surrendered herself with such passion that she cried: "Tie me up . . . I'm all yours." He found a cord and tied her wrists to the bars at the top of the bed. They both howled with pleasure. When the wild sex was over, she bathed, got dressed, and sat down in the armchair. He opened some cans of sausages and took out a piece of cheese, some bread, and cookies, and they began to eat. She thanked God and tried to eat slowly so she wouldn't vomit. The "Mute" finally decided to speak.

"Varinia, I need to talk to you. I forgot to tell you that I was going to spend Christmas in Munich with my children. I'm sorry."

"It was Christmas?"

"Yes."

"And how are your children?"

"They're fine, but we're not."

"We . . . who?"

"What I'm about to tell you cannot be repeated, not to anyone. Promise me."

"I promise."

"Germany is losing the war; even the generals are sure of it. It's just a matter of time. The planes flying over Auschwitz are Allied aircrafts. The Soviets have already entered Poland, and they discovered several concentration camps. They will probably liberate this one as well."

She closed her eyes and breathed a sigh from the depths of her soul; she couldn't hide her relief. "God, you finally heard me . . . and I'm still alive," she thought.

"The Russians are very close to Auschwitz. It's a matter of days. Many of my comrades—including Mengele—have already fled the camp, to South America, I've heard. No one's in control here anymore, they're all leaving. I don't know when Hitler will fall, but he'll be overthrown. Many people are abandoning him, especially those involved in these sick acts. Varinia, I want you to listen to me carefully. During the days we were apart, I thought a lot about you, about me, about us. I want you to run away with me. I want you to be my wife. You could take care of my children. But I need to tell you, in all honesty, that I'll have to live in hiding from now on; otherwise, they'll arrest me. My parents have a farm, and you could help me manage it, and we could live a quiet life together. This war has turned me into a hard man, a debased man, but I was just following orders. I swear to you by all that's holy that I never killed or sent anyone to be killed. That's why I have such a low rank. It's the murderers who are promoted here. And I ask you to forgive me if I ever yelled at you or forced you to have sex with me . . . I did it because I had to show authority, or because I was drunk and . . . I liked you a lot . . . too much, and I didn't know how to approach you. You don't have to answer me now. Take a few days to think it over. But tell me as soon as you can, because the enemy is getting closer and I need to flee."

She turned even more pale than she already was, and a deep silence fell, which made her feel even more confused. She didn't know what to say. Unconsciously, she began to shake her head back and forth.

"Oh . . . Nicolaus . . . I'm extremely flattered," she stammered, swallowing hard. "But I have a son, and after the war I need to find him and his father." She swallowed again. "I've survived a year and a half in this dump . . . in this camp of terror and death . . . stoically, sustained by love, and by the faith and hope that God will let me live to see them again, as well as my parents and my sister. The day they raided my house, they separated us, and I haven't seen them since . . . I have the hope that they're still alive . . . do you know how much we've suffered here? Do you know what it's like to live in uncertainty, on the threshold between life and death, knowing that you could be executed at any moment . . . on a whim of one of your people, who have frightened, humiliated, and intimidated us since we arrived in this hell? For a year and a half, I've been so hungry that sometimes I even thought it would be better to die . . ."

She suddenly realized that her hands, face, and entire body were perspiring, which she tried to conceal by putting her hands on her cheeks. Then she started to feel afraid. Would saying all this to the lieutenant bring consequences? He listened to her calmly.

"Nicolaus, I don't know you . . . we don't know each other. Other than the fact that we have intensely passionate sex, I don't know anything about you . . . this is the first time we've ever really spoken. I beg you to understand me. I'm grateful for your proposal . . . but I have to get out of here alive and resume my life. I want you to know that the only good thing that happened to me during this year and a half of terrible suffering and slavery was you. You gave me things I desperately needed, but I can't build a life with you. What happened between us needs to stay in the past . . . I'm sorry . . . I'm sorry, Nicolaus. I can't go with you. I can't leave Miriam either; she's like a sister to me. She knows better than anyone how much we've suffered, and we both value the deep friendship we have formed."

"Varinia, you're also the only good thing that has happened to me in this damned hell. For the first time in many years, I was able to sleep peacefully when we were together, I swear. I need to go back to Germany to get my children and rebuild my life, and I'm sure you're the right person to do this with me. I've never been so sure about anything before. I've felt this way since the first time I saw you in Kanada." He took her hands. "I can adopt your son, I'll even give him my last name, and I will treat him and love him like my own, and we'll have more children and we'll build a family together and I'll do everything in my power to make you happy. I promise. And we can take your friend Miriam with us. Think about it, please, give me a chance."

"Thank you, thank you, Nicolaus. I'll think about it." They embraced with all their strength.

"Thank you, Varinia. I hope your decision is the right one. Take this," he said, handing her a trinket box made of gold and enamel. "This is my Christmas gift to you. And take these chocolates. I'll be waiting for you tomorrow at the same time."

"I'll take the chocolates, but you keep the box for me; if they find me with it, they'll execute me."

"I don't want you to be in danger anymore. Please, let me know as soon as you decide."

246

Varinia went back to tell Miriam about the German's proposal, mentioning that she didn't know what to do.

"But . . . Varinia . . . have you lost your mind? How can you marry your enemy? Your naivety is infuriating! The Nazis aren't the Capulets and the Montagues . . . this is war. Remember that he took advantage of you. Can you imagine living with him? The SS will be remembered for all time as the worst thing human history has ever spawned. They've murdered our families, our people, in a way never before seen. You yourself have been a victim of their cruelty. Please . . . Varinia, get a hold of yourself. You'll forever be the tattooed Jewess he met at Auschwitz . . . and sooner or later he'll rub it in your face and you'll be forced to leave him with your tail between your legs. He might even be using you as a cover, because everyone says the war is about to end. Have some self-respect! How shameful!"

Varinia was stunned.

"He even offered to let you come with us. What would happen if the Nazis decide to kill us all before the Russians arrive?"

"I don't know. That's something I don't even want to imagine."

"The advantage of going with him is that we could save ourselves if something like that were to happen . . ."

Varinia couldn't sleep. She was more confused than ever. The next day she went to Kanada as she usually did. She and the lieutenant exchanged glances from afar. Oddly enough, trains with still arriving, carrying mostly Hungarian Jews. She noticed, however, that there were fewer high-ranking Nazis, and that the prisoners weren't being as tightly controlled.

New Year's Eve arrived. She went to see him as usual. She entered his office and saw that he was dressed in civilian clothing.

"Varinia, I have to flee tonight, taking advantage of the fact that everyone will be drunk. Even though I didn't raise the subject with you during the week, I wanted you to know that I can't stop thinking about us, and that I have feelings for you."

"Feelings?"

"Yes, Varinia. We've been closer than ever these past few days, and I've fallen in love with you. We have an extraordinary sexual connection. Although we don't know each other deeply, this could be the beginning of a relationship that lasts a lifetime. I have everything prepared for our escape, even for Miriam. I can't wait any longer. Please, Varinia, make a decision. Come with me . . . let's try, at least, to build a life together. Time is of the essence because the marches have already begun."

"The marches? What marches?" She frowned.

"An order has been sent from Stutthof, here and to all the other camps in Poland, to make the prisoners walk, to take them to Germany and Austria. The Third Reich doesn't want the Allies to find out about the concentration camps or the prisoners. They want to keep it a state secret. They even plan to destroy Auschwitz so there are no traces left. Tell me, Varinia . . . what's your decision?"

She was speechless. She looked into his eyes for a long time, and a shudder she could barely conceal went through her. Her instincts took over and she thought: "Once . . . a Nazi . . . always a Nazi . . . this man can behave unpredictably . . . can you imagine living with him?" She took the box he had given her, spun around, and headed for the door.

"But . . . Varinia!" He tried to grab her arm. She didn't stop, leaving the German in mute astonishment. He watched her go, then he slammed the door and kicked it furiously. She was overcome with fear and began to run toward the barracks faster than ever before, terrified that he would shoot her in the back. She wanted to hide in her own shadow. When she arrived, she buried the box in a corner and went to sleep beside Miriam, hugging her with all her soul and strength, but she didn't tell her about the march because she didn't want to cause her further suffering.

Chapter 11
Poland, 1945

The next day, Varinia went to clean the Nazi's office and found it
locked. Then she went to Kanada to look for him; he wasn't there.
She crossed herself and thought: "He left! Praise the Lord! He didn't
take revenge on me . . ."

A few days passed, and no one understood why men were being
executed left, right, and center. Everyone was afraid, more so than
ever. They were terrified of being the next to be killed. She wondered
if it would have been better to leave with the Nazi to save herself,
and then run away later. But it was too late. "I'm so stupid . . . how
didn't it occur to me before . . . well, Miriam wouldn't have wanted
to leave in any case . . . and I wouldn't leave her for the world."

Several days later, when most of the SS officers had fled Auschwitz,
the Wehrmacht announced over the loudspeakers that the prisoners
should line up to leave the camp and begin walking toward
Wodzislaw. Many of the prisoners' eyes filled with tears because this
confirmed that the war was ending. They had survived the holocaust,
and along the way they could escape and finally be free.

The Nazis instructed sixty thousand Jews to take their blankets with
them; they gave them a piece of bread and forced them to embark
on a snowy and icy journey through the forest, at ten degrees below
zero, surrounded by armed soldiers and dogs. They saw their ex-
captors escaping on bicycles, horses, and on foot, dressed in civilian
clothing. They also heard explosions all around them and felt the
earth shaking as the Russian tanks approached.

Nobody knew their final destination or what they would do with
them. Varinia spread the word that they were headed to a train
station from which they would depart for Germany and Austria
because the Russians were coming. The women were so sick, weak,
and tired that they crawled along the road. A woman would fall
suddenly, another would faint, and their captors would place them
back to back and shoot them both in the head. They saved bullets
this way. Others collapsed from exhaustion, and the Nazis left them
there to freeze to death. How could they endure what came to be
known as the "Death Marches" when they were so malnourished
from all those years living in starvation in Auschwitz? They were

more dead than alive, and they could barely move. Those who couldn't keep up with the pace imposed by the Germans were executed on the spot.

"Why are there more women and children than men?" Varinia asked Miriam.

"Because they're the ones who are least able to put up a fight, and it will be easier to liquidate them. Remember how many young men were executed before these marches began, and no one knew why? It's clear proof that they're still trying to eliminate us, right till the end."

The friends walked closely together to keep warm. They covered themselves with their blankets and ate their bread one crumb at a time. They saw women stumbling through the snow half dead, but they couldn't help them because it was forbidden; besides, they could barely stand themselves. Not even the act of walking heated them up. They had never felt so cold. They prayed to God over and over again for the strength and courage to keep going, and not to fall out of lack of sleep, because sleeping was also forbidden. They walked the entire day, through the night, and all of the following day. The friends were so exhausted that they reached the point of thinking it would be better to die. Varinia thought: "Why didn't I go with that damned German?" All of a sudden, during the second night, they saw low-flying planes emitting white smoke. It was a signal from the Americans to let the Jews know they had learned of the genocide. A couple of Poles had taken pictures of the executions, and those who were able to escape from Auschwitz had informed the Allies and the world of what they had experienced in the *Auschwitz Protocols*. They indicated where the gas chambers and crematoria were located. They even asked the Americans to bomb the railway to Auschwitz, but they didn't. The British also knew; the subject had even been discussed in Parliament. But they didn't do anything to stop it, either. When they saw the planes, the Wehrmacht officers shouted: "Get off the road! It's the enemy army!" Those who could move did so; those who couldn't where killed right then and there by the Nazis. Many soldiers began to run away. Amidst the confusion, and with the smoke obscuring visibility, Varinia told Miriam: "Let's go hide in the woods!" And they began to run. A Nazi saw them and started shooting at them, but he didn't manage to hit them. They ran to the point of exhaustion. They suddenly found themselves alone in the middle of the forest. They were free and alive. They hugged and shed the few tears they had left, swearing never to cry again. They were free, but they faced several problems: cold, hunger, and disorientation. They began to search for something, even though they didn't know what.

"What are we going to eat?"

"Mushrooms, whatever we find here. And we'll drink melted snow."

All of a sudden they heard troops passing by, and they climbed up some trees to hide. It was the Russians; they were closing in on Auschwitz. The women were afraid that they would harm them. "I've already been raped twice . . . and they say that these bastards gang rape women. God save us!" Varinia said. Once the troops had gone, they continued walking without knowing where they were going. They came across a humble farm with a small cabin and some alfalfa fields. Smoke billowed from the chimney, reminding them of the crematoria. Shivering from the cold, they knocked on the door. A stooped, elderly peasant answered; he was nearly bald, and what little hair he had left was gray. They begged him to give them shelter, but he took no pity on them and told them to leave.

"Listen, girls," he said. "Russian soldiers pass by here all the time looking for beautiful young women, and I don't want to be responsible for anything."

"But we can take refuge in the barn out back and sleep with the animals."

"That's the first place they look! They steal the animals."

Varinia took out the trinket box the lieutenant had given her, and the Pole finally acquiesced.

"Just for one day, though."

"Please . . . let us stay for at least three nights. We're exhausted from the Death March, which we barely managed to escape from."

"Okay, but you're going to have to work."

"We'll do whatever you ask," she said, handing over the box.

The women knelt down, crossed themselves, and thanked God. He thought: "They're not Jewish, they're my compatriots." He was touched by this, as was his wife, an elderly woman who was observing the scene from a wheelchair. They were Catholics, and above their fireplace hung an enormous wooden crucifix. He gave them each a slice of bread and accompanied them to the barn, where he showed them a wooden trapdoor in the floor that led to a cellar. He told them that if the Russians or the Nazis came, they should hide in there. There were goats, chickens, pigs, and some dogs in the barn. They rushed over to milk the goats. They gulped down the milk and felt revived. They settled into the small, windowless barn, lying down to sleep on the alfalfa and covering themselves with straw. Cuddling the dogs to keep warm, they fell asleep until the next morning.

The Pole woke them up early, and they washed themselves, which felt like a gift from God. He ordered them to clean and tidy up the barn. They did so with the remarkable meticulousness to which they had become accustomed. The peasant asked them to look after his crippled wife. They bathed her in a tub, washed her hair, and changed her clothes, leaving her impeccably clean. The woman didn't say a word. They asked her if they could take a bath afterward, and she consented. They both felt like they were in heaven. The woman gave them some clothes, and they tossed their prisoners' uniforms into the fireplace. She didn't give them any food, though; just a slice of bread at noon. At night, Miriam said: "I'm hungry . . . I've been hungry for years . . . I could eat a whole cow. I swear that once we have our normal lives back, I'd rather have a pantry full of food than a living room, and I don't care if I become fat. I'll eat enough to make up for everything I didn't eat during the years I spent in that hell."

When they were sure that the old couple had fallen sleep, they stole some potatoes and killed a chicken, which they plucked and quietly cooked in the barn. Once the food was ready, or still slightly undercooked, Miriam began to devour it down to the small bones. "Eat slowly," her friend told her, "You're going to make yourself sick." In a matter of minutes, Miriam gobbled down almost the entire chicken and all the potatoes. All of a sudden she started to gag and feel unwell; she suffered from vomiting, diarrhea, and chills, and began to howl from the stomach pains. Varinia put Miriam's arm around her shoulder and tried to walk with her to the cabin to ask for help. "Hold on, Miriam, hold on," she said, as Miriam struggled to breathe. As soon as they reached the door, Miriam fainted. The Pole opened the door and Varinia confessed that they had eaten almost an entire chicken. They brought her into the house and put her in an armchair. Varinia tried to wake her up, splashing water on her face, patting her cheeks, massaging her heart, giving her mouth-to-mouth resuscitation, but Miriam didn't respond. The Pole approached softly, took her pulse, listened to her heart, and said: "She's dead."

"What? That's impossible. Are you sure?"

"You girls haven't eaten for years . . . I think it's from eating so much . . . I don't know . . . she might have overeaten . . . or . . . maybe her insides got twisted . . . I don't know! She should have eaten little by little . . ."

"Noooooo!" howled Varinia, embracing her friend and weeping with such pain that the Pole was moved. Tears bathed her cheeks. He allowed her to stay in the living room next to her dear friend. She didn't leave her side; she sat on the floor beside the armchair and wept without pause. She wrapped her arms around her waist and thought: "It's not possible . . . this isn't happening . . . she survived the holocaust . . . the march . . . everything we've been through . . . and all to die from overeating . . . God . . . but . . . this isn't real . . . it's too much . . . Miriam . . . my beloved Miriam . . . I've never had a friend as loyal as you, as honest, as kind, as stoic. You were my conscience, you told me what I needed to hear, and what I didn't want to hear. Nobody helped me or supported me as much as you did. You were a sister to me, when I'm not even sure if my own sister is alive or dead . . ."

The next day, the Pole and Varinia wrapped Miriam's body in a sheet, placed her in a wheelbarrow, went into the forest, dug a hole, and buried her. Varinia made a wooden cross out of two sticks and some thread, and she place it over her grave. She wept profusely. They recited the Lord's Prayer, Ave Maria, the Nicene Creed, and Gloria. Then she thought: "Now I really am all alone in the world . . . I should have died too . . . nothing matters to me anymore . . ."

The Pole told her that he had to go to a town close to Warsaw to sell alfalfa, and that he could bring her with him, passing her off as his niece. She agreed. She helped him tie the hay into bales, which they loaded onto a horse-drawn cart. Then they said goodbye to his wife and set off. She tied a handkerchief around her head and put on the clothes the woman had given her. As everyone knew the Pole, no one gave them any trouble when they passed the checkpoints, and, after about an hour, they arrived at their destination. She helped him unload his merchandise, thanked him sincerely for his help, and said goodbye to him forever.

Varinia later learned that those who had survived the Death Marches had been packed into uncovered train cars bound for Germany, and nearly all had frozen or starved to death. Several days later, the Russians liberated Auschwitz.

She felt alone in the world once again. She climbed into the back of a truck heading to Warsaw with a group of people. She arrived in her hometown, which she found in ruins and still occupied by the enemy. She went to her house and found that a high-ranking German was living there. She went immediately to her neighbors' house, where her lifelong friends had lived. She rang the doorbell, and while she watched a gardener tending the plants, a German man dressed in civilian clothes appeared.

"Is this the Bieliks' house?"

"No, ma'am. No family by that name lives here."

"And where do they live?"

"I already told you. No Bieliks live here. Now, please go."

"Sir . . . please help me. I need to find that family."

"Get out of here! Otherwise, I'll call the authorities!"

She thought: "Damned German, he must be a Nazi, but he no longer wears his uniform because they're losing the war. God, help me! I have to find my son." Then she went to the houses of her grandparents, relatives, and friends, and every single one of them was occupied by Germans. No one gave her any information, and they all sent her away. She even went to the store in front of the university, but it no longer existed. She felt foreign in her own city. She had nowhere to go and no one to turn to. Finally, it occurred to her to go to St. Martin's. "God . . . help me to find some answers there," she prayed as she walked to the church. She rang the doorbell and a young man came to the door.

"Is Father Peter here?"

"No, ma'am."

"And who is in charge?"

"Bishop John."

"Please tell him that Varinia Horodinsky would like to speak to him."

"Come in, ma'am, and take a seat."

Bishop John appeared; he barely recognized her.

"Father . . . I'm sorry, Bishop, do you remember me?"

"But, Varinia . . . of course I remember you. Praise the Lord, you're alive!" He embraced her and ushered her into his office. He offered her a seat and took in her pitiful appearance, her missing teeth.

"I was in the Auschwitz concentration camp for more than a year. I've suffered unspeakable horrors. I'm looking for my son, his father, my family . . . for everyone, in fact."

254

"My dear child, Boris came looking for you and his family in December of 1943, together with Herr Moritz Hochschild, the man he works for in Bolivia. He went to the Bielik family house, your neighbors, to ask about you, and they told him that when they raided your house you refused to let go of your son, and they tore him from your arms. People say that blond, white children are sent to foster homes and passed off as Aryans."

"What?" she cried. "That's a lie, a terrible lie! On the day of raid, I was at my neighbors' house with my son, and when I saw them coming, I left my son with Ewa to go help my parents and sister, but they took us all prisoner and I was forced to leave my son behind. How could they tell such a lie?" Her heart pounded and her eyes bulged. "I need to find Ewa, she knows where my son is."

The bishop handed her a glass of water to calm her down.

"And where is that place?"

"I don't know, my child, but now that the Germans are losing the war, I'll have greater access to information."

"Bishop, I need to speak to Boris urgently. How is he?"

"He was devastated about not being able to find you or his family. He left the phone number of his workplace in Bolivia. He even left passports with visas for you, your son, and your families."

"I'm not leaving Warsaw until I find my son," she said. "What happened to my parents and sister?"

"I never heard from them again."

"It can't be true . . . and to think that all these years I've lived with the hope of seeing them again . . . and the Kominsky family?"

"About two years ago, the SS raided this sanctuary and took Olga, Sonitzya, and Sergei, who had been hiding here for several years. They also arrested Father Peter and Father Patrick. We never found out where they took them, and we haven't heard from them, despite all our efforts. We're hoping that they'll return at some point, just like you have. Dr. Kominsky has also been missing since they took him prisoner."

"I saw Sergei in Auschwitz, and I hope that he makes it out like I did. I asked him about his mother and sister, and he told me that he never saw them again. Does Boris know his father is still missing?"

"Yes."

"How is he? How did he react when he found out we have a son?"

"He's well. He wept profusely when he found out he had a son, especially because he couldn't find him, and I gave him the picture from his birth certificate."

"Damn this war," she said, her tears flowing. "Bishop, I'm full of resentment and hatred, even toward myself. I have sinned out of necessity, and I need the Lord to forgive me for my sins. Please absolve me. I'm searching for divine forgiveness."

She knelt down and the bishop recited a few words in Latin and made the sign of the cross.

"You don't need to confess. You're absolved, my child."

"Thank you, thank you very much, Bishop, although I know I'll need to carry these sins with me forever."

"God will absolve you."

"Yes, Bishop. I need something to eat and a place to live. Can I stay here?"

"Of course, my child, but no one can know. The war isn't over yet."

"Thank you, Bishop."

"This is Boris's card."

"I'll call him right now."

She ate a small piece of cheese with bread, recalling with a shudder. what had happened to her beloved Miriam, and asked the telephone operator to call La Paz, Bolivia. While she was waiting, they assigned her a room; oddly enough, it was the same one in which Sonitzya and Olga had stayed. She asked the bishop if she could use the clothes hanging there, which they had left behind, and he said yes. She took a very long bath, giving thanks to God as she did so. She spent hours trying to connect to Bolivia, but it was impossible. She eventually fell asleep from exhaustion.

She woke up early the next morning, ran to the phone, and again requested the call. She waited almost the entire morning and was finally connected to him. They could barely hear each other, and the connection kept cutting out, so they had to yell.

"Boris, my love . . ." she choked, drowning in tears.

"Varinia! You're alive! Blessed be God!" Tears ran down his cheeks. "How are you? How are you feeling?"

"Destroyed, with my heart and my head in tatters and an indescribable feeling of unease. I'm desperate to see you. I've missed you and our little Boris so much . . . I love you so much . . ."

"Me too, my beloved Varinia. I love as much as I always have. Where are you, love?"

"At St. Martin's, my love. I was at the Auschwitz concentration camp, but I survived."

"You're extraordinary! It's a miracle! God heard my prayers. I've been waiting for you every single day. I heard about that concentration camp . . . to be honest, I didn't rule out the possibility they had sent you there, even though you're Polish."

"I can't tell you about it right now."

"I understand . . . the time will come."

She was about to start talking about their son when the connection was lost; her heart shrank. Minutes later, it was resumed.

"Hello? . . . Hello? Boris, my love, I need you to come and help me to find our son . . . to find everyone . . ."

"Of course. Ewa said they took him from your arms."

"That's a lie! When they raided my house, I was with our son at Ewa's house, and I left him there. I ran over to my parents, and they took us all prisoner. I went to her house yesterday and they don't live there anymore, and no one knows anything and I don't know what to do."

"So maybe he's alive . . .!"

They were both so overwhelmed with excitement and happiness from speaking to one another that they couldn't stop crying.

"Try to calm down, my love. Have you heard from my family?"

"Just Sergei—I saw him in Auschwitz, but not Olga or Sonitzya. I know nothing about your father. Sergei and I looked for them at the camp, but we never found them. He told me that your mother was very ill when she arrived, and Sergei asked Sonitzya not to leave her side. He saw them go off together, but we never found out where. I worked in a sector that sorted through objects, and I recognized the vicuña shawl you sent us, which I imagine belonged to Olga or Sonitzya."

"So that means it could have been taken from one of them."

"Yes."

"And that means . . ."

"I don't know."

"We'll have to wait for the war to end and for them to come back like you did. And what about your family?"

"I haven't heard a thing."

"I'm so sorry. I'll come to Warsaw as soon as possible. My boss, Herr Hochschild, left Bolivia, and we've been put in charge of his office here. I'll finish up some urgent business, and we'll look for our families together."

257

Boris ran to tell Blum that he had spoken to Varinia. Blum told him to take all the time he needed to find his family. He even gave him the names of some friends and relatives and asked him to investigate their whereabouts. Then Boris called Hochschild in Buenos Aires and told him about the conversation he had had with his girlfriend. Both of them, however, remained very concerned about the fate of the child. Hochschild said it was impossible for him to accompany Boris to Europe at this time, but that he remained hopeful that his own family was still alive. He asked Boris to go to Cologne to see if he could find out anything about them. He also authorized him to withdraw the money he needed for the trip from the company account; Blum would take care of it. Boris insisted he would pay it back. Hochschild also gave him the number of a bank account in Cologne. "That's what money is for, my boy . . . for situations like this one," he said. Boris, who loved him like a father, responded: "I've never met a man as generous as you, Moritz. May God bless you, always." Hochschild warned: "Don't forget that the war isn't over yet . . . take care of yourself, and be very patient with Varinia . . . . she's a survivor . . ."

Boris took care of a few things in the office and flew to Warsaw on the next plane. He was anxious to see Varinia. He worried constantly about what had happened to his son and the neighbors.

Varinia, meanwhile, went to the orphanages to ask for information, but no one knew anything. She then pressed Bishop John to speak to his contacts. She ate lunch and dinner with the priests, but she hardly ate and said only what was absolutely necessary. She put very little food in her stomach. When one of them asked about her experience at Auschwitz, she requested that they not ask her about it again.

A few days later, Boris arrived in Warsaw. His itinerary was similar to the previous one. When he was in the taxi on the way to St. Martin's, he passed by the National Museum and the university, which brought back memories of Isaac in particular. He was overcome with nostalgia. The city, he observed, was in ruins. He arrived at the church just after nightfall. He rang the outer bell, and Varinia herself came the door. When he saw her, he said:

"Good evening, I'm looking for Varinia Horodinsky."

With war-weary serenity, she went out to the garden gate and opened it for him.

"It's me, my dear Boris. I'm Varinia."

"Varinia!" he cried. They hugged and kissed passionately, their tears intermingling with their kisses. He could feel every one of her rib bones and shoulder blades. She was skin and bones.

"My love . . . what have they done to you? . . . Forgive me, I didn't recognize you . . . you're so thin . . . your hair is so short . . . I've missed you so much! I've missed you all so much!" he said, shaking, wrapping his arms around her again in a loving embrace. After drying their tears, they walked to the parish door with their arms around each other. She didn't say a word. He observed that the years had taken their toll on her, and that she appeared downcast despite their reunion. She showed him in right away, and the bishop came to greet him. They embraced each other warmly because they had known each other since Boris's birth. The cleric withdrew discreetly, and Varinia served Boris a plate of food. She said next to nothing and remained looking at the ground.

"I'm sorry, I've gotten used to being silent."

"You don't have to force yourself to speak, and you don't have to tell me anything you don't want to. I'll respect your silence. I'll wait. I'm very worried about what might have happened to our son."

"I left him with Ewa when he was three years old. I would recognize him immediately. A child can't have changed that much in two years. Do you know what, my love? I think you're the only person in the world I have left."

"You, too, my darling, my Varinia, and my love for you is as strong as ever."

"I never stopped loving you, Boris." He stood up and they embraced again.

She took him to her bedroom. She had pushed the two beds together and made them up with double sheets. She got undressed, put on a nightshirt, and got into bed. He did the same. He wanted to make love to her, was eager to make her his. He started to kiss her, but she said:

"I'm sorry, I can't yet."

"Whatever you say, my love. I'm sorry, my desire for you got the better of me."

They lay in each other's arms and she slept like a baby. For the first time in years, she was able to fall asleep easily because she felt protected, loved, free, well-fed, and clean. Around three o'clock in the morning, however, she began to scream. He woke up, turned on the light, and found her bathed in sweat, so much so that her nightgown clung to her body. He had to wake her to make her stop. When she saw him, she embraced him with all her strength, breaking down into tears and thanking God that she had him.

"My love, you're the only thing I have left in life . . . never leave me . . ."

"I'll never leave you, my darling . . . never, I swear . . . you're also the only thing I have left in life."

He changed her nightgown and saw the number tattooed on her arm. "Oh God, please help her," he thought. "Poor Varinia, her head and her heart are tormented . . . full of incomprehensible horrors . . . God, how did you let this happen?" He barely slept. At one point, when he turned on the light to go to the bathroom, he looked at her and thought: "She hasn't lost her beauty, but she's withered, it's as if she had aged beyond her years . . . as if she were forty. She's a wreck . . ."

The next day they got up late, had lunch, and then Boris took her to a doctor and dentist recommended by the priests. After examining her and running some tests, the doctor said she was very sick and malnourished, and her immune system was extremely weak. He recommended that she be admitted to a private clinic because the hospitals were full of wounded soldiers. She was hospitalized and given saline solution for two weeks. She begged Boris not to leave her alone because she was terrified of falling back into Nazi hands. He never left her side. He even stayed overnight, sleeping in a bed next to hers. And, at her request, he locked the door. Even though he spoon fed her, she barely ate. Varinia slowly began to open up about her recent experiences, and she told him:

"My friend from Auschwitz died from eating too much when we were on our way to Warsaw, and I'm scared of dying in the same way."

"You're being looked after by doctors here, and nothing will happen to you. Trust them, and I'll take care of you, too."

While she slept, which was most of the time, he went out in search of information that would shed light on what had happened to his family members, as well as to the people on the long list of names he carried with him. All his efforts, however, were in vain. When she woke up, he would tell her about his life in Bolivia. He told her about his time in the Yungas with Isaac. He also told her how he met his boss, and how happy he was to be under the protection of such a successful and generous man. But he also told her how, all these years, he had felt very lonely as an expatriate, even more so because when the war broke out he had stopped receiving letters from her, his family, Isaac, or anyone else. Boris also read her light-hearted novels, acting out the characters, which made her smile. Often, however, she would stare off into space; she would stop listening, feel overcome by drowsiness, and fall asleep. She was trying to make up for all the peaceful and secure hours of slumber she had been denied over the last year and a half. The nightmares continued, though. Boris's love for her allowed him to comprehend and support her unconditionally. He thought; "God . . . you have to lift her out of this depression at some point," and he prayed for her constantly. They made plans for their future life together in Bolivia, after they had found their son. This filled her with hope and joy. He spent hours watching her closely, and he realized that he had never seen a face so marked by profound sadness; it seemed as if she were always on the verge of tears, and he caught her weeping silently many times. Whenever she sunk into a deep silence, he would tell her: "Let it out, my love, let it out . . . cry . . . it shows that you have a soul . . ." He was so worried that he spoke to the doctors, and they told him that her physical and mental recovery would take time, a long time. He needed to be patient. When the priests from St. Martin's visited her, they all prayed together.

Once she was feeling better, they returned to the church. They also went to the dentist, who replaced her missing teeth. Shortly afterward, he took her to have her photograph taken for her new Argentinian diplomatic passport. Everything was difficult to find. They finally found a photographer on the second floor of a building. He lent Varinia a wig from his collection and a lady who appeared to be his wife did her makeup. She looked like another woman. She smiled when saw her reflection in the mirror, which made Boris happy. Afterward, the same woman touched up her makeup and gave her the address of a house where they sold clothes. It was the apartment of a woman who had owned an antique store she had been forced to close because of the war. Boris bought her some tailored two-piece suits, blouses, undergarments, hats, gloves, shoes, a fur coat, and even a short wig the same color as her hair. "New clothes . . . what a gift, thank you, my love." He pasted the photograph to the passport, and she signed it. "Your name is now Patricia de Santiesteban. You're Argentinian, and you're my wife." She smiled again and kissed him. They hurried back to St. Martin's because it was getting dark.

She recalled that she had seen a gardener at her neighbors' house and thought that perhaps he could give them some information, so they went there the next day. They made sure that no one was home, and they approached the worker; he was a stooped old man whose hearing was almost gone. They gestured to him to come over to the fence.

"Sir," she said. ". . . but, it's you, Helmut . . . Helmut . . . do you remember me? I'm Varinia, the neighbor . . ."

"Of course, my child! How could I forget you? I watched you grow up!"

"Helmut, dear Helmut, what happened to my son Boris? You must know that I left him in this house that fateful day. You've been working here forever."

The man was reluctant at first, but then, seeing the look of desperation on Varinia's face, he said:

"My girl, your son is no longer called Boris; his name is Hans. Ewa married a colonel from the Third Reich, a man much older than her, named Friedrich Friderg. They adopted your son because, apparently, they weren't able to have children. He gave the boy his last name, and they remained living in this house."

Boris and Varinia turned pale.

"Swear to me by the Black Madonna that you're telling the truth!" she begged him.

"Varinia, I've known you all my life and I would never lie to you, especially seeing the anguish you two are in. I'm in charge of the house now because they abandoned it."

"When?"

"The same day you came here to claim the child. The man who came out to speak to you was the colonel."

"Do you know where they've gone? Have they gone to the country estate that the Bieliks had nearby? What happened to Maryla?"

"Before they left, I heard them talking about going to Lodz. I refused to go with them because by now I'm too old to work in the countryside; I can barely manage to take care of this garden. Maryla left with her parents, but I'm not sure where they went. Now . . . please go. If they find me talking to you, my life will be in danger."

Boris handed him a hefty dollar bill. The gardener refused to take it at first, but Varinia insisted that he accept it. He thanked them.

"God bless you, dear Helmut." She took and kissed the wrinkled hand resting on the fence, and they left.

"That awful Ewa stole our son, our Boris!" she exclaimed, her anger and anxiety growing. "How horrible! She even changed his name and gave him the Nazi's surname. Why would she do that? I would like to believe that it was to save him . . . but . . . why didn't she leave an address if her intentions were honorable? Why did they leave the same day I came to claim him and that man threw me out? And to you . . . Ewa told you that the Nazis tore him from my arms and that they would take him to an orphanage. But . . . how could this be? What wickedness! She and the Nazi lied to us and they've stolen our son! How could she do this to me? I trusted her more than anyone!"

"Calm down, love . . . God will help us," he said, trying to soothe her.

"God . . . I don't even know if God exists anymore . . ."

They were both devastated and found it difficult to assimilate the situation. They couldn't believe that such a close childhood friend would take their child away from them like this.

"Did that awful girl think I would die in the camps?"

"At least we know our son is alive and we have the German's name, so we can keep looking for him."

"I won't stop until I find him . . . I can't understand why Ewa did this to us . . . and on top of it all, she married the enemy . . . there are no words to describe this dirty trick . . ." She burst into tears. "Forgive me, Boris . . . I'm crying even though I swore I never would again. I've cried so much I thought I had run out of tears for good. In Auschwitz my fellow prisoners would tell us not to cry because we would lose the little salt we still had left in our bodies . . ." They hugged each other with all their strength.

"Varinia, I'll do everything possible to get out son back . . . I brought a lot of money with me, precisely for situations like this one," he said, thinking of Moritz.

The couple decided to go to Lodz the next day. They dressed in their best clothes to impress the authorities. She put on her mink coat, which she found unbearably warm, and Boris wore his vicuña coat. When they arrived at the train station, they saw with relief that there were no Nazis and no swastika flags hanging there. When they arrived in Lodz, they took a taxi to the Bieliks' estate. The trip took about twenty minutes. The car was stopped by Russian troops. Boris spoke to them in the little Russian he had learned from his dad, and he showed them their diplomatic passports, into which he had slipped a hefty dollar bill. They let them pass. The passports were useless—the Russians had no idea what they said—but the money spoke for itself. He carried the bills hidden in a money belt with a zipper. She quickly located the estate since she had spent many summer vacations there.

They got out of the taxi, and the driver agreed to wait for them. The estate spanned several hectares and was surrounded by century-old trees. The large house, entirely walled in, had a main gate that opened onto a dirt road. Boris rang the bell there, and no one answered. Then he picked up a stone and began to bang on the gate, trying to make himself heard, but there was still no answer. He forced the gate open with the taxi driver's help, and they went in. The house and the blinds were closed. Everything looked dirty, abandoned, and snow covered. There wasn't a soul in sight. They went over to the caretaker's house, which they also found empty, without even a guard dog. She remembered that there was a small back door they used to use when they went horseback riding or walking in the countryside. They opened it and found nothing. In the past there had been an abundance of cows, sheep, and horses. They supposed that the peasants, Nazis, and Russians had stolen them. They returned to the large house and forced a window open. Inside, everything was intact. There were lamps, furniture, and paintings covered in dusty white sheets. They walked around the house, but as there was clearly no one living there, there was nothing left to do but leave. They went to the estate next door, then to the one next to that one, as well as to warehouses, pharmacies, and stores in the town, asking if anyone had seen the Bieliks. No one appeared to know them, and Varinia didn't come across any familiar faces. "We used to be friends with the other girls who spent the summers here, but all these people are strangers to me," she said. Given the lack of answers, they decided to return to the city, and they took a room in the best hotel they could find. The hotel made Varinia think of the Nazi, and she became upset with herself. They ordered the set menu for dinner, and they went to bed. Even though they were exhausted, they hardly slept because they were so worried.

The next day, in Lodz, they continued asking around about the Bielik family, but no one knew them. They found this odd because Mr. Bielik was a wealthy cattle rancher. Nevertheless, they had no choice but to return to Warsaw, asking themselves: "What do we do now?

Where can we find this Herr Friderg, especially now that the Nazis are losing the war and they're all fleeing with their tails between their legs?"

"Let's pray, Varinia, let's pray . . . we'll think of something; something always falls from the heavens."

"I'm sorry, love, but I don't pray anymore. I spent so much time praying in Auschwitz that whenever I pray now it reminds me of what I went through there. I prayed in moments of intense pain and desperation, and those feelings come back to me every time."

He didn't respond. They were both suffering deeply. They sat with their arms around one other on the train back to Warsaw, and neither of them said a word during the trip.

That night, while they were having dinner, they told the priests about their sad experience. The couple asked the bishop to use his influence to find out who this Colonel Friderg was. He and the other clerics promised to do all they could. That same night, they also asked the priests where they might be able to find out what had happened to their families. Bishop John told them that the only way to find out was to wait until they were freed, just as with Varinia. He assured them that at least Boris's family knew they could count on the congregation and the parish. Varinia exclaimed, full of bitterness: "If they survive the concentration camps, that is . . . if they didn't send them to the gas chambers." Everyone was shocked by her outburst, and they fell silent. It was the first time she had spoken of the holocaust in public. She stood up and went to her room, and Boris went after her. She threw herself onto the bed. He took her in his arms and tried to console her, thinking: "Oh God . . . this will never end . . . and we've barely begun."

"I've been wanting to tell you that if Sergei didn't survive the Death Marches, I doubt he's alive. And I already told you about Olga and Sonitzya over the phone, so you can imagine what happened to them, as well as to my family. All we have is each other, and the search for our missing son," she said while he remained silent. "You're all I have in the world, and I love you with all my soul. I don't know what I'd do without you . . . never leave me . . ."

"I will never abandon you . . . my beloved Varinia. You don't have to worry about that . . ."

The couple decided to move to a hotel to have more privacy. Their dollars were worth the price of gold, especially now that the Germans were about to lose the war and the Russians were about to

265

occupy Berlin. In addition, Boris had to fulfill his promise to Hochschild to go to Cologne in search of his family. They embarked on the journey together, braving a tense and hostile environment. There were Nazi and SS officers all around, and every time Varinia saw them she became so terrified that she began to retch. They spent the night at the Dom Hotel Cologne. The day after their arrival they went to Planitz & Co. Hochschild to look for Krause, the engineer. He was there and recognized Boris immediately. They shook each other's hands firmly, and Krause introduced himself to Varinia.

"How is Herr Hochschild?"

"Well, he went to live in Chile. Have you heard anything about Hochschild's family?"

"Listen to me, Boris," he said. "There's no way of knowing what's happened to them. According to what my contacts have told me, they're sending survivors from the camps in Poland to Germany because they don't want the world to find out about the crimes against humanity and the terrible human rights violations they committed there."

"It's true," Varinia confirmed. "They're also sending them to Austria. I'm an Auschwitz survivor, and that's what I heard."

The engineer looked at her in astonishment, and an uneasy silence fell.

"What they've done is unspeakable, unforgivable, and the Nazis know it. These abominable people thought they would win the war, and they're about to lose it. All we can do is wait for the fighting to end and keep praying for his family's return."

"Tell me, what ever happened to Herr Hochschild's father's estate? I need to see it."

"I don't know, but I can take you there this afternoon if you'd like." Boris invited the engineer to lunch. Varinia ate with them, but terrified by the sight of so many Nazis swarming around in that grim atmosphere, she asked to stay behind at the hotel, where she locked the door to her room.

They made the short trip and discovered that the house was occupied by a German family. They looked for Franz, the caretaker, but he was no longer there.

"These bastards have seized all the houses and estates owned by Jews!" Krause spit out.

"They did the same thing in Poland. Not just to the Jews, but also to the Poles. My girlfriend lived in a mansion, and now it's occupied by a high-ranking SS officer."

"Was she the one you came to look for a few years ago?"

"Yes."

"You can't imagine how happy I am that you found her, Boris. Have you been able to find your family?"

"Not yet, unfortunately."

"Be patient. The war is about to end."

"I hope so."

They returned to Cologne later that afternoon.

"Thank you, Herr Krause. I'm living in Poland at the moment, and this is my telephone number. I'll leave these Bolivian passports with visas with you. All you have to do is add the name and a photograph. Give them to whomever you think would benefit from them."

"I still have the ones Herr Hochschild left with me."

"Yes, I remember."

"Thank you. Thank you very much. I'll let you know as soon as I hear anything. Please send my warmest regards to Herr Hochschild."

"I'll do that. Goodnight."

Boris went back to the hotel. He couldn't open the door to his room because Varinia had propped a piece of furniture against it. He had to knock for her to let him in.

"I'm sorry for putting the chest of drawers there, my love, but I didn't feel safe. How did it go, darling?"

"This war is like a plague . . . it has spread everywhere. Hochschild's house and farm have been taken over by Germans."

Varinia noticed a stronger Nazi presence in Germany than in Poland, and she didn't want to go down to the dining room for dinner, so they ordered room service. They ate and got into bed. He saw that she was calmer than before, and he began to kiss and hug her gently but passionately, and she consented. He took off her nightgown and she let herself be seduced by him. They gave each other long, deep, tender kisses, moaning and sighing with desire, but the moment he tried to penetrate her she turned away, breaking the spell.

"I'm sorry, my love . . . I don't know what's wrong with me . . . forgive me."

He got off of her slowly, lay down beside her, and covered his face with his arm, thinking: "Goddamn war . . . I hope she's able to put this trauma behind her . . . she only lets herself be kissed . . . but at the same time, it's tearing me apart . . . I think I'm the one who's going to end up going crazy . . . patience . . . Moritz told me to be patient . . . Goddammit!"

They returned to Warsaw the next day and Boris phoned Hochschild to tell him about his trip to Cologne. He was disheartened by the news.

"There's nothing left to do but wait," he replied, sounding as though he had almost given up hope.

"You can't imagine how sorrow I am. I'll keep looking for them."

"Thank you very much. And how is Varinia?"

"Not well at all. Auschwitz destroyed her. Sometimes I feel like she'd rather not be alive. We can't find our son, or her family, or mine. We can't find anybody."

"Courage, my boy. You'll find them. And be patient with her. Your love for her is the only thing that will give you the strength you need."

The couple pressed the priests to obtain information about the orphanages, and they decided to go to the headquarters of the International Red Cross. The organization had rented a mansion with extensive gardens that they had transformed into a hospital. They received all the survivors, whom they examined, bathed, fed, and administered intensive care to, especially psychiatric care. Many victims, they observed, had lost their minds; they were like lost souls wandering aimlessly, as if in a void.

They went to the reception office and presented their long list of names; none of the people listed there, however, had been heard from. Red Cross staff members had set up screens in a huge room where Jews, Poles and people of other nationalities hung pictures, messages, letters, cards, mementos, addresses, telephone numbers, and whatever else it occurred to them to leave as a sign in case their relatives turned up. Unfortunately, the couple had no pictures of their relatives, so they simply pinned up their names and the addresses of the places where they could be found. They spent hours there, looking at the survivors one by one to see if they recognized anyone and asking if anyone had seen their relatives. A man told them: "In the camps, we were just a number." No one knew anything about anyone. Boris was shocked by their physical appearance; they looked like corpses with just a breath of life left in them. Varinia told him: "You can't even begin to image what Auschwitz was like."

The couple heard how the Russians were left dumbstruck after the camp was liberated. The main survivors where the children Mengele had experimented with. They also learned that the Russians had authorized the Red Cross to rescue survivors from Auschwitz. Boris spoke to the organization's chief of personnel, asking for permission to go look for his relatives. He said his father was a doctor and that he had medical training, so he could help as a nurse. It was a white lie. The man replied: "Okay, we need volunteers." Boris was given credentials and a white apron, and they loaded food, saline solution, water, blankets, bandages, and medicine onto a convoy of green trucks with the Red Cross logo painted on the side. Alongside other doctors, nurses and volunteers, Boris headed to Auschwitz.

On the way there, they saw dead men and women lying on the side of the road in their striped uniforms; their bodies were swollen and deformed, sallow or ash colored. Some of them had been murdered while others had died of exhaustion or hunger during the Death Marches—or at least that's what Boris supposed, from what Varinia had told him. The chief doctor decided not to pick them up so that they could focus their efforts on the survivors. They also saw Russian troops everywhere, forcing the Nazi prisoners to walk with their hands behind their heads. It was impossible for them to escape unidentified: they were made to show the tattoos of their blood type on their arms, just as Varinia had predicted. They also saw convoys of Russian trucks packed with arrested German soldiers, as well as detention camps surrounded by barbed wire full of Nazis prisoners. Boris silently rejoiced, without asking for God's forgiveness.

When they arrived at Auschwitz they were greeted by the Russians who had taken control of the camp. They found themselves in the most horrific concentration camp in the history of humanity, where approximately two million human beings had been murdered. Boris managed to hold a conversation with the Russian soldiers, and they told him that the Nazis had left many of the weakest victims behind to die of hunger and thirst. They also told him that the survivors who had hidden when they set out on the Death Marches had hung the Nazis who stayed behind in the camp.

The Red Cross team approached the survivors, many of whom were lying near death on the ground in their striped uniforms or leaning against the walls. The dead were covered in flies; no one had collected or covered the bodies. The dying weren't even happy to see their rescuers. They had been reduced to eating the oil they found in tires, linseed, and coal. These were the first to be helped. They injected them with saline solution and gave them water to drink.

As Boris began to walk through the camp, terror seized him; it transformed into panic, making him struggle to control himself. He thought of Varinia, his father, mother, brother and sister, and Isaac. He noticed the peculiar smell of death, which resembled that of sewers. He began to feel as if someone were following him. A shiver went down his spine, and he began to retch. Trying to get a hold of himself, he closed his eyes and thought: "This isn't real." He tried to locate some information, but the SS officers had burnt all the records. Before fleeing, they had also managed to destroy the sector where the chambers and crematoria were. He spent a long time looking for his relatives. He peered into face after face, repeating the names of his friends and family members, but he didn't find anyone. His heart began to pound wildly, his hands and forehead began to sweat, and he felt sick to his stomach. "God . . . why did you allow me to be saved . . .? I can't thank you enough for letting me live . . . I'm a fortunate, privileged man . . . but I think I've lost everyone I loved . . . and . . . it looks like Varinia is the only one who has survived . . . how she must have suffered . . . and there seems to be no way to help her get her life back . . . she's completely lost . . . God, my Black Madonna, I'm so confused . . ." he thought, weeping. He went back to where the doctors were, and one of them told him: "Boy . . . the dead are already dead, come help us with the living." That helped him to get a grip on himself, and he began to follow instructions mechanically. They were forced to leave behind the victims who were on the verge of death—these were the majority. Those who still had a chance of survival were placed in the trucks lying side by side. Boris climbed in the back of a truck alongside some other volunteers, holding up the survivors' bottles of saline solution. Once the trucks were full, they sped back to Warsaw as quickly as possible in an effort to save those who still had a chance. "A life is a life," one of the doctors said as he held up the bottles of saline solution. No one spoke. Boris wept silently the whole way back.

They arrived at the Red Cross and Boris went to look for Varinia right away. When he found her, he hugged her with all his strength and said: "I admire you and I love you, you have no idea how much." She didn't want to ask him what he had seen so as not to increase his pain.

Seeing how much help was needed, the couple decided to volunteer. "It's the least we can go, after God let us live," he said. He donated a generous sum of money to help them buy what was necessary, although there was hardly any medicine available on the black market. They did whatever was asked of them, hoping all the while that a friend or relative would turn up. Every time one or more survivors arrived they would run to meet them, look them over carefully, and pronounce the names of their loved ones, but it was never them.

They learned from the BBC that Hitler, faced with the imminent arrival of the Russians in Berlin, had committed suicide. He knew defeat was inevitable and he didn't want to be put on display like Mussolini, whose body had been hung upside down alongside that his lover, Petacci, by the Italian people. Days later, the Germans surrendered. Never before had such joy been seen in the world. The damage they had done was abominable. The war continued in the Far East and the Pacific, however. The United States wanted to defeat Japan and was occupying the islands of the Pacific.

When the war ended in Europe, the couple learned that the Allies had set up offices to provide information, and they went to see if Colonel Friderg had been arrested. They were told that most of the Nazis were in hiding; they had fled and changed their names. They also went to the American Jewish Committee and the British Red Cross. They spent many days searching through records and photographs, and talking to survivors, but without success. They also checked the orphanages in the hopes that Ewa might have left little Boris there for some unknown reason. They learned of a program run by the SS called Lebensborn whose aim was to aid the expansion of the Aryan race, since many German soldiers had died in the war. They stole Aryan-looking children from their mothers' arms in the occupied countries, as well as from those entering the gas chambers, and, disregarding the fact that they were Jewish, they gave them to German families for adoption.

The couple decided to go to the Lebensborn office in northeastern Poland; after handing out money to several people, they were able to locate the place. They went inside and found no one. All that was left were huge rooms with rows of abandoned cribs. They went into the office and couldn't find a single record. Everything had been destroyed. Out of desperation, Varinia began asking the neighbors, but no one told her anything. Even though Boris offered them money, they were too afraid to talk. The only thing they told them was that the place had been an orphanage. All their efforts were in vain.

"I would recognize our son from a mile away," she said in despair. "I left him when he was three years old, and children don't change that much in one or two years. How could that evil Ewa do this to me . . .? A curse on her, a thousand curses! I will never forgive her! She deserves to go through what I did in Auschwitz for stealing my son!" she howled.

"Calm down, darling, calm down. Don't hate, my love, hatred only attracts more hatred."

"What do you know? You never even met our son!"

He was stunned. The remark pierced his heart like a knife, but he refrained from answering so as not to make an already difficult and awkward situation worse.

" . . . I'm sorry . . . forgive me, Boris."

Meanwhile, Boris noticed that Varinia was distancing herself from him. She asked him to respect her privacy and leave her alone. He did as she asked. At the same time, curiously enough, he saw that she was gaining confidence, and this pleased him. They kept alive the hope that it was a matter a time before their relatives appeared, just as she had. He even hired law firms in Warsaw, Paris, and London, with whom he shared the information from the list of names he carried with him. They made superhuman efforts. His life turned into a nightmare. In the depths of her heart, Varinia knew that if they hadn't turned up by now, the search was nothing but a heap of good intentions. Sometimes, to console herself, she would say to herself that at least her son was in the hands of someone she knew, and that she would recognize him and Ewa anywhere in the world. He tried to lift her spirits, but at times he, too, felt hopeless. "I can't bear this anymore . . . I'm sick of everything . . . it's too much to take!" he thought.

One night while they were having dinner at a table in their hotel room in Warsaw, Varinia decided to talk to him. She spoke without raising her eyes.

"Boris, I need to tell you something."

"Yes, my love?"

"All I ask is for you to try to comprehend . . . to understand me. . . ."

272

"What's wrong? Has something happened?" He stared at her without blinking.

"It's . . . it's . . . I wanted to tell you that . . . the truth is that . . . I'm pregnant."

His fork fell to his plate.

"Impossible! But . . . what are you saying . . . pregnant? But we haven't made love since I arrived! It's not possible, Varinia! And . . . don't try to tell me it's mine!"

"It's not yours."

"So . . . it's not mine . . ."

"No."

"Whose is it, then?"

"A Nazi lieutenant's."

"What?" he yelled. "You slept with the enemy?"

"Yes."

"Why?"

"He forced me to."

"Is that why we haven't had sex?"

"No."

"Then why won't you let me love you? Why haven't you wanted to make love to me? Do you think it's been easy for me not to make love to you when I desire you so much?"

"I don't know, and I ask for your forgiveness."

"And . . . why didn't you tell me about the baby earlier?"

"Because I just found out. A doctor from the Red Cross confirmed it."

A tense silence fell. Suddenly he threw his napkin down and rose abruptly from the table.

"This is it! This is the last straw! Fucking hell! This is collective madness! A Nazi . . . a German Nazi . . .! For God's sake!"

She began to tremble, her eyes still lowered. She had never seen him like this before.

"What happened?"

"I had to become his lover in order to survive . . . to find you and our son . . . and everyone . . ."

"His lover?"

"Yes."

Jealousy began to boil up inside him. He stood there for what felt like an eternity, doubting his relationship with her. "All this for nothing," he thought, feeling the urge to slap her for the first time.

"And the baby?"

"I'll have it, especially now that we can't find our son. This baby represents life, and even though it's not yours, all I want is to live and procreate. Life is the only thing that interests me because I've seen too many people die. I've lived with death for too long."

"And I'm not life? I'm more alive than you are! I'm a man with feelings . . . made of flesh and blood . . . look at me . . . touch me!" He went up to her.

She began to perspire, barely looking at him.

"The son of the enemy . . . do you know what that means?"

"Yes . . . but I won't have an abortion . . . I already had to give up one baby when I was raped by a kapo. When that happened, my biggest fear was that I would become infertile, but God has sent me this child, and I'm going to have it."

"Two rapes and both of them leave you pregnant!" he screamed. "My God, this is not happening . . ." He began to hit the wall with his right fist with such force that he broke his little finger. He let out a cry of pain.

She got up to see if he was okay and saw his finger hanging there limply. She scooped up some ice cubes from the wine bucket, put them on his hand, and wrapped them in a napkin. They stayed like that, in silence, for several minutes.

"I'll accept him . . . I'll adopt him and give him my last name . . . we'll never tell anyone, not even him, that his father is a Nazi . . ."

"You don't have to do that. I'll give him my last name." She finally looked into his eyes.

"Varinia, please calm down. I'll love him and we'll take care of him as if he were our own son, the son we can't find . . . the one who was taken from us . . . you love the children you raise, the ones you see growing up . . . you can be sure I'll love him like my own son . . . how couldn't I love an innocent baby, your child, a victim of this war, and after so much death, absence, and pain . . . I swear from the bottom of my heart," he said, trying to regain his composure. "Varinia, listen to me." He took her by the arm and they sat down at the table. "Let's be realistic. Nothing is working out for us here. We've exhausted all our efforts and we have nothing to show for it. We've lost our families, friends, and everything that we had here, and you, my love, have lost your soul and your youth. Let's go to Bolivia and start a new life there, far away from all this. This place only represents pain, so much pain. Let's go away forever and forget about this hell . . . we'll have the baby there, and we'll start a family, and we'll be deeply happy . . . we don't have anyone or anything to live for here anymore. We'll continue the search for our son from there, and we can come back whenever you want."

"I'm not going to Bolivia. I'm staying here, I'll keep looking for our little Boris until my dying day, and I'm having this baby. I'll work at the Red Cross, and I'll get my parents' house back."

"But . . . have you gone crazy? And who am I then? Didn't you tell me you loved me? What do I mean to you? So . . . you want me to stay and live in the ashes, in the ruins of a war, immersed in a vicious cycle of pain? Working as an unpaid volunteer because no one will give me a job? Money doesn't last forever; you need to work for it. I need to repay Moritz every penny I've spent. Varinia . . . Bolivia represents the future, freedom, tranquility, happiness, forgetting, starting a family . . . starting anew . . ."

"Boris, I love you and I will always love you . . . you're the best man I have ever known . . . you're the best thing that's ever happened to me in my life . . . but I'm asking you . . . please don't stay."

"What?" he cried, raising his voice again.

He was more confused than ever. He didn't understand how she could be so contradictory. "Be patient . . . she's a survivor," he thought, remembering Moritz's words.

"Varinia, listen to me . . ." He took her by the hands. "Don't nurture your pain . . . don't let sorrow blind you and lead you to make the wrong decision. Be reasonable. Don't you realize that the only thing we have in the world is each other? . . . that you are the only thing that gives meaning to my life? . . . you can't imagine the loneliness I've suffered these past six years, in a new, faraway country, where I didn't even know the language. All that kept me going was the hope of finding you, of finding everyone. By some miracle I found you, and now you decide not to build a life with me. Do you know what that looks like to me? It looks like you don't love me . . . like you never loved me . . . say something, Varinia . . . for the love of God, wake up! Let your wounds heal . . . try to forget the fucking war, the holocaust, and leave it all behind!"

"You didn't live through it, so you can't understand."

"You know, Varinia . . . suffering doesn't bring lucidity, and it doesn't bring back the dead, either. They say the League of Nations and the Allies will build refugee camps, and a Central Committee of the Liberated Jews will be created, so the situation is not entirely

275

hopeless. We have to have faith and be patient. You have nowhere to live here, the pogroms have begun again, and the Germans don't want to give the houses back to Poles who survived the war. I'm offering to stay with you . . . I want us to be together so we can find our son and our families . . ."

"You can stay, if you want, but I'm not going to live with you. And to be clear, I've never been so sure about anything in my life." Resolute in her decision, she bit her lower lip so hard that it split open. He put a napkin on her mouth to stop the bleeding.

"What? Now this? Varinia . . . what's happening to you?"

"Forgive me, Boris, but I'm a child of the war, as is the baby I'm carrying inside me. We're the children of a depraved war that continues to destroy us to this day, and that will continue to do so until the last day of our lives. The war made me like this. Look, I want you to go back to Bolivia to work. I'll be fine. If I survived the holocaust, I can survive now, especially now that I'm carrying a child inside of me, someone to live for . . . and another one I still have to find . . . they're all I have left in life . . . I can't love you more than my own life . . . or more than the life I carry inside me . . . or the one I lost . . ."

Chapter 12
Bolivia, twenty-first century

Many years have gone by, and I'm now in the twilight of my life. On this cold, clear morning, with the sun fully risen, I've come to the Jewish cemetery of La Paz in Villa San Antonio. From here you can see the city beneath a cloudless sky, surrounded by silent, snowy mountains. How it has changed since I arrived fifty years ago! As I enter the cemetery, I come across the memorial to the martyrs of the Holocaust. I greet my fellow Jews and Bolivians, who are wearing kippot and crowding the vicinity of the cemetery because there's no synagogue. I go directly to the room where the remains of the mother of some friends of mine lie; she was a Holocaust survivor. Her daughter, wearing a handkerchief over her head and a torn dress, weeps as she hugs her mother's body. The remains were washed by female family members and friends in a ceremony that took place earlier, during which they prayed and dressed her in a white cotton shroud sewn at the feet and hands and tied a lace cap around her neck. When I approach her to give her my condolences, she says to me in a voice hoarse from crying: "Boris . . . the Nazis are still killing us . . . when they tattooed the number on her arm she contracted hepatitis . . . she suffered from liver problems all her life, and the disease finally got the best of her . . ."

I look at her apprehensively; I've always had the feeling that death is pursuing me. I suddenly feel as if life, death, memories, even the most horrific ones, as well as moments of happiness and unease, however brief and singular, made sense, a sense that must be discovered. And I suddenly remember when I went to Auschwitz to look for my family and friends. I shudder. I've spent my entire life looking for them, especially for my son . . . the son I never knew . . . I went back to Warsaw and to many countries in Europe and Latin America, to the United States, even to Israel, but I never found them. I was left an orphan, with neither family nor friends. And I continue to miss them all, each and every day. It's an affliction I've had to live with all my life, a wound my heart has never able to heal. But I know I'll see them once again, because the soul does not die.

I decided to return to Bolivia for good and rebuild my life, but for thousands of my people who came to live here, this place was just a transit point. It's estimated that during the war, between two and three thousand Jews emigrated from Bolivia. And afterward several thousand more left, mainly for Argentina, which they saw as the most Europeanized country. But the majority of them obtained Bolivian citizenship, filled the quotas for US visas set by the American government, and immigrated there. Many of them returned to Europe in the hopes of being reunited with their families and recovering their possessions; most found neither. Others went to what was then Palestine, the promised land of Abraham. Today they go there to spend their final days because they finally have a country of their own: Israel, where they feel loved and protected. Today there are barely six hundred of us left in Bolivia. I'm still Catholic even though the Jewish community has become our family. Now that I've grown old, I thank God for giving me life, and I wonder if I've been a good man . . . a happy man . . . because I've seen and felt too much pain. God and my Black Madonna of Silesia gave me everything, took everything away from me, and then later gave it all back. At one point in my life I thought Varinia was everything to me. Was she? I wouldn't dare to say that today. Varinia was passion and pain; she was a chimera, a heavy blow to my soul, but now, from a distance, I finally understand her. Varinia was what infamy made of her. I wouldn't be able to understand who I am without remembering her, but I wouldn't have been able to become who I am without letting the trace of her perfume dissolve into the past. Only one thing is reserved for her: the sacred box of my inner world.

I've tried to be a good man, and I confess that I found happiness. It was scarce and fleeting, but I found it, because I married Misha and started a family with her. My wife and I have endeavored to celebrate life, and what better way to do so than to conceive life? That's what our children have been to us: a celebration. Today we are one enormous, united, and happy family. I have Bolivian-born children and grandchildren. They were educated in American schools. They didn't want to learn German, and they have no desire to go to Germany. I keep insisting that no fault lies with the new generations, and that the world wouldn't allow another Holocaust to occur. And I tell them over and over again that they should cultivate forgiveness, not resentment.

When Moritz left Bolivia I felt abandoned, even though I continued to work in his company for years and we stayed in touch. The

Hochschild group expanded, opening offices in Europe, Latin America, South Africa, Japan, and the United States. It had operations in twenty-four countries. Moritz was a visionary, a forerunner of globalization. He was a modern businessman who could easily have adapted to the twenty-first century. The thousands of Jews he saved and gave jobs to should have built a monument in his honor. It's a task that remains to be done.

When the Bolivian government confiscated his mines in 1952, I went to work for Philipp Brothers. A few years after leaving Bolivia, Moritz remarried Germaine, just as he had told me he planned to do when we were in Europe. But they divorced a second time. He was afraid of being alone. I don't blame him. How couldn't he be, seeing as his only son showed no interest in his companies? Moritz didn't grant him any decision-making power either; he decided everything himself. Consequently, he left no direct corporate dynasty behind. I later learned that his son, who had gone to live in Chile, took him to court, and that one of his grandnephews, Eduardo Hochschild Beeck, who lives in Peru, took over part of his legacy, presiding over the London-based Hochschild Mining Corporation. My beloved Moritz died of a heart attack at Le Meurice in Paris, where he was found dead one morning. Luckily, he didn't suffer. When I found out, I felt as if I had lost my father a second time. I immediately flew to France to attend his funeral. He was buried in the cimetière du Père-Lachaise. He was the best man I ever knew. Paul Hirsch succeeded him in the company.

I have tried to understand life, and to enjoy it. I've gone through so much suffering that I think the time has finally come for me to go. I feel no bitterness; on the contrary, I have only one hope: that what was promised will be given, that I will find that place of plenitude beyond death, because the soul doesn't die. My time is up. I'll be reunited with them there. I was able to live, to do everything my parents, my brother, and my sister were deprived of by those abominable men.

Made in the USA
Middletown, DE
14 August 2022